WESTMINSTER PUBLIC LIBRARY

P9-EDC-915

IR

# BROWN
# BOY
# NOWHERE

Westminster Public Library
3705 W 112th Ave
Westminster, CO 80031
www.westminsterlibrary.org

DISCARD

# BROWN BOY NOWHERE

A NOVEL

## SHEERYL LIM

**SKYSCAPE**

# ᴵᴵᴵᵤᴵᴵ SKYSCAPE

This is a work of fiction. Names, characters, organizations, places, events, and incidents are either products of the author's imagination or are used fictitiously. Any resemblance to actual persons, living or dead, or actual events is purely coincidental.

Text copyright © 2021 by Sheeryl Lim
All rights reserved.

No part of this book may be reproduced, or stored in a retrieval system, or transmitted in any form or by any means, electronic, mechanical, photocopying, recording, or otherwise, without express written permission of the publisher.

Published by Skyscape, New York

www.apub.com

Amazon, the Amazon logo, and Skyscape are trademarks of Amazon.com, Inc., or its affiliates.

ISBN-13: 9781542027762 (hardcover)
ISBN-10: 1542027764 (hardcover)

ISBN-13: 9781542027779 (paperback)
ISBN-10: 1542027772 (paperback)

Cover illustration by Kat Goodloe

Cover design by Faceout Studio, Amanda Hudson

Printed in the United States of America

First edition

*To Mia*

# 1

Adrenaline courses through my veins. I dig my feet into my grip tape and bend my knees, popping off into the sky. My skateboard does one, two, three rotations midair. With a whoosh I land perfectly centered on the deck and skate away fast.

Too fast.

The adrenaline gives way to utter dread. It rises up the back of my throat. I clench my core, trying my best to keep my balance, but the board wobbles. My foot slips. I hit the ground hard.

I wake up with a start. The car swerves, and my cheek hits the window. "What the hell, Dad?"

"Angelo. Language!" Mom snaps.

"Had to avoid the pothole." Dad scratches against the shallow pockmarks on his cheek. His tan skin is shiny, though I don't know why he'd be sweating. He's been blasting the AC since we drove through the blistering Lone Star State. "Go back to sleep. I'll wake you up when we get there."

"Kinda hard to sleep when you're driving like a maniac." My grunts are overshadowed by the rumbling in my stomach. "I bet this place doesn't even sell fish tacos," I repeat for about the thousandth time since we left San Diego. I salivate at the thought of those crispy pieces of mahi slathered in tangy *crema*. My digestive tract clearly hasn't caught on to what my mind already knows—I won't be eating fish tacos anytime soon.

"Eh, you can always go fishing and make your own." My mom's way too chipper considering we're headed to a place where casting a rod is my only option to get my favorite food.

Snorting, I glance out the car. "Yeah? In what ocean?"

"There are other bodies of water, Angelo," Mom clucks. "There's probably a nice creek somewhere in town."

"A creek?" I stare at the back of her head. "Are you serious?"

She gives a nonchalant bounce of her shoulders.

My life sucks.

It's nothing but people constantly trying to make it a living hell.

To my left is a green field scattered with grazing steer. On my right is more grass and more steer. Just add that huge flatbed truck with rolls of booger-colored hay piled in the back and I'm clearly on the way to the most boring, godforsaken town in the continental US.

Why anybody would want to live here, I don't know. Why my parents would want to uproot us from the paradise of our Southern California home and shove us into a tiny Prius with about a hundred suitcases and our dog, Nollie, to drive all the way across the country to some small-ass town right at the beginning of my junior year, I don't know either.

That's a lie. I do know. But as important the reason, it still doesn't lessen the blow. I glance at my phone, although it's been without service for the last thirty minutes.

*Amanda Panda:* Wish you were here, love!

I reread the text for what feels like the hundredth time.

I shut my eyes and picture my girlfriend's slightly crooked grin. The way it would quirk every time I entered the room or tug down anytime I told a stupid joke. I've always scoffed at the idea of falling in love in high school, but when I met Amanda in biology last year I was hooked. For some reason, the cute surfer chick was interested in me too, and we've been a couple ever since. I always pictured us going to senior prom and graduating side by side. But now here we are, miles apart. The good news is that we made a promise to stay together, which we consummated my last night in San Diego.

Heat creeps into my cheeks. I don't know what I expected losing my virginity would be like, but my fantasies certainly didn't include me blubbering like an idiot, telling her how much I'd miss her.

I toss the phone beside me, hitting the crate that houses our larger-than-life dachshund. Within seconds her high-pitched barks fill the car, ricocheting against my mom's out-of-style visor and rebounding off Dad's toupee.

"Angelo, shut your dog up!" Dad's clearly antsy after days behind the wheel. Except for a few pit stops at different motels (I will never be able to stomach another continental breakfast) and quick trips to rest stops along our cross-country trek, he's been driving constantly, seeing as Mom's anxiety is relentless and I only have my learner's permit.

I gesture out the window at the scattering of housing and expansive fields. "Why? Worried we're going to bother the five or so residents of Ocean Pointe? What kind of place names their landlocked town Ocean Pointe, anyway? The nearest beach has to be two hours away. I bet none of them have even seen a surfboard before." If we were back home, I'd be spending every day of my last leg of summer break at Pacific Beach with Amanda.

"Angelo," Mom pipes up in warning. She rubs against her temples with a sigh and glances back at me. "I know you're disappointed we chose to move—"

"Smack in the middle of high school!"

She takes another deep breath, which makes it sound as if she's at the end of her rope. "Angelo, you know we had no choice but to leave San Diego. We've discussed this."

"No, both of you discussed this. I wasn't part of the conversation, remember?"

"I know you aren't happy about this right now, but what you need to do is give this move a chance." I harrumph while Mom swivels her head to glare at me around the plants she's managed to secure on top of the center console. "Just think, besides the smog, it was getting congested and a bit too touristy. Not a great place to raise a teenager."

"Oh, you mean me?" I grunt.

"But this place . . ." She flails her hands as much as she can given the collection of ferns surrounding her. "You just need to open your eyes and there's no missing the beauty of it. *Ang ganda dito.*"

"Really? You think it's beautiful here?" I cringe at the pile of lawn clippings littering the edge of the road, wishing I were seeing the ocean instead.

"Plus, it will be a good bonding experience for our family before you leave for college."

She's full of crap, except for the touristy part. Somehow between my grade school years and high school, San Diego warped into an LA clone complete with miles of traffic and crowded beaches. Still, having a few thousand out-of-towners trickling in every day of the year isn't grounds to insult the only home I've known since birth. At least I don't think it is. Anyway, I think Mom should just be honest and admit the main reason they chose to move to Ocean Pointe—their real estate friend negotiated a great deal on a restaurant. Right now, saving money and making money are the most important things on my parents' minds. More important than considering the damage they can cause their poor son.

I press my head against the car's window and resume staring at the blurs of brown and green. There isn't a single person in sight. There's no way Ocean Pointe will ever be considered touristy.

I can feel Mom's still looking at me. After a beat, she sighs again. "This move is hard for us too, you know." She waits for me to respond, but my tongue is dry in my mouth. "It's not just you who has to start over. We have a new business to run!"

I frown. "I know."

"Do you?"

"Of course I do," I hiss.

"Don't talk back to me."

Mom settles into her seat and faces front. After a moment, she says, "Remember our agreement? We'll allow you to participate in that game in November . . . what's it called? Thanks Street?"

"Streetsgiving, Mom." I roll my eyes. "And it's not a game. It's only one of the biggest skateboarding competitions in San Diego."

One that I've been looking forward to for months. As bad luck would have it, the year I'm finally old enough to compete is the very same year my parents decide we'll move away.

"Oh, yes. Streetsgiving." Even after almost twenty years in this country, Mom still speaks with a Filipino accent, so it ends up sounding like "streets-*geebing*." "We'll let you fly back to San Diego during your fall break, but only if you actually try to enjoy this place and stop complaining all the time."

"Not gonna lie. It's going to be hard." Knowing I'll be back in San Diego in November is the only thing keeping me going right now, even though November seems so far away and I know I'll have to work hard to earn money to pay for a plane ticket.

"Golly, Angelo. I don't know why you're so worried about this move," Dad interjects. Unlike Mom, his Filipino accent is almost nonexistent. A member of the US Navy in his early twenties, he'd always tried his best to fit in with his shipmates, which I guess also meant erasing a part of him. It's a bit ironic that he and Mom opened a Filipino restaurant a couple of years after he left the military.

"We'll still give you the same freedom you had in California," Mom assures me.

"The same freedom? Are you kidding me?" Mom and Dad never once complained about the time I spent at the beach or skating the bowl. But now . . . "What about all the new rules and conditions you gave me?" I count down on my fingers. "I can only fly back to San Diego if I get good grades, don't get into any trouble, and—"

"You have to work hard at your new job." Mom shoots me a look. "But you'll do that anyway since you need the money, no?"

And that is an understatement. My parents know I need the money to fly back to San Diego to compete in Streetsgiving on school break. But what neither of them know is that I'm also planning to use the visit to convince my Tita Marie to let me stay with her for the remainder of high school.

*This really needs to work.* I slump back in my seat and knead at my eyebrows.

About ten minutes and three sporadic spurts of cellular service later, we finally pull up to our new house. Which I will not be calling a "home," as that's where your heart supposedly is, and right now mine is in the hands of a lavender-haired girl most likely surfing the California waves.

"Is this it?" I ask, even though I know it is. My hand is frozen on the door handle. I'm almost too scared to step out. Once I do, everything becomes more real.

Dad, however, immediately jumps out of the car, groaning as he pops his back. "Yup. Welcome home, son."

"Right." I still can't move.

The sprawling five-bedroom ranch, which is definitely bigger than our three-bedroom home in the Tierrasanta hills of San Diego (not to mention more space than our tiny family needs), looks nothing like it did online. If anything, it's even less inviting. I stare at the brick walls and slanted roof. I prefer the stucco finish and terra-cotta roof of my childhood home.

Nollie whines to be let out. I frown at her shaking crate.

"Are you really that excited to be here, or do you just need to pee?" I unlatch the crate and make sure I secure Nollie's leash to her collar before I finally open the car door and step out onto Ocean Pointe soil. I sidestep Mom, who's bent over in a weird stretch, and lead Nollie to the yard. "C'mon, girl. Let's do this together."

As Nollie pees, I stand and look around at our new street. The neighborhood seems nonthreatening enough. Though the houses are a bit farther apart than I'm used to, at least they aren't as spread out as they were back on the main road. However, it looks like about twenty different architects worked on this subdivision or a first-year contractor was in charge and ended up with a strange mix of houses made of materials like bricks, logs, or vinyl sidings.

Nollie yaps at me, tugging at her leash. I grimace at her in sympathy. "Guess this is our life now, huh?" We walk to the back of the house. "I'll bet you three dog treats I won't be able to find a skate park around here."

I watch Nollie sniff around, looking for another patch of grass to mark. If only finding a new place to piss on was my sole problem.

The metallic squeal of aged brakes echoes behind me.

A moment later, Dad comes hurrying around the side of the house. "Angelo, the movers are here. Do you want to help out?" Though he says it like a question, I know he's really barking out an order. Ex-military and all that. Tough luck for him, but I'm totally not in the mood to carry cardboard boxes filled with the past sixteen years of my life.

I walk Nollie back to the car, grab her things from the back seat and my skateboard from the trunk, and head for a nice shady spot under one of the big trees in the front yard. I settle her into the crate and pour her a bowl of water, telling her she can watch all the action from here but be safely out of the way.

"Okay, see you in a few hours, Nollie," I reassure her.

Dad calls out to me from inside the house, this time not even trying to hide the irritation in his voice. But I'm already rolling down the front walkway.

"Angelo! Where do you think you're going?" Even without looking, I know he's on the front stoop, a bright blue vein throbbing away at his temple.

Now if I were in a movie from the '90s or '00s (they're all I binge), I would do a kick-ass move and throw my middle finger in the air. But my life's not a movie, and Dad would probably take off his shoe to throw at my head. Instead I just shout, "Going exploring! Be back soon!"

"Angelo!" This time it's Mom's shrill voice screaming at me.

"I have my phone. Call me if you can even reach me!" I throw in the last part for good measure. With the way cellular service works around here, I know that if I skate even twenty feet away, I might as well be located in Middle Earth. This town probably only has half a cell tower erected, which is probably buried in half a ton of cow dung.

There's something relaxing about the sound of a skateboard's wheels as it cruises against the asphalt. With no real sense of direction, I pump faster. Right now, the familiar sound of my skateboard wheels is the only thing that gives me a sense of comfort, my own version of those Tibetan singing bowls my old neighbor used to play every morning.

I skate past more mismatched houses, which gradually are replaced by commercial buildings. Strangely, each building has a similar wooden sign with bold black lettering, reminders that there is nothing to do in this town.

### Jules's Glass Studio

### Glass-Blowing Workshop

### 1/2 Mile to Glass Sculptures

I wish I were surprised that every single business sells glass art, but then again in a town like this it totally makes sense.

I continue along and eventually come to an expansive brick building. Though it has no resemblance to my old high school and its palm tree–lined campus, I have a sinking feeling this is where I'll be spending my days until November. That is, if everything with my aunt goes as planned.

I skate to the main sign. **OCEAN POINTE HIGH SCHOOL** is written in faded vinyl lettering. Underneath is script so brand new, I swear I hear the high-pitched ding used when models in toothpaste commercials smile: **HOME OF THE TROJANS.**

Grimacing, I glance around. Ocean Pointe Middle School and Ocean Pointe Elementary School are on the same stretch of land. It doesn't take a genius to figure out that everyone here probably all know each other.

"Hey, brown boy! Are you lost?"

*Did he really call me "brown boy"? What kind of place is this?* I turn in the direction of the laughter. A group of five guys are huddled underneath a nearby tree, though because they're all wearing identical hunting camouflage, it'd be easy to mistake them for a single creature. Cigarettes glow from between their fingers as they stare me down, scanning me from head to toe. The husky blond one who I assume is their leader, or at least the chosen one housing their shared brain cell, steps away from the pack. Wisps of smoke dance around the boy's refrigerator-shaped body. "I was talking to you, kid. You lost?"

I jump off my skateboard, kicking it up so I catch it effortlessly in one hand. Digging my fingertips into the deck's rough grip tape, I walk straight up to the group, my jaw clenched and eyes narrowed.

I may be a skinny Filipino sixteen-year-old kid with sloppy hair, standing five feet nine on a good day, but I'm as strong as they come. Chalk it up to doing every single stereotypical SoCal sport out there—surfing, skating, snowboarding, skim boarding, hiking. So although I never had to deal with bullies back at my old high school with all its open-mindedness and diversity, obviously here I might have to. But I'm pretty sure I can hold my own.

Clearing my throat, I lift my chin. "Got a problem?"

"Yeah, my problem is that you're trespassing on our property." The boy's accent is the opposite of smooth.

"Your property?" I snort and motion at the newly power-washed brick building. "Didn't know you had rights to a *public* high school."

"The fact that we're seniors and at the top of the OPHS food chain makes all of this our property," he shoots back, practically foaming at the mouth. "So better take your little freshman ass and leave."

I may look young, but I don't look *that* young. "Of course, this would be the day I'd run into effing trolls," I grumble.

The leader stiffens, tosses the remnants of his illegal cigarette to the ground, and stomps down hard on it. Without taking his eyes off mine, he pulverizes the butt into miniscule ashes. "Care to repeat that?"

I open my mouth to respond, but before I can get a single word out the troll grunts. "Better watch your mouth unless you want your ass beat, kid."

Though I want nothing more than to show this boy I'm not scared of him and his friends, I know better than to pick a fight with someone who might make my life at school a living hell. Biting back a string of profanity, I shrug. "I ain't doing nothing but skating, dude."

"Dude?" The boy snickers. "Who the hell even talks like that?"

"'Dumbass' is more like it," one of his friends pipes in, earning a round of laughter.

The boy never loses his sneer and points behind me. "Hope you know how to read."

I roll my eyes and follow his stubby finger.

#### No Loitering

Is he that dumb not to realize it's exactly what he and his friends are doing? Then again, you can't knock sense into entitlement.

I'm in no mood to argue with stupidity. I place my skateboard on the ground and push off.

"Hey! We're not done talking to you," one of the background blockheads shouts after me, but I ignore him and pump my leg faster. The next thing I know, something jams against my front wheels. Before I can react, I'm flying off my board.

On instinct I stick my hands out to stop my fall, but I'm at a weird angle and land cheek first into the parking lot. A wave of heat spreads from the top of my cheekbone down to my jawline, casting electric zings along my skin.

I've had my share of road rash before, but these new gashes hurt way worse. Probably it's my pride that's taken a beating.

Growling, I push myself up with a swiftness that would make Marvel's Quicksilver proud and eye the rock wedged at the front wheel. "Did you assholes really just throw a rock at me?" I ask the bullies.

They hoot in celebration. A zit-covered boy cackles exceptionally loud and howls, "Take that stupid skateboard out of here! What are you? From the nineties?"

I fight the urge to point out their baggy jeans are the epitome of nineties fashion, kick away the jagged stone, and skate back home—oh, I'm sorry, I mean I skate back to my new house.

The movers are still in full swing when I arrive. I unlatch Nollie's crate and lead her into the house. Mom and Dad are so busy they don't even notice the cut on my face even though it's dripping blood. Or maybe they just ignore it. They're probably still annoyed that I ditched them.

"Are you finally ready to help us?" Dad snaps the same time Mom asks, "How was exploring? Did you find out what people do for fun?"

"Well, they seem to like racism." I rub the skin around my cut with a wince.

"Angelo! Racism's not something you should joke about," Mom snaps.

Annoyed she'd immediately think I was lying, I continue down the hallway and rush through the first open door I see. Then I spin around and call out, "They like glass blowing too."

Nollie runs into the room. I shut the door all the way and collapse onto the carpet with a groan. On cue, my sweet dog climbs on top of my chest and licks my face as if to shoo away this nightmare. Her ears flop over as I scratch between them and sigh. "Thanks, girl. But sorry. Nothing can make this sucky situation better."

# 2

A nother thing that sucks about this place—besides the constant odor of cow crap when we drive around and general sense of foreboding—is the absence of a good churro and carne asada fries. Two staples to my personally branded food pyramid, which consists of Mexican food, In-N-Out burgers, and some gluten-free, non-GMO snacks thrown in to appease my mother. Though I'd begged and pleaded with my two chef parents to open up a Mexican restaurant, figuring Ocean Pointe wouldn't have one (I was right), what did they go ahead and do? Buy an old fast-food joint. Not even a good franchise, but Sloppy's Pit Stop.

My head slams against the cool glass window as Dad takes a sharp turn. Our second day in town and things still don't seem to be looking up. A horn screams behind us. On instinct, I hold up a middle finger and am answered with another blare.

Mom glances back at me and scowls. "Angelo, put that finger down!"

"Did moving out here make you forget how to drive too?" I ask Dad.

Dad snickers sheepishly. "I forgot the turn is an unmarked one. The GPS didn't pick it up."

*Because we're in the middle of nowhere.* I bite my tongue, knowing Mom just might climb over her seat to knock me on the head if I answer back.

"I still don't get why you had to buy a crappy burger place—*ow!*" Okay, I guess I deserved that smack. One thing's for sure: Mom's got talent. I have no idea how she was able to reach me. Good thing I'm *matigas ang ulo* as she always calls me, which means "hardheaded" in Tagalog. Scowling, I rub my throbbing scalp. "If you didn't want to open a Mexican restaurant, why didn't you just open up a Filipino restaurant like the one we had in Mira Mesa?"

"You don't even like Filipino food," Mom points out flatly, clearly bored with the conversation.

"But I bet it's a lot better than some place called Sloppy's Pit Stop. I mean, shouldn't you be watching your cholesterol considering how old you both are?"

"*Bastos!* Stop it with that mouth of yours," Mom interrupts as Dad chuckles. "You don't think *lechon* clogs your veins?"

"Well, a roasted pig is better than an oily beef patty," I point out. "Probably more organic too."

"After what we went through back home—er, in San Diego"— Mom quickly corrects herself when I shoot her a knowing smirk—"we have to be more mindful of our business. Even with all our regulars in 'Manila Mesa,' we couldn't keep the business afloat. Your dad and I decided a Filipino restaurant just wouldn't do well in Ocean Pointe." Mom fusses with her already stick-straight bangs and huffs. "Not enough of our target market."

"And again, why did we move to Ocean Pointe?" I grumble as we take a final turn into the smallest parking lot known to humankind.

"We're here!" Dad happily chirps.

The seventh circle of hell must have been designed by a Ray Kroc wannabe. Well, if the McDonald's tycoon wannabe fused with S. F.

Bowser, the inventor of the fuel pump, to create the grimiest-looking truck stop on this side of the Mississippi.

With my jaw dropped, I slowly climb out of the car and stare at the dingy building. No way this brick slab with the blinding sign is our new business venture. "What . . . what . . . ?"

Dad throws a limp arm around my shoulder and gazes proudly at the monstrosity. It's a gas station, or rather, a restaurant *in* a gas station. The Sloppy's Pit Stop logo shines brightly, illuminating the four gas pumps behind us in a startling shade of red. "Welcome to your new job, son. I had the landlord keep the lights on so you can take a good look at it. What do you think?"

It's like someone shoved a handful of sawdust down my throat and expects me to recite Hamlet's soliloquy. Swallowing hard, I open and close my mouth, only able to get two syllables out. "I . . . uh . . . I . . . uh . . ."

Dad beams, clapping me on the back. "Let's go in and check the place out."

Coughing, my voice comes out even tinier. "I . . . uh . . . I . . . uh . . ."

My family shuffles into the beat-down, um, *restaurant-station*. Dad's on cloud nine with Mom just a few clouds below. Then there's me staking claim in earth's core.

Dad flips on the interior lights and spins around. "Not bad, huh?" He stomps to the overhead vent and smacks a heavy hand against it. "Had the landlord give us all new equipment before signing the lease. Spared no expense."

"Only because the standard of living is much lower here," Mom is quick to point out.

Dad ignores her and puffs out his chest. "They're even going to pave the grass lot behind the building next week. You know what that means—more customers. I did well, didn't I?"

"Way to toot your own horn, Dad." If I wasn't so horrified at the prospect of flipping burgers after school, maybe I could have admired the pristine fryers and grill. They're a heck of a lot better than the old pans we had at our former restaurant.

I walk through the tiny hybrid as if wading through a nightmare. It's as big as any standard convenience store, meaning there are only about five booths for diners to eat in. An orange counter bordered by metal racks beneath it, which I assume are meant to hold candy or chips for sale, separates the small dining area from the kitchen. I walk past the side of the counter into a corridor, which is stacked floor to ceiling with cardboard boxes, and see something I really wasn't expecting.

"Are those really . . . showers?" I gape at the clearly marked doors, reading and rereading the bold type.

Not singular, but plural. There are literally two showers between the men's and women's bathrooms.

"Who the heck takes a shower in a restaurant? Er, gas station?" I've officially wandered into the twilight zone.

"Truck drivers," Dad answers, without missing a beat.

"Truck drivers," I repeat, tasting the imaginary sawdust all over again. I spin on my heel and glare at my parents. "You don't expect me to pump gas for any of them, do you?"

"Of course not," Mom says with a snort. She's discarded her trademark visor and walks around the restaurant with a purpose. Running a finger across the counter, she cringes at the almost nonexistent layer of dust and shakes her head.

"Yeah, you just press those buttons right there and boom! They have gas." Dad points to an ancient-looking computer that looks like it still runs on DOS. Guess the landlord did spare some expense after all.

"Nice." This is downright horrible.

Dad claps his hands and rubs them together fast enough to make fire. "Are you ready for training day number one?"

I stiffen, staring at him blankly. "Wait, are you serious?"

Judging by the way he's turning on each machine he's more than serious—he's motivated. "Wash up. We're opening up in a week, and I need to teach you how to make a good burger."

"A good burger. Because that's what you think of when you hear the words *Sloppy's Pit Stop*, right?" I fall against a shower door and groan.

∿

"No, you smack it, *then* flip it! It keeps the flavor in."

It's been about two hours since the commencement of my "training session" and I want nothing more than to toss every box of frozen meat out onto the green pastures yelling, "Cows, see what they've done to your brethren. Attack!"

I have never felt more inclined to become vegan.

I glance at my mother, who looks just as frustrated as I am. Her thin eyebrows pull together as she pounds the side of her fist against the archaic computer, muttering Tagalog cuss words under her breath. I nearly laugh as she wishes damnation on the device: *"Lintik na computer ito."*

"Angelo, are you listening to me?" Dad says. "Smack and flip. Smack and flip! Flip!"

I want to flip something off all right.

"Yeah, yeah. I'm listening—"

"Hello, hello!" An old woman with faded red hair pushes through the door. She adjusts her oval-shaped glasses and looks around.

"Keep flipping," Dad tells me before stepping around the counter. "Can I help you, ma'am?"

I do as I'm told but never take my eyes off the stranger. Besides the bullies from the parking lot, I haven't seen another Ocean Pointe townie. At least not up close.

The woman's voice is raspy. "Name's Judy. I own the consignment shop down the road." She flails a hand behind her. "Thought I'd drop by and see who my new neighbors are."

"Oh, well, it's a pleasure to meet you, Judy. I'm Roman and that's my wife, Mila. Over there by the grill is my son, Angelo." I lift my greasy spatula. Dad's thick lips stretch into a wide grin. "How very nice of you to stop by. It's always great to meet the neighbors."

I bite back a snort. Dad's really laying it on thick.

Judy meets my gaze and shoots me a smile that doesn't quite meet her eyes. "Yes, well, I thought I should introduce myself early."

"Early? We'll be training all day."

"No, what I mean is the last owners left after only being here for a year. Business didn't do too well." Judy leans toward my dad, loudly whispering, "Or so I heard."

Mom, who's been too busy with the computer to pay attention to Judy, finally looks up with worry. "What do you mean? Why did their business fail?"

"Mila," Dad warns. "Maybe we shouldn't ask—"

"Hush, now. It's a valid question." Judy clearly loves gossip and flat out ignores Dad's deepening frown. She turns to Mom and explains, "You have to understand that it's a bit hard for newcomers to make a go around here."

"Why?" Mom demands.

"Ocean Pointe's all about tradition and routine. We're a tiny town. We don't see much change."

Remembering the parking lot bullies, I blurt out, "Or do you mean you don't handle change well?"

"Angelo," Dad snaps.

Judy pats him on the arm. "Ocean Pointe Diner's been a staple in this town since the beginning. Why go to any other place when it's only down Main Street? It's tried and true. Just good burgers and shakes. Traditional recipes. The last owners of this place couldn't compete with loyalty." She pauses and pastes a tight smile on her face. "But that was them, and now you're here. I hope business fares better for you."

"Er, thanks . . . ," says Dad.

The adults exchange a few more pleasantries before Judy leaves to go back to her store. Dad drags his feet to the grill, blinking slowly.

"You okay?" I flip a burger and nearly knock it to the floor. Dad's too dazed to notice.

"Did you hear what the lady said? Newcomers have it hard," he mutters more to himself than to me. "We have to appear traditional. Like we've been here all along. Good old-fashioned burgers and fries."

"What does that even mean?"

He barely gives me a glance. "We have to get this town to like us."

"People pleasing again, Dad? Are you sure that's going to work this time?" I smack a burger so hard it crumbles in half. Back in San Diego my parents went out of their way to make sure our customers were happy. It's good business practice in theory, until Dad started to give food out "on loan." Our regulars never paid us back.

"We're in the service industry, Angelo. Pleasing customers is what we do. And if they want old-fashioned and traditional, we can do that," Dad huffs.

Before I can respond, the front door flies open again. Something metal drops onto the floor.

"Oh, shoot!" A petite blonde, who looks about my age, stomps down her foot to block a can of spray paint from rolling away. She picks it up and quickly stuffs it back into her fallen tote bag, patting the canvas material for good measure. Her platinum locks are the same shade Amanda's used to be before she tinted her hair purple to look like a unicorn's mane. In fact, she looks so similar to my girlfriend that I rub my eyes to make sure I'm not seeing some sort of mirage . . . then quickly regret it when I realize I have cooking oil all over my fingers. Gross.

Probably still shaken by Judy's big mouth, Mom hardly waits for the girl to straighten and announces, "We're closed."

Surprise registers on Blonde Girl's face. She motions to the door. "But the sign outside—"

"Needs to be turned off." Mom whips her head around. "Roman, shut that thing off!"

"I'm sorry. I didn't know you weren't open yet. This place has been closed forever, so when I saw the lights finally on . . ." Blonde Girl realizes Mom isn't listening. She clamps her mouth shut and frowns. So much for people pleasing.

I feel a bit bad for the girl and scold, "Mom, don't be rude."

I slide out from behind the grill. "Sorry about that. We're a bit stressed with training, and that old lady from the consignment shop didn't make things any easier either."

"Consignment shop?" The girl glances at the window. "Are you talking about Mrs. Spellman?"

I shrug. "She said her name was Judy."

"She's harmless." Her lips twitch in amusement. Up close, Blonde Girl doesn't resemble Amanda as much as I thought. Big blue eyes instead of brown ones stare back at me from underneath her curtain of white-blonde hair. Whereas Amanda's locks came straight from a bottle, judging by this girl's lack of dark roots, she's a natural towhead. But with her tan skin, her light features make for an odd combination. It isn't until I notice the freckles covering the bridge of her nose, along with the patches of sweat lining her gray tank, that I realize she probably spends a lot of time outdoors.

"I hope I'm not adding to your stress. I was walking home from . . . um . . . painting and I saw your lights on," she explains. Her eyes linger on the flesh-colored Band-Aid plastered on my cheek, but fortunately she doesn't mention it. "Thought I'd swing in here for some water seeing as I'd forgotten mine."

"Oh. I can totally help you with that."

"Really? I don't want to be too much trouble—"

"On the house."

"Water's usually free," she reminds me with a laugh.

"Oh . . . yeah . . ."

"Angelo, come here for a second," Dad calls out from behind me.

"I'll be back." I tip my head forward.

But I do a mental face palm as I spin around and dutifully march over to my dad. Did I seriously bow?

"What is it, Pops?" I ask.

"Did I hear you say 'on the house'?" His toupee shifts as he shakes his head feverishly. "No. Nothing on the house. Do you want everyone in town thinking we're just giving things out? We haven't even opened yet."

I refrain from pointing out the hypocrisy in his statement and merely shrug. "It's water and she's thirsty."

"Or are *you* thirsty?" He gives me a pointed look.

"I have a girlfriend." I'm sure my already-flushed face becomes redder.

"Doesn't mean you can't look."

"Does Mom know you think this way?" I glance at the girl, who instantly locks eyes with me, and drop my tone. "Seriously, would you really let someone go thirsty because you're afraid of giving out water for free? I repeat, *water*. Not *lumpia* or *pancit*. Not even Sprite. Besides, do you want everyone in town thinking that the new owners of Sloppy's Pit Stop are stingy and mean? What happened to wanting people to like us?"

Guilt flashes over my dad's oily face. He finally nods toward a stack of cups, pointing with his lips. "Grab one of those and get her some water from the back sink. It's all we have right now until we set up the soda fountain."

"Roger that." I throw him a mock salute and slide across the floor to grab a Styrofoam cup. I make a mental note to remind my parents of eco-friendlier options and practically jog to the industrial-size sink in the back of the restaurant / gas station.

"Please don't come out brown. Please don't come out brown." I flip on the lever and wince as the faucet sputters loudly, not releasing my breath until a stream of clear liquid comes out. I fill the cup to the brim and hurry to the front of the store.

"Here you go." Blonde Girl's fingers graze mine. To my surprise, my stomach jolts. It's like I'm suddenly dropping in on the world's largest wave. I shake off the sensation.

"Thanks . . ." Before taking a sip, she sneaks a glance at my parents and gnaws at the corner of her mouth. A thoughtful expression flashes over her face, followed by a devious smirk. "Hey, do you mind going outside with me for a sec?"

"Huh? Why?"

"I need directions."

Feeling my parents' eyes burning into the back of my head, I rub my hair and shift awkwardly. "I'm actually new and I don't—"

She grabs my hand, pulling me to the door. "Come on." She leans in and whispers, "Just tell them you need some air. By the looks of things, you definitely need a break."

I turn back to see my dad lifting his arms in a *"What are you doing?"* fashion and motioning to the grill.

"You're right." I follow without protest. "Now that you mention it, I do need a break."

The air is as heavy as an MMA fighter splayed over your body in a guillotine choke hold. It's hot. Sticky. Somehow the air out here is even worse than the burger fumes inside.

Blonde Girl's ocean-blue eyes meet mine. "I'm Kirsten, by the way."

It isn't until she starts to shake my hand that I realize I'm still holding on to hers. I quickly let go and notice dried magenta paint coating each of her fingertips. "Angelo."

"Angelo." She taps against her chin. "I like it."

Chuckling, I relax for the first time since I arrived at Sloppy's. "And your name is Kirsten? Like the actress, Kirsten Dunst?" I quip, suddenly seeing the resemblance.

Kirsten's lips quirk at the corners. "Kirsten Dunst?"

"She was really famous in the nineties. She played a cheerleader in that one movie."

"I'm not a cheerleader," she snaps.

"Oh . . . uh . . . I didn't mean anything bad about it. I mean, I always thought Kirsten Dunst was pretty cute—I mean talented." I clear my throat. "It's a compliment."

Kirsten's laugh is strained. "Thanks. I guess."

My gaze wanders to her tank top. Splashes of color spread across the gray material. Green. Blue. The familiar magenta. It's a kaleidoscope printed across cotton.

Kirsten clears her throat, effectively snapping me back to attention. "You okay?"

"Uh, why wouldn't I be?" I blink.

She points to my cheek. "Looks like you're bleeding through your Band-Aid."

"I am?" My hand flies up to touch my face. I hiss at the sharp bite of pain radiating from my cheekbone.

"You're lucky your restaurant isn't open yet. That would *so* be a health code violation." Kirsten reaches into the pocket of her Daisy Dukes. The shorts, coupled with her cognac-and-turquoise-colored cowboy boots, make her come off as a Southern belle. "Here you go."

She slaps a new Band-Aid against my palm.

"Do you normally walk around with a first-aid kit in your pocket?"

She giggles. "I like to be prepared when I paint. Never know when I might fall."

"You paint houses or something?"

"Or something."

I peel off my used bandage with a grimace and toss it into the nearby garbage can. Opening the new one, I struggle to position it over my cut. Without a mirror, I'm a fumbling idiot.

Kirsten snorts. "Here, let me."

Before I can respond, she takes the Band-Aid from my fingers and places it onto my face, gently pressing down along the edges.

The hairs on the back of my neck stand up. A rush of goose bumps slides down my arm. Suddenly nervous, I clear my throat and step back. "I . . . uh . . ."

"That's a pretty bad-looking scrape." Kirsten gestures at the restaurant. "Didn't know cooking burgers was so dangerous."

I let out a strangled laugh. "Uh, no. Actually, I got it from skateboarding."

"Skateboarding?" Her eyes widen in interest.

"I don't usually fall," I say quickly. "But let's just say I found myself between a rock and a hard place."

Or hardheaded bullies, rather.

"Accidents happen," she murmurs.

"Yeah. Accidents." I shake my head with a grunt. I'm not one to be scared off so easily, but I also don't rush into conflicts either. Especially with entitled bullies. I scan the stretch of road in front of Sloppy's. It's not the most ideal place to skate, but it might just be where I'll find myself doing Ollies in the foreseeable future.

"You know, I've always wanted to learn how to skate."

"Oh, really?" I'm genuinely surprised. After my run-in with the bullies, I didn't think anyone in Ocean Pointe could give two shits about skating.

As if reading my thoughts, she muses, "I've always thought it looked cool, although I'm not saying a lot of other people around here would think so."

I let out a loud snort. "Trust me. I know."

She cocks an eyebrow. "Oh, do you now?"

"I mean I didn't know you thought it was cool." I shrug. "But I sorta figured no one else here would be into that kind of stuff."

"You got that right." She pulls her lips in and lets them out with a pop. "Ocean Pointe isn't really into trying new things."

Remembering what one of the bullies called me, I spit, "Like getting to know brown people, right?"

Kirsten's mouth drops open. Words tumble out like a cascading river. "*Omigosh*, I wasn't implying that at all. I just meant everyone here is so football minded and—"

"I'm kidding. I'm kidding. Trust me. I have to find ways to entertain myself now that I live in the boondocks. I mean no offense."

"None taken. Ocean Pointe is even beyond the boondocks."

"At least someone agrees with me." I glance at the restaurant. Mom motions for me through the window. "But yeah, I think I should get back inside. I'm sure burgers aren't the only thing my parents are flipping or flipping *out* about right now."

"Oh. Right." Kirsten gives me a tight smile. "I guess I'll see you at school next week."

"You go to Ocean Pointe High too?"

"It's the only high school around here." She hitches her tote onto her shoulder and throws up a hand. "Thanks for the water, Angelo. Oh, and be careful."

I freeze. "What do you mean?"

She doesn't answer and walks off, crossing the tiny parking lot, leaving her words hanging uncomfortably in the air.

I tear my gaze away from Kirsten's retreating figure and drag my feet to the restaurant entrance. But I pause as I'm reaching for the door handle. A magenta-colored graffiti tag is scribbled in paint beside the door. The color is hardly noticeable against the red wall. It's probably why I didn't notice it before. I lean in closer, examining the oval with two smaller circles near the top. A mouthless face. I look back to where Kirsten crosses the street and frown.

~

"Work, you stupid thing. Why won't you connect?" I barely stop myself from pounding on my laptop keyboard.

My mind is numb. My finger stings from the burn I suffered trying to dunk a basket of fries into oil. My legs are exhausted. I still smell like burned meat, and I swear a zit is forming on my eyelid. I spent all afternoon looking forward to this moment and even rushed into my room the second my family and I got back to the house. I really don't need my computer fucking up right now. And it isn't exactly. This connection problem isn't my computer's fault; it's the spotty Wi-Fi.

After about ten minutes wrestling with my router, a beautiful word flashes across the screen: *Connecting*. I settle into my chair and nearly burst with happiness once Amanda's sunlit face comes on.

"Hey, Lo-Lo." Only she could get away with calling me such a stupid nickname.

"Hey, Mandy. What are you up to? I miss you so freaking much." If I could kiss her through my screen, I would. "Where are you? What are you doing?"

"Oh, you know. Just hanging out with the fellas." She moves the phone away from her face and motions for someone off camera.

She didn't tell me she missed me too, but before I can start to dwell on that, the wide grin of my best friend, Mackabi, takes up my screen. "*Yo!* What's shaking?"

"Nothing much." I narrow my eyes, wishing I could see past him. But his brand-new veneers block my view. "Where'd Amanda go? We're supposed to be FaceTiming."

"Who knows?" He shrugs off my question and immediately dives into the same conversation we'd had the day before I left. "You still coming home for Streetsgiving?"

"Hell yeah!" I roll back in my chair so he can see me pump my fist. "Do you even have to ask?"

"Just checking, dude. Didn't know if those country folks already brainwashed you into walking around barefooted, shoveling hay. For all I know, you could already be engaged to a woman named Bertha-Ann or something."

"Stereotype much?" My lips twitch. "It's not even like that over here."

"What is it like?"

"You don't even wanna know, man." I let out a mournful sigh, followed by a smirk. "Besides, you should know better than to check on me. Even if there wasn't a skate competition, I would find my way home." *Back to Amanda.*

"Yeah, keep telling yourself that. I know your parents."

"And I know my aunt too," I fire back. My aunt is my mom's oldest yet coolest sister. If anyone can convince my parents into letting me finish out high school in San Diego, it's my free-spirited Tita Marie. "All I need is some time to talk to her alone, without my parents always butting in."

Mackabi sticks out his tongue. "For real. It's like your parents always knew what you were trying to do. Every time you tried to beg Marie to save you, your mom always showed up."

"Tell me about it. Why else do you think I need to have this conversation in San Diego? My parents can't stop the conversation if they aren't there." I grunt. "You'd think my mom would've been happy I was trying to spend QT with Tita Marie before we left. Especially since my parents are already committing one of the worst things a Filipino could do."

"Having an asshole for a son?" Mackabi teases.

I hold my middle finger up to the screen. "I was going to say move away from their family, dipshit."

Mackabi chuckles and shakes his head. "Yeah, I guess I can see that. I always thought Italian families were close, but yours got even mine beat."

"Family's important in our culture," I said.

"But that's exactly why I'm not so sure your parents will even let you visit alone. Watch your mom jump on that plane last minute."

"No, somebody needs to help Dad keep Sloppy's Pit Stop open. I doubt they'll trust some newbie to manage it."

"Sloppy's Pit Stop." Mackabi chuckles.

"Besides, Mom already promised I could go." If I can pay for my own ticket.

"Whatever you say."

There's no missing the hint of doubt in his tone. As much as I miss my best friend, I'm already over this conversation. I start to ask for Amanda, but like magic she grabs her phone back. "Hey, Mandy—"

"So sorry, Lo-Lo. I gotta go." The rush of wind distorts her already breathy voice. Lavender wisps dance across her face.

"Go? But I didn't even get to talk to you," I whine.

"Sorry," she says again. "But word on the street is there's a swell at PB. I need to grab my board before it flattens out."

"But—"

"I'll text you later, 'kay?"

"Uh, okay. I love—"

She ends the call, leaving me staring at a blank window.

"—you." I slowly close my laptop and slump forward. "Good God, can things get any worse?"

# 3

**One Week Later**

I'll pick you up right here. Right after school. Then we're going straight to Sloppy's," Mom instructs as I idiot check my bag to make sure I have my schedule.

I snap closed the buckles on the front of my backpack—the place I'd usually store my skateboard if Mom allowed me to skate to school instead of insisting she give me a ride. And yes, there's the skate magazine tucked in the side pocket of my bag. I never go anywhere without a little essential reading material.

Biting back a string of comebacks, I say instead, "Don't worry, I'll be right here. Right after school."

"Okay, *anak*. That's good." Mom's eyes glass over in that way reserved for parents who realize how grown their children have become. Maybe that's the reason why she called me "child." She reaches out and wraps her thin arms around my neck, pulling me into a tight squeeze.

"Mom!" I groan, trying to tap out. "Mom . . . let go!"

I'm vaguely aware of muffled laughter coming from outside the car, but I'm too embarrassed to look in case I find the entire student body watching this overly sentimental goodbye.

Mom finally releases me. "I'm just so proud of you, *anak*."

"For what? Going to high school?" I let out a choked laugh.

"No. Being brave enough to start a new school."

*Like I had a choice.* My jaw clenches as I give her a firm nod. "I'll see you later, Mom."

I finally push my way out of the car and, taking the first official steps into the Ocean Pointe High School population, maneuver around a line of almost identical pickup trucks in the parking lot.

I get my first good look at the high school sans bullies.

It's still horrible.

I continue forward and am rewarded with looks and whispers. Though I expected that, I'm still amazed at how small this school is. My last school had about four times the number of students and tons of diversity—black, white, brown, and even someone covered in purple tattoos.

As the buzz of conversations circles around me, I become confident this is one of those places where everyone's in everybody else's business.

I push through the front doors and let out a groan. Staring back at me are the bullies from the parking lot, only they're double in size.

A giant poster stretches from one wall to the other, surrounded by sparkling streamers. The bullies, dressed in full football regalia, grin back at me with obviously edited white teeth. There's no way those smokers have smiles that look like the "after" photo from an orthodontist office. I read the words printed at the bottom of the poster, SIX-TIME STATE CHAMPS, then scan the hallway full of letterman jackets and cheerleading uniforms. The students wearing them—the football players and cheerleaders—are greeted with a cascade of high fives and hugs from the other students. The lead jerk's words run through my head like an annoying song stuck on repeat: *top of the food chain.*

I once read that the trials you face in life make you the person you're meant to be. If that's the case, then this indescribable level of torture lying ahead of me means I'm meant to be pretty awesome.

I weave through the crowd of jocks to get to my locker on the second floor.

"Hey, brown boy. See you lost your skateboard."

I don't even have to turn around to know whom the voice belongs to. Ignoring him, I continue forward. In front of me is an overly excited group of girls. I watch the scene play out. Squeals, hugs, and a makeshift fashion show as friends compare their brand-new duds.

These girls are probably the type to write heartfelt messages in each other's yearbooks, only to go back to talking behind each other's backs once the new school year starts.

I wipe the smug smile off my face. There's no need for me to shit on other people's happiness because I miss my friends so much. I picture the latest string of texts in our group chat, full of inside jokes I'm no longer privy to. My throat constricts, but I allow myself only one mournful sigh. If I'm going to make it through the day, my head must be at a hundred percent.

I scan the different flyers littering the hallway walls. Drama Club. Student Council. French Club. Maybe Kirsten was wrong about this place being so football minded. I'm admiring a beautifully designed rainbow flyer for the school's GSA club when I plow right into a boy near the staircase.

Paper flies everywhere. A few books fall. My backpack slips off me and smashes to the ground.

"Whoa, buddy." On instinct, I reach out to grab the guy like I would anyone taking a spill at the skate park, but he slaps me away.

"If you weren't going so fast, maybe this wouldn't have happened." His Roman nose scrunches up. His caterpillar eyebrows furrow. Huffing, he bends over and scoops up his things.

I pick up my own stuff and argue, "I wasn't going fast."

"Then you're calling me slow." He straightens, as if to intimidate me.

"Sorry I bumped into you." I shake my head and walk away. I jog up the steps painted in alternate colors of maroon and yellow and wander the second floor in search of lucky locker number 277. It ends up being the farthest locker away from all my classes. Not so lucky after all.

Glancing at the three numbers scribbled at the top of my schedule, I quickly turn the dial a few times and throw open the locker door with a bang. I open my backpack and begin to transfer my extra notebooks inside but drop one.

"Hey, it's the water boy!" Kirsten's voice cuts through the air, then she's ducking underneath my arm to swipe my sticker-covered notepad off the floor. She grins as she eyeballs the multicolored designs. "Cool artwork. And why am I not surprised most of these stickers are skate brands?"

"What can I say? I'm predictable."

"Ah, don't sell yourself short." Kirsten hands me my notebook. Unlike before, her fingers are completely clean.

I remember the graffiti tag that Mom spent a half hour scrubbing off the wall of Sloppy's. "Hey, would you happen to know about some graffiti—"

A guy's deep voice interrupts me. "Well, if it isn't Kirsten the traitor."

"Don't you mean Kirsten the bitch?" a girl's nails-on-chalkboard shrill voice pipes in.

The tall brunette slings an arm around the leader jerk from the parking lot. It's a wonder I didn't smell his tobacco-drenched clothes approaching. Both wear identical grimaces and stare daggers at us.

I nudge Kirsten. "Who are these people?"

"No one worth knowing." Despite her stony face, there's no missing the sadness in her tone. I make a mental note to ask her about it later.

The buzz-cut, blockheaded boy whose shoulders look too big for his head eyeballs the now scabbed-over scrape on my face. His thin lips curve up at the corners.

"Guess Kirsten found a sidekick." The brunette makes a show of fake sniffing us. "Doesn't surprise me. Strays always find their way to trash."

It's the lamest insult ever, but the blood still rushes up to my face, rumbling inside my ears. When the jerk pipes in, "Guess that makes this here brown boy the dog, huh? You are what you eat," my vision narrows at the edges. Judging by his size alone I'm pretty sure he can take me. But I still pull my fist back and growl, "Guess that makes you a possum."

Kirsten tugs at my arm. "They're not worth it," she hisses, frowning at my newest enemies. "Justin and Maddie are just sad, small-minded people."

"Shut it, Kirsten. Justin and I are going to be big vloggers soon." Maddie's visibly offended. She swipes her tongue against her bottom lip with a sneer. "Just wait and see who's sad and small, *loser*."

Kirsten flinches.

Justin puffs out his chest. "We have a hundred subscribers on our channel. We're hitting it big already."

"Oh, I can only imagine what content you put out. Let me guess, hunting or football, right?" I reply with a laugh. If they only knew I just came from the mecca of vloggers, having rubbed elbows with some of the better-known influencers. In fact, Mackabi is pushing one million subscribers as we speak.

"I don't like your tone." Justin pushes forward. "I'm actually surprised you had the guts to come to school today. Especially after what me and my buddies did to you."

Kirsten shoots me a frown, but I roll my eyes and mimic the boy's accent. "Well, *y'alls* were very welcoming. How could I stay away?"

I can't help but grin as Kirsten snickers beside me. Justin isn't as tickled. "Here's a tip for you. Learn how to shut your mouth."

"Yeah, I think the ship's already sailed on that—"

"Mr. Henderson." A booming voice interrupts our little squabble. "Do we have a problem here?"

A slim man with a bald head and hippie glasses strolls up to us. Beside him, a short, scrawny kid wearing a wrinkled shirt and equally wrinkled jeans struggles with a tuba case almost half his size. He trips over his too-big feet to keep up with the man.

Justin stands to attention, looking more like the version of him from the poster. Managing to sound like a butt kisser and a snitch at the same time, he complains, "Mr. Holland, this kid—"

"Is new. Yes, I know. And I doubt he's stirring up any trouble this early in his OPHS career." The man—Mr. Holland—tilts his head toward me, lowering his glasses. "Are you, Mr. Rivera?"

"No, sir. And it's just Angelo, sir," I reply, using the tone I reserve for our restaurant's best customers.

"Angelo? Like Angela?" Maddie snickers, whispering "Angie" under her breath.

Mr. Holland's head snaps in her direction. "Miss Collins, don't you have somewhere else to be?"

"Sorry, sir." The girl purses her lips and tugs at Justin's arm. The two grudgingly walk away, throwing looks back at us until they round the corner and disappear.

Mr. Holland sighs, removing his glasses to wipe away some non-existent muck. "Those two will surely make me earn my pension." I let out a hesitant chuckle. The lanky man peers at me. "It's nice to meet you, Angelo. I'm Mr. Holland, your principal."

I extend my hand. "Nice to meet you, sir."

"Oh, a handshaker. Whoa, and a firm one too!"

Though Kirsten had laughed wholeheartedly at his pension joke, Mr. Holland glances at her as if just noticing her. Dropping my hand, he stares down at her from the tip of his crooked nose. "Don't you have homeroom to get to, Miss Nelson?"

*Kirsten Nelson.*

I don't know why, but it suits her. Like a movie star name I'd see on the credits of a classic movie, it's as elegant as it is ear catching.

Kirsten pats my arm. "See you around, Rivera. Welcome to OPHS."

"Yeah. Thanks." I rub at the goose bumps her brief touch somehow created.

"Angelo." Mr. Holland slams a hand on the short guy's shoulder. "This is Lawrence Buchanan. He's a junior like you."

"Larry," the boy corrects, wincing when Mr. Holland lifts an eyebrow. Larry shifts his weight from one foot to the other, and when he yanks at his shirt, I catch a whiff of body odor and nearly gag.

"Hi, Larry." I frown, guessing he's part of a buddy system for new students at OPHS. We had something like that at my old school, and thankfully I was never picked to be a "buddy."

Mr. Holland continues to fiddle with his glasses, peering at me from over the rims. "Seeing as you have most of the same classes together, we've taken it upon ourselves to assign him as your tour guide. To look out for you and whatnot."

I bite back a smile. I'm both impressed and confused that Larry's gangly arms can even hold up his gigantic instrument. From the looks of this kid it'll be *me* looking out for *him*.

Larry doesn't look too enthused about any of this. "Um, Mr. Holland? Do you think we can head over to AP English now?"

"Always nice to have students raring and ready to go." Our principal pumps a fist. "Go on and have fun, boys."

I hitch my backpack onto my shoulder with a nod. "Will do."

Larry waits until Mr. Holland is out of earshot. "Finally! I thought he'd never leave. Well, buddy, looks like it's just you and me now, huh?" he enthuses, about three energy drinks deep to my half a cup of green tea. He gestures to the stairs, hikes up his pants, and readjusts his tuba so he's holding it horizontally using both arms. "C'mon. I've had perfect attendance since I was in kindergarten, and I don't want to be late."

Larry jogs toward the stairs. Sighing, I slam my locker shut and follow him. Larry glances at me. "I think you'll like it here. The classes aren't too bad." He shoots me a grimace. "If they're too hard for you, maybe you can ask the office to switch them up for you. I wouldn't mind. I'd still be your buddy."

"Why do you think they'd be too hard for me?" I ask carefully.

We climb down the stairs. "I'm taking all honors and AP courses. Some glitch must've put you in all my classes," he says as if it's the most obvious thing in the world.

"Glitch?" I shake my head, unsure of whether to be pissed or amused. "You don't think I'm smart." I say it more as a statement than a question. This kid better watch himself or he'll end up on my list of bullies too. Alongside Justin and Maddie.

Larry gulps but never stops moving. "Mostly seniors are in my classes."

"Yeah, so?"

"And . . . um . . . it's just that . . . you look like . . ." He hikes up his baggy jeans again with his free hand, giving me a good view of the shoelace wrapped around his waist where a belt should be. Interesting. It's an old skater hack to hold up your pants without the risk of falling on a buckle, but I doubt he skates.

"I look like what?" If this is another crack at my race, I am jumping on the first flight back to California and never looking back. I'm sure Mackabi would get a kick outta vlogging about it.

He gestures at my Weezer shirt and ripped jeans with a shrug. "Not the type to know the difference between *Fahrenheit 451* and Blink-182."

"You've got to be kidding me." I let out a loud laugh to mask my growing annoyance. "Listen, dude. I'm a lot smarter than I look. I'm sure they put me in all honors because I was bored as hell in my old classes. Got a lot of z's, if you know what I mean."

The tips of Larry's ears turn bright red, but at least he nods. "Whatever you say."

"By the way, I know the difference between the two. So let me know if you want a hard-core discussion on classic literature or my music playlist."

"Should have known you're smart. I mean, you are Asian . . ." Larry's voice trails off as he looks at me in horror. He flinches, preparing for me to smack him.

But I decide to educate him instead. "I actually bust my ass and study to be smart. Don't discredit my hard work."

"S-sorry."

"It's fine, little dude. Just don't say shit like that again."

Larry's chest visibly deflates. "Where are you from, anyway?"

"California."

"No. I mean, where are you really from?"

*Good God. Are you serious?*

"If you're talking about where my parents immigrated from *twenty years ago*, then it's the Philippines," I snap. "Seriously, man. Most of us Filipinos are second or third generation. I was born in San Diego, so like I said, I'm from California."

Larry's ears aren't the only things that are red anymore. The flush almost camouflages the freckles on his cheeks. "I'm sorry. Sometimes I have a habit of speaking before thinking."

"Maybe try to break that habit, little dude."

"By the way, please stop calling me that." He grabs on to his faded waistband and hikes it up again so the frayed bottoms stop dragging against the tiled floor. "I have a bit of a complex about my height."

"Sorry, li—" At his look, I clear my throat. "I mean sorry, man. Obviously, I have a problem with speaking out my ass too."

Larry instantly relaxes. "No problem, *tall* dude."

I let out my first genuine laugh of the day. Guess my new tour guide isn't so bad after all.

We rush down the stairs until we're practically sprinting through the east wing.

"Class doesn't start until eight, right?" I ask between heavy breaths.

"Yeah, so?"

"So, we have time."

"If you haven't noticed, I'm kinda short. I need to get to class early so I can get a good seat in front to see the board."

Instead of telling him that people usually want the seats in the back of the room, I continue following him down the hall.

Around us people are moseying to class, most likely feeling the way I do—not wanting to be here. Larry and I rush past clusters of different friend groups. Every few feet questioning looks are thrown my way. Fortunately, none are as venomous as the ones from the jerk and his girlfriend. As if reading my mind, Larry glances at me and frowns. "What did you do to piss Justin and Maddie off?"

I shrug. "Nothing, man. I was just at my locker talking to Kirsten."

"Kirsten?" Larry's thick bottom lip juts out. "Makes sense."

"What's that supposed to mean? She not cool or something?"

We pass a row of lockers and take a turn into a corridor lined with classrooms. "Actually, it's nothing. Forget about it."

But judging by his tone it really isn't "nothing." And regretting not asking Kirsten about the graffiti earlier, I skid to a stop. "If I need to watch out for her, I want to know."

My new buddy slows down and throws his head back. "Can you pick up your feet, please? I'd leave you, but if Mr. Holland finds out . . ."

"What's that crack you made about Kirsten?" I insist.

Larry, one second away from pulling me down the hall, is shuffling along now. "Sorry, didn't realize you two were so close. Please. Come on."

I stand in place, firmly rooting myself so only a huge linebacker can take me down. "I'm not moving until you tell me what you mean."

Larry's shoulders sag forward as he lets out a loud sigh. "Fine. But only because you asked so nicely."

Kid's got sarcasm. I like it.

"You're new, so it will probably be in your best interest to stay clear of Kirsten," Larry explains. "She has a bit of a reputation for being . . . uh . . . a bitch."

I shake my head and cluck, "You really shouldn't call a girl that."

Larry shifts uneasily. "All I'm saying is that if you don't want to be guilty by association, I'd turn the other way. Especially if you're planning on trying out for football or something."

"What makes you think I wanna try out for football? Hell no! Team sports are so not my thing. Especially with people like Justin on the team."

Larry shrugs. "Everyone wishes they could be on the team."

I gesture at the giant black case he's holding. "Something tells me that doesn't include you." I turn and nod at a group of kids belting out show tunes. "Doubt they'd wanna be on the team either."

"Well, I can't speak for them, but I'm practically on the team. I mean, I play tuba at the games."

I picture Larry with a ridiculous hat with a feather on top and chuckle. "Yeah, I guess that's the same thing."

"You know what? As your new buddy, I'll ignore that and instead usher you"—he tugs at my arm, forcing me to take a step—"toward better decision-making."

I follow him to the end of the hall where our classroom is. But I stop before going through the doorway. "Larry. I'm intrigued."

"Kirsten may seem nice, but she pissed off the whole cheerleading squad by leaving them hanging before nationals last year. It was a bitchy move. She was captain and left them right before the competition."

"No one ups and leaves without a good reason," I point out.

"Kirsten does. The squad was down a man—er, girl, and couldn't even compete. I think it's really messed up that she bailed on them. Besides, those girls have been her friends forever." He glances longingly at the classroom and sighs.

"If most of those girls are like Maddie, then I don't really blame her for it," I reply with a snort.

But Larry's beyond listening to me. "If I were you, I wouldn't even try to be friends with her. She'll probably drop you in a heartbeat one day when you least expect it."

"No problem. I wasn't planning on it." I tap my watch. "Anyway, it looks like we got one minute 'til the bell rings."

Larry's eyes widen in alarm. He spins around to hurry into the classroom and smacks right into a wall. Well, not a real wall but a giant kid wearing a maroon fedora.

The tuba case crashes to the ground, and Larry splays onto the floor beside it. Sighing, I grab on to his arm and pull him up. "Here you go, buddy."

The giant barely gives us a glance. Humming softly under his breath, he continues down the hall as if nothing happened. "Is everyone in this school rude or just all the football players, like that guy?" I ask.

Larry straightens and picks up his case. "He wishes. That's just Aiden Brinkman. Smart guy. Shy. Definitely not one of Justin's friends or on the team."

Larry heads into the classroom. "By the way, this teacher's been known to give a quiz on the first day. Hope you're read up on Gustave Flaubert. That's AP English for you."

I step into the empty classroom. Larry plops into his coveted seat in the front row, and I take the desk in the back corner.

And then a familiar voice carries in from the hall, and Justin and a couple of his friends walk into the room. I'm surprised they're in AP. Maybe they're not as dumb as I thought they'd be.

The bully's harsh glare lands on my face. "*Lookit* here, guys. The brown boy's in our class."

A rush of heat washes over me.

One of the other bullies breaks out into a grin that would make the Cheshire Cat proud. "This should be fun."

I throw my head back and sigh. God, can this day be over already?

# 4

I should've known better than to wish away the school day, because sweating over the grill is way worse than bombing a test I had no idea to prepare for.

Then again, I should be happy I even have any burgers to make. We've only had a handful of customers all afternoon, even after Dad put his all into advertising Sloppy's Pit Stop's grand opening today. The multicolored balloons lining the entrance pound against the glass doors with each blast of wind. Dad, decked out in a bright red wig and equally bright grin, stands at the corner waving a giant **Now Open** sign to passing cars. But despite all his efforts, no one's busted a U-turn to check us out.

It's nearing the end of my shift, and I'm dying for our new trainee, Chad, to take my place. I'm drenched in sweat and pull my shirt away from my stomach, like peeling off a sticker from the paper backing. Desperate for relief, I'm *this* close to ripping my sopping shirt off all the way, but Mom's nasally voice calls out above the annoying elevator music she insists on playing. "Angelo! I'm busy helping this gentleman cash in his lotto tickets. You mind taking their orders?"

A disgruntled old man with ebony skin and startling white hair watches my mother feed his pile of wrinkled tickets into the machine one at a time. He scowls in impatience. It looks like he'll be here for a while, so instead of complaining I walk over to the counter.

"Well, well, well. If it isn't the brown boy from California." Justin eyes me up and down, then glances at his friend, whom I recognize from AP English. I'm suddenly thankful for the large counter separating us.

"What can I get for you, Justin?" I ask, purposely ignoring the gang of football players who'd come into the diner with him. Except for their one black teammate, the rest of the players all pretty much look the same. All the way from their pristine letterman jackets to their bad haircuts and irritating smirks.

The guy from AP English pushes away from the pack, pressing up against our newly cleaned counter. He looks almost identical to Justin, but his head is more oval than square. A pinkish scar runs through his right eyebrow all the way down to his cheekbone. He taps against the cleft in his chin, taking his time to read the illuminated board as if it isn't like any other fast-food joint's menu. "What do you serve that doesn't have dog in it?"

"Nice, Grayson," says one of the football players.

"Woof," barks another.

My mouth drops open. Everything slows. Even the jocks' annoying cackles sound like Charlie Brown's teacher, warped and low.

I glance over at my mother. To my relief, she's busy with her customer, completely oblivious to the bigotry going on right under her nose.

"You know I don't have to serve you, right?" I point at the front window.

The Grayson jerk follows my finger and laughs. "Am I supposed to see something there?"

To my embarrassment, Dad must have ripped down the huge black-and-red sign left behind by the last owners. **WE RESERVE THE RIGHT TO REFUSE SERVICE.**

Fantastic. Dad's probably worried to lose any kind of business. Even from bullies.

I clench my jaw. "Never mind. Do you want a burger or not?"

"Hey, I don't like your tone," he snarls. "You should know my dad's the sheriff."

"Am I supposed to be impressed by that or something?"

The boy sneers. "You better watch how you talk to me, because he's only one phone call away."

He makes a show of plucking out his cell phone, which looks like a child's toy against his oversize palm.

"Guess Superman's gonna save the day, eh?" I joke, paraphrasing one of my guilty pleasure songs.

I'm met with blank looks.

I have to consciously stop myself from sagging forward in disbelief. "Seriously? Do you guys not listen to good music down here?" I shake my head and cluck. "It's a song by Charlie Puth. A classic." I pause for a beat, scanning the crowd's blank expressions. "Shit, it's not even that old of a song. I can't believe you don't know it."

Grayson isn't impressed. "Some of us actually have lives, nerd. So don't go thinking you're better than us just because you listen to some indie artist nobody's heard of."

I press my lips into a smirk. "He's mainstream."

"That smart-ass mouth of yours is gonna get you in trouble." The bully makes a show of pulling up his contact list on his phone. "It won't take much for me to convince my dad to shut this place down."

He holds the phone at an angle so I can see DAD displayed in bold letters on the screen. I'm surprised his phone number isn't labeled ATM or ONE PHONE CALL.

"Dude, this is a burger joint, not a money laundering scheme. Doubt he'd have grounds to close it down," I say with a tired sigh.

"I bet it's a scheme all right. Tricking people into eating dog or cat, that is," Justin pipes up, high-fiving the snickering guy next to him. He turns back to me, takes a gumball from the glass jar Mom insists on keeping near the register, and pops it into his mouth.

I've never been much of a fighter. I never had to be. With my old circle of friends who'd rather spend their energy surfing the waves than wasting it on stupid arguments, I never had a reason to raise my fists. But seeing the way these guys are looking at me, *judging* me, I have an inkling all that is about to change.

"We can have this place shut down for poor health conditions." Grayson leans across the counter toward me and sniffs loudly. "And bad hygiene if you're not careful."

"Says the grade A the health inspector gave us?" This time I point to a sign I know is there. My dad posted the inspection grade proudly last week.

"Only takes one hygiene complaint to bring it back down to an F. You wouldn't want this poor excuse of a diner to be shut down right after opening, would you?" Daddy's boy bares his teeth.

It's a trick question. To be honest, I do want it shut down. Maybe then my family can move back to California and forget this stupid idea of country living. Money matters aside, I'm sure my parents can scrounge up enough to build a tiny taco stand by the beach. Shit, I wouldn't even mind living in a hut on the sand if we needed to.

But a glance at my mom shows me that she and Lotto Guy have gotten the whole cashing-out debacle figured out, and now she's all smiles and is even shaking the man's hand. As ridiculous as this whole "uprooting the family" plan was, my parents put everything into making our move successful. I can't let them lose out because of someone who probably doesn't know the difference between Caesar the emperor and Little Caesars.

As much as it pains me, I clench my jaw and look back at Grayson. "What do you want?"

"Ah, a man willing to negotiate. I like that." His cronies chuckle behind him.

I cross my arms tightly against my chest, trying hard to make them appear bigger and more intimidating than they usually do. "I'm waiting."

Justin takes the lead, of course. He grins wickedly. "We want the combo number five. For free."

"For *all* of you?" My arms drop to my sides. There have to be seven guys here. All that food will come out to be more than my whole shift's pay. "Are you serious? I can't just give you free food!"

"Funny, because once I start talking and people find out what a trash restaurant this is, you'll have to give your food away for anyone to eat it."

I'm stuck. Blow my entire check, a.k.a. my plane ticket money, on giving these bullies free food or risk these guys making major trouble for my parents. I glance at Mom again, then look outside at my dad who's busy twirling his sign in the air. But telling on these guys will only make matters worse.

"We're waiting." Grayson drums his fingers against the counter. I swear they're so huge the coins inside the register rattle.

*I'm going to regret this,* I think as I suck in a deep breath. "Fine. I'll give you all free food—"

"Not free. Paid for." Kirsten seems to appear out of nowhere. I didn't notice her walk in. Then again, I was distracted.

Her petite body pushes through the menacing group, working her way to the counter. We all watch in surprise as she slams a few twenties on the counter. "I think this should pay for all of it."

I gape at her and shake my head. "I can't take your money."

"Yes, you can." She stands a bit straighter, eyeballing the sneering jerk across from me. "As for you, Grayson, what you can do is drop the whole 'call your daddy' routine. It's getting old."

Grayson shrugs. "Sure. Free food is free food. Besides, paying for me is exactly how you got me into your pants in the first place, right?"

The guys bust out laughing, and I clench my fists, but Grayson doesn't even crack a smile. If anything, he seems a bit dejected.

But Kirsten ignores him. "You better get cooking, Angelo," she tells me. "The quicker you make them food, the quicker they'll leave."

"Yeah, Angie. Make my food. I'm hungry," Justin says with a snicker.

The jocks' voices all become white noise to me. Dad in his red wig peeks in through the window, shooting me a thumbs-up. If he only knew they aren't customers but freeloading extortionists.

"Angelo," Kirsten repeats, nodding to the grill.

I grit my teeth and walk to the back.

~

"You didn't have to do that, you know," I grumble as I pluck a mayo-crusted piece of tomato off the booth closest to the door. Kirsten's right beside me, helping to gather the crumpled wrappers the jocks left behind.

"A simple thank-you would do. And stop saying you'll pay me back. I don't want your money." She tilts her head, her hair swinging across her face.

"Thank you," I say.

Her eyes sparkle as she winks.

I blush and focus on the fries strewn across the table, picking them off one by one. "And now I repeat, you didn't have to pay for them."

"It was nothing. I'm always here to help someone in need," she says brightly.

*That's not what Larry said,* I think. "You sure you don't mind?"

"Why would I mind?" She snorts. "C'mon, Rivera. It's only forty bucks."

"It's a lot of money," I argue, cringing as I pick up a snot-filled napkin. I shudder, tossing it into the rolling trash can at the edge of the booth.

"No, it's not."

To me it is. Coughing up forty bucks to feed those bullies would have put a big dent in my "get back to California" savings account, which is still a couple of hundred dollars below my goal. It doesn't help that my parents are only paying me minimum wage.

"It's still money you gave to me when you didn't have to." I swipe my arm across the table, knocking everything into the trash can. The pile may or may not include some reusable trays. I'm hoping Mom doesn't do an inventory count on our supplies later.

"Seriously. Enough. Why can't you just let this go?" Kirsten steps back as I push the trash can past her.

"I don't like taking handouts," I answer.

"Then don't think of this as a handout."

"What other way should I think of it?" I kick the trash can the rest of the way, then give the rolling bin one last monstrous kick to put it back where it belongs. Taking a deep breath, I wipe my hands across my dingy apron and throw her a pointed look. "Just let me pay you back for it."

This time her bubblegum lips curl slowly into a wide grin. "Since it doesn't seem like you're going to drop this anytime soon . . ."

"I'm not," I agree.

She nods. "I actually have some other form of payment in mind. But it isn't money."

"Well, that isn't scary or anything," I reply with a laugh. "Do you need a hit man or something?" Then, suddenly, I feel awkward. Is she flirting?

"Not scary at all," she purrs. "Just a future favor I can cash in whenever I need it."

"Need to wait until the next blue moon or something?"

"Actually, winter solstice," she shoots right back.

"Well, if you're looking to sacrifice a virgin, you gotta use someone else," I play along.

"Thanks for sharing. But totally TMI," Kirsten says, rolling her eyes. She leans up against the closest booth. "But I don't do sacrifices. Didn't you hear? I'm vegan."

"Wait, you're vegan?"

"Yup." She narrows her eyes suspiciously. "Why? Want to joke me about it or something? Believe me, I've heard it all."

"No." I shake my head, surprised at her sudden shift in mood. "Actually, I'm just wondering why you're even in a burger joint to begin with. Shouldn't you be against this place?"

And just like that, her scowl disappears. "Oh." Her mouth forms a circle as she lets out a breath. "I actually came in here to see if you wanted to hang out."

"Uh, I can't today. I'm busy." As soon as I clock out I'm going home to FaceTime Amanda.

Kirsten doesn't look at all disappointed. Instead, she takes a marker from her pocket and grabs a napkin from the table's dispenser. I narrow my eyes as she scribbles a phone number in bright magenta.

"Hey, Kirsten. I've been meaning to ask you something. Do you tag walls—"

"Here." She springs up and thrusts the napkin into my chest. "Now you can text me to let me know when you aren't busy."

I tighten my hold around the napkin. "Kirsten, um, I have a girl-friend back home."

Kirsten's eyes widen in surprise before tightening at the corners. She clears her throat and smirks. "A bit cocky of you to assume I wanted to hang out like *that*, Angelo."

My cheeks warm. "I . . . I thought because you . . ."

"Yeah, yeah, yeah." Despite her smile, Kirsten's icy blues remain hard. "Actually, let me get your number too."

"Why?"

"So I can phone in my favor when I think of what I want."

In a daze, I pluck my phone out of my apron and plug in Kirsten's number. I shoot her a quick text: It's me.

Within seconds her phone chirps. She glances at the screen and beams.

My stomach churns. This doesn't feel right. I'd hate it if it were Amanda giving some random guy her number. Then again, I do owe Kirsten a favor. This is pure business.

I push my phone back into my pocket. I can't wait to get home and call my girlfriend.

~

I walk into my bedroom, collapse into the chair behind my desk, and power up my laptop. I pick up Nollie, placing her on my lap. Amanda's always loved my little ginger dog—even if the feeling isn't really reciprocated. Maybe seeing her will make Amanda want to stay online for a bit longer this time.

Our video chats, which are supposed to be nightly, now only happen about every other day. They're always cut short for some reason or another. Good waves at the beach, meeting with her friends, skate practice—even Amanda's texts are becoming sporadic. I called her out on it, but she insists staying busy is the only way she won't miss me too much. You'd think actually speaking to me would be better.

I stare at the dots on my screen waiting for the call to connect. Nollie fidgets in my lap, growing as restless as I am. After another round of rings, Amanda's sweet face appears.

"Lo-Lo!" She grins, but there's something off about her smile. It's stiffer. Then again, maybe it's just the added pixels on my screen.

"Aren't you a sight for sore eyes." I lift Nollie up to the camera. "Look who wants to say hi to you."

"Nollie, my girl. How are you, cutie?" Amanda giggles, and I push away the day's stresses—the bullies, Kirsten's mysterious favor, and even dealing with Larry's clinginess at school.

Wanting to hear her laugh for just a second longer, I tilt Nollie from left to right so it looks like she's dancing. "Nollie misses you, but not as much as I do."

Amanda's laughter comes to a stop. "Yeah, it's been hard, huh?"

"Knowing I'll be talking to you at night makes it easier." I try to smile, but it comes out wavery. I clear my throat and lower Nollie onto the ground. "Mandy, do you think we can try harder to talk every night? When I left we promised we would, but it's been two weeks since I got here—three weeks since I left San Diego—and we've only FaceTimed a handful of times."

Amanda sits straighter. "I've been busy, Lo-Lo."

I lean back and sigh. "Trust me. I know."

"Don't give me attitude," she snaps.

"I'm not giving you attitude."

"It's hard having a boyfriend so far away. Like, I don't even know the kind of people you're around. I need to stay busy so I don't think about it."

"Well, if we talked more you'd know," I say as kindly as possible.

She scowls. "What happens if you meet a girl over there?"

Kirsten pops up in my thoughts, but I quickly push her away. "C'mon, Mandy. Don't you trust me? Besides, you're around guys all the time."

"Yeah. Our friends. Guys you don't have to worry about."

"And there isn't anyone here you have to worry about either."

As if on cue, the G note from My Chemical Romance's classic song "Welcome to the Black Parade" plays from my phone. I glance at the Instagram notification: Kirsten Nelson requested to follow you. I turn the phone over on my desk as if Amanda could see it.

I briefly shut my eyes and take a deep breath. "Mandy, do you remember our last night together?"

"How could I forget?" Even with the pixels there's no missing the pink spots on her cheeks.

I swallow hard and grin. "It was the best night of my life."

"Because of the sex?" she grunts.

"No! But yeah." I shake my head. "My point is, it was amazing because it happened with you. I loved you before, but after that night I love you even more. What makes you think I'd throw it all away for someone else?"

"I guess . . ."

"No. No guessing. I'm being honest."

Amanda glances over her shoulder and sighs. "Angelo, I'll talk to you later, okay? I'm running late to something."

"What? Are you serious? You're going to end our conversation *now*?"

She reaches for the screen. "I'll talk to you later."

"But—"

"Bye."

I stare at the blank screen in surprise, unsure of which to be mad at more: the fact she cut our conversation short *again* or that she called me by my real name.

# 5

"I see you stepped out of your meth lab." Maddie snickers and shoulders me as she walks by my locker. I whip around.

"Hey, buddy. Ready for your second day of school?" It's like Larry manifests out of thin air.

I jump about five feet, somehow slamming my locker shut in the process. I lose my grip on my skateboard. It flies in the air, landing upside down.

Grabbing my chest, I take three deep breaths to calm myself down. "What the hell's your problem, man?"

"God, you're jumpy." Larry smirks in amusement. "Are you always this weird?"

"Sorry. Wasn't expecting your magic act today."

"Magic act?"

"Never mind, Houdini." I snort and reach down to grab the side of my skateboard. Not a "mall grab" because it's lame holding on to the front trucks, the metal in between the wheels.

Larry peers at my board, pausing at the deep scratch marks on the bottom of the deck and trucks. Telltale signs of grinds conquered and lost. He flicks at an old Padres sticker and gazes at me curiously. "You skateboard?"

"No, I just carry this around to pick up girls."

His eyes widen in surprise. "Really? Does that work?"

"No!" This guy can't be serious.

I glance at my locker. I could leave my skateboard inside, but I always lugged it around with me at my old high school. As did all my friends. Granted, we used to skate around in the quad at lunch, and though I doubt I can do that here, I'm not about to change my habits now.

I lower my backpack onto the floor and place my skateboard, wheels side out, against the front of the bag. I clip the first set of straps underneath the top trucks and tighten the other set below the bottom ones.

He squints. "No, it doesn't work? Or . . ."

"Try 'or,' dude." After I give a slight tug to make sure the board's secure, I grab my bag and push past Larry. I'm beyond needing a tour guide and just want to be left alone.

I fly down the stairs and see that Maddie's now focused her attention on another poor soul. She's black, which makes her only the third other BIPOC I've seen so far in this monochrome institution. The girl frowns. She pushes her red cat-eye glasses up her curved nose bridge, practically leaning back as Maddie barks at her. "I told you the squad needs the auditorium that day, Stella! Or can you not read your emails?"

"I . . . I'm sorry." Stella reddens as she clutches her binder tightly against her chest with one arm. She bounces from one foot to the other. "I didn't know."

Maddie's lips pull into her usual snarl. "I hope you know the only reason we voted you student council president is so you'd do what we want you to. Now start doing what we want you to!"

I open my mouth to say something, but once again Larry pops up behind me out of nowhere, effectively distracting me. "Well, excuse me if no one I know actually skates."

I reluctantly tear my gaze away from Stella. "Honestly, I wouldn't have thought any different," I tell Larry.

Larry gives a half-hearted shrug. "All people care about around here is football."

"You sure about that? I saw some flyers for other clubs yesterday."

"Clubs hardly anybody ever joins. Why else do you think they advertise using cheap little flyers when the football team has a giant poster in the front of the school? It's not hard to tell who the favorites are around here. Popularity equals club funding, and club funding equals a higher shot at being popular. It's a vicious cycle."

I grunt. "Football's big in this part of the country, huh?" We're standing in front of the school's huge trophy case. The overshined football trophies almost blind me.

"I guess. At least it is in Ocean Pointe."

"Why?"

Larry shoots me a bewildered look and says, "Because it's cool?" He shakes his head. "It's just the way it is. Ocean Pointe High's been obsessed with football ever since the school was erected. Then again, it is about the only sport we ever win in."

"Maybe think twice about using the word 'erected.'" I smack my mouth.

Larry gestures at my beat-up board. "Guess it's a California thing to skate, then?"

"Not really," I mutter, easily dodging a group of cheerleaders who plow right into Larry. The redheaded one nearly knocks him to the floor. Larry barely flinches, as if it's an everyday occurrence.

Regaining his balance, he drops his head and mumbles something under his breath.

"Dude, are you talking to me? You gotta speak louder than that." I glance over my shoulder and stare at the cheerleaders' swishing skirts until they disappear down the hall. I shake my head and frown at the boy who's supposed to look out for me. "And while you're at it, maybe you shouldn't let those pom-poms walk all over you."

As we resume hurrying to class, Larry clears his throat and talks only a decibel higher. "Do you think you can teach me how to skate?"

Wait, what?

I don't know whether to laugh or cry. "Are you serious?"

"Of course I'm serious." He stiffens, shrugging uncomfortably. The chaos of the hallway and our squeaking sneakers fill the awkward silence between us. "Is that a weird question or something?" He gives a strained chuckle. "Am I too old to learn?"

"It's not weird. And you're definitely not too old." I stare at the floor until the alternating maroon and yellow tiles make me dizzy, remembering the first time I even hopped on a skateboard. I was about seven, and I'd been begging my parents for a board ever since I saw my neighbor Tyler do a kickflip in the middle of our street. My parents finally caved and drove me straight to the toy store after 24/7 pleading. "I mean, I learned when I was a kid. Most of my friends did. But I don't think it would be any different for you."

"Then what's with the look?" Larry shoots back.

"Like I said, I didn't think anyone in Ocean Pointe would care to learn." Well, besides Kirsten. But what are the chances I found the only two other people in town who like skateboarding?

I turn down the hall, slapping a hand against a low-hanging banner advertising the first game of the season. "Before me and my skateboard came along, all you cared about was football, right?"

"And band," Larry retorts.

"Right."

We make it into the classroom a bit later than Larry wanted and find a sprinkling of students already scattered around the tiny room. Three girls huddle in the back, comparing pictures on their phones. I walk to my usual desk in the corner, and to my surprise Larry gives up his precious seat in the front to sit next to me.

"Are you going to teach me or not?" he presses. Larry watches me place my bag on the floor, resting the back of it against the legs of my desk so my skateboard stays vertical. "I'm free today after school. I only have band practice on Mondays, Wednesdays, and before games on Fridays."

"Why do you want to learn so much?"

Larry mumbles something.

"What?" I lean over and shoot him a frown. He mumbles again, and this time I cup my ears. "Say that again."

"Because I'm sick of doing what's expected of me," he bites, straightening when the jocks glance our way.

I roll my eyes partly because of Justin and his buddies and partly because of Larry's pathetic scowl. "Says the guy who runs to every one of his classes because he doesn't want to break his perfect attendance record?"

"Maybe I'm stuck in a rut. School, band practice, football games, home—maybe I just want to do something exciting for once. Do something different. High school's supposed to be about fun and discovering yourself, right? What if I haven't done any of that?"

A wadded-up paper ball hits my temple, bouncing off and landing just a few feet in front of me.

"Hey, brown boy. Why don't you go ahead and pick that up?" a deep voice rumbles from across the room.

I kick the wadded-up paper toward Justin's desk. "Larry, if you want to do something different, maybe start standing up to these cheerleaders and jocks."

Larry shifts uncomfortably. "What if I start out smaller?"

"By skating," I say.

He nods excitedly. "And when you teach me, we have to find a place to skateboard in private. Hate to say it, but if the badminton team is considered bottom tier, skating in public would be committing social suicide."

"First of all, I don't recall even agreeing to teach you." I slump against the uncomfortable plastic chair and groan. "And seriously? A *Mean Girls* reference?"

"I streamed the movie," Larry mumbles. "I like old teen flicks."

"You do?" I'm impressed. "That's pretty cool. I binge old movies too."

Larry's eyes brighten. "Does that mean you'll teach me?"

"Whoa. I'm still not agreeing to anything." I pull a notebook onto my desk just to have a buffer between us. "Also, good luck finding a good place to skate around here. Private or not."

Just this morning I was racking my brain trying to figure out a way to practice for Streetsgiving while living in a town whose version of a skate park is the potholes littering the streets.

Larry clears his throat. "Listen. Angelo. You're new here, and I don't have many friends either. So think of this as a win-win. I get lessons. And you get—"

"A waste of time?"

Larry bristles. "I was going to say a friend. Isn't that what new kids want? A friend?"

"New kids don't always want friends," I tell him. Especially new kids who are planning to leave.

"I beg to differ. You seemed pretty cozy with Kirsten yesterday."

"We weren't cozy," I say through gritted teeth. "And I don't want to be cozy with her." After our conversation last night, I don't know what I'd do if Amanda thought I was into another girl. "She was just being nice."

"Kirsten's never nice."

"So you say," I shoot back with a scowl. "But she saved my ass yesterday." I explain to him what happened at the restaurant.

When Larry looks surprised, I suggest, "Maybe try to get to know Kirsten better."

A group of OPHS cheerleaders gathers by the door. The flood of yellow hair ribbons swarms around the entrance like a bunch of bumblebees surrounding their hive.

"Kirsten used to be one of them. Those cheerleaders. The top of the hierarchy," Larry says, watching them.

He turns back to me. "And for your information, I do know her. I've known her since kindergarten. And so I also know that it doesn't matter that she jumped ship and is no longer part of the popular group. She's a 'popular girl' at heart. You know, entitled and judgy. I've seen all the games she used to play before she turned over this 'new' leaf," Larry says, making air quotations as he says the word "new," which irritates me for some reason. "And she's not going to change now."

"This sounds like the plot to a cheesy teen movie," I scoff.

Larry scowls. "Hey, I'm trying to help you here. Trying to be a friend."

I can't hold back my disbelieving snicker. "Oh, is that what you're doing? Sounds to me like you're talking shit."

"More like saving your ass."

"Kirsten saved my ass," I remind him. "Without putting anybody down. Right now, the only mean person is you."

Larry's bottom lip trembles, but he never takes his eyes away from me. "Even if Kirsten saved you, getting with her almost guarantees getting your ass beat."

"Whoa, whoa, whoa." I hold my hands up. "Who said anything about 'getting with her'? I have a girlfriend, dude."

"You do?" Larry's nose scrunches up.

"Is that so hard to believe?" I ask.

"I guess not." Larry shakes his head. "Anyway, it's a good thing you're not after Kirsten. For the reasons I just explained. Plus it'd be breaking the OPHS bro code to even look her way. All the guys in school know not to go after her. Grayson would be so mad. Actually, it might be better if you aren't friends with her at all."

"Wait a minute. She dated Grayson?" The thought of her with that jerk annoys me.

As if on cue he walks into class. Grayson tries to toss a balled-up piece of paper into the wastebasket as he heads for his seat. Upon missing, he groans loudly, as if he's just blown the state championship for his team.

Larry's eyes bug out as if I've just committed the worst infraction by not already knowing every detail of the OPHS royalty's lives. "They dated on and off for almost three years."

I nod, but really, I can't wrap my head around the idea. Sure, Grayson hinted at some kind of . . . relationship with her during his visit to Sloppy's Pit Stop, but I'd just chalked it up to him being stupid. Kirsten doesn't strike me as the type who'd bother to give the meathead the time of day.

Grayson easily shoots a second wad of paper into the wastebasket and lets out a loud whoop. Snorting, I nod toward him. "Why is he in this class? I doubt there's much going on up there."

"Angelo. Focus. Did you hear what I said about becoming friends with her? Will you give it up?" Larry insists.

"Honestly, I stopped listening." I wink.

Ignoring my jab, Larry hisses, "Kirsten dropped her friend group like a hot potato. Then she dumped Grayson right after. Who's to say this new phase in her life's gonna last? Is it really worth getting beat up only for her to ditch you right after?"

"I never said I wanted to be friends with her, let alone want any friends to begin with, remember?" I snap.

"Right. I believe you." Larry busies himself with setting up his desk for class.

My eyes zero in on Grayson's profile and narrow. "And if the bullies want to be pissed at me, they can go right ahead."

Another wad of paper flies across the room, landing on my desk. Larry reaches over and flicks it off. "Yeah, I don't think you'll have to worry about that."

# 6

B urger Boy, your food sucks!" Justin shouts from his table.
I grit my teeth and keep moving, though what I really want to do is throw my food in his face. Kirsten wasn't the only one who found me on Instagram. Justin and Grayson spent all of last night DMing me sorry memes and insults. I ended up blocking them, but that didn't stop them from finding one of my old unlocked profiles that I mainly used to post about skateboarding. It might make me look chickenshit, but I ended up deactivating the account just so I wouldn't have to deal with them.

Justin's laughter is lost in the white noise of cafeteria chatter, but there's no ignoring his glare burning into my back. I scan the cafeteria, looking for a place to sit. I see Stella, the girl Maddie was yelling at. For a moment I'm tempted to join her and maybe apologize for not stepping in when I had the chance. The big kid with the fedora, I think his name is Aiden, is sitting beside her. But the mean guy I bumped into on the stairs . . . he's sitting at the same table, and there's no way in hell I'm in the mood for his level of drama today.

Larry magically appears by my side yet again. His tray bumps into mine, sloshing some soup onto my plate. "Where'd you eat yesterday, Angelo? I didn't see you."

"I don't remember," I lie, not wanting to admit I'd spent the entire hour in the library, wishing I were anywhere but OPHS.

"I bet," he muses, sounding skeptical.

Annoyed at his slight smirk and the almost mustache on his lip (I can only grow peach fuzz), I shoot the same question back at him, expecting an equally sad answer. "Where'd you eat, superstar?"

He doesn't disappoint. "Over there." He points with his chin to the lone table in the corner by the row of trash cans. It stands empty, and I doubt it'll have more than one occupant today.

*Or just maybe two,* I think as a round of laughter booms from what I can only guess is the popular table. Like those *National Geographic* photos of fish swimming around a shark, there's a radius of space surrounding the jocks and cheerleaders.

Grayson glances up and catches my eye. His thin lips spread across his annoying face as he leans back and rubs at his nonexistent belly, no doubt a crack about our time together at Sloppy's Pit Stop.

"Yeah, yeah. Free food," I grumble.

"What's that?" Larry walks in front of me, intent on leading the way to his sorry table. Unfortunately for him, I've officially lost my appetite.

"You know what? I'm not really hungry."

Larry freezes on the spot. "You're not?"

"Nah, I think I'm gonna head out and use lunch to text my friends. In California." I'm not sure why I feel a need to clarify, but either way it doesn't stop Larry's face from crumbling.

"But I thought we'd eat lunch together so we can talk more about skating."

"Sorry." I feel a bit dickish, but coming to the cafeteria was a bad idea. I need to get out of here before my head explodes.

I walk over to the nearest trash can, dump in the nasty lump OPHS is trying to pass off as Salisbury steak, and toss the empty tray onto the rack beside it. I adjust the straps of my backpack, tightening them against my shoulders. "I'll catch you later, okay?"

"Yeah, whatever." Larry frowns, bumping into my arm on the way to his table.

I weave my way between the rounded tables filled to the brim with my classmates. Back in my old school, we didn't have a cafeteria. We had a half hour of eating on top of palm tree–lined green hills that stretched throughout campus. Once again, I can't believe I traded in paradise for this circus act.

I burst through the exit into the main hallway and lean against the wall. I've never been the type to feel claustrophobic, but this place is ridiculous.

When my spinning head is screwed back on tight, I pluck my phone from my pocket, open my texts, and click on the thread at the very top.

I eye the blue bubbles, cringing at how many times I've texted Amanda this morning alone. All but one of my texts have gone unanswered. The silence is a bit unnerving. At the risk of being even more clingy, I shoot her another message.

Hey, Mandy . . . just want you to know I miss you and I love you.

Almost immediately, a bubble with the bouncing ellipses pops up. My heart leaps to my throat. I wait for Amanda's reply, but the ellipses disappear, and I'm once again left with nothing.

"Are you serious?" I grit my teeth, wanting to chuck my phone, when I notice a familiar head of blonde rushing to the school's exit. I zero in on the bulging tote bag bouncing against Kirsten's thigh.

In my mind's eye I see the magenta face on Sloppy's Pit Stop's wall. I'm pretty sure she's the artist behind the doodle, and though I doubt she'll tag Sloppy's again, what other buildings will she target?

She pushes through the front exit, and I'm tempted to go after her. Skipping school isn't something I usually do, but the glimpse of the blue sky calls to me. From behind the cafeteria doors the buzz of students seems to grow louder. Claustrophobia creeps up again. I need to get out of here. Besides, I'm curious what Kirsten can possibly be up to.

I glance from left to right. No teachers. I unbuckle my skateboard from my backpack and rush to the door.

# 7

I crouch low in an attempt to make myself more aerodynamic, but I'm tense. The scrape of my wheels against the asphalt is far from relaxing. I have to weave around cracks and dodge loose pebbles and twigs as I desperately try to keep up with Kirsten. Not only does she have a couple of minutes' head start on me, but she's pretty fast on her bicycle.

My calf muscle burns as I push forward, watching the land fly by. Everything looks identical. Green grass upon green grass, and cows upon cows.

When the scenery does change, it isn't anywhere as serene. Trees morph into sprawling houses intermixed with rusted trailers. On one side of the street sits a ranch-style house not unlike my own, made entirely out of bricks. It has colorful wind socks hanging off the eaves with streamers dancing in the air. I pray it's where Kirsten's headed off to, but considering how fast she's pedaling I highly doubt it, so my lungs continue screaming for air and I'm sorely reminded of my lack of practice. Thanks to all my mandatory training sessions at work last week at Sloppy's, the last time I was on a board was my first day in Ocean Pointe. Well, not counting the short ride to school this morning. At this rate, I have no hope of even placing in Streetsgiving.

Kirsten takes an abrupt turn down an unmarked road like the one near the restaurant, and I turn to get onto the road.

But immediately I skid to a stop. The asphalt ends abruptly, with hardly any transition into a gravel pathway. I gulp, staring at Kirsten's back as she bikes up the hill and immediately disappears over the crest.

"Well, I've come this far. No use in turning back"—I pick up my board and shuffle forward, kicking up dust around my ankles—"says every person in a horror movie."

The afternoon sun beats against my shoulders, burning through my T-shirt, which is already drenched. Chest heaving, I finally make it up to the peak of the hill. My mouth drops open.

An abandoned industrial lot stretches out as far as the eye can see. Small buildings that look like warehouses surround a large one, which I'm guessing used to be the main warehouse. Except for its chipped paint and rusted aluminum siding, it's far from decrepit. I have no idea what Kirsten's doing here, but I thank God I followed her.

Gaps.

Rails.

Stairs.

Banks.

Ramps.

This is a skater's paradise.

Like a kid stumbling into Santa's secret workshop, I run down the hill, clasping my skateboard tightly against my body. I practically drool, staring at each obstacle, wondering which I should tackle first. It isn't until I hear a curious noise that I remember why I'm even here to begin with. I tear myself away from the obstacles—it's almost physically painful to do so—and follow the sound to the big building. It intensifies, alternating between long hisses and short, sporadic spurts.

I walk up to the entrance. The two door handles are wrapped together in oxidized chains. Orange flakes of rust fly off as I yank the gigantic lock, but it barely budges.

I walk the perimeter of the building and notice a window with one of the glass panes missing. Placing my board against the wall, I wipe my hands against my shorts and grab on to the ledge, hoisting myself up. I've barely cleared the windowsill—I've propped one foot on top so I can throw my other leg over—when I spot Kirsten inside, crouched over and *spray-painting?*

"Whoa . . . *WHOA!*"

I lose my balance and tilt forward. My body hits the cement floor with a sickening thud.

"Angelo! What the fuck are you doing here?" Kirsten shrieks.

Groaning, I push myself up. Kirsten is hastily walking over to me. Her teeth bared, eyes blazing—she looks furious.

Ignoring the waves of anger radiating from her body, not to mention the pain radiating from my forearm, I look around.

The warehouse resembles one of the cool alleyways in Los Angeles or New York City. Giant bubble letters, thin script, doodles, and even some abstract designs cover the otherwise bland concrete walls.

Kirsten comes to stand near me while my eyes roam the walls. "Did you follow me?" she barks when my eyes return to her.

"Yes. I mean no. I mean, yeah?" I wince, scratching at the sweat coating my chin.

She puts one paint-covered hand on her hip and with the other hand aims a spray can at me. "Well, which is it? Yes or no?" Her voice trembles, possibly in anger. And her hand is trembling too, I guess. Because she actually loses her grip on the can. It falls onto the concrete with a loud clang and rolls to me. Like she did at Sloppy's, I stop it with my foot and pick it up. The nozzle's still wet with bright-turquoise paint that matches the giant letters on the wall behind her.

## JUST ME

"Looks nice," I comment, nodding at the words. I shift uncomfortably as she narrows her startling blue eyes even more. "You have skills."

She swipes the can from my hand. "You didn't answer me," she growls. "What are you doing here?"

I bow my head. "If you must know—"

"I must."

"—I did follow you. I saw you skip school, and I wanted to know where you were going."

"Why?"

I flinch. Is this the mean girl Larry warned me about? "Because I wanted to know if you were the one who tagged Sloppy's Pit Stop's wall."

Pink circles sprout on Kirsten's cheeks, but her tone remains abrasive. "I guess you found your answer, huh?"

My gaze lands on a magenta squiggle on the other side of the room. "Yeah, I guess so."

Kirsten crosses her arms and taps her toes. "What are you going to do about it? You gonna tell on me?"

"I—"

"Actually, you know what? I think I'll cash in that favor you owe me." Her eyes narrow into menacing slits. "Don't tell anyone about my work. More specifically, don't tell anyone about this place."

"I wasn't going to say anything." I blink in surprise. The words *"friends wouldn't snitch"* tease the tip of my tongue. But saying them out loud would be admitting to something I'm not ready to. "Besides, who would I even tell?"

"Are you saying if you had someone to tell you would?"

"Wait, what?" I gape at her. "Please don't put words in my mouth."

She cocks an eyebrow. "Are you going to keep your mouth shut or what?"

"I'm not going to tell anyone!" Figuring this argument will just run around in circles, I decide to lighten the mood. I gesture to the paintings around us. "Guess this explains why you always have stains on your fingers."

Kirsten doesn't crack a smile.

I suck in a deep breath. "Listen, I promise I'm not going to say anything. You have absolutely nothing to worry about." She harrumphs but looks relieved. "Besides, no one in Ocean Pointe even likes me enough to want to speak to me. And even if I did have people to talk to, I wouldn't do you dirty like that."

Kirsten considers it for a moment and shakes her head. "That's not true."

"It's not? But it is. I wouldn't . . ."

"No, not that. The bit about no one here even liking you. I like you."

"Oh, um . . ." My heart throbs against my rib cage. "Okay." I move away, look around at the walls, and change the subject. "Now that we got that all settled, let's talk about your artwork." I move even farther from her. "You did all these yourself?"

"Yeah." Her lips finally curve into a full smile. "My afternoons and evenings have cleared up, so I like to come here and paint." She points to a lopsided daisy on the opposite wall. "That's my oldest piece from last spring. Not my best, but I was just starting out. With spray paint, I mean. I dabbled in art since I was a kid."

"Does that include glass blowing?"

"Are you kidding me?"

I shrug. "Everyone seems to like glass art here. I saw the signs."

She snorts. "I don't."

"Yeah, you only like tagging abandoned buildings and restaurants, right?" I half joke.

"I . . . I . . ." Kirsten grimaces. "Listen, I'm sorry for tagging Sloppy's Pit Stop. I did it about a week before you guys came, and when I saw the lights on when I was walking by that day, I knew I had to clean it up. Why else do you think I came in for water?"

I narrow my eyes. "Wait a minute. You weren't really thirsty?"

She smiles sheepishly. "To be fair, I was. But I did need the water to clean up my work."

"Water takes off graffiti paint?"

"No, but the paint marker I used at your restaurant was acrylic-based. It comes off with water. Takes a little elbow grease, but it cleans up eventually."

"You still didn't clean it up, though," I point out.

"I was planning on it," she protests. "I got distracted talking to you. Anyway, I'm sorry for the trouble."

"Don't apologize to me. Apologize to my mom. She's the one who cleaned it up."

Kirsten's eyes widen. "Oh, shit. Is she mad? I'll go to Sloppy's Pit Stop later and—"

"Dude, I'm kidding. Don't worry about it." Though Mom had been angry, she'd already have forgotten about it. Reopening the topic wouldn't be good for anyone.

"I'm really sorry. I won't do it again. Obviously."

I gesture toward the walls. "I'm surprised you even did it to begin with. Looks like you have your own private studio in here."

Kirsten follows my gaze and murmurs, "After a while you get tired of hiding."

"Why do you have to hide?" The girl Larry described doesn't sound like the type to be scared of anything. Shit, I saw her stand up to Grayson when I couldn't.

"It's complicated." She takes a deep breath and forces a smile. "But part of the reason is because no one really supported my art. It's a lot easier to paint in secret without having to worry about public scrutiny."

I snort. "Is that why you chose this medium?"

"Huh?"

"Graffiti. The artists usually use symbols in place of their names or other pseudonyms. Like they're hiding behind a mask. At least from the pieces I saw in California."

Kirsten mulls it over for a beat. "Yes. And no. I like the anonymity, that's for sure. But I also like how different street art is from the art I used to do. Well, what little art I used to do when I was stuck in my box."

"Box? What box?" I ask.

"Cheerleading," she answers as if it's the most obvious thing in the world. "Ever since I was in peewees, cheerleading ate me up mentally and physically, not to mention eating up all my time. It was my niche." She stopped and looked around at the walls for a moment. "Luckily, I'm not pigeonholed in that box anymore."

"Oh, yeah. I heard about that."

She blinks in surprise and flashes me a smile that warms me to my core. "Oh, did you now? You asking around about me, Rivera?"

I shake off the warm sensation swimming in my gut. "Isn't that how Ocean Pointe rolls? Everyone knows everybody's business, don't they?"

"You can say that again." Kirsten spins around, walking back to her unfinished piece. "Speaking of knowing people's business, what are you even doing here?"

"What do you mean what am I doing here?" I pick up my feet, following her. "I already told you. I wanted to see what you were up to."

"No, I mean why are you in Ocean Pointe?" She stops in front of the unfinished mural and turns around, scanning me from head to toe. "Unless you're related to one of the old bloods, no one comes here voluntarily. Trust me. My dad's Ocean Pointe's only real estate agent, and with his repeat customers, I know."

"I guess that's what Judy meant about Ocean Pointe being all about tradition and routine."

"Mrs. Spellman speaks facts . . . and gossip." Kirsten smirks. "Before I painted on your restaurant wall, I had to make sure she wasn't at her shop to see me."

"Gossip or not, I should've paid more attention to her when she said newcomers have it hard here."

"But isn't it like that anywhere, though?" Kirsten asked.

"I'm not so sure." I stare at the bright-blue lettering behind Kirsten, getting lost in its swirls. It reminds me so much of the ocean that I'm

Sheeryl Lim

hit with a pang of homesickness. "Anyway, to answer your question, my parents thought it would be a good idea to move here."

"Why?"

"Why do parents do anything?"

"That's not an answer." She chuckles, bending over to swipe a painter's mask off the floor. "Here." She hands it to me. "Wear this unless you want to get high off the fumes while I paint."

"Maybe if I get high, I'll forget I'm in Ocean Pointe." My fingers graze hers, and I pull back in a hurry.

"Sorry to tell you, it doesn't help," she teases. "Now go ahead and tell me why you moved here."

"It's not an interesting story," I warn, putting on the mask. I breathe in and cough out the industrial smell. "Uh, I think paint fumes would smell better than this. Was this doused in silica gel or something?"

"Just tell the story." Kirsten's voice is muffled through her mask, as if she's talking from the far end of a tunnel. She shoots me a pointed look and starts to spray more turquoise paint inside the unfinished letters.

"Okay, but remember I warned you." I bite the inside of my cheek, wondering why I feel almost embarrassed to tell her our old restaurant failed miserably. Actually, that's far from the truth. It wasn't so miserable. Rivera's Kusina used to do really well, and we tried our best to hold on until the very end. But like the tide ebbs and flows, I guess businesses do too. Still, it's hard to believe that our family restaurant—our first one—is nothing but a memory.

I frown remembering the conversation my parents sprang on me. I'd just finished shooting the shit with my friends at PB and rode the bus over to our restaurant. It was bustling as usual, with the same old customers. Lolo Ben and his eerie but cool colorless eyes. Auntie Josie and her endearing cackle. Tony and Lou, the college-aged twins. Nothing seemed out of the ordinary until Dad motioned for me to join him and Mom in the kitchen. It was *sinigang* night, and he knew better than to

72

put me in charge of mixing the no-recipe-just-by-taste tamarind-based broth. I knew something big had to be going on for him to ask for me on such a special night.

"What's up?" I asked, frowning when I noticed the dark crescents bordering his bloodshot eyes. He didn't look as stressed out when I'd left the house that morning. "Are you okay?"

He twisted an oily dishrag in his hands repeatedly, almost as if he didn't realize he was doing it at all. "Um, yes. Your mom and I need to talk to you."

"Okay . . . ?"

His Adam's apple bounced each time he swallowed. "You see . . . er . . . your mom." He shook his head and took a deep breath. "Your mom and I have made a big decision."

"You're getting a divorce." Looking back, I don't know why that was my go-to response. It's ridiculous to think my parents, who've been best friends since they were five, would even think of separating at this old age.

"No! *Bastos!*" Mom clucked with a quick shake of her head. "Your dad and I aren't divorcing. Our family is moving."

I gaped at her for a moment before bursting into laughter. There was no way I could've heard her right. "Wait a minute. I thought you said we were moving."

"We are."

I stared at her blankly but found nothing. Only pure seriousness etched on her already stern face. "Like up to Rancho Bernardo?"

"A little farther than that."

I gulped. "Temecula?"

Mom sighed, rubbing at her temples as if our little guessing game exhausted her. "Across the country."

"But . . . but that doesn't make any sense."

"I'm sure you've heard your dad and me talking about how we're not making much profit anymore. So we sold Rivera's—"

"You sold the restaurant?" My voice boomed across the tiny restaurant, startling our regulars, who immediately started to whisper among themselves.

"Mila!" Dad hissed to my mother. "We said we'd ease him into the idea. Not spring it on him!" His eyes darted in the direction of the dining area. "More importantly, I wasn't ready to tell the customers yet."

"Can you stop worrying about customers and for once worry about me?" I said, but Mom's voice rose above me.

"Ay! But you were taking so long, Roman. He thought we were separating! He should know we have a new place."

While the two bickered, all I could do was focus on how life as I knew it was slowly unraveling. My phone had buzzed in my hand—Amanda asking if I was still joining her for dinner at Taco Hut that night. As a testament to my warped mind, I hadn't even been able to answer the text.

"And before I knew it, I was on a cross-country trip to this town. All because of some bad business decisions my parents made."

I don't know how I expect Kirsten to react, but her one question surprises me. "Who's Amanda?"

That's all she got out of my story?

"She's my girlfriend."

"Ah, the infamous girlfriend." Kirsten finishes the *S* in **JUST ME** and glances back at me. "That's cool you guys stayed together even with your move. A lot of couples can't make it through big changes."

Those damn ellipses from Amanda's non-text pop into my head. I shake it off and reply, "You sound like you're speaking from experience."

"I won't even deny it." Kirsten bends over and pokes at her tote, perusing her collection of spray cans. Deciding on one, she grabs it and tosses it in my direction. "Here." I barely catch it before it hits my face. "Why don't you help me paint?"

"I don't know how." Not to mention I really want to get back outside and skate. There's a ramp with my name on it, just waiting for me.

"It's easy. Just spray where I tell you to." She catches me looking over my shoulder and grunts. "Don't worry. No one's going to catch us. This place has been abandoned for years. They used to bottle soda here or something until they went out of business."

"I know the feeling." I smirk at her, despite the mask still covering my face. "But I wasn't worried about getting caught. I was actually thinking about skating."

"Skating?" She squats and busies herself with spraying more blue on a blank space on the wall.

I nod. "I don't know if you know this, but right outside there's a ton of places I can practice."

"Practice for what?"

"A skating competition," I explain. "I'm planning to enter one in November with my friends."

She turns from her piece and eyes me curiously. "With Amanda, you mean?"

"Wait, what?"

"Never mind." She gets up, brushing off her frayed shorts, which only smears paint on them. "I'm guessing it's a competition in California, right?"

"How'd you know?"

She pulls down her mask so it hangs below her chin. "Obviously, Ocean Pointe would never hold a skating competition."

"Obviously," I repeat with a grunt. "No one here sees it as a sport."

"Because it's not."

Scowling, I whip off my mask. "Don't go turning all Ocean Pointe on me now, Kirsten. Just because it isn't football doesn't mean it's not a sport." I picture Grayson in his stupid letterman jacket and feel the sting of face-planting in the school parking lot. "Tony Hawk, Steve Caballero, Daewon Song—I'd like to see someone tell them skating's not a sport. They don't just have huge competitions and followings for nothing. Who cares if it's not under Friday night lights?"

Kirsten stares. "Well, no one can ever say you're not passionate about skating, that's for sure. Sorry if I offended you. I obviously don't know much about it."

My nostrils flare, and I shoot her a tight smile. "Yeah, I guess I do get pretty defensive about skating."

She snorts. "You think?"

"What can I say? It's one of my last lifelines to California."

"I guess I can see that," she says quietly, looking up at me through hooded eyes. "Sorry if I upset you."

"Nah, don't worry about it."

She rights her mask, positioning it over the bottom half of her face. "I'll tell you what. Why don't you help me finish this piece, and when we're done you can show me some moves outside?"

"You really want to watch?"

"Voyeurism is underrated." She winks.

My jaw goes slack. Is she for real?

She snickers and points to the outline of the *T*. "Stop fooling around and paint."

I pop off the lid, stare at her mural, and throw out an innuendo of my own. "Where do you want me?"

# 8

Painting is euphoric.

I've never been the artsy-fartsy type, but there is something soothing about seeing an otherwise boring space transform into something beautiful.

But as beautiful as Kirsten's finished piece is, I know I can most definitely turn the rusted rails and dusty ramps outside the building into masterpieces.

Kirsten steps up beside me and follows my gaze. "What are we looking at?"

She's so close I can almost feel her heat penetrating the thin layer of my *Thrasher* shirt, which I happened to wear today. Talk about manifestation. Clearing my throat, I shift away. "Just figuring out which obstacle to take on first."

"For practice."

I nod. "I was starting to worry I wouldn't have a place to skate. But this is great."

My gaze roams over the gaps between buildings. It is paradise. "How'd you find this place, anyway?"

"Like I said, it used to be a soda bottling plant. The only bustling thing in this town. But no one's ever really come back here after it was shut down five years ago. I thought it'd be the perfect spot to paint since it's a ghost town. Private."

The word "private" sparks something in my memory. I push away the thought of Larry begging me to teach him in secret and place my board on the ground. "Well, another man's treasure is someone's trash. Glad you commandeered this place."

Kirsten bursts into laughter. "I don't think that's how the saying goes. Isn't it one man's trash is another man's treasure?"

"Well, er . . ." I shake my head and jump onto my board.

The thing I love most about skating is the rush. The humid wind hits my face as I grind my feet into the grip tape for a Nollie Frontside 180. My stomach practically flies into my mouth as I jump into the air. It's been a while since I attempted the move, but I land on the bolts and roll away clean.

I cruise by a yellow-painted curb and stare hungrily, wishing I'd packed some wax. Then again, it's not like I knew I'd end up in a skater's wonderland.

*I'll just bring some next time.* The moment the thought flies through my mind, I slow to a stop. Will there be a next time?

I swallow hard and skate back to Kirsten. She claps, whistling loudly. "That was really good. Who says you need practice?"

"The judges." I kick my board up and catch it midair. I drag a palm down the length of my face, wiping away sweat.

"Hey." My voice cracks. I wince, trying my best to calm my nerves. "Uh, speaking of practice, do you . . . um . . . maybe think I can roll through here sometimes?" I scrunch up my nose. "I know this is like your spot and all, but it's pretty ripe for skating."

Her eyes twinkle. "It's not really *my* spot. Abandoned, remember?"

"You sort of marked your territory." I gesture to the main building. "Remember? You chewed me out when you thought I'd snitch on you."

She cocks her head. "That was more for my paintings than this actual lot."

"Same thing." With her head tilted she reminds me of another painting. One I learned about in art history last year. *The Birth of Venus*. I have to focus on spinning my board against the ground so she doesn't catch me staring. "What do you say? Is it cool?"

"Tell you what. I'll say yes if you do something for me."

I stop fidgeting with the board and narrow my eyes. "Guess I'll owe you another favor, then, huh?"

"Nah." She flashes me a bright smile that in no way, shape, or form would need any photo editing. "Consider this the same one. Honestly, you just caught me by surprise earlier. But I know you'd never tell anyone about my work. You don't seem the type."

"What do you want, then?"

She nods at my board. "I want a skateboarding lesson. Or les-son*ssss*"—she drags out the consonant like the spray from her cans— "depending how this one goes."

"You wanna learn how to skate?" The smile wipes off my face when I remember Larry asking me for the same thing. Then again, it's not as if I owe him anything.

"Like I said, I don't like being kept in boxes. Former cheerleader. Artist. Why can't I be a skater girl?"

"True that."

Wagging her eyebrows, she saunters to me, stopping just a few inches away. She never loses her smile and reaches for my board, grazing my fingers along the way. She bats her eyelashes, flagrantly using her old cheerleading charms on me. "Shall we start?"

This girl is dangerous.

But not as dangerous as skating with her heeled cowboy boots.

"Wait, you can't skate like that." I motion to her feet.

"Like what?" She scowls.

"With those boots!" I cringe at the red faux leather covering her calves. "Don't you have sneakers lying around somewhere? Something without heels and with a good grip?"

"Trust me. I know how to work these boots." To make her point, she does a little jig and taps her heels in the air.

I cross my arms and shake my head. "No lessons until you change."

Her mouth drops open. "You're serious?"

"Please change."

She throws her head back and groans, stomping back to the building. Moments later, she reappears wearing those ugly white sneakers all cheerleaders seem to own. "Happy now?"

"See? That wasn't so hard, was it?" I hand her my board as she snorts.

"You're lucky I still had these in my bag from PE this morning."

"No, *you're* lucky."

She mimics my earlier stance and places the board by her feet. "Okay, teacher. What do I do first?"

"First things first. Let's see if you're Reggie or Goofy."

"I'm sorry, but what?" Kirsten's nose scrunches up.

I circle her like a fly on a fallen Sloppy's Pit Stop fry. She stiffens, straightening her neck. I can see each indent of her muscles as they pull tight. She keeps looking forward, but her eyelashes flutter as she peeks at me from the corners of her eyes. I grin and give her a little shove. With a high-pitched squeal, she stumbles forward, taking a large step with her right foot.

"What was that for?" She spins around, baring her sparkling white teeth.

I point to her feet. "You're Goofy. Just like me."

"Wow, you're two for two today, Rivera. First you sneak up on me and then you insult me."

I bite back a laugh. "What I mean is your right foot will be your lead foot. Like this." I grab the board and hop on, placing my right foot in between the two bolts on top. I push off with my left foot before plopping it onto the tail and gliding in a circle around her. "Knowing which one to put in front will make skating more comfortable for you. It helps with your balance and how easily you can do certain tricks."

She watches me closely, taking in each of my movements as if embedding the images in her brain for safekeeping. My body burns under her focus.

"Okay," she finally says after a few beats of silence. "I think I get it. Now what?"

Where to begin?

No one ever taught me how to skate. I hopped on, fell off, and suffered a few bruises and scrapes until I figured out the mechanics of it all. But the point is, I learned. And sometimes the best way to learn something new is to get hurt. Unfortunately, judging by the way she's looking at the board as if it's a land mine waiting to explode, Kirsten might not be as open to injuring herself as I was.

Suddenly feeling the heat, I yank the bottom of my shirt away from my stomach. It's already soaked in sweat. "Does it ever get cold around here?"

"Be careful what you wish for, because December through March sucks."

"Nah, I think I'd rather be cold. You can always put on more clothes to stay warm," I point out.

"Or you can just wear the right clothes to stay cool," she counters back. "Look at me. I'm doing fine in the heat."

She spins around, showing off her signature short shorts, and kicks her foot out behind her.

I tear my gaze away from her long legs and clear my throat. "When you're done with your fashion show you can get back on the board."

Kirsten stops her little dance and frowns. "With both feet?"

"Yes."

"Are you sure?"

"Yeah." I point to the board. "One in the front and the other in the back."

"But what if I fall?"

I gape at her. "Weren't you a cheerleader? Didn't you get thrown in the air all the time? I'm sure you took a couple of bad falls."

"I wasn't a flyer, Angelo," she snaps.

Whatever that means.

Her eyes flash with worry. "Besides, taking a tumble on a mat is way different than ripping your skin off on concrete."

"Okay, what if I hold you until you're ready to do it on your own?" I suggest.

Shit. Instantly I regret the offer. Skating lesson or not, I really shouldn't be holding on to another girl. I'm about to take it back when Kirsten carefully climbs onto the board and it jerks forward. I rush behind her and wrap my fingers around her waist. "Whoa, watch it."

"Thanks." She releases a breath and relaxes into my grip. "Don't let go, all right?"

"I . . . um . . ." I shake off the unease and remind myself again that this is business plain and simple. "Okay. You ready?"

"Born ready." She shoots me a wink. "Let's do it."

I stand on the right side of the board behind her and push her slowly, keeping an eye on the ground for any rocks or cracks, maneuvering the board to avoid any potential hazards. "Don't lock your knees. Spread your legs wider. It'll help with your balance."

"It's been a while since I heard someone say that to me," she jokes. "At least it's been a while since a boy's said it to me."

I cough so hard it burns my eyes. Kirsten bursts out laughing, and I growl, "Can we be serious right now? C'mon."

Truthfully, skateboarding doesn't have to be *that* serious. It is supposed to be fun. I just don't know how much more of her smart mouth I can handle.

"F-fine," she stammers as I wrap my fingers around her hips again. I tighten my grip on her, accidentally slipping my finger above the waistband of her shorts below her cropped top. My finger brushes her soft skin before I have a chance to pull away.

"Oh, um, sorry about that." I quickly readjust my hands so they sit on her belt loops.

She shakes in my hands. The board wobbles. I brace myself in case it shoots out from under her feet. But like a natural she fixes her posture and regains her balance.

Once I'm sure she won't fall, I take a deep breath and nod. "Okay, okay, that's good. I guess we can move on."

"To what?"

"Um . . . I guess you can try it on your own now."

"On my own?" Her eyes bug out before her pale lashes flutter closed. "I was kinda hoping you'd be my handlebars for a while."

My lips pull into a smile. "I can't always be there for you, Kirsten. Skating is a one-person job." To make my point, I release her. "Go on. I believe in you."

"At least one of us does." She jumps off the board. "But you're the only one. I'm not sure I'm ready to skate by myself yet."

"I thought you were born ready," I tease with a laugh.

But she doesn't laugh along with me. She looks nervous.

I nod to calm her down. "Seriously, the only way you're going to learn how to skate is to just do it. Remember how your parents taught you to ride a two-wheeler?"

"My parents made sure to hold on to me until I was ready." Her eyes narrow. Her tone is sharp. "Angelo. I'm really not as ready as you think I am."

I'm surprised at her sudden change in attitude. "But—"

"I know myself," she interrupts me with a snap of her fingers. "Back when I first started tumbling, my coaches would spot me until I felt comfortable enough to do it on my own. Nothing's changed. I need more time."

I gnaw at my lip. "Fine. We'll keep working at it until you feel you can do it on your own."

"But how will I know when I'm ready?" She eyeballs the board.

"You'll just know." I tap her arm, surprised to find goose bumps there. "C'mon. Let's try it again. With me as your handlebars."

I push her around for a bit, explaining the basics. It doesn't take long until her confidence returns. Kirsten finally gets impatient enough to want to try it on her own. Though I doubt she'll be doing kick-flips and Ollies anytime soon, she takes to cruising solo fairly quickly. Within ten minutes, she's effortlessly navigating around the narrow lot, making sharp turns around the corners.

"See, I can roll around pretty good." Kirsten circles me triumphantly, giggling as I spin around to keep up with her.

"Cruise, not roll," I correct. "But yeah, you're doing pretty good."

"Cruise," she repeats good-naturedly, continuing her donuts. "So what else do I have to learn today?"

"Nothing much. Just continue to practice." I wince at the word. It's what I really should be doing instead of standing around watching somebody else skate.

As if she can hear my unspoken thoughts, Kirsten comes to an abrupt stop. "What about you?"

"I can practice later," I say, more to convince myself.

"No, what I mean is that I doubt you'd be satisfied just rolling—cruising," she corrects, seeing my face. "Don't you know any cool flips or tricks you can teach me?"

"Says the girl who begged for handlebars?" I tease.

She purses her lips. "That was different. I wasn't comfortable enough with the board before, but I am now."

"You may be comfortable cruising around, but doing tricks is a whole different monster. Like, you can't expect to just jump from tinkering around with 'Twinkle, Twinkle, Little Star' to performing 'Waves of the Danube.' You need to master your scales before you move on to chords and progressions."

She whistles in appreciation. "You seem to know a lot about piano."

"My parents were convinced that learning to play would teach me discipline."

"Did it?"

"Skateboarding taught me the same thing."

"Makes sense." The corners of Kirsten's mouth tug down as she nods. "Do you like playing piano? Ever think of auditioning for band? I'm sure Larry would love it."

I picture his large tuba case and laugh. "Nope, can't say that I have."

"Well, maybe you should think about it. I heard they need a new keyboardist."

"What is it with you and Larry trying to awaken my school spirit?" I shake my head incredulously. "Besides band not really being my thing, it's been years since I played. My piano's practically just an expensive piece of furniture now."

"Yikes, sorry I mentioned it." Kirsten lets out a high-pitched whistle. She digs the tail of my board into the ground and cuts too sharp of a turn. She stumbles off the board, accidentally flipping it over. Huffing, she bends over to pick it up, giving me an excellent view of her back pockets. I look away. "It's just that you might actually enjoy it. *And* everyone at OPHS is either on a sports team, a cheerleader, or in the band."

"You're not," I point out, glancing back at her. "And do I look like I want to be any of those things?"

"I don't know. You'd look pretty great in a cheerleading skirt." She wags her eyebrows.

I chuckle. "Skating gives you awesome legs, I'll give you that."

Kirsten's face burns a bright red.

I rush to explain. "I mean, it doesn't give *you* awesome legs."

She frowns.

"I mean, you do have awesome legs. Not that I'm looking or anything." My ears ring. I slump forward and let out a loud breath. "Can we just pretend I didn't say any of that?"

Kirsten snorts. "But you're right."

"I am?" A knee-jerk reaction, my gaze drops to her legs.

"I'm not a cheerleader anymore, but I still have a bad habit of assuming all people want that lifestyle." She shrugs. "I blame OPHS brainwashing."

"Lucky for me, I'm immune to that type of gaslighting."

"Then you're one step ahead of most of the people at our school."

"I don't know. That girl Stella doesn't seem to like cheerleaders that much either—or at least one in particular."

Kirsten places a foot on the skateboard, rolling it back and forth. "Stella? You mean Stella Thompson? The mayor's daughter?"

I shrug. "I guess."

"You're right. She doesn't want anything to do with sports and cheerleading. She'd rather follow in her mom's footsteps."

"See—"

"But that's why I said 'most of the people.' Not all of them." Kirsten points to the board. "Did you want to skate around?"

"Nah. Go ahead."

Grinning, Kirsten jumps onto the board and skates away. She really does seem to be enjoying this. Though I'm dying to fly down one of the rails, I let her have her time with my board. Honestly, it's nice to have another person in Ocean Pointe appreciate skateboarding.

*Larry appreciates it too.* Guilt sucker punches me in the gut. I ditched him to follow Kirsten. To be fair, I didn't know following her would end up in a skating lesson. But still . . .

"God, I'm a jerk," I mutter with a sigh as Kirsten circles back to me.

"What was that?" Like a veteran she rolls to a stop and kicks up my board, catching it easily.

I scan the grounds, which, as Kirsten's secret artwork is a testament to, are as private as it gets. I bite the inside of my cheek until I taste iron. "Hey, I know I said I wouldn't say anything about this place—"

"Angelo," she warns in a sharp tone.

"But someone else wants to learn how to skate, and I was thinking that maybe I can bring him here too." I wince, waiting for her reaction.

"Hell no!" She pushes the board into my chest and shakes her head fervently. "What part of 'don't tell anyone about this' don't you get?"

"But he wouldn't tell anyone," I protest. At least I don't think he would.

"Funny, but that's what you said about yourself earlier. And look where we are now." She crosses her arms and taps her foot against the pavement. "My answer is no. Find somewhere else to teach him."

"Don't you want to find out who I'm talking about before you make a decision? He's harmless."

"I don't care if he's a guinea pig. This is *my* place, Angelo."

"Funny, but that's not what you said earlier," I shoot back, mimicking her tone. Apparently, it was the wrong thing to say and do.

Her eyes flash in anger, whites blazing. "That was before I knew you wanted to invite the whole block here!"

I picture the piece we just worked on. A six-feet-by-six-feet turquoise monstrosity made up of giant bubble letters reading: **JUST ME**. Maybe I should've known she'd react this way.

"I'm guessing my invitation to practice here is revoked now?"

Maybe it's the tone of my voice. Or maybe it's the utter desperation I'm sure is seeping out of my pores. Whatever the reason, Kirsten instantly calms down. "Depends on whether you have a big mouth or not."

"Kirsten, I—" I'm interrupted by the loud blare of "Let's Go Surfing" by the Drums.

I scramble for my phone, plucking it out of my pocket. I turn it over and look at the screen. The blood drains from my face. "Crap!"

"Who is it?" Kirsten asks tentatively.

I shut my eyes briefly, but I know I have to face Judgment Day sooner or later. I force my eyes open and swipe against the screen to answer. "Hi, Mom."

# 9

The air is heavy. Like a thick slab of frozen meat you need a sharp cleaver to hack through. Beef patties sizzle on the grill. Their collective smoke winds into a cone shape that burns against my nose hairs. Beside me, Chad hums along to the corny music blasting from the speakers. A college student at the local community college, he's only a few years older than me but swears he's a sage, always acting like an annoying know-it-all. With his mop of curly red hair, he reminds me of the pro snowboarder Shaun White but less athletic. He wouldn't be too bad to work with if it weren't for his never-ending need to carry on a conversation. It's only been a week since Chad started and I'm already over working with him.

"Heard your parents are pissed off at you for ditching school today," he yells, as if the bubbling oil in the deep fryer would somehow make it hard for me to hear him. I flinch, peeking into the dining area. Our only customer, a young mother with her toddler, shoots me a disapproving look.

"Can you say that a bit louder? I don't think the people across the street heard you—shoot!" I yank back my hand as a splash of oil hits my skin, let my spatula fall onto the grill (as is becoming my habit), rush to the sink, and quickly turn on the cold water. Growling, I push my hand underneath the icy stream and watch my skin begin to pucker and redden.

I scowl back at Chad, who's watching me with interest. "And this is why we shouldn't talk during our shift!"

He makes a show of rolling his eyes. "Oh, please. It's called multitasking, Padawan."

"I'm not your trainee," I retort, though I wouldn't mind being a Jedi.

Chad ignores me. "Multitasking is something you need to master to even think about getting into college."

I hardly stop myself from pointing out he goes to a college with a 100 percent acceptance rate. I shake out my hand, but it still stings so fucking bad. Holding it over a hot grill again is the last thing I want to do, but there's no way I can leave the patties to burn. Besides the bullies' meals yesterday, the mother's family-size order is the largest I've had to put together since Sloppy's Pit Stop's opening. Can't risk giving my parents something else to yell at me about if I ruin our only other big order.

I drag myself back to the greasy slab and push the now oily spatula away with a clean one. Chad's stare burns into my cheek. I whip around and hiss, "What's your problem, man?"

He doesn't flinch. "Are your parents still mad about you skipping?"

"Why do you even care?" I grumble and smack the hell out of a patty before flipping it over.

He shrugs and lifts the basket of newly cooked fries. "Just making conversation."

"Yeah, of course you are." I snort and flip over another burger, which is now too crispy for company standards. "It doesn't matter if they're still pissed. They'll get over it. They know it's partly their fault anyway."

"Ah, playing the victim now, are we?" Chad snickers as he dumps the perfectly golden fries onto the warmer and starts to salt them. Even after a couple of weeks working at Sloppy's, my mouth still waters from the smell of crispy potatoes. I lick my lips and fight the urge to grab a handful of them to stuff into my mouth. At the rate I'm eating them, I'll look like Santa Claus by Christmas.

"They forced me to move across the country, hence basically forcing me to meet new people," I remind him. "And you know what? I went ahead and did just that."

He snorts. "Well, you're obviously bad at picking friends if your new one made you ditch on the second day of school."

Friends? Is that what me and Kirsten are now? Either way, I feel a need to defend her. Especially after how we left things off this afternoon. "She didn't force me to do anything."

"Ah, now it makes sense . . ."

"What does?"

"Why you were so willing to skip." Chad grins. "You like this girl, huh?"

I roll my eyes. "Chad, you know I have a girlfriend. You see me texting Amanda all the time. I don't 'like' Kirsten."

Chad nearly drops the basket. He hurries to place it back in its holder and whips around with wide eyes. "Kirsten? As in Kirsten Nelson?"

I cock an eyebrow. "You know her or something?"

"Who doesn't?" Chad lets out a high-pitched whistle. "She's so freaking hot, man. Now I totally get why you skipped school. I'd do it too if it meant getting to hang out with that hottie all day. I mean, have you seen her butt?"

Still feeling protective of my new "friend," I grab a dish towel and ball it up, throwing it in his direction.

"What the heck was that for?" He cringes, plucking the stained towel off his face. Smacking his mouth in disgust, he drops it to the floor. "There's dried oil on that. I'm probably gonna break out now."

"Zits will be the least of your problems if you keep talking about women that way, man."

"What? I'm speaking the truth. You have to be blind not to see how hot she is." He smirks.

"I have a girlfriend," I repeat more slowly this time.

"Aw, c'mon. Admit it. You spent all day with her. You checked her out, didn't you?"

"Dude, just shut up about Kirsten, okay? Actually, just shut up in general." I shoot him one last pointed look and turn back to my overcooked patties.

I wish I could say the rest of my shift goes easier, but it doesn't. Not that we're busy. In fact, we're the definition of the phrase "slow as a snail." Chad does not let up about my so-called friendship with Kirsten, and my shift lasts a couple of more hours than usual, a penance for today's truancy. By the time seven o'clock finally hits and my parents come in to do the books, I grab my skateboard and hightail it out of Sloppy's faster than Chad can make another inappropriate comment about Kirsten.

The still-humid air slaps me across the face as I weave around potholes. But even the asphalt's calming noise can't distract me from thinking back to Larry.

I'm a jerk.

After all the crap I've been getting from everyone else in my life, I really should've looked in a mirror and realized I've been shoveling my own pile of cow dung too. Larry's been nothing but nice, and I did the one thing my friends back in California are doing to me.

I ditched him.

My phone vibrates. Amanda returning my texts? No, it's probably Kirsten.

An hour or so ago, figuring I wouldn't be able to sleep tonight with guilt festering inside my belly, I had used the one phone number I told myself I wouldn't. I texted Kirsten to ask for Larry's address. She might not be besties with him, but as the daughter of the only real estate agent in town, she'd probably have ways of finding his number.

I stop and yank out my phone.

*Kirsten:* 4516 Cherrywood Road

Straight and to the point. I type out a response. I haven't had any problems with coverage since my parents insisted I drop my California area code in favor of a new Ocean Pointe number from one of the local carriers.

*Me:* Thanks. Appreciate it.

My phone buzzes again before I can open my map app.

*Kirsten:* Guess Larry's your other student, huh?

Before I can respond, she texts again.

*Kirsten:* I'll think about it

My lips twitch.

I plug Larry's address into the app. Once I see his house is farther away than I expected, I stuff my phone back into my shorts pocket and mentally prepare for the long trek.

The rush of wind and sound of rolling wheels do nothing to ease my guilt. I've been skating for what feels like forever, and suddenly the calm country road morphs into something straight out of those crime shows Dad likes to watch.

I read the numbers etched on the front of each rusted trailer. "Forty-five hundred . . . forty-five hundred and two . . ."

The farther I travel, the farther apart each residence is. I shudder. This would be a perfect backdrop to being hacked to death by a masked monster wielding a chain saw.

I pump harder, flying down the bumpy road. When I finally reach trailer number 4516, I skid to a stop. I scramble for my phone to text Kirsten.

*Me:* Are you sure Larry's place is 4516 Cherrywood Road?

It takes Kirsten no time to reply.

*Kirsten:* According to my dad's records, yeah.

Why?

My fingers freeze above the keyboard. I stare at the slab of a trailer, which is much shorter than the ones I've passed. It's white, or rather it would be white if it weren't for the rusted panels and splatters of mud on the sidings. It also stands on what looks like a tall pile of cinder blocks and hasn't any steps. Larry must need to take a running leap to make it to the front door.

And just like that his oversize jeans and wrinkled clothing make complete sense. Back in California I've seen people dress way worse by choice (see definition of "beach bum"). I assumed his purely effortless look was for fashion. Guilt, that bitch, worms inside my gut yet again. I try to shake it off and stare at the high entrance.

*Me:* Never mind

Cracking my neck, I sweep my board off the ground and walk toward the trailer. The tall grass rubs against my bare calves. I fight against the foliage and dodge a pile of broken lawn ornaments.

I manage to pull myself up onto the makeshift porch and knock lightly on the thin aluminum door. Within seconds, high-pitched shrieks pound against my eardrums. Cats breaking out into the song of their people. There's a slight movement at the window, so I lean toward the brown-tinted glass and peer inside. I do my best to avoid grazing a silvery web but still brush against a bug's decomposing thorax. "Gross."

It's hard to see through all the filth, so I inch just close enough that my nose isn't pressed against the gunk.

A pair of wide gray eyes align with me.

"Holy shiitake mushrooms!" I stumble back, falling off the porch into the grass.

A harsh metallic screech fills the air as the door flies open. "Angelo?" Larry's voice is as hesitant as it is accusatory. "What are you doing here?"

Tiny insect legs scamper across my thigh. I brush off my shorts and flick away a wad of mud with tiny grass blades sticking out of it. "Enjoying the wildlife."

"But there isn't any cool wildlife in my yard."

"Never mind." I jump back onto the porch and grab my board. "I was actually looking for you."

"Me?" Larry asks. A fat orange cat squeezes between his legs. "Why?" The cat presses its bushy tail against the torn denim and turns its head, staring straight at me. When it hisses, I grimace and take a step back.

"I came to apologize."

"For what?" I open my mouth to reply, but Larry's tidal wave of accusations crashes down on me. "For ditching me at school? For being mean to me? For not being a buddy at all?"

"Y-yes to all of the above."

He lifts a hand. "You know what? Don't even worry about it. I'm used to it. It's not as if I haven't spent the last fifteen years of my life being ignored."

"Fifteen?" I ask. "You're only fifteen?"

He shrugs. "So I skipped a grade."

No wonder he's so tiny. "Then why are you letting people bully you? You're smart! In ten years, you'll probably be their boss."

"That's not how Ocean Pointe works. Brawn over brains, remember?"

I stare at him blankly. "I don't understand why one has to matter more than the other."

He shrugs. "That's just the way it's always been. It's the way of life here."

"So what you're saying is people are just complacent to bullshit?"

"It's less complacency than it is knowing trying to change anything here is impossible," Larry replies in a cold tone. "But it's fine. I've already made peace with my fate."

"Dude." I toe against a raised plank, unsure of how to respond.

"But thanks." His head drops, ruffling his crazy curls. "For the apology, I mean."

I sigh, looking over the part of the trailer where I'm just now noticing bullet holes scattered along the aluminum wall. "So . . . you live here?"

He lifts his head and shrugs. "With my mom. But she's at work right now."

"Oh."

"This used to be my grandpa's trailer," Larry says. "We moved in right after my dad died." With a curl of his lips he comments, "Not because of a drug overdose, mind you."

I hold up my palms. "I wasn't even thinking that."

"Most of the town does."

My eyebrows fly up. Maddie's weird "meth lab" remark at school finally makes sense.

Larry jams his hands into his pockets and brings his sharp shoulders up to his ears. "Guess I'm used to everyone assuming the worst. Kind of goes with the territory of having a drug dealer as a grandfather."

I look back at the bullet holes, imagining what kind of shady business the patriarch might've been involved in. "Well, you're not a drug dealer, are you?"

"Hell no!"

"Cool. Because I'm all about hugs not drugs." I hold out the board to him. "Here."

He looks down at the board and then back at me. "I'm confused."

I roll my eyes. "You wanted to learn, right?"

"Yeah . . ."

"Then let's go."

Larry's eyes are comically wide and resemble one of those characters from the 11:00 p.m. block on Cartoon Network. "Now?"

"Ain't no better time than the present."

Cringing, he glances over his shoulder. "But I was in the middle of watching a movie."

I'm tempted to ask him which one, but instead I walk behind him and give him a slight shove. He steps out with his left foot. "Reggie."

"What?" Slack-jawed, he stares at my outstretched arms. As if feeling imaginary fingers along his waist, he hikes up his pants even higher than usual. "My name's Larry."

Chuckling, I shake my head. "Never mind. Let's get this lesson started."

~

About twenty minutes into our lesson, Larry yanks at his drenched V-neck. He fans it from the collar so it looks more like the letter *u*. Even from three feet away, there's no mistaking his personal scent of Gouda cheese and sweat. "I can't believe you talked me into skating without protection."

"Sorry, I didn't have any Magnums hanging around," I shoot back with a chuckle.

Larry scratches his chin. "Like the ice cream bar?"

"No." I shake my head. "Why are you even worried? If you keep skating as slow as you are, the worst you'll get is a scrape on the knee. If that!"

"Easy for you to say," he mutters. "I bet you came out of the womb knowing how to skate."

"Ha! I wish. I'd probably be pro right now if I did."

"Might as well be." Larry climbs onto the board with wobbly knees, but to my relief he stays upright. "You're good."

"But am I good enough to win a competition? That is the question."

Larry stomps his foot down on the ground, coming to an abrupt stop. "What competition?"

"There's a street skating competition in San Diego this November. Streetsgiving."

"Heh. Good pun."

"I'm planning to compete."

Larry's visibly impressed. "Are you going up against the pros?"

"Some." I rub against my nostrils with a sniff and lift my chin in pride.

"Wow."

"Which is exactly why I need more practice. What sucks is that places to skate around here are limited." I scan the dark road in front of us. Out here, like all the streets in town, there are way too many potholes to do any of the cool tricks that'll score high in competition. And for as awesome as Kirsten's industrial park is, it's nowhere near the level of a professionally built skate park.

Larry bites his lip in thought. He hands me my board. "Wait here."

"Oh, yeah, sure then." I scratch my head as he disappears into the trailer. The orange cat peeks its head around the door and hisses at me. Grimacing, I jump back. "And this is why I'm a dog person."

Shaking it off, I decide to cruise around while I wait for Larry to do whatever the heck he's doing. I'm just about to do a kickflip when I hear something bang behind me. I whip around and burst out laughing.

A thin slab of metal rests on top of an empty drum, forming a makeshift ramp. I stare at the drum's chipped blue paint, grimacing at the metal's rusted edges. "What the heck is that?"

Larry gestures to his creation in pride. "Something for you to practice on. Don't skaters jump down ramps and stuff?"

"Yeah, something like that." For the first time since I've arrived in Ocean Pointe, my heart swells in emotion. My buddy isn't so bad after all.

My phone breaks out into the G note, interrupting the moment.

Larry frowns. "That's your phone? Sounds like a piano or something."

"I got a new text." I check my phone. This time I expect it to be Kirsten, but to my surprise it's one of my long-lost buds.

*Mackabi:* Hey stranger, you practicing?

Leave it to my best friend to sense what I'm doing from all the way across the country.

With a shake of my head, I put my phone away. I'll text him back later.

# 10

I stay at Larry's for another thirty minutes. By the time I get home the streets are completely dark, but fortunately my parents are still at the restaurant doing the books—or so they say. I'm sure they're staying late because they don't trust Chad to manage the closing shift alone. I don't blame them.

Exhausted beyond belief, I drag myself to the front door and throw it open. Nollie comes bounding to me, and I fall to my knees and take her furry body into my arms. She always has a knack for recharging my empty battery. She's usually excited to see me, but as if she can sense my depleted energy, she's extra attentive and licks my face more aggressively. I plant multiple kisses between her ears and sigh.

"Girl, thank you for being the only thing constant in my life." She answers with a sloppy lick stretching from the point of my chin to the tip of my nose. After kicking off my shoes, I carry her into the kitchen and grab her bag of treats. I hold up a piece of jerky and smile as she grabs for it.

"Yeah, that's a good girl," I murmur as she chomps down on the piece of meat.

After planting one last kiss on her tiny head, I place her back onto the floor. She scampers off toward another one of her little adventures.

Another text comes through as I scoop up my skateboard and head to my room.

Probably Mackabi pissed off I haven't texted back yet. Damn hypocrite. I yank out my phone.

But it isn't Mackabi.

*Kirsten:* Are your parents home?

It's a random question, but I text back:

No. They're still at Sloppy's Pit Stop.

*Kirsten:* Awesome! I'm coming in.

"Wait, what?" I reread the short text three more times because there's no way I'm seeing it right. It isn't until I hear Nollie's crazy barking that I realize Kirsten's not kidding.

I have no idea what to do. Of course, I've had friends over to my house in San Diego before, but none of them have ever let themselves in without asking. And besides Amanda, none of them were females. I spot a few pairs of used boxers strung across my carpet and try to kick the closest pair under my bed. The material gets tangled around my foot. I hop around, scrambling to dislodge my underwear, when Kirsten's amused voice calls out, "Come out, come out, wherever you are."

How the hell did she get inside?

Nollie scrambles into my room, settles on her tiny bed, and barks at the doorway. Groaning, I swipe for the boxers, but no.

It's a nightmare come true. Kirsten pauses at my doorjamb and takes one look at me, bursting into laughter. "Need help?"

"Got it!" With flushed cheeks, I ball up my underwear and shoot it over to the laundry bin by my closet. I rush over and scoop up the remaining boxers, tossing them into the bin as well.

Kirsten examines my sparsely decorated room. Her fingers graze a cardboard box, running along the black marker labeling it MOVIES, BOOKS AND STUFF. "How long have you been in town, again?" she asks.

"A couple of weeks. Why?"

"And you still haven't unpacked?" She scans the empty white walls and my bare desk, which only has a laptop placed in the middle. Even my bed doesn't look fully lived in yet with only one pathetic pillow and a crumpled bedsheet on top.

I shrug, following her gaze. "Just haven't gotten around to it."

"Or just hoping your parents will change their minds and suddenly move you back home?" She shoots me a conspiratorial wink.

I make note of her use of the word "home" and smile back at her. "Maybe."

She pulls her lips inward and nods thoughtfully. Not waiting for my invitation, which seems to be her running theme for the night, she sashays to my full-size mattress and plops right on top. The metal springs squeak underneath her weight. A familiar but not entirely unwelcome sensation begins to swim around my stomach.

I clear my throat and as I take a seat on my desk chair across from her, Nollie jumps up from her bed on the floor and leaps up onto mine.

"Nollie!" I'm about to warn Kirsten about Nollie's antisocial tendencies but am rendered speechless when my dog settles right into Kirsten's lap.

"Aw, aren't you a sweet girl?" Kirsten scratches in between Nollie's floppy ears, who in turn nuzzles against Kirsten's neck.

I blink in confusion. "That's . . . strange."

"What's strange?" Kirsten asks as she places a kiss on Nollie's head in the same spot I did earlier.

"Nollie's a rescue and basically only likes my family. And my best friend, Mackabi. I'm surprised she's taken to you so well." What I don't mention is that Nollie never liked Amanda, always barking whenever she was around. One time Nollie even snapped her teeth at her.

"Well, you know. Us girls got to stick together."

As if understanding her, Nollie gives a little yip. Kirsten giggles and carefully places her on the part of my mattress that's pushed up against the wall. Once Nollie's settled, Kirsten kicks out her legs, stretching them out. She's changed from earlier and now wears new jean shorts, a cropped OPHS T-shirt, and her signature boots. She's also pulled her hair up, exposing the swanlike curve of her neck.

"Why are you here?" My question comes out a lot harsher than I intended. To soften it up a bit, I rephrase. "I mean, how do you even know where I live? How did you get inside?"

Like a sassy magician, she wiggles her phone in the air, showing me a picture of a computer screen. "My dad's the town's main real estate agent, remember? Your parents bought your house from him."

"Yeah, I know. I think he helped negotiate a deal for Sloppy's Pit Stop too." Damn him. "That's why I knew you could help me get Larry's address earlier."

She nods. "And while I was in Dad's files, I decided to look you up."

"That doesn't explain how you got inside here," I point out.

She shrugs, stuffing her phone into her back pocket. "You left the front door open."

"Are you serious?" I drop my head with a groan. "I've never done that before. Wouldn't have been able to get away with it back in San Diego either."

"Eh, this is Ocean Pointe. Nothing to worry about."

Not true. If I've already grown complacent enough with country living that I'd forget something as simple as locking the door, next thing you know I might be okay with the whole brawn over brains thing too.

Kirsten pulls her legs into a crisscross applesauce position. The soles of her boots scuff my bedsheet. I wince. "Hey, um, do you mind removing your boots? We usually take off our shoes at the door."

Kirsten quickly yanks off her boots and starts to climb off the bed. "Oh, shit. Sorry. I'll put these out there—"

"You know what? Just toss them on the carpet."

"Are you sure?"

"Well, you've already walked inside with them. Just not on my sheets, please."

She carefully lays the boots on the floor and climbs back onto my bed. "Sorry about that. I'll take them off at the door next time."

I frown. She's planning to come over again?

I fidget awkwardly. "Um, enough about your shoes. Can you tell me why you stopped by?"

"I wanted to talk to you."

I snort. "I kinda gathered that."

"About the warehouse site," she clarifies. "We never finished our conversation about you practicing there."

"Maybe because my mother called to chew me out for skipping school." I grimace, thinking about the call. It was Mom's usual tears—the angry kind—followed by a string of Tagalog cuss words and a proclamation to figure out where they went wrong in parenting me.

"You didn't need to answer the phone right then and there," Kirsten points out.

"You obviously don't know Filipino parents that well." Speaking of Filipino parents, mine can come home at any time. I glance out the window. I need to get Kirsten out of here.

"What you're saying is it's like a Tiger Mom sort of thing?"

My head whips around and I scan Kirsten's expression to see if she's joking, but she's totally serious.

"You really shouldn't use that expression. It's kind of offensive."

She blinks quickly. "Huh? Why?"

"It perpetuates an Asian stereotype." When her face folds in embarrassment, I quickly say, "But hey, you didn't know and now you do. Growth."

"I definitely won't make that mistake again."

"Appreciated." I nod. "As for my parents, they just have extra-high expectations."

"Don't all parents?"

I think about how Mom always expects to see straight As on all my report cards. "I'm not so sure."

Kirsten fiddles with her thumbs and frowns. "Take mine, for example. They were ready to disown me when they found out I wasn't cheerleading anymore. Then again, why wouldn't they? They signed me up for peewees, forced me to try out in middle school and high school . . . hell, they always expected I'd get a scholarship and cheer at their alma mater. Guess they assumed I'd be fine blindly following this grand old plan they have for my life. If that isn't a high expectation, I don't know what is."

I stare at Kirsten's flushed cheeks. For a second I think she's on the verge of tears, but no, it's more like she's angry. "Um, Kirsten. Are you okay?"

She clears her throat and changes the subject. "I just hope your parents aren't too pissed off at me. You wouldn't have ditched school if it weren't for me."

"Hey, it was my decision to skip school. You didn't know I was following you."

"Most adults, mainly parents, only see things in black-and-white," Kirsten says. "They'll only care that I was there with you. An accessory to a crime, if you will."

I huff. "You've been watching one too many crime documentaries."

She ignores me. "I'd hate for your parents to, well, already hate me before I got to know them better."

"Why would you even want to?"

"Because . . ."

I wait for a beat, but she remains silent. "Because what?"

She shakes her head and smiles. "It's only a matter of time until I do. Everyone in Ocean Pointe knows each other."

I chuckle. "Yeah, okay."

"And it's also only a matter of time until we know each other better too. You know, outside of skateboarding."

"And vandalism?" I joke.

She chuckles. "Sure."

I shrug. "Maybe we will."

"Why 'maybe'?" She flips onto her stomach, resting her feet on my pillow. At least she's bootless this time.

"Because I'm not planning on sticking around here for much longer," I answer truthfully.

"Really?" She frowns. "But what about Sloppy's Pit Stop? It just opened."

"My parents aren't leaving, but I will. Hopefully in November." I motion to my calendar. The one thing I hung on my wall. "Remember that competition I told you about?"

"In California, right?" There's a strange edge to her tone.

"Not just in California, but in my hometown," I explain. "Besides competing in it, I'm planning to use that time to ask my *tita*—*aunt*—if I can live with her for the rest of high school."

Something resembling disappointment flashes over her face. "You think she'll go for it?"

"Maybe. If not, at least I tried, ya know?"

Kirsten stares at the calendar. "Can I ask you something?"

"Well, we are getting to know each other better, aren't we?" I joke.

She smiles, but it doesn't reach her eyes. "I get that California was your home and that you have this competition to attend, but why are you in such a hurry to leave? You've only been here for a couple of weeks. November's only a couple months away. Why don't you give it some time? Maybe you'll end up liking Ocean Pointe."

"For one, my girlfriend's back home."

"Oh, yeah. Your girlfriend . . ."

"And also it's kind of hard to see myself liking Ocean Pointe when I had a *hell* of a welcome on my first day."

"What happened on your first day?" she asks in alarm.

Only now do I realize I never told her about my first run-in with the bullies. Honestly, I don't want to tell her. A zing of phantom pain burns my cheek as I recall the gnarly road rash. It's something I'd rather forget.

I change the subject. "Hey, remember what I said about my parents being strict? They might be coming home soon—"

"Angelo!" As if on cue, I'm interrupted by my mother's brash voice.

"Whose bike is that at the curb?" Dad pipes in.

Nollie instantly awakens and jumps off my bed, bounding through my door.

"I'll assume Filipino parents don't appreciate girls in their sons' bedrooms?" Kirsten whispers out of the side of her mouth. With wide eyes, I shake my head slowly and she groans. "I thought so."

Kirsten points to the window and I nod, saying a silent prayer of thanks that we now live in a one-story ranch as opposed to our old two-story adobe-style house. As she grabs her boots, not bothering to put them back on, I rush to slide the window open, and Kirsten does an amazing ballet-type leap and practically swan dives out the window. Just in time too.

"Didn't you hear us calling you?" Mom pops her head inside and scans my room as if she can sense trouble brewing.

Though Kirsten's nowhere in sight, Nollie scratches at the wall beneath the window, whining loudly. I carefully nudge her out of the way and slide in front of the window to block my mom from seeing outside. "Oh, no. I was . . . um . . . I was doing homework."

Mom purses her lips and looks me up and down. I stiffen, waiting for her to call me out on my BS, but all she says is, "Good boy," and turns to leave.

Most likely hearing the word "good" and expecting a treat, Nollie rushes after my mom. I take one last peek outside and watch Kirsten bike down the street. She really needs to get a skateboard, I think, sniffing at the whiff of perfume still lingering in my room.

Once she's out of sight I grab my phone and dial Amanda's number. It goes straight to voice mail.

# 11

Larry slams his tray onto the table beside me with enough force to knock over my bottled drink. "Why's she coming over here?"

"Who?" I ask, barely pulling my gaze away from my phone.

"Queen Kirsten herself." Larry's face does a weird thing where it looks like an invisible fan is blowing all his skin back. "You know how you told me to stand up to the cheerleaders?"

"Yeah . . ."

"She was one of the girls who always picked on me."

I put my phone down. Considering Amanda hasn't answered any of my texts and missed my call last night, there's a high probability she won't message me back anytime soon. Fear and annoyance bubble in my gut, but I push away the feelings.

"Who knows? Maybe she's coming over here to apologize to you."

"Like that would ever happen. She's not the type to apologize for anything. She's not that nice." Spit flies out of the corners of Larry's mouth in foamy bubbles.

"You'd be surprised."

Larry narrows his eyes. "I'm not buying it. All I know is that she better not push me again or I'm going to say something."

I start to respond but think better of it. Sticking up for himself is exactly what I advised Larry to do. Besides, I'm sure Kirsten won't do anything to hurt him.

Kirsten approaches our table and pauses as if unsure what to do now that she's staring Larry in the face. Shaking out of it, she lifts the hand gripped around her sack lunch and greets us. "Thought I'd join you today."

If this were a movie scene, the camera would pan the now almost silent cafeteria. It'd slow on the glob of pudding falling from Aiden's mouth and fly over to the boy from the stairs, zooming in on his wide eyes. It'd move across Stella's shocked face and Maddie's gritted teeth before finally settling on Grayson's clenched jaw.

Don't even get me started on the sound effects. Hollywood would probably choose cricket chirps—no, exaggerated gasps—as a soundtrack to Kirsten's unexpected appearance at our table.

She sits down on the uncomfortable plastic chair and begins to unload her lunch, solidifying her intent to stay. I make note of her little meal prep containers filled with an array of multicolored vegetables and fruit. "Thanks for having me, guys."

"Whatever," Larry mutters. "Just be nice and we'll be okay."

"Um, sure . . ." Kirsten props her elbows on the table, clasping her hands together so her thin fingers intertwine. Her nails are plain, devoid of even clear polish. Amanda always paints her nails a bright blue to "match the ocean."

Kirsten shoots me a look, and I shake my head as if to say, *Just go with it.*

Taking the hint, she clears her throat and regroups with a smile. "So, Rivera. Why is it that every time we're having a deep conversation, your parents interrupt us?"

"Maybe because every time I'm with you it involves breaking some sort of rule."

"Figures," Larry mumbles as he takes a bite of his lunch.

I kick him underneath the table and ignore his whimpers.

Kirsten frowns at Larry. "Are you saying that's my fault? As we agreed, I didn't make you ditch and follow me," she says to me.

"Well, I didn't ask you to join me in my bedroom," I shoot back.

Kirsten's blue eyes widen. I can make out the little gold flecks scattered along her irises. The colors run together like the high-noon sun on the Pacific. "Touché."

"Wait. You let Kirsten into your house? Into your bedroom?" Larry's head bounces between the two of us. He grimaces. "Why?"

"Dude . . . ," I murmur.

Kirsten clears her throat and concentrates on one of her containers, flicking at a dried piece of kale. "Better watch your mouth, Larry. Or I might change my mind."

Larry lowers his sandwich. "Change your mind about what?"

Though Kirsten answers Larry, she keeps her eyes on me. "Angelo mentioned that you wanted to learn how to skate and need a place to practice—"

"Wait a minute," I interrupt. "How did you figure out it was Larry?"

Kirsten purses her lips. "Besides the fact you asked me for his address, he's also your only other friend."

Friend. There goes that word again.

Shooting me a wink, Kirsten unscrews the top of her water bottle and leans toward Larry. "But as I was saying, how would you like to be invited to my sacred place?"

Larry's eyes grow comically wide. "Be invited to the what now?" The tips of his ears turn bright red. "You mean to your vagina?"

Kirsten nearly spits out her drink. "No!"

"Inappropriate much, Larry?" I growl in annoyance. "You do not speak to a girl"—Kirsten gives me a look—"a *woman* that way. Don't be nasty."

Larry holds up his hands. "Hey, it's not my fault she likes to speak in innuendos."

"Okay, enough about my woman parts," Kirsten says, rolling her eyes. "Do you want to skate or not?"

The outline of Larry's ribs pops out through his shirt as he puffs out his chest. "I already skate."

"I like the confidence." I slap a hand against his shoulder. "But I only gave you one lesson, dude."

Larry's face crumbles. "I thought I did pretty good."

"You did," I say in a rush at the same time Kirsten asks, "Do you want to get better?"

Larry's head snaps in her direction as if she tugged an invisible string attached to his forehead. "What do you know about skating?"

"Probably about as much as you," she admits. "But like I said, I have a place you can practice, Laurie." She props her pointed chin on top of her fist. "A place that isn't my vagina, by the way."

Laurie? Since when does she use nicknames of the Louisa May Alcott variety?

My eyes narrow. "Kirsten, what's with the sudden change of mind? Yesterday you almost bit off my head when I asked to bring him around."

"I decided it's part of the favor you owe me," she answers in a nonchalant tone.

I stare at her incredulously. "I thought giving you lessons was the favor."

She straightens her shoulders. "Well, I changed my mind."

"How many times are you going to change your mind? And why change your mind about this?" It hits me that I'm practically talking Kirsten out of letting Larry skate with us. But I can't keep up with her 180.

"Think of this as an addendum. I still want the lessons, obviously." She smiles at both of us. "But you can teach Larry and me together. At my place. But only if you make sure he keeps his mouth shut about it. As for why I'm letting him . . ." She tilts her head from left to right. "Let's just say it feels right."

Larry looks equal parts tentative and curious. "Is this secret place gonna get me in trouble?"

"What makes you think I'm going to get you in trouble?" she snaps.

I lift a finger. "Actually—"

"Don't listen to Rivera. I didn't even know he ditched." Kirsten leans back, crossing her arms tightly across her shirt. The neckline of her tank top folds over, giving me a good view of the top of her polka-dotted bra.

I look away and grab my phone.

*Me:* Mandy, where you at?

Larry flicks his hand toward the popular table. "To be fair, you haven't really had a good track record."

"What do you mean?" she asks in a careful tone.

"Oh, c'mon, Kirsten. Everyone knows you left your squad hanging. And no offense, I've seen you skip school."

"You have?" Kirsten's eyes bulge out.

He nods. "On more than one occasion."

"Shit."

"What are you doing that's so important you have to miss class?"

Kirsten sighs in relief. "It doesn't matter. What does matter is that you don't know what I'm doing, which means other people probably don't either. And for your information, I didn't leave my squad hanging. They kicked me off the squad."

I blink quickly. "But I thought you said you quit the team."

"I never said I quit the team." Her nostrils flare. "It's just what everyone else has been saying since they don't bother to learn the truth."

Larry casts his eyes down and fidgets. "Oh, um . . . that doesn't answer my question."

"Listen to me, Laurie." She tucks in her chin and drops her tone. "I'm not going to get you in trouble. Regardless of what Justin, Maddie, or Grayson"—she flinches when she says his name—"may be saying about me, there's a reason I'm not on the squad or am even friends with them anymore. As for what I do outside of school . . . well, you have to come to my place to find out."

Doubt is still etched on Larry's face. I jump in. "I can vouch for Kirsten on this. You're going to want to go to her . . . place."

Kirsten catches my eye and bursts into laughter. I blush and look away. Unfortunately, my gaze land's on Grayson's table, and he's glaring at me.

I clench my fists against my sides, mentally preparing the excuses I'll give my parents in case a brawl breaks out. *He threw the first punch!* Or my favorite, *He fell into my fist!*

To my relief, all Grayson does is flick me off. But before he turns away, he shoots what can be interpreted as a longing look in Kirsten's direction.

A feeling of protectiveness for Kirsten comes over me again, but before I can dwell on it, my phone vibrates with a new text. I scramble to pick it up.

Kirsten taps her fingers against the table. "What do you say, Larry? You comin' out to play or what?"

"I'm not sure . . . ," Larry murmurs.

I read Amanda's message. "What the fuck?" I blurt out.

Larry startles. "Sheesh, okay. I'll say yes."

I sigh. "No, that's not what . . ." I reread the text.

*Amanda Panda:* Angelo, we need to talk

Larry reads over my shoulder. "Are you mad because Amanda Panda said she wants to talk to you? Isn't that a good thing?"

Kirsten eyes me curiously.

I scowl. "Not when it's your girlfriend saying it like that."

"Like what?"

"Like *that*." I tighten my grip on my phone. "In that tone."

"Tone?" Larry glances at my phone again. "Um, but she texted."

"And she also called me Angelo instead of the dumb nickname she always uses," I grumble, crossing my arms.

"Which is?"

"Now's not the time, dude."

Kirsten clears her throat. "Okay, then. So . . . you guys want to take a field trip to my spot or what?"

Larry slumps against the table. "Why are you so persistent?"

Kirsten's eyes slide over to me. "Just an inkling we all need some fun," she says firmly.

My fingers fly across my screen.

*Angelo:* Let's talk right now

*Amanda Panda:* I'll call you when I'm ready

Kirsten snaps her fingers in front of my nose. "Angelo. You okay?"

"Peachy," I mutter.

Another text comes through.

*Mackabi:* Heard Tyler Park's entering the competition. You scared, bro?

When it rains, it pours.

I slam a fist against the table. Larry jumps in his seat but grabs my drink before it rolls onto the floor.

"Are you sure you're okay?" Kirsten places her hand on top of mine, squeezing lightly.

I pull my hand away and grit my teeth. "I need to skate."

Kirsten swallows and forces a smile. "Is that a yes to fun?"

"It's a yes to practice," I correct.

She nods slowly and looks at Larry. "What about you? Did you make up your mind yet?"

He holds out my drink for me, but I shake my head. He stares at the bottle like it's some sort of crystal ball that will tell him the right answer. "If I go I won't get into trouble, right?"

Kirsten sags forward. "You're not going to get into trouble, Larry. At least not if you keep your mouth shut about it."

His Adam's apple bounces. "Fine. If it means I can skate again, I'll go."

"Then it's settled." Kirsten nods. "Meet me by the flagpole right after school. We're taking a field trip."

"We have to stop by my house first," I interject.

"Why?"

"You need boards, don't you?" Now that I'll be competing against Tyler I can't keep giving up the board I'm using. It'll only waste precious practice time.

Larry beams in excitement. "Awesome."

I glare at Mackabi's text. "Yeah. Awesome . . ."

# 12

Tyler Park.

My old neighbor and newly knighted pro skater.

We've had an unspoken rivalry ever since he stole my bucket of Legos in kindergarten and I ran over his G.I. Joe action figure with my bike in retaliation. Obviously, being pro he's currently "winning." But it would be nice to take the Streetsgiving trophy home and wipe the stupid lopsided grin off his face. The only problem is I have to make it back to San Diego to do so. I trail behind Larry and Kirsten and stare at my banking app, letting out a mournful sigh.

$347.69

Even scrounging up every penny from my paycheck, my leftover birthday money, and Lola Irene's belated Christmas gift, my California fund isn't anywhere near where I want it to be. Today's certainly not helping either.

I check my phone and roll my eyes at the string of smiley face emojis.

*Chad:* I'll be at Sloppy's 4pm on the dot :) :) :)

*Me:* Thanks Chad. I'll return the favor

*Chad:* Nah, I need the money

As do I. I think about not only my plane ticket but also the entry fee for Streetsgiving. Maybe I shouldn't have impulsively agreed to this "field trip" after school today.

It's close to 3:30 p.m., but the air is thick with humidity. Despite being mid-September, the sun still hangs high, beating down on us with its harsh rays.

Kirsten glances at the road behind us and snorts. "You trying to lead people to us, Hansel?"

What? I glance back. A swarm of flies gathers around one of Larry's fallen fruit snacks like vultures stalking a dead wildebeest. He stuffs another handful into his mouth and mumbles something inaudible, but I barely pay attention to him or Kirsten or putting one foot in front of the other as we head to the warehouses. My mind's buzzing. It's like the circuits in my brain are intersecting freeways, and I'm stuck on the I-5 during rush hour.

It's Amanda. As much as I try to convince myself that she wants to talk for a variety of reasons that don't involve her breaking up with me, I can't ignore how weird she's been or how many of my calls and texts she's missed. But if she really is trying to end things with me, I need to know and I need to change her mind.

"Earth to Angelo," Kirsten calls out in a singsong voice. "Care to share your thoughts with the class?"

I blink. "What?"

"You've been quiet since we left your house."

"Actually, he was quiet at his house," Larry pipes in. "He didn't say a word when he was putting our boards together."

Well, not *their* boards but two of mine. Together all three of us walked back to my house after school to tear through all the unopened boxes in my room until we found the extra decks that I don't mind ruining or snapping in half. I attached new trucks and wheels in record time.

"I was hurrying in case my parents decided to stop by," I explain. "Dad would've talked shit if he found out I gave my shift to Chad so I could skate."

"But isn't he going to find out anyway?" Kirsten hugs her skateboard. "Obviously your coworker's going to clock in and not you."

I shrug. "I told my parents I have some homework to do."

"Tsk, tsk. Lying to our parents now, are we?" Kirsten teases.

"You would know about lying, wouldn't you?" Larry crumples his empty snack bag with one hand, holding his skateboard with the other.

Kirsten's eyes flash. "What the hell are you talking about, Larry?"

"Oh, c'mon. You know." He tosses the bag onto the ground. Kirsten scowls and picks it up.

"I obviously don't." She shakes the plastic in front of his face. "And you should know better than littering."

"What *are* you talking about, Larry?" I ask, thankful to take my mind off Amanda for a bit.

His face flushes, but he never looks away from Kirsten. "Didn't you throw Maddie under the bus for something you did? That's why you quit the squad, right?"

"I told you I didn't quit!"

"So what you're saying is that you did throw Maddie under the bus." Once again Larry finds a way for *x* to mean *y*, but this time, I don't mind.

My eyes dart toward Kirsten. "Wait, is that true? Is that why she's mad at you?"

Instead of answering me, she shoots Larry a sneer. "Maybe you shouldn't listen to OPHS gossip so much. You should know how hurtful it is."

I look between the two of them. "I'm so lost. What gossip are you talking about?"

"Never mind." Kirsten spins on her heels, kicking up a cloud of dust. "We're here."

Larry's frown disappears. He pauses at the peak of the hill, taking in the monstrosity of the industrial park. "Whoa!"

"Told you this was a special place." Kirsten pokes him in the shoulder. "Don't make me regret inviting you."

Larry ignores her and asks me, "What tricks are we going to learn today?"

"I . . . uh . . ." Thoughts of Amanda, Tyler, money, and now practicing and teaching novice skaters are muddled in my brain. Favor or not, maybe I bit off more than I can chew agreeing to teach both Larry and Kirsten.

"Hey, Rivera, why don't you show me and Larry a few things, and then we can all branch off on our own."

I blink in surprise. "Are you sure? Because I owe you lessons—"

"Forget about the favor for now. Today's supposed to be fun." She shoots me a pointed look and pats against her tote, rattling the cans inside.

"What's that sound?" Larry tears his gaze away from the main warehouse and looks down at her bag.

Kirsten shifts her tote so it rests on the opposite hip and changes the subject. "This place is pretty old. It's probably safer if we don't wander into any of the buildings and stay in the lot."

Catching the warning in her tone, I readily agree. "Yeah. We don't know what's inside them. At least out here we have a good view of everything."

Kirsten mouths a thank-you from over Larry's head. I nod and walk to the center area between the buildings. "You guys ready to learn a trick?"

As usual Kirsten wears her bright smile, along with a straw cowboy hat that sets off her bronze skin perfectly. Larry, however, looks a bit more nervous than he did in front of his house. "Nothing too crazy, right?"

I drop my own board onto the ground and place my foot on top. I push it back and forth. "Right. Nothing insane. I'll teach you a basic move, and from there you can decide what to do."

"Um, okay." Larry makes a face.

"Hey, where's that excitement you had last night? Or at school when you first asked me to teach you?"

Larry shifts his weight from one foot to the other. "I . . . This . . ." He shakes his head and motions toward the rusted handrails bordering the concrete ramps at the buildings' different loading docks. He turns and frowns at the main building's metal staircase. "This just seems more real."

"You skated for real in front of your house too," I remind him.

"Yeah, but this place looks more out of a skate magazine than the front of my house did."

I nod in understanding. "Don't worry. Today will be just as easy. Today you will learn how to pop an Ollie—"

"Like Oliver?" Larry blinks.

"Uh, no." I make an effort not to roll my eyes. To be patient. To be respectful of their inexperience. "The Ollie is fundamental to every skateboarding trick—kickflips, gaps, rails. And you do it like this . . ."

I skate around my students, building up speed, and stomp down on the tail end of my board while simultaneously lifting my front foot so the board does a slight leap. I land back on the ground and skid to a stop. "That right there is an Ollie. Looks hard, but it's not. Now who wants to try first?"

Kirsten's hand shoots up in the air, but to my surprise, Larry's does too. I can do this. I can focus on this and help them learn to skate. Somehow I push aside my worries and grin. "All right, then. Let's begin."

~

About an hour into our lesson, Kirsten lands one Ollie and immediately sneaks away, no doubt itching to paint an addition to her already awesome-looking wall. Larry's still rusty but insists on learning a kickflip.

"No, you stomp and drag your front foot to the top of your board." I step back and watch Larry build up speed. "Flick your ankle! Flick! Flick!"

I'm vaguely aware of how similar my instructions and tone are sounding to the ones I got on my first day of training at Sloppy's. Apparently, the apple doesn't fall far from the tree, and Dad and I have the same style of teaching. I rub my hair, just to make sure I'm not losing it like he did.

"I am flicking!" Larry's board tumbles to the ground. He uses his momentum to run to avoid tripping over it. To my relief he manages to stay on his feet, but he slumps forward in exhaustion. "Why am I not getting this?"

"It's okay if you don't master a kickflip on your second lesson. For some people it takes years."

"Years?" he gapes at me. "Guess I shouldn't feel too bad I've bombed it for the past two hours."

"*Two* hours?" I repeat dumbly, glancing at my watch. "I thought it's only been one."

I've been so caught up in teaching Larry, celebrating in his triumphs and getting irritated at his defeats, that I completely forgot to practice.

"Yeah . . ." Larry's voice trails off. He tilts his head to the side. "Weren't you supposed to prepare for your competition or something?"

"Or something."

I shake my head and glance at the different obstacles around me. But I'm too tired to conquer any of them right now.

We still have about an hour before sunset, a.k.a. the time Amanda's set to call me, but the sky's already a pale pink splashed with burnt orange. It reminds me of one of Kirsten's graffiti pieces. I stretch my arms and let out a loud yawn. "Hey, you think we can call it a—"

"Guys! Come here." Kirsten sticks her head out of the broken window and motions us to her building. "I need to show you something."

Larry frowns. "Hey, is that where you went? I thought we weren't allowed inside the buildings."

I snort. "It's Kirsten's place. She makes the rules."

Larry cups the side of his mouth and mock whispers to me, "Is she going to show us her special place?"

"Dude, shut up."

He shrugs and jogs ahead of me. With my lanky legs, my normal strides let me catch up with him without even really trying.

Larry stops in front of the window and shoots me a pointed look. "Well?"

"Well what?"

He gestures wildly. "Is this the only way to get inside? I'm too short to climb in."

"Says the guy who needs to pole-vault to get onto his porch." I roll my eyes but squat down, pushing my palms together. He stares at me blankly. "What are you waiting for? C'mon. I'll give you a boost."

He smacks his mouth. "No, thanks."

My hands fall to the ground. "Quit stalling, Larry."

"There has to be another way inside."

"There's not. I looked."

"Not hard enough." He walks away.

I stand up and yell after him. "I'll give you five minutes before you're back here." He disappears around the corner. "Suit yourself."

I grab the edge of the window and hoist myself inside. Unlike the first time, I land on both feet. "About time you got here."

"Larry!" I whirl around and gape at him. "How'd you get in here so quick?"

"The door, of course." He snickers and points his thumb at a doorway partially blocked by a pile of wooden pallets.

"How did I miss that?" I rub the back of my neck.

"Beats me. It's how I always get in." Kirsten walks up to us and laughs at my perplexed look.

"Then why did we go out the window last time?"

"Because I thought it was fun. But enough of that. Look." I follow the direction of her pointed finger. My eyes bug out at the new swirls of colors spray-painted on the back wall.

"Is that . . . is that . . . ?" I stare.

Kirsten beams. "I was inspired by our lesson today. Thought I'd make a tiny change to the piece we worked on." She tosses her spray can in the air, catching it effortlessly. "What do you think?"

"Wait a minute. You guys did that?" Larry nudges me.

"Mostly she did it." I blink, running my gaze over the giant red X spray-painted over the word ME. I should be mad considering how much time it took me to color in the bubble letters, but how can I be?

I smile as I read a new word painted below the X-ed-out ME. "Us. Just us."

Kirsten looks at her modified piece with pride. "I guess after all my time spent alone and hiding, I forgot how nice it feels to hang out with other people."

"Other people you aren't forced to spend time with," Larry agrees. "Like some of my bandmates." After a pause, he adds, "They don't all like how I play."

"Don't you follow the notes?" I crack my knuckles, suddenly feeling the urge to run my fingers against piano keys.

He smiles sheepishly. "I do, but they say I get a bit overexcited."

"I can't imagine," I shoot back with a laugh.

"Just us." Larry gestures to the wall. "Is this like a pact or something?"

"If you want it to be," Kirsten answers, shifting awkwardly. "I was, um, thinking about what I said earlier about gossip. I had no right to be mad at you when I was talking shit about you too. You know, about all that drug dealer stuff."

Larry and I exchange glances.

"But I haven't done it for a while," Kirsten adds quickly.

"Not since people started talking bad about you too?" Larry suggests.

"Yeah . . ." She grimaces. "Anyway, I'm sorry. It was a bitchy thing to do. I won't do it again."

Larry closes the gap between them and places a hand on her shoulder. "I appreciate that. Thank you."

"You're welcome." Kirsten presses her lips together.

"Too bad the other kids at school still think I'm a drug mule or something."

"Why don't you start standing up for yourself? Tell everyone to shut up?" I pipe in.

Larry drops his hand and shrugs. "I don't like conflict."

Kirsten considers it for a moment and finally nods. "Lucky for you we're a team now."

"A team?" Larry narrows his eyes.

"Yes, a team."

"Like a skating team?" Larry's eyes widen in delight.

"Or what if we start small and just be friends?" Kirsten suggests. She glances at me and presses, "We might as well be something since I trust you guys with this place. What do you think, Rivera?"

I stare at the painting behind her and am compelled to agree. "Sure. We're whatever you want us to be."

"Friends." Larry says the word as if trying it out for size.

Satisfied, Kirsten announces, "Teammates, friends—they protect each other. So if you want, stand up for yourself, Larry. We'll be here to support you."

My phone goes off.

*Amanda Panda:* I'm ready to talk now . . .

I curl my fingers tightly around my phone. My new friends shoot me questioning looks. As timing goes, it's a good thing they're here. I have a feeling I'm going to need a lot of support.

# 13

I sit at my desk, waiting. I wipe my palms against my thighs.
In the living room, my parents bicker about making budget cuts
at the new restaurant. Judging by how intense the argument sounds,
they'll be at it for a while. But just in case they decide to check up on
me, I get up and lock my door.

I pick up Nollie and sit back down at my desk, making room to
set my dog on my lap. Not for Amanda's sake this time but mine. With
trembling fingers I pet her, which calms me down a bit, and wait for
Amanda to answer my video call.

"Hey, Angelo." Her tone is unreadable.

I admire her newly dyed hair. Gone are the lavender locks I used to
bury my face in. Now her hair is light blue, which is fitting considering
my heart feels as cold as ice.

I take a breath. "Mandy, what's going on?"

She looks everywhere but at the camera. "This isn't easy, Angelo—"

"I know it's not easy," I say quickly. "We both knew being apart
would take a lot of work. But we can get through this, Mandy. And I'll
be home soon so—"

Now it's her turn to interrupt me. "No, Angelo. Th-that's not what
I mean."

I choke up. "What do you mean?"

"I . . . I think we should break up." She winces. She still doesn't look at me.

Though I was expecting it, I still feel stunned. "Why?"

"You've been gone for almost a month, and it already feels like eternity. I can't do this anymore. I can't sit around missing someone who might not come back."

"But I am coming back!" My voice comes out loud. Flinching, I glance at my door, but no one comes.

"Yeah, for Streetsgiving. But after the competition you'll be gone again."

"You know I'm going to ask Tita Marie—"

"Like she and your parents will ever go for it," Amanda scoffs.

"I'll try my best."

"Right."

I put Nollie on the floor and clasp my hands in front of the camera, leaning in. "Mandy, please. We can work through this. It just takes some getting used to, and I will be coming back to stay—"

"I think this is what's best for us," she interrupts in a firm tone. "I can live my life without missing you, and you can finally focus on settling in Ocean Pointe."

"But I don't want to settle in." My voice cracks. "I want you. We made a promise, remember?"

Amanda finally looks at the camera, but I almost wish she hadn't. The look in her eyes is something I've never seen from her before. They're distant. "Angelo, we're only sixteen. If this didn't happen now, we probably would've broken up before college anyway."

It's like I've been slapped in the face. "But what about our plans to go to SDSU together?"

"I . . . I never wanted to go to SDSU," she admits.

"Are you kidding me?" I explode. "What about all the plans we made? Were those as fake as your love obviously is?"

She winces. "I meant them . . . at the time."

There's a tempest inside me. Anger. Sadness. Defeat.

I choke back a sniffle. "This is it, then? After a year together you want to end it like this?"

At least she has the decency to look apologetic. "I'll still hang out with you during Streetsgiving, okay?"

I remain silent.

"Angelo . . ."

I tap my mouse and end the call.

# 14

Last night was one hell of a night. I couldn't sleep, which made school today almost unbearable. At least classes are finally over and I can focus on skating.

I lean against the flagpole, waiting for Larry and Kirsten, and watch the football team on the practice field.

Yes, practice field.

This high school football team has an actual *stadium* for their games.

A wall of yellow closes in on a single player dressed in maroon. He plucks the ball out of the air and then, clutching it to his chest, Maroon somehow pivots on one foot, completely avoiding his opposing teammates. He sprints away, easily making a touchdown.

Maroon's moves are pretty impressive. I'd kill to move as fast as he can. It'd probably make pushing off into some of my tricks a lot easier.

The player takes off his helmet.

*Maroon is Grayson?*

My mouth grows sour. Like Tyler, his cockiness and assholishness easily overshadow his talent.

"Hey, sorry to keep you waiting." Kirsten jogs up beside me and follows my gaze. I ignore the evil looks Grayson keeps throwing at me from the field. Kirsten stiffens when some of the cheerleaders, who are also practicing on the field, glance over at us. The redheaded one, the

girl who bumped into Larry before, starts to lift her hand, but Maddie
pulls her away.

Kirsten snorts.

"You going to tell me what actually happened between all of you?"
I nod in Maddie's direction.

"Only if you tell me why you look like a zombie." She scans my
face and frowns. "Your eyes are all red and puffy. I'm taking it your call
didn't go well last night?"

I'm too sad to be embarrassed. Not to mention furious.

I open Instagram and click on Amanda's newest photo. "Here."

Kirsten takes my phone. "Who am I looking at it?"

"Amanda."

She stiffens. "Your girlfriend?"

"*Ex*-girlfriend." Even saying it out loud doesn't make it feel any
more real. "She broke up with me last night."

Kirsten's eyes widen. "Oh, Angelo. I'm sorry."

I shrug because what else can I do? Lie and tell her it's okay?

Kirsten squints at the screen. "If she broke up with you last night,
then who the heck is this guy with her? And why did she use this
caption?"

I don't even have to read it to know what it says. I've looked at the
photo so many times after Amanda posted it. "Oh, you mean, 'You
can't fight destiny'?"

"Yeah," Kirsten whispers. "Is she dating someone new already?"

I glare at Tyler's dumb face. He somehow beat me again. But he
won't win in Streetsgiving. I'll make sure of it.

"I can't wait until I see him at the competition. I'm going to wipe
that stupid smile off his face and take the trophy. I'm gonna beat him
so hard . . ."

"Ah. I see." Kirsten nods slowly. "This is why you were so hell-bent
on going to the warehouses today, huh? So you can practice and win
your girlfriend back?"

"I'm not trying to win her back," I say truthfully. "I did all I can to try to make the relationship work, and she's the one who bailed on me. Fool me once, ya know?"

Kirsten works her lips and nods.

"Besides, she's with Tyler now. That fucker. He wins at everything! But he's not going to win this time."

The G note plays.

"You gave up your shift again?" Kirsten hands me my phone. "I didn't mean to read your text. It popped up when I was looking at the photo."

I look at the screen.

*Mom:* Why is Chad working your shift?

"I need to practice." Not bothering to text Mom back, I put my phone away.

It's probably stupid of me to skip work again since I need the money for the ticket. But Sloppy's Pit Stop still isn't getting a lot of customers, and I'd go crazy having all that time to think about Amanda and Tyler. If I'm going to think about them, I might as well do something productive like practice my ass off.

"A-Angelo." Kirsten places a hand on my arm. "You're shaking."

"Oh yeah?" I say through gritted teeth.

Kirsten opens her mouth to respond but—

"Sorry I'm late. Band ran over . . ." Larry frowns at me. "Uh, did I miss something?"

I wriggle away from Kirsten and place my board on the ground. "Let's get to the warehouses. I have some practicing to do."

I ignore their shared glance. Digging my back foot into the ground, I push off and fly down the sidewalk.

"Rivera! Wait up!"

"Yeah, hold on a second."

Their voices become white noise to me. The streets fly by in a blur. By the time I make it to the hill in front of the lot my left leg is screaming. But I'm too jazzed up to be tired. I run down and immediately jump into a trick, grinding down the nearest rail.

Sometime later, Kirsten jogs up to me, panting heavily. "Angelo! The heck?"

Larry stops beside her, bends forward, shoulders heaving. "Why didn't you wait for us? We were calling for you."

I land my trick and jump off my board. "Oh, were you? I didn't hear."

Kirsten's nostrils flare. "We need to talk."

"Not the first time I heard that," I mutter.

Larry lowers himself onto the pavement. He lays back, taking deep breaths. "Y'all can talk. I'm gonna lie here for a minute, okay?"

"Take your time." Kirsten frowns at me. "Angelo and I are going inside to cool down a bit."

"No. I need to practice." I start to climb onto my board, but Kirsten kicks it out from underneath me. I stumble back. "Hey! What was that for?"

She tugs my wrist. "We're going inside. Now."

"What if I don't want to?" I shoot back like some elementary schoolkid.

"My place, my rules."

"What happened to 'Just Us'?"

Kirsten sighs. "Trust me. It's exactly why we need to talk."

Something about her tone snaps me out of my rage. I nod and follow her into the main building.

"I hate it here, you know." I squat against one of the columns, staring at the wilted daisy. I've never related to an art piece so much.

Kirsten lowers beside me. "Didn't seem that way when you were practically begging me for permission to practice here."

"I was talking about Ocean Pointe." I sit at her side.

Kirsten's chuckle is strained. "I know."

"From day one all it's been is crap." I flick against a crack in the floor and mutter, "I wish I never moved here."

"That's right. You never told me what happened on your first day." Kirsten shifts to look at me. "You going to tell me now?"

With an exaggerated sigh, I grind out, "I ran into Justin and his friends in the school parking lot. Let's just say they were very welcoming."

Kirsten winces, picking up on my tone.

"Not only did they make fun of my skateboard, but they also poked fun at my skin color." I take note of her horrified expression and add, "Then to top it all off, they threw a rock at my board. I ended up flying off and scratching up my face."

"That explains the Band-Aid you had on your face," she gasps.

Echoing one of her first jokes, I reply, "It's not like cooking burgers is dangerous or anything."

Instead of laughing, Kirsten bites the inside of her cheek and frowns. "I promise everyone in Ocean Pointe isn't as narrow-minded as those guys make us out to be."

"I know you're not. And Larry isn't. But they called me 'brown boy,' Kirsten," I say in a flat tone.

Her eyes drop down for a moment as if she's gathering her thoughts. "They . . . they were probably just scared of you."

I motion to my skinny body. "Of me? Are you serious? You do realize our size difference, right?"

"You have to understand something. Everyone at OPHS knows everybody else."

"What does that have to do with anything?"

"Don't you get it? We all sized each other up a long time ago. The football team. The cheerleaders. Everyone who attends OPHS practically met in day care. I've known Justin and his friends since we were in diapers, so I'm sure them seeing an ultracool dude from California freaked them out."

"Did you really just call me 'ultracool'?" I snicker despite knowing Kirsten's probably as serious as you can get.

"Remember what Mrs. Spellman said about routine and tradition? Ocean Pointe runs off the familiar. It's the reason old stores like her consignment shop stay in business even if she still sells stuff from the eighties. And why—"

"New places like Sloppy's Pit Stop are suffering?" I suggest, remembering how empty it's been.

She nods. "The same goes with new people, I guess. Change is scary, and like it or not, you're an outsider. No one really knows you."

"Then why don't they get to know me?" I snap.

"The only way guys like Grayson and Justin know how to handle being scared or facing the unfamiliar is by treating it like a football game and attacking it."

I consider it for a second and grunt. "That's bullshit. Being scared isn't an excuse to be racist. That's just damn ignorant. You don't call someone 'brown boy' or say he eats dogs just because he's new to town and 'unfamiliar.'"

"I wasn't using it as an excuse," Kirsten says quietly.

"I really miss San Diego." I bow my head with a breathy sigh. "I never had to deal with this much crap at home."

"San Diego is a big city," Kirsten agrees. "Bet there weren't any racists there, huh?"

I mull it over for a second. "There's a huge navy base in town. Not to mention all the tourists. It's pretty diverse."

"I see."

I let out a deep breath. "But if I'm being honest, I had to deal with it there too. Not to the extent I'm dealing with it here, though."

"What do you mean?"

"A big city means more different-minded people. I can't speak for everyone, but personally what I faced were microaggressions. Kind of like when I first met Larry and he asked me where I was *really* from."

Kirsten's lips pucker. "Ooh."

"Or when someone would say I was cute 'for an Asian.'"

"Well, you are." I shoot Kirsten a pointed look, and she corrects, "I mean in general. Not just for an Asian . . ."

My blush matches hers. "Er, thanks."

She gives her trademark wink. "You're welcome."

"But anyway, I also used to deal with people saying they don't see race."

"Isn't that a good thing?"

"No," I say truthfully.

Kirsten scratches her head. "I'm sorry. I'm not following."

"I get that some people who say it mean well," I explain. "But saying you don't see race disregards my identity. I'm Asian. I'm proud of it. If you don't see race, then you're ignoring that part of me."

"Oh, okay . . ."

"And if you don't see race, then you're turning a blind eye on racial injustices. Because colorblind or not, racism does happen. And why be colorblind? We're all different, and diversity is a good thing. But tell that to Justin and Grayson, who point out my skin color like it's bad."

I shift against the column. "I used to ignore the microaggression. But thinking about it now, I don't really know why I did."

"This town has been playing like a broken record ever since it was first built," Kirsten explains. "It's the same thing, but it's a different day. But now you're here. And you can change things up. Show us things we've ignored before."

I scan the different paintings around us. "Were you trying to change things up?"

"What are you talking about?"

"What happened between you and your old friends?" I drop my tone. "The real reason, Kirsten."

She inhales deeply. "It's actually what I wanted to talk to you about."

"Oh?"

"I know you're really mad about your ex."

"What gives you that idea?" I mutter.

"But I can tell you're really sad too. I was in the same boat, but unlike you it was my fault."

"Now what are *you* talking about?" I throw back at her.

"Larry was right. I did throw Maddie under the bus." She gulps loudly. "I let her take the fall for me because I was too scared to tell my parents what I was up to. It was my fault my whole squad was disqualified from competing in the finals, and now they all hate me."

"I'm so lost right now," I admit.

She turns so she's completely facing me, but I get the feeling she's not actually *seeing* me but studying old memories as they flash inside her mind. "You know how I said I always dabbled in art?"

"Yes."

"I lied."

*Another lie?* I murmur, "Oh."

"I didn't just dabble in it. I'd sneak it in any chance I got. I'd order supplies online. Do YouTube tutorials. I even followed one from the 'happy trees' guy."

"Bob Ross? My *lola*—grandma—used to watch him on public television."

She nods. "But when I was promoted to captain of the squad, my time was limited. It was then I realized which was more important to me."

"Art?"

She nods. "My squad qualified for nationals, which happened to be around the same time as an art competition I wanted to attend. Same city too. It was actually only a few streets down from the hotel we were staying at."

"Oh," I murmur, figuring out where this is going.

"My coach was so gung ho about being focused. No distractions. She would never have been on board with me entering the art competition, so I decided to register and attend without her knowing. But our trip was heavily chaperoned. I made my ex–best friend cover for me when I snuck out."

"Ex–best friend? You mean . . . Maddie?" I take a wild guess, remembering the first day of school. The amount of venom the mean girl had for Kirsten could only be explained away by a ruined friendship. Thin line between love and hate and all that.

She nods again. "Long story short, our coach called a last-minute practice that night, but Maddie couldn't get ahold of me. I guess my phone died or I didn't have service. Maddie tried to leave the hotel to look for me, but one of the chaperones caught her. As luck would have it, I'd already snuck back a few minutes before." She grimaces. "My whole squad suffered because I snuck out. But I was chickenshit and let the chaperones think it was Maddie who did, and she got in a boatload of trouble. Anyway, we were disqualified for breaking the rules."

"Wow, that sucks."

"I tried to make it up to them. I apologized. I even told our coach the truth. Eventually." She grimaces. "It's why I was kicked out and Maddie took over as captain."

"But they never forgave you . . ."

"No." Kirsten forces a smile. "I know it might seem hard to get over Amanda. But it'll get easier. Look at me. I lost all my friends. Even my parents are still mad at me, but I'm doing okay."

"Did your parents find out about the art competition or something?"

"Oh, yeah. My coach told them. That was not a good night." She lets out a half-hearted chuckle. "I don't know what they were angrier about. That I snuck out, that I got kicked off the squad, or that I'd rather do art than cheerlead."

"Why would they be mad at you for liking art over cheerleading?"

"Because I'm deviating from their life plan for me." She shrugs. "I'm supposed to follow in my parents' footsteps. Cheerlead all through high school and college like my mom and become some real estate tycoon like my dad when I'm older. Remember? It's all about tradition."

"Damn. You weren't kidding about them having high expectations." I frown. "Do you even want to get into real estate?"

"All I know is right now I want to paint." She looks down and sniffs. "It's kind of stupid considering I didn't even win the dumb art competition. The judges said there was nothing special about my pieces. Nothing different. One of them even suggested I take up a new medium since charcoal apparently was not working for me."

I motion to the walls. "Is that the real reason you decided to spray-paint?"

"None of the other pieces that I went up against were created with spray paint." She smiles. "And I ended up loving it more."

"No offense, because it's cool you shared this with me, but what does this have to do with my breakup?" I ask carefully.

"I was just getting to that," she replies, but not unkindly. "After everything with the squad went down, I told Grayson I was thinking of pursuing art since I wasn't cheerleading anymore. I even told him I was almost glad I'd been kicked off the squad because it'd give me more time to paint. I expected him as my boyfriend to support me. I mean, he knew I did some drawing before, and he wasn't opposed to it."

Catching her tone, I prod, "But?"

"But you know what he said? That I should beg for my spot back on the team since cheerleading is probably all I'm good at."

"Fuck." I clench my fist. "What an asshole."

"Of course, I tried not to let him get to me. I told myself he only said that because he was disappointed I ruined the whole 'jock dating the head cheerleader' thing. So I took it a step further and dumped him altogether since keeping up with appearances mattered more to him than what I wanted." She bites her lip. "But I did lose my first art competition. And he still made me feel a bit insecure. It's why I paint in private. I'm not ready to show the world my pieces again. Maybe not ever, but at least not yet." She smiles sheepishly. "Except the tag I did on Sloppy's Pit Stop. But I met you because of it, so I don't regret it."

I can't believe what Grayson did to her. It makes me see red. "If he loved you," I blurt out, "he should've built you up instead of tearing you down."

"But don't you see? It's exactly what Amanda's doing to you. Instead of supporting you while you're away, she tore down what you guys had." Kirsten's tone shifts. Placatingly she says, "I know it doesn't seem like it right now, but what she did was a blessing because now you can rebuild yourself. And you can surround yourself with people who will support you."

"You mean you and Larry?" I glance at the far wall, feeling the true meaning of the words seep into my very core.

*Just Us.*

Her pale eyelashes brush against the top of her cheekbones as she looks down. "Yeah. You, me, and Larry—we have a lot in common. We're all pretty much loners."

"Wow, thanks," I say.

"We're all doing our best. Me trying to piece together my life after cheerleading. Larry living in his grandfather's shadow. And you . . ."

"And me what?"

She bounces one shoulder. "The new kid trying to make it day by day."

"Yeah, that's me," I grunt.

"Maybe we were destined to find one another. Pick up the pieces. Together."

I don't respond. The sound of Larry's skateboard wheels against the pavement echo from outside.

"You should really show off your artwork," I finally say after a few beats of silence. "These ones are really good. Don't listen to those dumb judges or what Grayson said."

Kirsten's answering smile warms my core. "And you shouldn't let Amanda get to you either. Anyone who'd drop you like that isn't worth your time."

I look at my skateboard and grumble, "Oh, this isn't about Amanda."

"It's not?" Doubt laces Kirsten's tone.

I push myself off the floor. "It's about kicking Tyler's ass during Streetsgiving."

"That's the spirit," she says dryly.

I hold out a hand for Kirsten. She takes it with a frown.

# 15

With vengeance as my sole motivator, I spend the next week skating harder than I've ever skated before. I land kickflips I never had the guts to try. My hardflips, which I'd always had trouble with, are now superb. But as important as practice is in my plan to humiliate Tyler on the podium, money is equally if not more vital in the overall scheme of things.

As much as it pains me to admit, Chad is right. Multitasking is needed to succeed. So instead of giving him all my shifts, I'm learning to master the art of juggling practice with work.

I look up at the clock above the lotto machine. Only ten minutes to go before I can clock out from my Thursday night shift and go to the warehouses to practice.

"Instead of standing around, why don't you clean?" Mom tosses me a rag and points to the dining area.

"It's already clean, Mom. No one's come in here since—"

"Shhh." Mom nods toward Dad, who's behind the counter, reading today's newspaper. Dad tosses the paper on the counter and slams his fist on it.

"Damn, Dad," I whistle. "What that paper ever do to you?"

"Took my money, that's what." He picks it up and flicks against a black-and-white ad. "I paid extra to put a Sloppy's Pit Stop advertisement in the sports section. Everyone in town likes football so much, I thought it was a no-brainer. They'd see the ad and come in. But not even those boys from your school came back."

"Good," I mumble.

"What was that?"

"Er, um, let me see what ad you used, Dad."

I take the paper and look at the generic photo of a burger underneath plain white type reading: SLOPPY'S PIT STOP OLD FASHIONED BURGERS.

I grimace. "See, that's what our problem is."

"That you're not cleaning?" Mom snaps.

I purse my lips. "There's nothing special about Sloppy's Pit Stop. It's just a burger and fry place. What makes it different from the other joint up Main Street?"

Dad huffs and grabs the paper from my hands. "This 'burger and fry place' will pay for your college tuition."

"And your plane ticket," Mom pipes in.

I bristle. "I know, but what I'm saying is if you want more customers, you need to offer something different."

"Different?" Dad's strained laughter is almost sinister. "You heard what Judy said. Newcomers don't do well. We need to fit in."

Remembering what Kirsten said about change, I snap, "Maybe instead of trying to fit in all the time, you can try to stand out for once."

"Angelo," Dad says in a sharp tone.

"Why would anyone come in for a regular burger? You can get one anywhere," I argue. "Besides, you guys are both great cooks. Why don't you offer some fusion pieces or something to shake things up?"

"We sell burgers. We do what makes the customers happy."

"What customers?" I huff.

Mom lowers her dishrag and looks between me and Dad. "Angelo. Maybe you should clock out early."

"No." Dad points to the clock. "He has eight minutes to go. He needs to learn responsibility and work his full shifts instead of giving them away all the time."

"And you need to learn that bending over backward for your customers isn't always a great thing either. Isn't that why Rivera's Kusina went under? Because you were too worried about keeping people happy than running an actual business? That's why you let our regulars put it on 'their tab' all the time, right?"

Dad's nostrils flare. He points a trembling finger to the computer. "Clock out. Now."

"Fine by me."

I whip off my apron and punch my employee number into the register. I grab my skateboard and head off to the warehouses, where Larry and Kirsten are already waiting for me.

~

I wipe a bead of sweat off my brow and frown.

"You okay?" Kirsten touches my arm.

"I'm fine."

"I don't believe you." She drops her hand. "No offense, but you skated pretty bad today. You didn't even skate this bad when . . ."

"When Amanda broke up with me?" I nod. "I'm fine. I just got into a little argument with my dad. No big deal."

The corners of Kirsten's mouth pull down. "I know how that goes."

"He's so stubborn about business."

"I know how that is too."

I nod in solidarity. "He always puts business first. Even when his family suffers because of it. We moved here to make a go of Sloppy's Pit Stop, and it's not even doing well!"

"To be fair, it was your mom's decision too."

I narrow my eyes.

"I'm just saying." Kirsten touches my arm again. This time her feathery touch sends goose bumps trickling down my arm. "Listen, I can't blame you for being mad about moving. But I want you to know I'm really happy you're here." Her fingers trail down my skin as she pulls away.

"At least one of us is," I respond grumpily, but now I'm forcing it a bit, distracted by her touch.

Kirsten holds my gaze and whispers, "Give it time."

My breath hitches.

Larry, who up until this point has been cruising between the different buildings, slows in front of us. He jumps off his board. "Are you guys done skating already?"

"Already?" Kirsten gapes at him with a laugh. "We've been at it for at least an hour."

I throw my head back and look up into the sky. It's nearing dusk. "Actually, I think I'm gonna head home. I have some homework to do."

Kirsten glances at her watch and arches an eyebrow. "It's only seven thirty."

"Got a lot on my mind," I say with a shrug.

"I guess I should leave too." Larry picks up his board and starts to walk away. He glances back at us. "You two coming or what?"

Kirsten shoots me a tentative smile and follows after Larry. I scoop up my board and trail behind them.

Kirsten has on the same outfit she wore the first time I met her. I never noticed how good those jean shorts looked on her. Her back pockets are hypnotizing. We make it down the gravel path and climb onto our boards as soon as we hit the pavement. The autumn sun hovers along the horizon, casting a dull orange glow on the street. Our trio skates in silence with only the scraping noise of our wheels as a soundtrack to our ride. Larry's in the lead, followed by Kirsten, and me taking up the rear. Never one to be quiet for long, Larry whistles a tune, matching the beat with each turn we make.

The newly lit streetlamps illuminate Kirsten's hair, making it appear whiter. She weaves around a giant crack in the road, barely missing a broken tree branch.

"Maybe you should slow down a bit," I yell at her above the whizzing air. I push faster and align my board with hers.

She glances at me, and I bite the urge to demand she keep her eyes on the road. "Doubting my skills already?"

"It's not about your skills. Do you see this street? It's gnarly. And we're getting into the center of town. There might actually be some traffic. Especially when we go past the high school toward the neighborhoods."

Kirsten turns her attention back to the road but not before rolling her eyes at me.

We cut through a path in the town park, which offers nothing more than a primary-colored swing set, and turn onto Main Street, where all the other restaurants, a.k.a. Sloppy's competitors, are located. The familiar scent of burgers hits my nostrils. Ocean Pointe Diner is located in the middle of the bustling block and is teeming with customers. One thing's for sure: Sloppy's needs to do something big in order to compete with them.

I'm so deep in my thoughts I almost don't hear Kirsten's sharp gasp. I look back just in time to see her board dip into a large crevice. Though she's going fast enough to come out of it, her board wobbles toward the center of the street. A car horn blares in warning.

It happens so quickly. In a move that belongs in one of the *Fast and Furious* movies, I jump off my board, race back, and somehow grab on to Kirsten's arm, yanking her off her board and pulling her toward the sidewalk. Her board shoots across the street, narrowly missing the passing car, and I fall back, thumping hard across the curb. Thankfully, I don't hit the back of my head, and also thankfully, I'm able to break Kirsten's fall as she drops on top of me.

"K-Kirsten?" I smack at my mouth, trying to get her hair out of it. I'll probably be sore as hell tomorrow, but I don't mind all the scratches and bruises if nothing worse has happened and she's okay.

"Holy crap! Guys!" Larry turns around and skids to a stop beside us, breathing heavily. "Do you need to go to the hospital? Is anything broken?"

I feel Kirsten's shuddering deep breaths, but otherwise she's pretty much frozen against me. For a moment I forget where we are. On the cool street, barely dodging a few broken bones. I tighten my arms around Kirsten's curves, hugging her even closer into me. I can feel her heart beating against my chest, racing almost as fast as mine.

"Get a room!" someone shouts from a passing car, jarring me back to reality.

I ignore a car horn and loosen my hold on her. "Kirsten? Are you hurt?"

Kirsten scrambles to her feet. She grabs her cowboy hat off the ground while Larry runs across the street to grab our boards.

"Wow." She blows away some tendrils of hair covering her face and places her hat back onto her head. She grabs me by the elbow, helping me up. "That was intense."

I rub my tailbone and wince. "Ah, I've had worse."

"Worse than that?" Larry jogs up beside us and motions to some gnarly road rash running down my arm. My skin's already puckering and reddening around the scratches. Fortunately, the pain's still masked by adrenaline, but I know it'll hurt like hell later on.

Not wanting to look like a total loser, I shrug. "Nothing but a scratch."

"If you say so."

The sun has gone down while we're regrouping. A pair of headlights comes around the corner.

"Guys, why don't we get off the street." Larry motions to the oncoming car.

We hop onto the sidewalk as a police car drives by. A young-looking officer peers at us curiously. I hug my skateboard tightly. Back in San Diego I'd gotten in trouble a handful of times for skating in the business district. I'm not sure if the same rules apply to Main Street, but I'm not in the mood to find out.

"I think we should leave." I try to keep my tone light. The adrenaline starts to wear off, and a sharp pain radiates from my bicep, tingling down to the bone. I wiggle my fingers, double-checking for any breaks, but the burning sensation across my skin only intensifies.

"Angelo, are you sure you're okay?" Kirsten reaches for my scraped arm but, as if thinking twice about it, pulls back in a hurry. "We can stop by the drugstore and get you cleaned up before we head home."

People peer at us through the diner's windows. Mostly strangers, but I notice some of Grayson's friends eyeballing me in amusement.

Not wanting to look like a total wimp, I suck in a lungful of air, trying my best to breathe through the pain. Circling my lips, I let the air out slowly. "Nah, let's go."

"Only if you're sure." Kirsten winces at my purpling skin and shudders.

"I've had worse," I repeat, puffing up my chest to prove my point. Too bad my arm's screaming for mercy. I end up grimacing in pain.

Kirsten visibly swallows and nods, positioning her board. "Um, okay then."

Larry looks sorry for me but jumps onto his board without further argument. In unison, we set off, remaining silent along the way.

We reach the turn to Larry's place first. He jumps off his board and scoops it up in one arm, lifting the other to bid farewell. He runs off while Kirsten and I continue on a little farther past some fields until we reach the turn to the more affluent part of town. I expect her to keep going, but she slows to a stop in front of me. Curious, I stop as well.

She keeps one foot on the board, rolling it back and forth. "I . . . um . . . just want to say thank you."

"For what?" I reach up to scratch my head, immediately regretting it when my arm screams bloody murder.

"Thank you for breaking my fall." She presses her lips together into a tight smile and nods.

I let out a strained chuckle. "It was nothing."

"No, it was something. It was . . ." She shakes her head and lets out a deep breath. I frown curiously as she takes a giant step toward me, letting out a soft gasp when she presses her soft lips against my cheek.

"Thank you," she whispers.

Though she's pulled away, my cheek still thrums from the heat of her lips. Swallowing hard, I whisper, "Kirsten? What was that?"

"I'll see you tomorrow." She turns quickly and jumps onto her board, skating away frantically.

I start to call out to her, but the G note pings loudly from my phone. It goes off a few more times. Cringing through the pain, I take my phone out of my front pocket. My blood runs cold. "What the hell?"

*Blake Hart:* Saw you getting down and dirty with Kirsten on Main Street

*Maddie Collins:* Guess Kirsten downgraded

*Cole Sterling:* Wait until Grayson hears about this

One thing's for sure: I'm gonna have to block a lot more people on Instagram tonight.

# 16

"What's up, Angie?" Grayson sidles up next to me, his wide-set eyes narrowing threateningly. I sigh and slam my locker shut. If he wants to scare me, he needs to try harder. Not only is it too early in the morning to deal with his bull, but I can barely focus on anything after last night.

Clenching my jaw, I glare right back. "What do you want, Grayson?"

Like a villain from all those old movies I watch, the jock looms over me. His fist flies past my head, hitting the locker with enough power to dent it. I glance to the side, but to my surprise I find no blemish in the thin metal.

"Word on the street is that you were all over Kirsten," the testosterone-fueled boy growls in my face, coating my nose with the stench of minty toothpaste. Who knew the Neanderthal cared a lick about dental hygiene? Then again, it's probably just to mask the smell of tobacco on his breath.

Blood pounds in my ears. Though I don't have much experience dealing with ex-boyfriends, I'm still sure about one thing: Grayson has no right to question me.

I shrug. "Why do you care? Last I heard she dumped you."

His eyes tighten, flashing in pain. He clears his throat quickly. His voice comes out a bit tinier than his normal behemoth drawl. "A relationship isn't over until I say it's over."

"Last time I checked a relationship takes two people." My shoulders bounce. "Or more if you're polyamorous."

"What are you getting at, Angie?" For someone in AP English, he doesn't seem to understand big words.

"Kirsten obviously doesn't want to be with you anymore." I make a sweeping motion with my hand. "Move on, dude."

Grayson's scar shifts as his frown deepens. "You want me to move on so you can mess around with my girl, *dude*? I gave you a pass before when you two were only doing that stupid skating crap. But making out with her in public like that? Nuh-uh."

"Again, she's not your girl," I say with a laugh. This guy's ridiculous. "Besides, we're just friends, and we weren't making out. Not that I need to explain anything to you."

"Fuck that. I heard how you were getting all nice and cozy on Main." His upper lip trembles. "Hope you're okay being one of her stray dogs. You know that's all you are to her, right?"

I bang the side of my head softly against the locker and groan. "Dude, why do you guys keep bringing up dogs?"

"The hell are you talking about?" Either Grayson's a good actor or just too stupid to realize how offensive half the things coming out of his mouth are.

"Let me guess, you're going to make another crack about me eating them, right?" I shake my head and let out a strained laugh. "It's like you guys are grasping for any racism straws you can reach. At least come up with new material."

The blood drains from Grayson's face. "I-I'm not racist."

"Are you for real? You seriously have the balls to say that to my face?"

His knuckles pop as he clenches his fist to his side. "It's the truth!"

"Then what about calling me 'brown boy'? And, yeah, those jokes about me eating pets? Don't tell me you can't see how racist that is."

"You're being too sensitive," he argues. "Besides, I see people say things like that online all the time. Can't be too bad."

"Actually, it is bad," I growl, in awe at how ignorant some people can be.

He glances around as if to make sure no one's listening and spots Larry strolling our way. As soon as the little dude sees Grayson, he screeches to a stop. The jock turns back to me. "I wasn't making a crack about a dog, Angie."

"Maybe if you say it a couple more times, I'll actually believe it."

His gelled hair barely moves as he shakes his head with ferocity. "What I mean is you're just another hurt animal to her. A stray puppy or a kitten. A pet for her to rescue. It's metaphorical. You know she once jumped out of a moving car to save a rabbit running across the street?"

My heart warms at the idea. "That's . . . actually nice."

My response makes him angrier. "Heard she's taking Larry under her wing too." The gears behind Grayson's eyes start clicking. His voice grows louder, harsher. "She's just nursing you both because she sees what everyone else does. You guys are broken. She likes broken."

I let out an exaggerated yawn. "Guess that's why she dated you, huh?"

"Fuck you, Angie." He closes the gap between us. "Just admit what you already know. Even for as weird as Kirsten is now, she's still way too good for you. You ain't shit."

Okay. Now I'm done with this little heart-to-heart. "At least I don't put up some *machismo* act, pretending I'm better than everyone just so I can wear a dumb crown during prom."

Grayson falters a bit but regains his composure and stands a bit straighter. "Don't act like you know me, *dude*. I don't even like going to prom."

As if that's a redeeming quality.

"Using your daddy's connections to get your way? Threatening me? If anybody's broken it's you. You're nothing but a scared little boy with a silver spoon up your ass, expecting life to go your way all the time. But you know what? It doesn't. Shit, I'm the poster boy for that. I'm stuck here in freaking Ocean Pointe."

"You don't know a thing about me. So why don't you shut your mouth and leave Kirsten alone, *brown boy*."

"Ah, here we go. Back to the racist comments when your back's up against a wall." I snort, dropping my head with a tired sigh.

"Go back to where you came from, loser. No one wants you here."

"Pretty sure Kirsten does—"

I don't even get to finish my thought. A blinding pain hits me square in the jaw. Sharp and intense. I stagger back, grasping for anything to hold on to, only to smack my open palms against the cold locker. I try to blink away fuzzy stars, but it only leaves me with double vision.

Three Graysons loom over me, followed by two, and finally only one. But the hunting camo on his shirt keeps whirling around, so I'm nauseatingly dizzy.

Grayson keeps his fist up to my nose. His knuckles are bright red.

"Stop it!" Larry shouts, but neither me nor Grayson pay any attention to him.

My jaw is throbbing, but I try to ignore the pulsating pain, which probably would be worse if it weren't for the aspirin I took this morning. I move it around a bit, but my cheek's swelling up fast. Trying to hold on to some of my pride, I manage to lift my chin and smirk at him, fully aware of all the new eyes and whispers surrounding us. Guess it's the punch heard round the world. Within a matter of seconds, we've accumulated quite an audience, which may or may not include all the people who DMed me last night.

"Didn't we warn you to keep that stupid mouth shut?" he tells me.

"You're the one who came up to me, or did you forget already?" I say. "Maybe I'm not the stupid one here."

A chorus of nervous giggles and shocked gasps circles us. Grayson's eyes widen in anger. Or maybe it's embarrassment. At this point I can't tell.

"You must have a death wish, brown boy." Grayson pulls his fist back, but I don't flinch. I won't give him the satisfaction.

"Ooooh," answers the crowd.

And I say, "You just called me a brown boy. Again."

"Yeah, because that's what you are." Grayson pauses, glancing at the crowd as if noticing them for the first time. But instead of causing him to step away, their presence only riles him up. "He is a brown boy, ain't he?"

Groupthink. It's the only phrase that flies through my head as I take in all the dropped gazes and awkward shifting. I've heard of mob mentality before, but I guess it's worse in high school.

"Yup," I reply with a pop of the *p*. "I am brown. And you know what? I'm proud of it! So you better try to think of another insult, because that one's not it."

Grayson grabs on to my collar, pushing me against the locker. But I'm not intimidated. Not even the slightest bit. My vision tightens, turning black around the edges. Every muscle in my body tenses, and I clench my fists, straining to hit something. Judging by Grayson's stiffening stance and the collective inhale around us, everyone's expecting a fight. I'm sure the overall boredom experienced in Ocean Pointe accounts for the bloodlust. Unfortunately for them, I like using brains over brawn.

Never taking my eyes off his, I don't unclench my fists but I lower my tone. "I dare you to call me a brown boy one more time." As his mouth opens to form the words, I cut him off. "But before you do, I should ask if you know the definition of a hate crime."

Grayson shifts uncomfortably but doesn't back down. "This ain't a hate crime, Angie. I'm beating your ass because you're messing with my girl."

"Wow, you are one delusional dick," I mutter.

The toe of his shoe hits mine as he leans into me. "Want to say that louder?"

"I'll scream it." Mustering up an imaginary megaphone, I yell, "Grayson's a delusional dick!"

This time I smile as the crowd coughs uncomfortably. "You and your friends keep acting like my skin color is such a bad thing. News flash, it's not. You swear you aren't racist or that you aren't picking on me because of my skin color. Yet here you are calling me brown and punching me. Hate to break it to you, but violence spurred on by race is officially a hate crime. Now go ahead and call me 'brown' one more time."

If only my phone wasn't in my backpack, I'd grab it and snap a photo of Grayson's widening eyes and slack jaw. I'd probably print the picture and hang it on my wall to commemorate the day I outsmarted a bully.

"N-no," he stammers, looking at the crowd for support, almost all of whom seem to immediately avoid his gaze. "I punched you because of your obsession with Kirsten. N-not because of your race."

"Kirsten? The girl *everyone* knows you're not with anymore. Am I right?" It's my turn to look at our audience, and given their awkward fidgeting, I hit the nail right on the head. "Besides, everyone here heard you call me 'brown boy.' And I'm pretty sure they can see how jacked up my face looks right now. Seems to me I got a lot of witnesses."

My proclamation has the opposite effect I wanted. Instead of running away with his tail between his legs, Grayson shoots me a wicked grin. "Witnesses? Who do you think's going to back you up? No one here would dare talk against me. You think anyone will take your side over mine? You're forgetting whose photo is hanging downstairs on the wall. I'm respected. You're just some newbie."

Crap. He might be right. I may have underestimated the perks of being the big man on campus. Maybe the whole brains over brawn thing didn't work this time.

I try to remain expressionless, silently praying for Mr. Holland or one of the teachers to storm in. We had security guards back at my old school. There would have been no way this could have carried on for this long. And I probably look pathetic, all red and swollen, waiting for anyone to side with me.

I start to lose hope when someone calls out, Spartacus-like, "I'll talk against you, Grayson."

"Who said that?" Grayson challenges, and *holy shit!* Larry steps up from behind a redheaded cheerleader, pushing his way to the front of the crowd. As touched as I am that he'd try to help, I also know his fear of conflict. "Larry, what are you doing?" I hiss. I try to break free, but the bully's still got me wedged against the locker.

And Larry, ignoring me, lifts his phone. Grayson gasps, his grip on me loosening as my buddy plays the video of the punch heard round the world.

"What do you think the local news outlets would think about seeing their star football player committing a hate crime?" Larry roars. "I'm sure your daddy would be pissed to know you might lose all those scholarships you've been gunning for."

The air is thick with tension. I don't think any of our classmates are even breathing at this point. A few hightail it down the hallway.

Grayson's Elvis-like snarl returns in full force. "Aren't you forgetting my dad is the sheriff? You think he'd let anyone see that video? He'd probably arrest you for blackmailing me!"

"You go, Grayson!" a deep voice shouts from the back, eliciting another round of uncomfortable giggles.

But a surge of satisfaction rushes through me when I realize Larry's not backing down. "He might control this town but not the country," Larry says. "Why don't you say we skip the dinky ole Ocean Pointe newscasts and go national?"

*"National?"* Grayson and I exclaim in unison.

"Apparently CNN and *GMA* look down on hate crimes. Who woulda thought?" Larry shoots me a wink. "I'm sure you'd enjoy being a guest on *Good Morning America*, wouldn't you, Angelo?"

"Seems fun," I agree, playing along.

But Grayson doesn't know when to quit. "You ain't got the guts, Larry. Don't think I don't know your druggie ass is scared of me. I'm sure my dad will be glad to finally get a Buchanan behind bars."

A second wave of anger surges through my veins. Enough is enough.

"Hey!" I roar. "You're talking about your dad charging Larry? What if I sue you for aggravated assault?"

Grayson's head snaps back in my direction. "Remember what I told you I'd do to your parents' business? What do you think about that?"

"So you're back to threatening my family with stupid lies? Fine. Then let's add extortion and blackmail to the hate crime and aggravated assault charges." I shake my head and grunt. "Grayson, you're obviously not thinking clearly. This can't end well for you. Just back down already, man."

Grayson stares at me for a beat. I frown, wondering what's going through his mind. He finally releases me. Coughing, I crash onto the floor, and when I do, a jock from the crowd dives forward and grabs Larry's phone.

"Ha!" The stiffness in Grayson's neck relaxes. He glances between me and Larry. "Guess you have nothing on me now, do you?"

Before I can respond, Larry chuckles and then all-out laughs. About fifty pairs of eyes stare at him as he wipes away a few tears rolling down his cheeks.

Grayson's lips tremble, but he maintains a calm tone. "What's so funny?"

"Do you think I'm an idiot?" Larry chokes out between snickers. Beaming victoriously, he continues, "Do you think I'm stupid enough to literally dangle my only playing card in front of you without having a backup?"

Grayson laughs, but it doesn't sound believable. "You've been here the whole time. Do you really expect me to believe you had the ability to back up that file? What are you, Superman?"

*"Lame comeback"* comes from somewhere behind me, and Grayson actually flinches.

"There's something called the cloud, dumbass," Larry announces proudly. "My files are automatically saved."

Once again, there's a chorus of *oohs*, and I can't help but cup my mouth and join in with my own loud, "Ooh!"

Grayson shifts his weight from side to side. Finally he throws up a white flag. "What do you want, Larry?"

Larry's ready. In a firm tone he says, "I want you to leave us alone: Angelo, his family, Sloppy's Pit Stop, and me."

"And me!" Kirsten appears out of nowhere, squirming out of the crowd to take a stand beside us.

Grayson's eyes darken, but he shakes his head and grinds out, "And if I do all that, you'll delete the footage?"

Larry shrugs. "Call it collateral. I'll keep it on file."

My eyebrows shoot up, and I elbow Larry in the ribs. "You're crazy, dude." But he merely shrugs again, clearly enjoying being on top for once.

"How do I know you won't just post it on the internet?" Grayson asks, that vein stretched along the middle of his forehead looking a second away from popping.

"Because unlike you I'm a man of my word." Larry holds out his hand. "Do we have a deal?"

Grayson scans the crowd, but no one makes a move to help him. Even the deep-voiced jock looks unsure. Call me a bad person, but I love seeing someone so obviously used to getting his way being shut down so coldly. Call it my new kink.

Groaning, Grayson reaches out to shake Larry's hand, but the little dude suddenly pulls back and gestures at Grayson's friend. "I'll be needing my phone back first."

Grayson motions to the jock, who slumps forward and slams the phone back into Larry's palm. Grinning widely, Larry shoves it into his pocket and grabs Grayson's hand, shaking it firmly. "Guess we have a deal."

As if on cue, the first bell rings signaling the start of homeroom, and the crowd of students quickly disbands, shuffling their feet and murmuring among themselves. I don't know if Larry realizes it, but he just made himself a badass among the OPHS student body.

Grayson catches Kirsten's eyes just as Mr. Holland strolls on by. The principal pauses midstep, swiveling on his feet to turn toward us. "Is there a problem here, children?"

"No, sir," I say quickly. My friends shake their heads.

Mr. Holland peers down his long nose and frowns at my jaw. I'm sure it looks pretty bad. "Are you sure, Angelo?"

I grin past the throbbing pain. "Definitely."

I'm sure Mr. Holland doesn't believe me, but he nods and gestures to the staircase. "Well, then get to class before I have to start handing out tardy slips."

Grayson is the first to leave. He stares at Kirsten as he walks by, but she ignores him and claps her hand against Larry's back. "Way to go, Larry! That took some guts."

"Yeah, man. That was purely epic," I say.

Kirsten lifts Larry's arm in the air like a prizefighter and doesn't even flinch at his usual stench of body odor.

"Friends protect friends, remember?" Larry watches Grayson intently until he's out of earshot. He smiles proudly. "Didn't know my acting skills were so lit."

I raise an eyebrow. "What do you mean?"

"When Cole grabbed my phone, I thought I was dead, but luckily I'm a quick thinker." He taps against his temple and then laughs at my incredulous expression.

"You mean there wasn't a file in the cloud?" I don't know whether to be shocked, relieved, or impressed. But I guess I'm a combination of all.

"Nope. My mom has my log-in information, and I hated her seeing any photos I saved, so I disabled the connection."

Kirsten hoots in amusement. "Do I even want to know what kind of photos you have on your phone?"

Larry wags his eyebrows. "I plead the Fifth."

Kirsten bursts into giggles. "Gross!"

"You're low-key savage," I tell the little dude as we head off to class.

"Maybe just a little." Larry beams.

# 17

There's definitely a shift in Larry. A group of cheerleaders jumps out of his way as we walk to our usual lunch table. To our surprise, there are already three people sitting there: Aiden, Stella, and the mean kid from the stairs.

Kirsten blinks. "Uh, can we help you?"

Aiden slides off his fedora, opening and closing his mouth. He visibly swallows but doesn't say a word.

I glance at Larry, who shakes his head in wonder.

"Don't worry, Aiden. I got this," a vaguely familiar voice cuts in.

The boy from the stairs slaps a magazine against his palm. My eyes zero in on the familiar cover with the bent corner.

"Wait a minute. That's my skate magazine!" I blurt out in surprise. "I haven't seen that one in weeks. Ever since the first day of school and . . ."

"And you bumped into me?" The boy wiggles my magazine in the air. "It got mixed in with my things."

"Oh . . ." I eye the Ichabod Crane–looking boy suspiciously and take a seat. Larry and Kirsten do the same.

The boy cocks an eyebrow. "Name's Wyatt."

"Angelo." On instinct I extend my hand, but he merely looks down at it and sniffs. I drop my hand and frown. "What's up?"

"We saw what Larry did with Grayson this morning. It's about time someone stood up to that asshole."

"Everyone saw what Larry did with Grayson," Kirsten interrupts with pride. She whacks her arm against Larry's chest. He grunts, nearly falling off his chair. "Our friend here is a star."

"Sure, if you want to see it that way." Wyatt's narrow nostrils flare as he looks back at me. "But I'm sure your 'celebrity' friend"—that makes Larry chuckle—"wouldn't have had the guts to do all that without you by his side."

I flinch, waiting for Larry to react, but he just shrugs in agreement. "What's your point?" I say.

Wyatt gestures to him and Aiden. "We need your help."

"Doing what?"

"Taking down the football team," he answers.

I nearly choke on my own spit. "I—I'm sorry?"

"Let me explain." Stella speaks up, sounding somewhat determined but looking incredibly shy. Now, I'm sure Stella's really smart, and running the student council takes guts, but I see how Maddie's able to walk all over her. There's no mistaking Stella's insecurity. You can sense it from miles away. "What my brother here was trying to say is—"

"Hold on a minute." I slide my gaze between her and Wyatt. "Brother? You're related?"

"Are you saying we don't look alike?" Wyatt glances at his sister and cracks a grin when she rolls her eyes.

I take in Stella's beautiful mocha complexion and Wyatt's almost porcelain face. "I . . . uh . . ."

"*Step*brother," Stella clarifies.

"Oh," I say again, feeling dumb.

"Anyway, what Wyatt was trying to say is that we want to take the football team down *a notch*. And the cheerleaders." She glances at Kirsten, whose expression never changes.

"I still don't know what that means," I admit.

Stella nods empathetically. "I wouldn't expect someone new to understand. But let me break it down for you. The football team and cheerleading squad rule OPHS."

"Everybody knows that," I shoot back.

She nods. "But did you know none of the other clubs would ever dare to hold an event the same time as a football game?"

"Because they know no one would attend?" I offer.

"Yes, and because the PTA would have the clubs' asses if they scheduled anything that overlapped with game time. The football team is the favorite around here. Most of the school budget goes to them. Once the season's over, whatever's left is split up among the other teams and clubs for the rest of the school year. That includes student council."

"It's because the school board thinks football is the moneymaker," Wyatt grumbles. "I heard a rumor that every time the Trojans win a championship, OPHS gets more state funding."

"Long story short, even if I'm president, my decisions are always undermined. By Maddie and her boyfriend . . . the other council members always vote for what they want because, again, the jocks and cheerleaders always get what they want."

"Like that time in the hallway," I comment.

"What?"

I shake my head. "Never mind."

"And if not by them, by other people who are too scared to speak up against them." Stella bites the inside of her cheek. "I guess you can call it complacency."

"Okay," I say. "That makes sense."

"So we need something to topple football in this school." She flicks her finger against my magazine. "That's where you and skating come in."

"I'm not following . . ."

"Don't you get it? None of the other clubs can hold an event on Friday nights because they're funded by the school. But skating isn't."

"Okay . . . ?" I look at Kirsten and Larry, who look as confused as I do but intrigued.

"Can you imagine what a statement it would make if another sports event was held the same time as a football game? It'd be epic!"

I shoot Kirsten a cheeky smirk. "Someone thinks skating's a sport," I whisper.

But Kirsten isn't paying attention to me. She's thinking hard. "Wait a minute . . ." Her eyebrows fly up. "Are you suggesting what I think you're suggesting? You're saying we should hold a skate competition, aren't you?"

Wyatt's voice comes out louder, faster. "I read through your magazine, and skateboarding competitions are pretty big. What if we hold one here and show the football team they're not the only stars in town? What if we take their audience away so they're left with nothing but empty bleachers?"

"Okay, hang on. Stop right there," I say with a laugh. "First of all, I don't think anyone in this town will ever say no to football." I flail my arms wildly toward the numerous banners hanging around the cafeteria. "Plus, we can't just hold a competition."

"Why not?" Kirsten demands.

"Those things take a long time to plan." I hold up a hand, counting down on my fingers. "You'd need insurance—"

"Not if you make people sign waivers," Stella cuts in, proving she's presidential material after all. "It excuses you from liability."

I hold up another finger. "You'll also need money."

Wyatt and Stella exchanges glances. "Money?"

"Yes, money." My whole head moves along with my eye roll. "For prizes, venue rental, advertising—competitions aren't cheap."

"We're not on a schedule," Wyatt argues. "We can make that money and then some."

"I respect your optimism, but making the amount you'd need is no easy feat." I picture my savings account. "Trust me. I know."

"Is that it?" Stella asks, clearly ignoring my point. "Is that all you need?"

"No." I laugh again. "It also helps to have skaters."

"Skaters?"

"Yes, skaters. You can't hold a competition without people to compete in it." I glance at the popular table and at the other students watching the jocks and cheerleaders longingly, probably wishing they were part of the clique. "As hard as making money is, I bet finding skaters in this area is just as hard if not harder."

"I'll skate." Aiden's soft voice catches me by surprise. Melodic with a soft timbre, I wouldn't expect such an angelic voice to come from a giant guy.

I blink incredulously. "Wait a minute. You know how to skate?"

"No," he confesses. "But I can learn. We all can."

"Yeah." Stella nods in solidarity.

Aiden fiddles with the brim of his hat. "I saw you guys on Main Street."

A strained laugh bubbles in my throat. "Did everyone see us?"

"Probably . . ." He swallows so hard I can make out the muscles moving in his neck. "Skating looked fun."

"It is fun."

"Besides, if skating can give Larry the guts to stand up to Grayson, then I'm all for it," he says quietly.

Larry thinks it over. "Maybe I'm just a kick-ass person."

Kirsten bites back a snort.

"You've never stood up to anyone before. Not that I've seen," Aiden points out. He flips through the magazine. He taps against a photo of a skater who'd taken a spill after a fakie flip attempt. "But I think with skating you're prepared to crash and burn. No fear."

"No fear," Larry repeats with a satisfied nod. "Guess skating did do that for me."

Skating's always been a passion of mine. A way to stay fit, to escape reality, and to have fun. But of course, it does demand some level of bravery, especially when it comes to conquering death-defying tricks. Maybe skating let Larry realize he does have some innate courage. And all it took was him tapping into this courage to stand up to Grayson despite his fear of conflicts.

I clear my throat. "Skating is great, and if you want to learn you should do it. But I don't think holding a competition's going to work out. Especially for the reason you want it to."

"Angelo, let me encourage you to reconsider your stance," says Stella in true presidential fashion. "Now, we've already gone over the reasons why you think we *can't* hold the competition, but we haven't discussed the reasons we can."

I lean back and cross my arms. "Do go on."

Stella motions to her friends. "Wyatt, Aiden, and I will learn how to skate and sign up for the competition. That's already three contestants. And if you, Larry, and Kirsten sign up, that's six altogether. We can also check to see if people in neighboring towns want to compete."

"As great as all that is, no one's going to watch a bunch of newbies skate. And it's not only the skaters you need to worry about," I remind her. "I already told you how hard it would be to plan a competition and . . ."

"I was just getting to that," Stella snaps. "We'll handle that. Just leave it to us. But obviously someone needs to teach us how to skate. And that'll be your job."

"How'd I know this was coming?" I sigh.

"Listen, we'll handle everything else. It'd be all you'd have to do." Stella leans forward, clasping her hands. "Do we have a deal?"

"First of all, why would I agree to teach you? I'm already busy enough as it is."

Stella frowns. "You're teaching Larry and Kirsten."

"Exactly! And three more students will cut into my practice time."

"Practice for what?"

*Winning back my pride.*

I change the subject. "And what do you mean by 'we'll handle everything else' exactly?"

"Everything we need to do to make a competition happen, of course!"

I shake my head. "Still one major problem. Like I said earlier, no one's going to watch a bunch of newbies skate."

"But they'll want to watch you." Kirsten leans into me, coating my cheek with her warm breath. At my doubtful look, she presses, "Think about it. You want to fly all the way to California to compete in some stranger's event, but now you can compete in your own."

"Yeah, because that's completely ethical."

"Then you can be the judge but still do an awesome demo to show off your skills."

I snort. Between her and Stella, they have an argument for everything.

She ignores me. "This Tyler guy you're so keen to defeat. If you're so worried about that, what better way to show him up than to hold your own competition? I bet he's never done that before, right?"

"True," I admit.

"Maybe this way you wouldn't even have to go back to California."

"Oh, I'm still going," I blurt out. "I still have to convince my aunt to let me live with her."

Kirsten falters. "But you're not with Amanda anymore . . ."

"California's still my home."

Kirsten averts her eyes. "Well, at least this can be more practice for you."

"How can it be more practice if I'll be teaching three more people how to skate?" I eye the group in dismay.

"Angelo, please," Stella pleads. "This is important. I'm sick of playing second fiddle to Justin and Maddie. This isn't just about holding a skating event. It's showing them that I'm no longer scared to stand up for myself."

Wyatt clears his throat. "Like Stella said, this will be a statement. Made by all of us. And even if only one or two people decide to watch us newbies, it's still more than us doing nothing."

I hate to be the bad guy, but sometimes you have to put your foot down so you don't find yourself in a regrettable situation. "I'm sorry, guys, but between teaching Kirsten and Larry, my own practice, school-work, and my shifts at Sloppy's, I'm already spread thin enough as it is."

Stella shakes her head. "But—"

"I'm sorry but no," I say firmly.

Wyatt's the first to leave the table. Stella and Aiden exchange glances and quietly follow after him. Kirsten and Larry shoot me hesitant looks.

"Why are you looking at me like that?" I grumble. Before either of them could answer I remind them, "The more students I have, the less time I can focus on you."

"But we already know how to skate," Larry argues.

Not wanting to knock him off his high horse, I agree. "You're right. You do know how to skate. Which frees up more time for me to practice."

Larry looks like he wants to say something more, but I tear into my lunch, hinting that the conversation is over.

# 18

"I can't believe you talked me into this." My voice gets stuck somewhere between my larynx and esophagus. Kirsten and I walk the gravel pathway to the industrial park. I tighten my grip on my skateboard and drag my feet up the hill and spot my three new students waiting for me in front of the main warehouse. Larry's beside them; he jumps up from the metal staircase and waves at me excitedly. "I thought I made myself perfectly clear. I don't have time for this."

"Then why did it take no convincing at all when I brought it up again at Sloppy's?" Kirsten pinches the wrinkly skin on my elbow. I think it's called the weenus.

"Oh, you mean when you barged into the restaurant and gave my parents some lame excuse about needing my help for school? Thought you'd be over lying by now."

"Okay, 'lying' is a strong word. I prefer to think of it as embellishing the truth," says Kirsten.

"Or when you blackmailed me by saying unless I taught—what did you call them again? The 'other outsiders'?" I shake my head. "Unless I taught them and helped with their competition, you were ready to revoke my access to the warehouse?"

"'Blackmail' is another strong word." Kirsten stops midway down the hill.

I step up beside her. "Why is it so important to you that I help out with this grand scheme of theirs?"

"Because it's for the greater good."

I scoff. "Seriously? So it isn't just a way for you to get back at your old friends?"

"You should talk." She smirks as my cheeks flush. "Remember what I said about this town not wanting to change?" She points to my new students. "They want a change. And you'll be as complacent as everyone else if you don't help them out."

"But why do *I* have to help them out? It's not my problem."

"You live here now, so it is your problem." Kirsten's lips split into a wide grin. "Besides, you're the only one who can help in the way they need."

I turn to look at Larry, who's gesturing to us impatiently. He'd looked so proud after he stood up to Grayson this morning. Can I really deny Stella, Aiden, and Wyatt the chance to do the same thing?

I throw my head back and groan. "Fine."

"Fine?" Kirsten claps her hands. "I knew you'd make the right choice."

"Blackmail aside, I felt like a bad guy for not helping Stella when I saw Maddie being mean to her," I confess. "I owe her this. Besides, it might be fun to have a competition to look forward to that my ex's new boyfriend isn't competing in."

Kirsten squeezes my shoulder, and warmth flows to my core. "You're crazy if you think you're anywhere close to being a bad guy. And you're right. This will be fun."

"What are you guys doing? C'mon!" Larry shouts.

I cup a hand around my mouth and yell back, "Be right there!"

Larry throws his arms in the air.

I chuckle and turn back to Kirsten. "You really don't think I'm a bad guy, eh?"

"You adopted a rescue, Nollie."

"What does that have to do with anything?"

"You can tell a lot about a person by their love for animals." She winks. "You're good. That's why I keep you around."

Butterflies attack my stomach again. At a loss for words, I say the first thing that comes to mind. "I heard you rescued a rabbit once too."

She blinks in surprise. "Where'd you hear that?"

"Grayson."

"Huh."

A sudden thought floods my mind. I straighten like a marionette being tugged. "*Are* you rescuing us?"

"What are you talking about?"

"Grayson said you like fixing broken people. Is that why you've been hanging out with me and Larry?" I gesture to the others. "And now them? I'm actually surprised you let them in on this place."

Irritation flashes across Kirsten's face. "First of all, you guys aren't broken. And second . . ." Her sharp features relax, and she releases a breath. "And second, maybe you're the ones rescuing me."

"That's . . . so corny. Totally cheesy!" I tease, leaning in close. Her pale eyelashes flutter in surprise, almost mimicking each beat of my heart.

She breaks into laughter. "Maybe a little," she admits. "But it's true. Me, you, and Larry aren't really loners anymore, are we?"

"Guess not . . ."

"Because the three of us are together. And yeah, Larry got Grayson to back off, but the three of us are still mostly treated like outsiders in our own school. So why not band together with other outsiders. Add more people to the mix."

Before I can reply, she rushes ahead of me and greets my impatient students.

"Finally! Took you guys long enough," Wyatt complains as I walk up.

"Attention!" Only a banshee's wail even comes close to Kirsten's shriek. The newbies watch intently as she places her board at her feet.

"You have been entrusted with the knowledge of this sacred space. We only have one rule here. Can anyone guess what it is?"

Aiden starts to raise his hand but thinking twice about it jams it back into his pocket. Stella rises onto her tiptoes, waving her hand in the air. But Kirsten doesn't call on either of them. She saunters over to Wyatt, who is decked head to toe in safety pads. From his thick helmet down to his elbow pads, wrist guards, kneepads, *and* shin guards, it's as if he's trying to protect himself from a hoard of zombies rather than just skating around an abandoned warehouse. I mean, don't get me wrong, I'm all for safety and all that jazz, but part of skating is getting hurt.

"Wyatt? What do you think?" Kirsten crosses her arms and taps against the cracked concrete with her foot. "What is our number one rule?"

Wyatt licks his chapped lips. "The first rule is not to speak about this."

"That is correct," Kirsten says at the same time Aiden shoots back, "But that's from *Fight Club*."

"You've seen *Fight Club*?" I ask in surprise. No offense, but Aiden doesn't seem like the kind of guy who'd watch the cult classic. He comes across as a softy, and the movie is . . . well, somewhat harsh.

His bulky shoulders bounce. "Who hasn't?"

"I haven't," Wyatt snaps in annoyance.

Aiden lifts an eyebrow. "Well, maybe you should."

I clap my hands to get their attention. "Okay, okay. Enough of that. Let's get this lesson started. Kirsten, Larry, you can lend your boards to these three. But two of them have to share."

I lead Kirsten, Larry, and the three new skaters to the center of the lot. Once they're settled around me, I place a foot on top of my board and clap my hands. "*Hola, estudiantes.* Are you ready for today's lessons?"

Scrunching up his nose, Wyatt sticks a finger in the space between his helmet and forehead and scratches against his shiny skin. "Um, do Filipinos speak Spanish?"

Stella's head snaps in his direction. "Seriously? How is that even relevant?"

"He spoke Spanish," Wyatt mumbles, casting his eyes down to his feet.

"No, it's okay to ask," I assure him. "At least you're taking the time to get to know me. Unlike some of the other people in this town."

Kirsten meets my gaze and opens her mouth. But she quickly shuts it again and nods in understanding.

"I did speak Spanish this time, but Filipinos have their own language. Multiple languages, actually." I smile fondly, remembering all the different conversations that used to float around our old restaurant. Tagalog, Ilocano, Bicolano—it was beautiful to hear.

Lost in nostalgia, I explain, "But a lot of words do sound like Spanish because Spaniards conquered the Philippine Islands a long time ago."

"Oh. That's interesting," Wyatt murmurs, finally meeting my gaze again.

I doubt Wyatt really is interested, but his sister is fascinated. "Do you speak any of those languages? Can you say something for us?"

I wince. "Yeah, about that . . . I can only understand Tagalog—fluently, by the way. But I can't actually speak it."

"How is that possible?" Stella asks.

I shrug. "Beats me. It's just the way my mind works. I can't seem to string together the right words to make a sentence. I guess it's because my parents never really talked to me in Tagalog, so I never really practiced speaking it back to them. I only learned the language because my aunt always used to talk to me in Tagalog when she babysat me."

"Why don't your parents talk to you in Tagalog?" Stella wonders.

"They use some words but really only talk in English. It's probably because they're in customer service. We may have owned a Filipino restaurant in California, but we had a lot of non-Filipino customers too . . . at least we used to have a lot."

She nods slowly. "That's interesting."

I chuckle. "You know what else is interesting? About the only time I can speak Tagalog is when I'm really pissed off about something."

"Must be subconscious," she ponders.

I shrug. "But enough about all that. Let's start for real. We've wasted enough time already."

"You got that right," Wyatt says with a straight face. "I should've watched a tutorial on YouTube. I'd probably be a pro by now."

I don't know him well enough to be able to tell if he's kidding or not. Either way, I deadpan right back, "A YouTube tutorial wouldn't look out for you to make sure you don't need all these." I flick against his elbow pad. "Where'd you get all these pads, anyway?"

"They're my dad's. He took up biking recently."

"Cool." I kick the tail end of my deck and grab on to the board as it flies through the air, pressing my fingertips against the grip tape. "Back to business. Let's see which foot is your lead foot."

"Lead foot?" Aiden, who I am now dubbing our gentle giant, murmurs under his breath.

Knowing what's coming next, Kirsten and Larry are practically giddy with excitement. Like two kids waiting for Christmas morning. I walk behind Stella and give her a gentle shove. She squeals in surprise as I announce, "Reggie."

Now it's Aiden's turn. He stiffens once I place both hands against his back. I grunt, using all my might to push him, but I can't budge him. "Dude, how are you not on the football team? It'd probably take five guys to tackle you."

The tips of Aiden's ears turn bright red. "Football's not really my thing."

"It's not mine either." I chuckle.

"Or mine," Kirsten pipes in at the same time Larry announces, "Me neither."

I try again, taking him by surprise, and he takes a tiny step. I wipe the sweat out of my eye and take a deep breath. "Goofy."

"Like us!" Kirsten holds up her hand and gives me a high five.

Aiden's voice is as quiet as a mouse. "What does Goofy mean?"

"It means you put your right foot forward," Larry answers quickly. "To help you balance better."

"Can't I put my left foot forward?" he asks, never taking his eyes off the board.

"Like this?" I push off on my board and jump in the air, landing so my left foot's in front. Kirsten's whistles of appreciation give me butterflies. *What is going on with me?* I wonder, and yet I speed up and push off again, landing back in my usual stance. And I know I'm showing off, but it's kinda hard not to knowing Kirsten's cheering me on.

I cruise around the center area of the lot until I'm back in front of my students and place my back foot on the ground to stop. "That's called a switch or switchfoot for novices. But since you're just starting to learn, your balance will be much better using your right foot as your lead foot."

"Switchfoot? Like the band?" Wyatt smacks a bug flying beside his ear with a sickening thwap.

"No, not like the band. And for that failed comparison . . ." I walk up behind him with my arms outstretched, but before I can even get my hands on him, he jumps out of my way with a screech.

"What the hell kinda noise did you just make?" I ask. "Some pterodactyl crap?"

Wyatt rubs at the only patch of skin exposed between his kneepad and shin guard. "I don't like to be touched by other people."

Stella peers at her stepbrother with sympathy. "He's been like this for years."

"I have to figure out which is your lead foot," I remind him.

Wyatt stares at me as if I'd just suggested he jump off a five-story building. "Why don't I just take a step forward?" He takes an exaggerated step and smirks. "There. Left foot."

I don't have the energy to argue at this point. "Fine. Whatever. Let's just do this."

As if sensing my growing irritation, Larry steps forward and motions for Kirsten. "Why don't we help Angelo out and teach these guys the basics?"

Kirsten catches my eye and nods. "Yeah. It'll give you some time to practice, Rivera."

"You sure?" I dig the end of my board into the ground.

"We can handle it."

Relieved, I don't bother to argue. Once everyone heads off to skate, I take out my phone. I don't know why I bother to check my savings account knowing perfectly well I hardly made any new money since the last time I opened the app. But like a masochist I stare at the bold type.

**$390.69**

I have no one to blame but myself for giving away some of my shifts. Leaving work early today isn't helping either.

I sigh and put away my phone. I head over to my favorite curb and walk past our version of David and Goliath. Aiden's outstretched arms tremble as Larry pushes him near the loading docks. I pray Aiden doesn't fall and squish Larry like a bug.

I watch Stella, who is only a smidge more relaxed than Aiden. Kirsten holds her by the hand and pulls her along the cracked concrete.

I head over to one of the three ramps toward the back end of the lot. Wyatt is by the nearest one, halfway hidden in the shadows, alone. He fidgets awkwardly by the railing.

I glance at the others and then back at Wyatt. I slump forward with a groan.

Kirsten's right. I'm not a bad guy. But maybe things would be easier for me if I were.

I really should take advantage of my friends' offer to let me practice, but seeing Wyatt's pathetic stance there's no way I can.

I drop my board in front of him and hold out my hand, but he only slaps it away. "Nope. No, no, no. You ain't touching me, buddy."

"I'm trying to teach you. How do you suggest we do this?" I snap, not bothering to hide my annoyance. I gesture toward his ridiculous pads, cringing at the bright neon patterns. "You're obviously afraid of falling. I'm just trying to prevent you from getting hurt. Look! Everyone's being guided around."

He watches Stella complete a turn and bites his dried bottom lip. "Fine. But just stand there"—he points a few feet away—"and get ready to dive forward in case I fall."

Sticking a finger in my ear, I wiggle it around with a scowl. "Did I hear you correctly? You want me to break your fall? Act like your floor mat?"

Wyatt's almost goatee seems to flutter in the wind as he lifts his chin. "Exactly. You did it for Kirsten, right?"

I shut my eyes, pinching the bridge of my nose, and take deep, methodical breaths. My yoga-instructor cousin would be proud. "Whatever. Let's just do this. And remember, left foot—"

"Left foot first," he has the audacity to interrupt me. "I got it."

I throw my hands in the air and back away before those safety pads really do take a beating.

Wyatt's foot trembles in the air. He hesitantly plants it onto the top of the deck. The board wobbles a bit. Cringing, I take an automatic step forward. Wyatt shoots me a look as if to say *Don't even think about it*, so I hold my palms out in surrender. Wincing the whole time, I watch him place his other foot on top of the board and groan when it slides out from underneath him.

"Ow! Crap!" Wyatt's on his back, rubbing the meaty part of his butt. Guess for all the safety equipment he used he forgot an ass pad.

"Here." I hold out a hand for him, but he merely smacks it away and struggles to stand by himself. I step back with a grunt. "Fine. Do what you want. Again."

"Wyatt! Are you okay?" Stella, who has been cruising around by herself slowly, races over to us. She jumps off her board and scans Wyatt's body as if looking for injuries. "Are you hurt?"

"Forget it!" An almost guttural wail escapes his thick lips. "I was stupid to try to do anything physical!"

I run my fingers through my damp hair and let out a loud groan. "Dude, you can't expect never to fall. Especially on your first try. Do you know how many bones I've broken before?"

Kirsten runs up beside us as Wyatt's face pales to a startling shade of white. "Yeah, Rivera, that's not really helping."

Wyatt doesn't wait for me to apologize. The snapping sound of Velcro rebounds off the empty buildings as he rips off his pads and prepares to storm off. Sighing, I jump in front of him. Wyatt walks straight into my chest and falls back, but this time I catch him by the wrist before he can push me away.

"Look, I'm sorry if I'm being pushy," I tell Wyatt, quickly letting go of his wrist. "I'm just in over my head trying to balance everything right now. I even left my shift early to be here."

Kirsten flinches. "I'm sorry."

I shrug as Wyatt demands, "You call that teaching?" Foamy spit gathers at the corners of his mouth like a rabid animal.

"Yes, I do." Wyatt shifts uncomfortably, but I go on. "I even offered to hold you like Kirsten was doing with Stella and Larry with Aiden."

"And I said no, didn't I?" he snaps.

I clasp my chest in mock pain. "That hurt. That really hurt."

"Like I'd want your hands on me."

"Oh, you'd be surprised how gentle my touch is." I grin, wagging my eyebrows suggestively.

I'm not sure what response I was expecting. Maybe annoyance. If I was lucky a laugh. But as I take in his quivering lips and downcast eyes, I'm surprised to find sadness etched on his long face.

"Good to know you can joke around at my expense. Everyone always seems to." He focuses on an unknown spot as if indicating the conversation is over.

Being bullied seems like the running theme of our little group. Kirsten's right. Us outsiders need to stick together.

"Wyatt, c'mon. I'm just not sure how to handle this situation the best way, so I went for humor. Let's talk about this." I pause for a response but am met with nothing but silence. A wave of heat floods my veins. But soon, my growing annoyance is overwhelmed by downright exhaustion. Wyatt's truly giving Amanda a run for her money in the drama queen department. "If you don't want to be here, we won't force you. We're all here only because we want to be."

"It's not that I don't want to be here," he finally says. "It's just that I had no idea this would be so hard."

"Learning to skate can be hard, but—"

"No, it's not just that," he cuts me off with a sigh. "I'm talking bigger."

I catch Kirsten's eye, and she shrugs. "What do you mean by bigger?"

"I haven't been entirely honest with you." His Adam's apple bobs as he swallows. "I . . . I don't just want to take down the football team. I want to be . . . um . . . I want to be, uh . . ."

"Don't tell me you want to be on the team," I say dryly.

"No. I want to be different. Faster." And then he says something unexpected. "I saw you guys flying down Main Street. I want that. Especially after what's happening in gym."

"Wait, what's happening in gym?" Kirsten asks.

Wyatt toes the ground, embarrassed. "I, um, come in last during the fun run. The mile run. Every week. All the time."

I grimace. "Doesn't sound like fun to me."

"Trust me. It's not. Especially since I never hear the end of it. The fun run's held at the end of class, and I have gym right before football practice."

I get it. I can connect the dots just fine.

"I guess this explains your vendetta against the team," I say with a slow nod. "Is it safe to assume they're the ones who keep making fun of you?"

"I just want things to be different." He kicks at a pebble.

Banishing all thoughts of practicing myself, I ask, "Okay. So what do you say? Care to give it another go? We'll take it slow this time."

The lot is quiet. The fact that he and I have completely switched stances and now it's *me* trying to convince *him* to take my lessons is not completely lost on me.

"Fine," he finally answers. "But if at any time I don't feel comfortable, I'm out of here."

*Ditto,* I want to say. But I don't.

I bend over and swipe a fallen kneepad off the ground, tossing it against his chest. "Then let's begin."

# 19

**To-Do List:**

1. Find a venue
2. Brainstorm fundraising ideas
3. Recruit skaters
4. Spread the word
5. ~~Get Angelo to tell Kirsten how he feels about her~~

I walk around the counter to peer over Larry's shoulder. Grabbing his pen, I quickly cross out the fifth item. "Number five? Really? News flash—I'm not into Kirsten like that."

"Sure you're not."

It's Saturday night, and Larry's hanging out with me at Sloppy's. It's not only been about a week and a half since the punch heard round the world, a.k.a. Showdown at Angelo's Locker, but also a full eleven days since the newest outsiders joined our crew.

I look into the dining area at the only full booth—a two-seater near the trash cans. The couple picks at their fries, talking and laughing, lost in their own world. It's weird to think anyone would actually want to spend their free time in this place, but then again it would be nice if more people did.

"What are you even doing, anyway?" I ask Larry as he taps his pen against the counter.

Larry's buckteeth become even more noticeable with his wide grin. "What do you think I'm doing? Putting a list of things together that we need to do to make the competition happen . . . *ah!* Thought of another one."

6.   Think of a cool name

I let out a puff of air from my nostrils. "You really don't have much experience in this, do you?"

"Do you?"

"No. And that's the point. None of us do." I grab a dish towel and toss it into a sudsy bucket. "I admit, holding a competition's a cool idea, but it's never going to happen."

"Why are you being so negative?" Larry snaps.

"Take a look at your list." I lean over and knock against it. "Most of those things cost money. Money that we do not have."

"Hence the fundraising," Larry counters.

"Fine. But do you really think we'll make enough money—in Ocean Pointe of all places—to fund a skateboarding event? Money's hard to come by, and right now money's one of my main problems."

Larry doesn't look a bit fazed. "Kirsten's family's loaded."

"What does that have to do with anything?" I snap.

"I'm sure she wouldn't mind donating to the cause. What if we consider it her entry fee?" Larry's eyes light up. "That's it! We can charge each skater an entry fee!"

"Hate to burst your bubble, but even if we charge every skater who signs up, we'll still have a large amount of money to front. Especially if it ends up that there are only five skaters in the whole competition!"

"Then we'll just get Kirsten to ask her family to front it."

I shoot him a pointed look. "Really?"

"What? Like I said, they're loaded."

I shake my head. "That's messed up, and you know it."

Larry considers me for a moment and snickers. "The only reason you don't want to take her money is because you like her. *Like* like her," he teases.

"Shut up, man. I do not like her. Or *like* like her. How old are we again?" I'm sure my flushed cheeks give away what I've been grappling with for the past week. I don't know when it happened or even how it happened, but I can no longer deny it. I have a crush on Kirsten. Maybe it was inevitable considering the time we spend together and the fact that she's funny and smart, not to mention beautiful. And the thank-you peck she gave me after I broke her fall on Main Street didn't hurt either. But it's way too soon after Amanda for me to even think of getting with someone new. Besides, Kirsten's my friend. I can't let these swoony feelings jeopardize that.

Larry grunts and rewrites the bullet point underneath the scratched-out line. "If you keep telling yourself that lie, you might actually believe it. I sure don't."

I grab the dish towel and flick it, sending drops of water toward his mocking grin, but Larry's quick to move away, completely missing the soapy spray. Guess skating's doing him well. "Who knew all it took was standing up to one bully to make you even more of a smart-ass."

His grin widens even more. "I think you mean confident."

"Confident or not, I can still kick you out of here, you know."

"But you wouldn't."

I snicker. "You're right. I wouldn't."

"It's not as if you're busy anyway."

I squeeze the soapy dish towel in my hand. Cold suds spill out from between my fingers, covering the already spotless counter. Larry picks at a dried zit on top of his upper lip with a smirk. "You've cleaned this counter about four times already." He swipes his finger against the surface and lifts it up for me. "See? Clean."

I blush, drying the bubbles from the counter. "Can't be too clean."

Larry's curls bounce as he chuckles. "Do your parents know how big Kirsten's role is in keeping this place up to health code?"

I shift uncomfortably, trying to play it off. "Why are you going on about this again?"

"I know you're thinking of her while you clean—"

"Only because you mentioned her," I mutter.

He smiles knowingly. "How about the way you're always hanging on to every word she says, even if her stories are lame—"

"They're never lame," I grumble.

"Or the way you're practically drooling every time she does . . . well, anything?"

"I was thinking maybe we can forgo cash prizes." I change the subject, not really wanting to talk about my love life, or lack thereof. "Maybe if we hit up a few companies online, they can donate some gear for a prize pack."

Fortunately, Larry goes along with it. "I'll add it to our list."

As Larry bends over the sheet of paper, Mom pokes her head out of the back office. "Angelo, can we speak to you for a moment?" A deep frown mars her otherwise pretty face. She rubs both her cheeks, which look a bit more hollowed out than usual. Dad steps out of the office and fidgets uncomfortably. I've only seen them this anxious when they told me we were leaving San Diego.

And at that thought, call it PTSD or whatever, my stomach drops like it's about to fall out of my butt. "Uh, okay sure." I turn to Larry, who's already backing away.

"I'll see you tomorrow." He throws his hand in the air and is out the door.

I turn back to my parents. My armpits break out in a cold sweat. My lungs constrict. If I didn't know any better, I'd say I was scared. But of what?

Mom motions me to the kitchen and near the sink, a good place for privacy that still gives us a good vantage point of the restaurant. She positions herself so she can see the front doors and Dad can keep an eye on the dining area. Not that he really needs to considering we only have two customers.

My mouth feels like it has a swarm of angry bees in it. "What's up?"

"Your dad and I have been talking . . ."

*Uh-oh.*

". . . and we noticed you're not pulling your weight around here."

It's as if someone yanked out a plug. I release the breath I didn't realize I was holding. "Oh," I say, relieved. "If this is about me giving my shifts to Chad—"

"It's more than that," Dad cuts me off. He and Mom exchange that look reserved for parents who are sorely disappointed in their kid.

"I made friends," I say simply.

"We know. And we're happy for you. But do you remember why we moved to Ocean Pointe to begin with?"

"Because Rivera's Kusina went under and you had no choice but to sell it?" I don't mean to sound so cheeky about it, but it's partly their fault for always allowing our regulars to "put it on their tab" all the time. If those tabs were actually paid, I'd probably still be in San Diego right now.

Fortunately, Mom doesn't whap me on the head for being a smart-ass. "Sloppy's Pit Stop isn't doing as well as we'd like."

"I kind of figured." I frown, scanning the dining area.

Mom follows my gaze. "We get customers, but not enough to break even. This is exactly what happened before."

"Don't tell me we're moving again." The joke loses its humor, sticking to my tongue like bugs on one of those sticky papers.

"Of course not," Mom snaps.

"Cool." I can't deny how relieved I feel, which is plain weird.

"At least not yet."

"You have to be joking." My gaze bounces between the two of them. "You're joking, right?"

Mom dodges the question and says, "Angelo, we need your help."

As much as I'm not ready to let go of her truth bomb, I ask, "What kind of help?"

"We need you to brainstorm ways to get more customers," she explains, patting my dad's shoulder as if tapping him into the ring.

"Great. More brainstorming," I say under my breath.

"What was that?" Dad asks. When I shake my head, he continues where Mom left off. "We also need you to stop giving your shifts to Chad. This is a family business, Angelo. That's what our brand is. *Family.*"

"Is it?" My chuckle is strangled. "I thought it was making sure the customers love us."

"Of course we need customers to love us, Angelo. And they will if we show a united front. Not a mom, a dad, and their missing son." His tone is as stern as it is disappointed.

"How about a mom, a dad, and their surrogate ginger child?" I'm surprised I can keep a straight face.

"Eh, no one would even believe Chad's a love child."

Dad stumbles forward from Mom's hard shove.

"*Bastos!* This is serious, Roman!" she complains.

"Ay, I'm being serious, Mila."

She clicks her tongue in annoyance and turns to me. "Starting this week, you will no longer give your shifts to Chad. We put you on the schedule. More hours. And you're working that schedule. Like your dad said, this is our family's establishment, and we expect you to work here."

I should be happy for the bigger paycheck. Heck, dollar signs should be flashing before my eyes . . . so why is the first thing I see my friends' faces?

"But I have people counting on me."

"Your family is counting on you." Mom snaps her fingers in front of my face. She pulls back and examines me curiously. "I'm actually surprised to see that frown. Aren't you saving up for San Diego?"

"Mom," I whine when she grabs my chin.

I pull away and she drops her hold. "Didn't you say you wanted to compete in that game?"

"It's a skate competition, Mom."

"What about visiting your *tita* and cousins? Do you not want to do that anymore?"

"I wanted to. I mean I *want* to. I do!" I grimace. I'm sure Freud would have a field day analyzing that slip of the tongue.

"You know we don't have the extra money to buy your ticket. We agreed you'd go only if you can pay for it." She points to a piece of paper tacked to their office door. The company schedule. "With all these extra shifts that shouldn't be a problem for you."

I force a smile and whisper, "I know."

Dad walks over to the overhead vent and pats against it almost lovingly. "But more importantly, our family restaurant needs help, Angelo. So we need to work hard as a family. Unless you want a repeat of San Diego."

"You mean the business going under?"

His thick lips press together. "I doubt you'd want to move again so soon. This business is our one shot in this town."

My parents return to the office together, leaving me in the kitchen, alone. And confused.

# 20

Look at those jocks, thinking they own the place." Wyatt shifts in his seat and stuffs a spoonful of mashed potatoes into his mouth. Chunks splatter on the table as he spews, "Wait until Street Wars is the hottest ticket in town and no one goes to their games anymore."

"Street Wars? What the hell is that?" I ask, although even as I ask I'm getting an inkling.

"What do you think? Our competition."

Our competition.

Not his. Not hers. But *ours*.

I push my fists into my forehead and let out a groan. Wyatt swallows his food and eyes me curiously. "What's wrong with you?"

"Oh, nothing." I drop my hands against the table with a deafening smack. "Just that I barely have time for anything anymore, and now my parents want to increase my shifts too."

"That answers your money problem," Larry points out, shoveling in his own food.

Kirsten eyes me with concern. "What money problem?"

"Never mind . . ." A sweet, melodic tone captures my attention. I whirl around in surprise as Aiden sings between bites. "I didn't know you could sing."

Aiden's fork stops midair. His mouth remains frozen around the last note. He swallows hard and squeaks, "Do you want me to stop?"

"No. Actually, your voice is pretty soothing. Keep going." I rub against my eyelids and take a deep breath. "God knows I need some comfort."

But of course, Aiden doesn't continue. I should've known better than to call him out.

He blushes and puts down his fork. "Soothing? Nah. But I can carry a tune," he almost whispers.

"Why are you selling yourself short like that?" I ask. "Your voice sounds really nice." But my words are drowned out by Grayson's boisterous laugh. Annoyed, I glance over at him. Even our fight at my locker didn't do anything to diminish his popularity. He still has students—and some teachers—kissing his ass every time he walks through the halls. Right now a few of my classmates from the AV Club are filming him for God knows what reason.

All this time I'd wondered what Kirsten ever saw in him. He's a creep! But just past the little crevice where the question lingers in my brain is another one that's been nagging at me. I've done my best to ignore it. But there's no pushing it away anymore.

Hypothetically, if I were ever to decide to try my shot with Kirsten, what would she see in me? Obviously, Amanda never saw anything special enough to try to make our relationship work.

"Angelo? Why are you looking at me like that?" My vision focuses, and I realize I've been staring at Kirsten. Her eyes tighten, but there's no mistaking the slightest grin. I clear my throat and look away, but Larry bursts into laughter.

"It's because he has a thing—*ow!*" Larry sags forward, rubbing his shin under the table. He scowls at me. "Did you really have to kick my pushing leg? I need it strong for the competition."

The competition.

Right.

I clear my throat and shift awkwardly. "Hey, you guys. I know this sounds corny, but I believe you can accomplish anything you put your minds to."

Kirsten scrunches her nose in confusion, but Wyatt salutes me. "Thank you, Mr. Motivational Speaker."

"Rivera," Kirsten says in a steady voice. "What are you getting at?"

I wasn't planning on saying this. It certainly isn't premeditated or whatever cops call it. But my mouth starts to form the words before my brain catches on. "You know you don't need me to hold the competition . . . right?"

Everyone stops what they're doing and looks at me.

"Sure, I may have helped inspire the idea. But I really don't have to be around for it to come to realization."

Kirsten grabs my wrist. Her touch sears into my skin. It's hard to focus on what she's saying.

"Are you planning to ditch us? After everything?" I flinch from the accusation in her tone.

"Why are *you* surprised?" Larry says to her. "It's not like you didn't flake out on your old friends . . ." He clasps his hands over his mouth and grimaces. "Did I say that out loud?"

Kirsten rolls her eyes. "One, I was kicked off the squad. And two, this is different." She spins around, straddling her seat so she's staring directly at my profile. I can practically feel the waves of anger radiating from her body. This time it's easy not to look at her. "Angelo. Hey, look at me. We're all counting on you. You can't go back on your word now."

"Listen, it's not that I don't want to hang out with you guys," I say, trying my best to explain. "But it's like what I've been saying all along. I don't have the time to help you with the competition with everything else going on in my life."

"Then multitask," Wyatt interrupts.

I purse my lips. "When did you start talking with Chad?"

"Who?"

"Can you guys calm down for a second?" Kirsten waves an arm between us. I finally look in her direction. Her top teeth dig into the delicate skin of her bottom lip. The sight does weird things to my stomach.

"Rivera," she pleads. "You can't bail on us."

I try to ignore the guilt pooling in my gut. "To be fair, I was coerced into being part of this."

"Which part? The lessons? The competition? Or the friendship?" There's no bite to her tone. No more accusation. Just hurt.

"The competition, of course." I grip the edge of the table so tightly my knuckles turn paper white. Like a pathetic version of King Arthur, I look around the table. "I'm not going to pretend I was on board from the start. I told you guys a competition would be a bad idea."

"No. It's a good idea." There's a determination in Wyatt's eyes that's almost scary. "And you know what? You're right. We don't need you. We don't need anyone who's negative."

"I'm not being negative," I argue. "I'm being realistic. A competition takes a lot of work—"

"That we're going to do. That we're all going to do," Kirsten cuts in.

"Everyone except Angelo, you mean." Wyatt's ready to take on Maddie in the scowl department, that's for sure.

"Even Angelo." Kirsten pats my shoulder. This time her touch is gentle. "We'll figure this out, okay? No need to jump to rash decisions."

"But—" I start to say, but she cuts me off.

"What about we do the heavy lifting and you can be . . . a . . . um . . . consultant."

"A consultant?"

"Someone we can run to whenever we need advice about skating while we're continuing to make our plans. You can still be a judge too. If you want."

Something stirs inside me. I wanted out, but now I feel like I'm getting kicked out of the group in more ways than one. A wave of sadness hits me. Is this how Kirsten felt when she was pushed out of her cheerleading squad even after she'd decided she wanted more time to do her art? "Hey, I'm not saying I won't skate with you guys *ever*. I just can't help with the competition."

But it's no use. I can tell that none of them believes me. Not even Kirsten.

Maybe there's a part of me that doesn't believe it either.

*"Nerd!"*

*"Loser!"*

*"You better not change it, Stella!"*

Ignoring the insults, Stella walks past the popular table and plops down next to Kirsten. Her eyeglasses are as crooked as the slight snarl of her lip.

"Everything okay?" I ask carefully, thankful for the distraction.

She doesn't answer me and concentrates on smoothing out a crumpled piece of paper. Someone chucks an empty water bottle, missing the trash can adjacent to our table. The plastic bottle topples in front of us, and without looking up Stella flicks it away.

I catch Wyatt's eye, and he immediately nudges his stepsister. "What's up?"

She straightens her glasses and places both palms on top of the paper. "My meeting ran late. What'd I miss?"

Larry barely looks up from the Tre Flip tutorial playing on his phone. "Angelo's existential crisis."

"It's far from an existential crisis," I shoot back.

"More like his inability to manage his time." Wyatt's tone cuts as sharp as a knife.

"Actually, it's more the worry that Sloppy's Pit Stop might be going under," I blurt out without thinking. I immediately regret it once I see my friends' faces.

"Wait a minute. Sloppy's is going out of business?"

I don't know what I hate more: Kirsten's obvious shock or her pity.

Stella scrunches up her nose. "Yeah, that would make me worry too."

"At least someone gets it," I grunt.

"Now that we know about it, we get it." Kirsten nods firmly. "We get why your family's suddenly so gung ho about you working more."

"But do you really think increasing your shifts will help the business?" Larry's never shy to play devil's advocate.

"Honestly, no." I grab the water bottle and absently turn it around in my hands like a makeshift fidget spinner. "But my dad wants to work on our brand."

"What the hell's your brand?"

"Family." It sounds even cornier now that I'm repeating it.

"Family." Stella shakes her head. "But that's like *every* Ocean Pointe business's brand."

"Probably the reason why my dad wants to use it." I let out a strained chuckle.

"Wait a minute." Kirsten grabs my arm again, and this time I turn without a second thought. "As much as I'd like to think Sloppy's can recover from this, what happens if it doesn't? What's your family going to do?"

Dad's cryptic warning runs through my head. "Who knows? Maybe move again. Find another town our business will do great in."

"But of course, that wouldn't bother you since you're planning to go back to California anyway," she replies more as a statement than a question.

Kirsten's reaction is such a low blow. "Of course it bothers me! I don't want my parents to suffer."

"Hmm." She turns away before I can say anything else.

"This is great!" Wyatt's sudden outburst bothers me for a different reason.

"How is it great?" I ask through gritted teeth. "This is my family's livelihood you're talking about!"

"Well, I thought all this complaining about shifts and time was just your way to weasel out of helping."

"I'm not weaseling out of anything!"

Wyatt rolls his eyes. "That's what I'm saying. You aren't making excuses, which means this is a problem we can solve. Lucky for you, you're in the presence of some of the smartest kids in school . . ." Wyatt's voice trails off as he glances at Kirsten. "Well, mostly the smartest kids."

"What's that supposed to mean?" She reaches over the table and smacks him against the temple.

"Okay, okay, sorry. I'm joking," Wyatt chokes out between laughs. "Anyway, why don't we all think up ways to help Sloppy's Pit Stop? Maybe if Angelo's parents see an increase in business, they'll lighten up on his shifts. Hence, giving him more time to help us."

I shift uncomfortably. Wyatt must notice because he asks, "That's what you want, right?"

"I mean, I do get a bigger paycheck . . ."

"But?"

I take a moment to respond, gazing at each friend one at a time. "But I will miss hanging out with you guys."

"I'll miss you too," Kirsten throws back without hesitation, and I try hard not to read too much into it.

Quiet blankets our table. Lost in my thoughts, I absently pick off pale pieces of pepperoni from my pizza and push them to the side of my plate. "If you keep that up, I may turn you vegan," Kirsten says, breaking the silence.

I drop another piece of meat. "Nah. The best Filipino food has meat in it. Besides, my parents would freak. We sell burgers, remember? Vegan is bad for our business."

She grimaces at my pizza and shudders. "Well, you all should think about adding some vegan items onto your menu. Or at least vegetarian. That would be a start."

Stella gasps. "That's a great idea!"

"What's a great idea?" I turn to Stella with raised eyebrows.

She clasps her tiny hands together in excitement. "You need to add nonmeat items on your menu. It'll help you expand your target market."

I scratch my head with a grimace. "Are there a lot of herbivores in Ocean Pointe?"

"There are plant-based eaters everywhere, Angelo," Kirsten says haughtily. "And I agree with Stella. None of the diners in town sell any vegan foods. Ocean Pointe Diner sure as hell doesn't. You'd be ahead of the game. Just watch, Sloppy's Pit Stop will be called an innovator."

"Thought this town doesn't like change."

"But you're here to shake things up, remember?"

I frown, remembering my dad's reaction when I'd suggested a fusion menu. "I don't know if my parents will even go for it."

"You'll never know if you don't ask." Kirsten flashes me a wide smile that leaves me tongue-tied.

"O-okay. I'll suggest it."

I shake my head and continue to pick at my food, but Wyatt begins drumming his long fingers on the table. "That idea is good, but you need to put something into action now to get the buzz going about your restaurant."

Stella sighs and takes a marker out of her backpack. She stares at the neon paper she's been toying with ever since she sat down and suddenly makes a face of disgust. Uncapping her marker, she slashes a giant $X$ on the flyer. Then does it again with even more enthusiasm.

"What'd that piece of paper ever do to you?" I joke.

"What? This?" She flips the paper so we can all read it. "I'm redoing Maddie's flyer. If she thinks she can change the theme for homecoming without checking with me, she has another thing coming!"

"She wants to use 'Walking the Red Carpet'?" Kirsten grabs the paper and reads it, then slams it back onto the table. "Ha! Sounds exactly like something she would do." She points to Stella's marker. "Hey, can I borrow that for a second?"

Stella hands the pen to her. "That's why I was late today. We had an emergency student council meeting. Maddie has been pushing for us to change the theme, even though we all already voted for 'California Dreaming' a week ago."

"California?" I automatically perk up, but unlike before I don't feel the slight pinch of my heart anytime someone mentions my home state.

Deep in thought, Kirsten undoes her messy bun. She flips her hair over her slim shoulder, exposing the heart-shaped freckle on the side of her neck. My fingers tingle. What would it feel like to trace the smooth outline of that heart on her skin?

I blink, trying my best to refocus on Stella.

"Obviously, you inspired it." Stella smiles brightly.

"Oh. Wow."

"It was actually my idea," Aiden says in his usual soft tone. "Ever since the first day of school, all anyone's been talking about is the boy from California."

"Better than the brown boy." My eyes slide over to the popular table. "California Boy's a lot better."

"You attract a lot of attention. So I thought if people saw the word 'California' on a flyer, it'd make more people want to come to the dance—"

"Oh my God. That's it!" My sudden outburst startles everyone at our table. I grab the flyer from Kirsten's grip.

"Hey!" she protests. "I wasn't done with that!"

She's already drawn a beach landscape on the flyer, but ignoring her, I flick a finger against the neon paper. "Sloppy's Pit Stop needs flyers! My dad's done every other marketing ploy he could afford, but he hasn't done flyers yet."

Wyatt glances at Stella. She shrugs. "I guess it can work."

I nod excitedly. "Kirsten, you're good at art."

"Gee, thanks."

I ignore her sarcasm. "Do you think you can design some flyers for me? Something different. Eye-catching. Not just a plain burger and fries?"

"Do you even have to ask?" She winks, and my cheeks grow warm.

"How much do you think it'll cost to print out about a hundred copies?" I ask the gang.

"Nada," Stella answers. "I'm the student council president, remember? I have free rein over the laser printer in the teachers' lounge."

"Pays to have friends in high places." I give her a high five. "Now what do I do about passing them out? I'm already pressed for time."

"Isn't it obvious?" Larry reaches for his board and places it on top of the table. "We'll pass out the flyers while you're at work. We'll take turns borrowing your extra boards."

"Uh, you and Kirsten have been riding those boards for weeks now. I think we've more than established they're yours now." I look at Wyatt, Stella, and Aiden thoughtfully. "We really need to get you guys some boards of your own too so you don't have to keep waiting on Larry and Kirsten."

"We'll worry about that later." Stella waves me off. "For now, concentrate on your shifts. We'll take care of the rest."

"Thanks, guys." My throat constricts.

"No need to thank us." Wyatt grins. "Helping you out only helps us out."

I shake my head with a snicker. "That sounds both selfless and selfish at the same time."

"What can I say?" says Wyatt. "You *are* going to shake up this town whether you like it or not. We'll make sure of it."

# 21

W hat the hell is that?" I cry.

It's after school, and my friends are gathered around the flagpole looking extremely proud of themselves. A flutter of aqua burns my retinas. Stella passes the ostentatious flyers around, pushing a thick wad into Larry's chest. I grab a piece of paper off the top and gape in horror.

"Why is my face on this flyer?" I demand.

Well, it isn't my real face but a cartoon depiction of it. But even drawn in Sharpie, there's no way anyone in our school wouldn't recognize it's me.

"California Boy, remember?" Kirsten wags her eyebrows. "Sorry to say, but you're the face of Sloppy's Pit Stop. Own it."

"Own what?" I read the words under the Sloppy's Pit Stop logo. "Own the fact that this says we'll be giving people a free small fry for every purchase? Are you trying to get my parents to kill me?"

"Why are you so mad?" Wyatt tucks his pile under his armpit.

"Uh, for one, we're going out of business, remember? We can't afford to give away free food." The words are vaguely familiar. I catch Kirsten's eyes and am transported back to a little over a month ago when she'd saved me from the bullies. I shift uncomfortably. "We're trying to save Sloppy's, not burn it to the ground."

"Trust, man. Trust." Wyatt holds up a flyer and drags his finger across the text. "It says *a* small fry. As in one fry."

I drop my head, shaking it slowly. "What?"

"No one ever counts their fries. Just add an extra one into the carton and boom! A free small fry."

"That . . . just sounds like false advertising."

"Ah! But that's why we put this asterisk on the bottom of the flyer." I lean forward and read the sentence, which is written in really small type. "See? It says one extra fry will be added to their carton."

I shut my eyes and let out a loud breath. "Oh my God."

"Angelo, quit complaining." Kirsten gives me a little shove. "It's too late. We already printed out a hundred copies."

"I can't believe you agreed to draw this," I grumble.

"Seemed like a good idea to me." She shrugs and tugs on my arm. My synapses fire at her touch. "Aren't you going to be late? Just go to work and leave the flyering up to us."

Like pounding an invisible gavel, her words have us breaking off, going our separate ways. Unfortunately, each way requires us to head past the practice field.

I try to concentrate on just skating, on thinking about heading out for some practicing, and do my best to ignore the bustle of helmets and shoulder pads in my periphery. But Justin is intent on getting my attention. "Where are ya freaks headed?"

I tell myself not to look, but I can't help it. I glare at Captain Jerk, biting back the urge to flip him the bird. But he makes it hard. Really hard.

Hearing his crap is a great reminder why this competition needs to happen.

Grayson stands beside him, takes off his helmet, and starts to gyrate his hips because . . . I don't really know why, actually. Technically, I guess he's still within the bylaws of his and Larry's agreement since he's not actually picking on us. But I kinda wish he would cross the line because then I might—

"Ignore all of them," Kirsten mutters, skating past me.

"All of them?" I tear my eyes away from Justin and Grayson and notice we've garnered a larger audience consisting of first- and second-string players. Luckily, Coach Shappey blows his whistle. Like droids, the players follow the noise, gathering in the center of the field.

I grunt, pushing my leg hard to get away from them as quickly as possible. They may be poking fun at us now, but I can't wait to see what they think of us once our competition becomes a reality.

~

*"What's up? Welcome to vlog number whatever the hell this is! I'm here with my homie, Amanda, and her new bae, Tyler . . ."*

I tap pause on the video, waiting for the pain to come.

It never does.

I've been waiting for my heart to break all over again ever since I saw Amanda's newest Instagram post. A photo of her and Tyler eating burritos in front of Taco Hut with the caption: True love ♥ ♥ ♥

But it doesn't bother me.

Not one bit.

I play the rest of Mackabi's newest vlog and find that the spark of long-awaited jealousy does make an appearance—but it isn't because a now pink-haired Amanda's sucking face with Tyler but because they're all having fun at the skate park. I sigh, tearing my eyes away from my phone as Mackabi pans the crowded bowl.

It's about two hours into my shift, and the restaurant's as empty as it was on our first day here. Wait, no. That's a lie. Back then we had Judy and Kirsten pop in.

I sigh, leaning over the counter, praying for someone—anyone—to distract me from the growing longing in my gut. But all I get are five empty booths and a plate of half-burned fries I made myself about twenty minutes ago.

Something's changed in me. A flip of a switch. A rewrite of a script. And it's not something I want to admit to myself, let alone thought would ever happen. Though I want to go back to California, it's mainly to wipe Tyler Park's ass on the grass and nothing more. I haven't really been thinking about moving back for good anymore. Being alone in Sloppy's while watching Mackabi's vlog only solidifies what's been brewing for weeks.

I want to hang out with my friends—my new friends.

I want to roll my eyes at Wyatt's sardonic remarks and laugh at Larry's sarcastic ones. I want to listen to Aiden's secret songs and watch Stella come into her presidential role. Moreover, I want to spend any time I can with Kirsten.

Desperate for a distraction, I click on Tyler's profile. As expected, there are new action shots of him skating gaps and dropping in on a vert ramp. One caption in particular gets my blood boiling:

> Still waiting on someone worthy enough to be
> dubbed COMPETITION

"You want competition? I'll show you competition." I switch over to my banking app and cringe at my savings account. The good news is that the total amount hasn't gotten any lower. The bad news? It hasn't increased by much either. I'm still about a hundred short. "At least I'm making money off this BS shift."

I lift my gaze to stare out the oversize windows. I swear a tumbleweed rolls by. I turn around and look out the back door, which I always keep propped open to air out the otherwise hot kitchen. The excess lot still sits as empty as the day it was paved. Now an entirely different feeling pinches at my gut. How long can I count on paychecks if Sloppy's Pit Stop goes under?

I look around the restaurant and picture the place boarded up and closed. If my family loses its business, I can kiss Streetsgiving goodbye. But the thought doesn't hurt nearly as much as the possibility of moving away from Ocean Pointe.

Why would I mind leaving Ocean Pointe? It's what I wanted from the start, wasn't it?

True. But it seems it's not exactly the town I don't want to leave. It's the artistic ex-cheerleader. The sarcastic tuba player. The snappy runner. The unsure president. The shy singer.

My skating crew.

I swipe back on to Mackabi's vlog and watch my old skater friends in action. I really don't want to leave my new crew. But if things don't pick up with Sloppy's Pit Stop, I might end up losing them too.

# 22

"A re you sure you passed out *all* the flyers?" I ask for about the mil-lionth time.

My friends and I climb the stairs to lucky locker number 277, which has become our unofficial meeting place every morning. Larry balances his skateboard in one hand and uses his other arm to carry his tuba case. "Yes. Well, at least I passed out all mine. I went right after band practice."

"You don't need to ask me." Wyatt lifts his chin in pride. "I even taped mine up around Roy's."

One by one, my friends stare at him as if they've seen a ghost.

I look at Wyatt, then at the rest of my friends, and then back at him again. "Um, am I missing something?"

Kirsten purses her lips. "He's talking about Roy's Corner Mart."

"What's so bad about that?"

"It's straight out of the 1800s."

"As opposed to the rest of this town?" I mutter under my breath.

"Roy doesn't even have a scanner. He literally has to type in every price into a calculator. You only ever go there as a last resort." She shoots Wyatt a bewildered look. "Unless you're a senior citizen . . . or Wyatt, apparently."

"Hey, I don't shop there," he says pointedly. "But there's no point in discriminating against our technologically inept neighbors. You ever stop to think they might want a burger or two?"

"Touché."

"Besides, I posted a photo of the flyer on Instagram." He looks down at the ground in embarrassment. "At least my ten followers saw it."

I grab my locker's dial. I turn it three to the right and seven to the left. "Too bad none of the flyers worked. Or your post." I glance at Wyatt and sigh. "We didn't get a single new customer last night. Not one!"

"But you did get some customers, right?" Kirsten places her hand on the small of my back, and my legs turn to jelly.

"Not enough."

Kirsten slides her hand off me. "Try not to worry about it too much. It's only been one day. Just give it time."

"Yeah. You're right." I open my locker. "I bet by this weekend more people will—what the hell?"

A flood of aqua spills out of my locker like a waterfall. We all jump back except for Kirsten, who bends over to pick up one of the crumpled flyers. "There have to be sixty of these in here!"

Aiden bows his head, cradling it in his hands. "All that hard work. My step counter logged me in at ten thousand. That's never happened before."

"Look on the bright side. At least that means there's still forty flyers floating around out there." Larry hikes up his pants and bounces his shoulders in response to our glares. "There's still a silver lining."

I swipe the flyer from Kirsten's hand and crumple it into a ball. "This has Grayson written all over it."

"Do you really think he'd do this, though?" Kirsten muses. The pain I expected to come from seeing Amanda with her new bae washes over me at the thought Kirsten might be sticking up for her ex.

"Why wouldn't he do it?" I shoot back. "He's had a vendetta against me from the start. He's even threatened to shut down Sloppy's! Maybe he's the reason we don't have any customers."

"He doesn't have that much power."

"A football player doesn't have power in Ocean Pointe? Please."

"Besides, that really isn't proof." Kirsten shakes her head. "What I'm trying to say is that Larry still has the video. Why would Grayson even risk messing with us knowing that we can get him in a load of trouble?"

I consider her argument and nod. "Yeah, I guess you're right."

Larry squirms, losing his hold on the tuba case. It lands with a loud crash.

Kirsten spins around and glares at Larry, who winces under her stare. "Wait, you still have the video, right?" When he doesn't respond, Kirsten shrieks, *"Right?"*

Larry scrunches up his nose. "I . . . I may have accidentally deleted it when I was updating my phone."

"Larry!" we shout in unison.

"Talk about being technologically inept," Wyatt mutters.

"Hey! I couldn't help it! My phone's old." Larry hikes up his pants again and scowls. "I'll have you know, I'm really good with computers. I have to be, considering my mom shares a laptop with me. Do you know how many viruses she downloads by accident?"

"If you're so good with computers, how the hell didn't you know not to update your phone?"

Larry ignores him. "What does it matter? Grayson doesn't know the video is gone."

As the two bicker, I catch sight of Grayson, Justin, and Maddie at the far end of the hallway. They're all looking in our direction, pointing and laughing at the pile of flyers by our feet. Grayson catches my eye and shoots me a smug grin. Circumstantial evidence or not, it's enough for me to know he's behind this.

"Everybody relax!" I shout above their voices. They clamp their mouths shut, staring at me. I crumple the flyer even more. "The only people who ever mess with me are Grayson, Justin, or one of the other assholes from the football team. I know they did this, and I'm sick of it! *Mga tarantado talaga sila!* They're messing with the wrong man."

"Man?" Wyatt snickers.

"Whoa. You spoke Tagalog, Angelo." Stella gasps in wonder. "You must be really mad."

"What does it mean what you just said?" Larry scratches his head.

"I called them jackasses," I mutter.

I'm on the verge of blacking out.

*Nerd rage.*

That's what Mackabi used to call it. Keep a laid-back dude down long enough and his temper will spike up until he's out for blood.

I'm sick of being picked on. Moreover, I'm tired of it affecting the people I care about.

Hardly looking, I throw the balled-up paper toward the nearest wastebasket. It goes in with a swish.

"Wow. That was impressive." Wyatt nods in approval, but I don't care.

In a clear, steady voice I grind out, "We are going to hold that damn skating competition."

Wyatt snorts. "Tell me something I don't know."

I grab another flyer off the ground and clench a fist around it. "No, you're not hearing me. We are going to hold the competition as soon as possible." I whirl around so fast that Larry nearly stumbles back. "When's the next football game?"

He flinches, scratching at his temple. "At the end of the week. They have an away game at HHS."

"Nope," I say with a pop of the *p*. "That won't do. We need a home game."

My friends exchange weird looks. Kirsten licks her lips and says, "Um, there's one in two weeks."

"Perfect!"

Kirsten narrows her eyes in suspicion. "For what?"

"We aren't only going to be taking the football team down a notch . . ." Warm sweat starts to pool above my brows. My voice shakes, mimicking the thundering of my heart. "We're taking them down period! We'll show them that us outsiders are sick of falling in their shadow. Those Friday night lights will be shining on us!"

"He really is a motivational speaker." Wyatt elbows Larry.

I look Kirsten square in the eye. "You said that their stupidity is because they're scared of me. Well, we'll give them something to be scared about. Nothing scares people in power more than the possibility of losing it."

Stella's eyes grow comically wide. "I think I created a monster."

"And if those jackasses think they can sabotage Sloppy's, they have another thing coming because I'm making Sloppy's Pit Stop the number one sponsor!"

"But I thought Sloppy's was going under?" Larry murmurs.

"How about I give away some fries at the competition? *A small fry.* At least people will see our logo." I shoot him a smug smile. "Our flyers were torn down, but an event can't be. Two birds with one stone. We take over a Friday night, and the crowd will be hungry for Sloppy's afterward!"

"I guess . . ." Larry kicks against the floor.

I ignore him and pump a fist in the air. "We have two weeks to plan the best competition we can. Now who's with me?"

Crickets.

I drop my raised fist and say through gritted teeth, "Who's with me?"

Wyatt shrugs. "Of course I am. But I didn't think we'd be holding an event so soon. We've been so focused on trying to learn how to skate that we hardly even started planning for it."

"What's 'hardly' mean, exactly?"

Wyatt grunts. "Put it this way. We haven't even bought our own boards yet."

Maybe the adrenaline coursing through my veins is screwing with my brain. He's right. There are too many things we need to take care of in order to pull this off.

I suddenly droop. I'm about ready to throw in the towel.

But Kirsten steps up. "Holding the competition in two weeks might still be possible. We never said it had to be a big event, right?"

"No," Stella admits. "But it still needs to make a statement."

"And it will." Kirsten gives a firm nod. "Why don't we give it a little bit more thought. Think of ideas and reconvene at lunch."

"Yeah, that sounds good." A worried crease settles in the middle of Stella's forehead. She tugs at one of her spiraled tendrils. "We're on a time crunch, so make sure whatever ideas you think of are completely doable."

I sense a backhanded insult hidden somewhere in her words, but I shrug it off. Wasn't it me telling them that in the beginning? Oh, how the tables have turned.

Larry nods. "I can come up with some stuff by lunch."

"Hell yeah." I toss the new ball of paper into the trash can. This time I miss. I sure as hell hope it isn't a bad omen.

# 23

I walk up to our usual lunch table by the row of trash cans and do a double take. All five of my friends sit primly, waiting for me with a ton of paper spread out over the table in front of them. Guess brainstorming has a different meaning when it comes to them. They came prepared.

"What's all this?" I pick up the nearest paper and cringe at my cartoon depiction. "My face? Again?"

Kirsten holds up her palms in defense. "Hey, as of now you're the brains behind this operation. Like it or not, you're the face too."

I set my backpack down and fling my legs over the seat. I flip through the different flyer mock-ups and shake my head. "No. These won't work. None of these are right."

"Why not?" Kirsten crosses her arms and lifts an eyebrow. "My designs are awesome."

"It's not so much about the design as it is about me." Heat creeps into my cheeks. "The bullies hate me, that much is obvious."

"Yes, it is," Larry agrees.

I roll my eyes. "We need people to know about the event. And Sloppy's. But in order for this to work, we can't let the bullies know what we're up to until the day of the event. Otherwise they'll rip down our flyers again."

"We still can't prove it was them," Kirsten pipes in.

Not in the mood for arguing, I clench my jaw and force out, "Fine. Whoever the culprit is might rip them down."

Kirsten slowly nods. "Okay . . . so what do you suggest?"

"Maybe if . . ." I shake my head. "Um . . . What if . . . uh . . ."

Kirsten tilts her head. *"Yessss?"*

"I . . . uh . . ." I groan, slumping forward. "Why are we already deciding on designs? We're still like two steps behind all that."

"Yeah, I guess you're right." Kirsten gathers her papers, straightening and stacking them. "At this point, the flyer would probably say 'Come to the middle of nowhere.'"

"The middle of nowhere?" I blink incredulously. "Aren't we going to hold the event at the warehouses?"

Kirsten nearly drops the paper. "Why the hell would we do that?"

"It's the only place in town that's good for skating. Where else would we hold it?" Larry chimes in.

Kirsten opens her mouth to respond, but Larry cuts her off. He grabs one of the papers off her stack and stares at my cartoon counterpart. "If Angelo doesn't want his face on the flyer, maybe we can use all of ours."

Wyatt snorts. "A bunch of nobodies—"

"Who are about to make their mark on OPHS," Larry finishes proudly.

Nobodies . . .

I spring up, for once startling Larry. "Holy crap, that's it!"

He barely catches his tuba case from toppling over at his feet. "Uh, what's it?"

Excitement floods through my veins. I'm practically shaking. "Kirsten, instead of my face—"

Larry clears his throat.

I roll my eyes. "Or any of your faces, why don't you not use a face at all?"

"Not use a face?" she repeats incredulously. "I have no idea what you're talking about."

"Make it look like the tag you painted on Sloppy's Pit Stop's wall. Two eyes in a circle. That's it."

I can see the precise moment it clicks in Kirsten's head. But it still doesn't quell her doubt. "I don't understand why you'd want to use that on our flyers. That was only a quick tag I made to prove I can paint in public."

"Because that tag is as faceless as we are." I point to Kirsten, Larry, Stella, Wyatt, and Aiden. "Nobodies."

"It kind of hurts when you say it," Wyatt grumbles.

"Yeah, but it's not just us but everyone else in this room who isn't part of the football team." I gesture around the cafeteria. "Just look around and you'll see what I mean."

Begrudgingly, everyone scans the room. The popular table sits in the middle of the cafeteria like a castle surrounded by a moat made up of the other lunch tables. I motion to the one beside it. "Look there."

"You mean at the people who keep trying to get Grayson's attention?" Wyatt asks. "That one girl in the plaid pants looks like she's a second away from tackling him. And I'm not talking football."

I glance at Kirsten, wondering what she may be thinking, but she remains expressionless.

"No!" I point to the table on the opposite side. "That one."

Kids with their heads tilted down sit huddled together. Their voices barely audible. They fade into the background, though I'm not sure if it's on purpose. Truthfully, besides my friends I haven't given much thought to any of my other classmates. With everything else going on in my life there wasn't really any extra room in my brain for me to. But I think it's time to change that. Starting with our competition.

"And look at the table beside that one," I insist, pointing to the right.

Different kids, same story.

Kirsten cracks a smile. Like me, she probably senses a kinship. After all, she has a good eye for outsiders, and these students are most likely nobodies just like us.

I lower my voice. "We all know some of the people we'll attract to the event are those too scared to go against the jocks otherwise." Stella shifts uncomfortably. "To the bullies, we're all faceless losers. So why don't we use that against them?"

"But how is using a faceless picture going to help our cause?" Stella asks quietly.

"We need a flag to unite under. An outsiders' mascot." I hold Kirsten's gaze. She's always believed I could make a difference in this place. "Remember what Grayson said when Larry stood up to him? He didn't think anyone would go against him. If the bullies want us to blend into the background and be invisible, then we will. And we'll use it to our advantage because they won't know who's holding the event until we're ready to unmask ourselves."

"There's one thing you're forgetting, though." Hearing Aiden speak never ceases to surprise me.

I turn to look at him. "And what's that?"

"It's a skateboarding competition. Who else in this town skates? Everyone will know we're behind the mask . . ." His eyes widen. "Unless . . ."

I cock an eyebrow. "Unless what?"

"I think I know how to get our message out there. All I need is some time and a computer."

"Well, you got two weeks." My gaze slides over to Kirsten. "Now, about the warehouses . . ."

Kirsten's hair whips across her face. "No." She shakes her head even more. "Absolutely not."

"Why not? You were down to hold the competition from the start," Wyatt reminds her.

"Not at the warehouses!"

"But it's a given," I argue. "Where else would we hold the event?"

"Exactly," says Stella.

"Oh, c'mon, Kirsten." Larry's whine is almost ear-piercing. "The lot is perfect! It's large enough to fit a crowd and already has enough obstacles to make the competition a good one."

"It also has all my artwork inside."

As soon as Kirsten blurts this out, she gasps and cradles her head in dismay. It suddenly dawns on me. Other than Larry and me, who both love her artwork, she's never let our other friends in on the secret. We always stayed outside the main building.

"What artwork?" Stella nudges Kirsten. "Am I missing something here?"

Kirsten slowly lifts her head and squirms. Swallowing hard, she clasps her hands underneath the table and squeaks, "Promise not to tell, all right?"

"We haven't told anyone about the lot," Wyatt deadpans. "Rule number one, right?"

"Right." Kirsten cringes. "But there's more. I . . . um . . . sort of . . . spray-paint in one of the buildings." She winces, waiting for everyone's reaction.

Aiden frowns. "Spray-paint? Like graffiti?"

"Yeah, like graffiti," Kirsten almost whispers. "Now you know why we can't hold it there."

"But why? It's so cool!" Aiden breaks out in a wide grin.

"It is pretty awesome," Stella agrees. "Why didn't you tell us about your art before?"

"I'll tell you more about it soon." Kirsten visibly relaxes. "But cool or not, I can get in a lot of trouble if the sheriff finds out about it."

"But it's art," Aiden argues.

"Art that he'll consider vandalism." She looks around the table and shakes her head. "Sorry, guys. I can't risk it."

"No one knows it's your artwork, Kirsten. We can definitely hold Street Wars in the lot without getting you in trouble." Larry stares at her with wide eyes, almost as if trying to hypnotize her.

"Street Wars." I smack my tongue in disgust. "The name doesn't do it for me anymore."

Wyatt's familiar scowl makes an appearance again. "I resent that. You know, it took me hours to come up with that name."

"Hours?" I snicker.

Wyatt smacks his lips and grinds out, "You think you can do better? What do you suggest, oh wise one?"

"I'll think of something cool," I shoot back with a smirk. "But first we need to get the venue tied down." I shoot Kirsten a meaningful look, but she quickly turns away. Bristling slightly, I try to keep my tone light. "Oh, and we need to figure out how to get competitors too."

"Remember what I said about checking with neighboring towns," Stella pipes in. "I can email some of my student council contacts at other schools to see if anyone there is interested."

"The good thing is skaters don't have to be local." Larry takes out his phone and taps on the screen. "Look at you."

"What about me?"

"You're planning on flying back to California for Streetsgiving. Why wouldn't other skaters come here?"

"Because it's Ocean Pointe?"

Wyatt lifts a finger. "I read in your magazine that skaters go to competitions in different places all the time to get their names out there."

"Is that true?" Stella asks.

"Well, yeah . . ." I shrug. "It's self-promotion. The more competitions a skater attends, or better yet wins, the more likely they'll catch a sponsor's eye."

"So why would our event be any different than the other ones?" Wyatt prods.

"Um, because we don't have a professional setup? And no household names competing."

"But all competitions have to start somewhere," he argues.

Larry flips his phone over so we can see what's on the screen. "We can post about it online. Call it a start-up or something. In skate forums like this one. We can even come up with a hashtag to get it trending."

"Hashtag?" I can't hide my doubt.

"Yes, hashtag." Larry rolls his eyes. "Trust me. It'll work."

"If you say so . . ."

"And you have skater friends, right?"

My lips quirk. "Is that even a question?"

"Can't they help get the word out?" Larry scrolls through the different posts in the forum. "Imagine getting all these skaters talking about our event. Then we'll be the ones who'll need a stadium."

"Mackabi would love vlogging about it," I muse. With his million followers, I'm sure we'll be able to get some traction.

"Excuse me. Y'all are forgetting about one thing," Kirsten says in a cool tone. "I didn't actually agree to letting anyone else into my secret place."

"Is she talking about her vag?" Wyatt whispers, earning a hard shove from his sister.

"If you're so worried about people seeing your pieces, why don't we close up the building for the competition? We can even board up that broken window and the side door to make sure no one can get in."

"But can you really promise no one's going to see my paintings? Especially if we get a big crowd?" Kirsten insists.

I smile, hoping to bring down the tension a notch. "I'll tell you what. We can do our absolute best. I don't have to be at work until five today. Why don't we swing by the hardware store after school and grab some boards. We can start securing it today."

"That's actually not a bad idea." Stella pushes her lunch to the side, placing her notebook in front of her. She whips the cover open and

217

starts scribbling inside. "If we're really planning on holding this in a couple of weeks—"

"We are," I cut her off.

She nods. "Then we'll need to nail down all the logistics too. No pun intended."

"What do you mean?" Kirsten asks.

"Like deciding which obstacles in the lot we're including in the event and in what order." Her eyes widen and she jots down another string of notes. "If we are going to get more expert skaters, maybe we should have a special area where newbies like us will skate. Like maybe the novices can stay near the loading docks and the experts can use the area by the stair rails. Oh! We can also rope off a section by the main building for spectators."

I nod in approval and look around the table. "Who's down for going to our secret spot after school?"

"I have a student council meeting," Stella admits, sliding the notebook to me.

"Band," Larry says a bit too loudly.

Aiden shakes his head. But Wyatt lifts a finger. "I—*ow!*" He hisses, bending forward to rub his shin. I look over to my left and see Larry smirking.

"What did you do?" I mouth.

"Wingman," he mouths back.

I shake my head but can't ignore the sudden rate increase of my pulse. I haven't been able to spend any time alone with Kirsten in days.

I catch her eye. "Guess it's just us."

"Guess so."

# 24

After all this, are you still planning to go back to San Diego next month?" The whizzing air muffles Kirsten's voice.

I hug the wooden boards we picked up at the hardware store tighter against my chest. I push and kick harder, aligning my skateboard with hers. Now that we're on the outskirts of town near the warehouses, we don't have to worry too much about any passing cars. "I never changed my mind about competing."

"Even now that you have the Skate Event to Be Named Later to host?"

I think of Tyler Park's smug face. With his jet-black hair and K-pop boy bander–worthy looks, he's always had me beat. But I really want to outskate him this one time . . . so much so he'll cry. "You know I have some unfinished business to take care of."

"Tyler." Kirsten adjusts the plastic bag carrying our hammer, nails, and a giant lock around her wrist and pushes ahead of me. "But do you still want to talk to your aunt about living with her?"

They say first love never dies. To some people it's a person. A few weeks ago I would've thought it was Amanda. But for me, it's my hometown. I doubt I'll ever stop missing California completely, but now that I'm back to skating with Kirsten it's easy to forget why I want to travel across the country so badly.

My throat constricts. I'm not paying attention to where I'm going and hit a divot. I jump off the board just seconds before I would've hit the ground.

"Wow!" Kirsten whistles, slowing to a stop. "You're pretty fast on your feet."

"You learn to be quick when you're used to running from the cops," I say with a soft chuckle.

"Are you an ex-felon?" Her eyes are as wide as saucers.

I burst into laughter and walk back to retrieve my board. "No! Of course not."

"You aren't?"

"I'm not," I repeat. Her obvious relief makes me laugh even harder. This is just plain ridiculous. "But when you skate around private property as much as I used to, you have no choice but to learn how to run, make excuses, and pop chain-link fences."

"Didn't know you had such a checkered past, Rivera." She smiles. "Maybe I should get some pointers from you. You know, in case I get caught painting."

I'm not sure why I get off on it, but a surge of adrenaline rushes through my veins, and I'm suddenly speaking louder and quicker. "One time, a cop threatened to bring me downtown after he'd caught me skating illegally in an abandoned parking lot."

"Yikes." She grimaces. "How'd you get out of it?"

"First, I tried to feed him a story about being stressed out with high school finals and needing an outlet for my energy."

"I'm guessing that didn't work?"

"Of course not. That's why I ran."

She giggles, and I decide it's officially my new favorite sound.

We opt not to skate the rest of the way to the warehouses, and I savor the extra time it takes us to get there. But my enjoyment slips away once we hit the peak of the hill near the lot.

A random crow caws from the top of the nearest building, then swoops down so low as it flies past us that it nearly hits our heads. As bad omens go, this one's right up there, but I pray this isn't one of them. But my Third Eye, which according to Filipino superstition is an intuition like the sixth sense, buzzes so hard my head starts to hurt.

"Hey." Kirsten pinches my side. "You okay? You look a bit green."

"Oh, yeah. It's nothing." But it doesn't feel like nothing.

Chalking it up to stress, I head down the hill with Kirsten. We cross the center lot and walk to the main building.

I point to the plastic bag. "You hammer and I hold up the boards?"

"Actually, let's go in here first. I have an idea I want to run past you." She sprints to the window. She tosses the plastic bag inside and rests her skateboard against the wall. She hoists her body onto the sill, slides through, and disappears inside the building.

"What happened to using the door?" I place my board beside hers and climb through the window. Once both of my feet are on the ground, Kirsten tugs my wrist, leading me to the middle of the empty building.

"What's your big idea?"

I'm not surprised to see a few new pieces on the wall. A wave of sadness, or maybe it's annoyance—no, it's definitely longing—hits me when I imagine her in the building alone, all the while I'm stuck waiting on nonexistent Sloppy's Pit Stop customers.

She drops my hand and clasps hers together. "Okay, so hear me out."

"I listen to everything you ever tell me," I reply truthfully.

Despite her answering smile, Kirsten's eyes tighten. "I've been doing a lot of thinking today." She opens the plastic bag and takes out the lock. "I want to use this."

"Yeah, I know. I was there when you bought it." I point to the narrow door. "We can use it there—"

"No, listen to me," she says. "I don't only want to use this for the competition. I want to use it forever."

"What are you talking about, Kirsten?"

She bites her lip and leads me to the opposite side of the building. We walk to an art piece made entirely of broad strokes. The maroon and yellow stripes are almost dizzying. "This represented my cheerleading days," she explains.

I wince at the harsh colors. "Oh, yeah. I can make out the pom-pom streamers."

She nods and points to another piece on the far wall that resembles a broken heart. "I don't have to tell you what that's about."

"No. You don't." I tear my gaze away, but once again Grayson's specter overshadows me. "Kirsten, I appreciate you giving me a thorough walkthrough, but I still don't understand what your idea is."

"Everything in here represents a part of my life. But most of these pieces represent my past." She points to the giant turquoise piece with the red X. "If I had to pick one of these pieces, I'd say that one best represents who I am right now."

"Still not following . . ."

She briefly shuts her eyes and nods, as if to convince herself. "We're holding this competition to show everyone that we're through hiding in the shadows. Well, I'm through hiding this part of me. I don't care that the judges thought my pieces were crap. I don't care that Grayson never believed in me or that my parents think I'm throwing my life away. I'm ready to get back out there and show the world what I can do."

She raises the lock. "No more handlebars. I'm locking myself out of this building and throwing away the key. This way, even if I'm tempted, I can't run back inside to hide."

"Are you sure about this?" I ask cautiously.

She doesn't hesitate. "No more handlebars."

I consider her for a moment and finally nod. "No more handlebars."

"Now let's go lock that door and board up that window." She spins around, but the short heel of her cowboy boot catches in a crack on the floor. I reach out and grab her, pulling her into me before she falls.

Her body's both warm and cold. Her heart pounds erratically against my arm as she struggles to breathe. "A-Angelo . . ."

"I got you," I whisper against her coconut-scented strands.

Her head's pressed against my chest. She grabs on to my forearms, and it's suddenly me who needs to catch my breath. She slowly peels herself off me, but I keep my arms wrapped around her waist. She doesn't complain.

Like we're dancing to our own private music, she turns in my arms and looks up at me. Her warm breath coats my collarbone as my own breath ruffles her already tangled hair.

"Ki-Kirsten," I stammer, suddenly losing all ability to speak. I gulp past the cotton feeling in my mouth, but my throat becomes even drier.

"What's happening right now?" she whispers.

My gaze flits down to her bottom lip.

I want to kiss her.

I want to kiss her more than anything in the world. More than skate competitions, burger patties, and even plane tickets to California.

I step back, putting some space between us.

There's too much on the line right now. I can't risk ruining the dynamic of our group over a stupid crush. Sure there are times when I think Kirsten might be a little fond of me—she did give me that peck on the cheek—but I thought Amanda loved me, and I was obviously wrong about that. If I act on my feelings and Kirsten doesn't feel the same way, will she still want to hang out with me? I care too much about her to gamble our friendship away.

As if waking from a dream, Kirsten blinks quickly and moves even farther away. "I . . ." She clears her throat and forces a smile that doesn't reach her eyes. "I think I'm going to head on home after I lock the door. Is that okay? Or do you need help boarding up?"

I rub the back of my neck. "Oh. Um, no. It's fine."

She nods, quickly crosses the room, and disappears out the door, leaving me standing alone in the colorful building.

# 25

Wyatt was right. Teaming up with some of the smartest kids in school to advertise our competition does have its advantages. In a matter of a few days, not only has Larry got #NobodyNowhereSkateEvent (dubbed by yours truly) trending in skating forums, but the hashtag also caught the attention of a few pro skaters who are voicing interest. To top it all off, our very own whiz kid, Aiden, was able to set up a new website, Countdown to Nowhere, that's got everyone in school buzzing. It's where we're going to make the big reveal listing the event's location.

With only hours to spare before the announcement, everyone in school's glued to their phones, watching the bright red numbers count down.

*"I heard it's a military experiment."*

*"Well, I heard it's aliens."*

*"It's something shady, guys."*

It takes a lot of effort, but I somehow keep a neutral face as I walk into the cafeteria. I look around, internally celebrating as I see even the popular table with their phones pinged onto our website. In an effort to blend in, Stella also has her laptop open. My friends' eyes are glued to the screen. Everyone but Aiden is anxious to see what the big reveal will look like.

"I have to say, I'm impressed." I scoot in next to Larry and try to catch Kirsten's eye, but she quickly looks away. Ever since our almost kiss, she's been acting really weird around me. I try to dial back my disappointment and focus on Stella's screen. "How many visitors do you think we've gotten on our site?"

Aiden's dimple deepens with his grin. "I don't know . . . *everyone from school!*"

I clap softly. "Now tell me why we didn't think of doing something like this to advertise Sloppy's Pit Stop."

"Because it wouldn't have trended," Larry says matter-of-factly. "The thing that everyone likes about this website is that it's the unknown. It's not your boring, run-of-the-mill Ocean Pointe crap."

"They don't like run-of-the-mill, eh? So maybe this town isn't as hell-bent on tradition as everyone thinks it is." I'm only half kidding.

"Maybe all it took was something special enough to show everyone that different can be good," Kirsten replies. We lock gazes, but she quickly looks away.

Before I can start to feel too sad about it, Wyatt elbows me in the gut. "I have to admit, your whole faceless symbol idea really worked."

"Yeah, who would've thought posting a picture of a plain mask with eyeholes on a burner account—"

"Catfishing," Wyatt corrects.

I roll my eyes and rephrase. "Posting it on a *fake* account and tagging a URL would get people from school to visit the website?" Despite the weirdness still hanging between me and Kirsten, I reach across the table to tap her arm. "Thanks for designing it, by the way."

She presses her lips together into a tight smile but doesn't say anything.

I sigh and allow myself to get lost in the red digital numbers. "Looks like we only have a couple more minutes to go." I peer at my friends one by one. "Everyone set for tonight?"

"Yes, sir," Stella answers. "We all have our new skateboards."

"Express shipping for the win!" Wyatt raises a fist in the air.

His sister nods. "And I also have the package you had your friend send us." She shakes her head with a grimace. "Tell me again why he had to ship it to our house?"

"My parents are still keeping a close watch on me. They want my attention focused only on school and Sloppy's," I explain. "Seeing a giant box from Mackabi would raise their suspicions. Besides, do you know how hard it was trying to explain why I was frying a ton of fries? I had to tell them it was for a pep rally." I cringe, thinking of the dent all those fries made in my savings account.

Stella scowls. "Well, seeing a box from a boy raised my mom's suspicions!"

Wyatt whoops in amusement, but I only grimace. "Sorry about that. But hey, he sent a lot of merch. I'm sure the winner won't mind if you take a shirt or two from the stash."

Wyatt's smile fades. "Yeah, about that. Do you really think people will want *Mackabi Vlogs* merchandise as a prize?"

I was actually surprised Mackabi would donate a bunch of stuff to our cause. But like he said, *"Anything for skating, bro."*

Then again, I did have to endure about twenty minutes of listening to him call me a country bumpkin. So I guess it wasn't all that free.

"It was either that or shell out our own cash as a prize." I chuckle as Wyatt recoils in horror. "Yeah, I thought so."

Justin's voice booms above the cafeteria chatter. "It's almost time!"

A hush falls over the room. Everyone's hunched over their phones and computers, practically salivating as the numbers fall back.

. . . 5

. . . 4

. . . 3

. . . 2

. . . 1

Everyone takes a collective breath, only releasing once a string of numbers flashes across an image of a featureless mask.

"What the hell?" Justin's voice echoes across the cafeteria. "More numbers? What the fuck is this?"

"Wait, it also says eight o'clock on the bottom." Maddie taps against her computer screen. "But that's when the game starts tonight . . ." She shoots everyone at her table a suspicious look. "You guys did this, didn't you? Is this some kind of sick joke?"

"Like we'd know how to make a website," Grayson barks back. He gestures to the screen. "I don't even know what all this means!"

I can't bring myself to listen to their bullshit argument anymore and frown at Aiden. "Coordinates?" I whisper-yell at him, looking around to make sure no one can hear us. "Why the heck would you use coordinates? We want people to actually show up, remember?"

Aiden's cheeks flush. "It went along with my theme."

"Are you kidding me? I don't care about your web design. Coordinates just make it that much harder to get people to come to our event. Who the heck can even figure it out?"

"People who want to be there," Kirsten interjects.

I turn to her in surprise. "Huh?"

"As much as we want a large audience, we also want people who'll make it a fun time. At least the first time around." Kirsten stares at the screen and smiles at the dancing mask graphic. "I think Aiden did a good job on this. The only people who will show up are the people who can figure this out."

Larry clears his throat. "Don't worry too much about it, Angelo. I already posted the actual address on the skate forums earlier this week. Not that anyone in school would bother checking those message boards out."

"Wait, what's that?" Maddie squeals as a new graphic pops up on the screen.

Everyone stares at their devices intently. Me included.

"Aiden. What did you . . . oh my God!" I gasp.

A masked skater cruises across the bottom of the screen, doing a kickflip right before it fades to reveal the following words:

*Nobody*
*Nowhere*
*Skateboarding Competition*
*Prepare to thrash*
*. . . Sponsored by Sloppy's Pit Stop*

The cafeteria is silent. In my periphery, I can feel everyone's eyes on me. After a beat, Maddie whines, "All this for a *skating* event? This is all you, isn't it, Angie?"

"So much for being a nobody," I grumble. But I can't be mad. In fact, I hold my head much higher. If the outsiders need a martyr, then I'll be that guy for them. Besides, it got word out on our restaurant, which I wanted in the first place.

But Stella smacks Aiden on the arm. "Why would you do that?" she hisses. "*Sloppy's Pit Stop?* What happened to being faceless? Now everyone knows Angelo's part of it."

Aiden lowers his fedora, hiding his eyes. "Angelo said he didn't want anyone to find out who's behind the competition until the day of the event. It's the day of the event."

"I'm sure he didn't mean it literally. And if he did, I'm sure he meant *at the time* of the event."

"No, no. This is okay," I say more to convince myself than anything. "I only wanted to keep it a secret until then in case anyone wanted to sabotage our plans."

"Anyone as in Grayson?" Larry suggests.

I nod. "But with their game tonight, it's too late for him to do anything to hurt our event now."

I dare to glance at the popular table and spot Grayson glaring at me. I widen my smile. *Take that.*

# 26

The subtle glow of my fluorescent necklace has nothing on the bright Friday night lights shining in the distance. It's a little after dusk and nearing time for our Nobody Nowhere Skate event. Everyone except Kirsten stands in front of Stella and Wyatt's house, buzzing with energy. I once read that anxiety and excitement elicit the same physiological response, but the emotion is based solely on how your brain interprets the sensation. Right now, I don't know where anxiety ends and excitement begins.

"How are you feeling?" Larry snaps his own glowstick necklace, activating it. He places the purple ring around his neck and shakes his head. "I have to say, it's weird not sitting on the football bleachers right now."

"Was your band teacher salty about you telling him you'd be missing tonight?" I ask, unsure how to answer his question.

"That's an understatement," he says with a chuckle. "Then again, I've never missed a game before."

"Oh."

"You didn't answer my question," he points out. "How are you feeling?"

"Isn't that a loaded question?" I snicker in an attempt to mask my nerves, but Larry isn't buying it.

Once everyone at school figured out who was behind the mysterious website, it felt like I had a sword hanging above my head all afternoon, just waiting to fall down on me. Questions whizzed through my mind, like sports cars on an LA freeway—

Had it been too soon to reveal that I was the one behind the mask?

Was it a good idea to name Sloppy's Pit Stop the sponsor?

I'm used to people here staring at me or whispering behind my back. It was a bit odd to have classmates I've never spoken to before asking me about the event. Then again, I did promise myself that I'd talk to more people out of my friend group. And interest in the event is what we wanted in the first place.

"Angelo? Are you okay?" Kirsten's voice is like a jumper cable to my heart. My nerves slowly melt away, pooling in a puddle at my feet.

"Kirsten, you're here!" I cringe. "I mean, you made it. I mean . . ."

"Why wouldn't I be here?" Kirsten steps up next to me. She's dressed like the rest of us, in a plain hoodie with glowstick jewelry hanging around her neck and wrists and a magenta mask ready to be slipped on. She even ditched her trademark cowboy boots for a pair of dark sneakers. But even in the dimming light of dusk, she stands out like the sun.

Larry watches our exchange and quickly turns away. For once, I'm happy he's so perceptive.

I lower my tone so none of our other friends can hear. "It's just that things have been weird between us. You know, ever since . . ."

"Yeah, ever since . . ."

After a few beats of silence, Kirsten sighs, saying, "I'm sorry."

"Wait, *you're* sorry?" I'm floored. I wasn't expecting her to apologize. Especially since it was me who almost initiated the kiss . . . and it was me who pulled away before I had the guts to do it.

"Angelo, I . . ."

I'm on the tip of my toes, waiting anxiously for her to finish her thought. But she clamps up all over again and walks over to Stella, who's busy stuffing Mackabi's package into the back of her mom's car.

I bow my head but am distracted by the loud cheers echoing from the football field for the pregame. Even standing blocks away, the sound's almost deafening.

I turn away from the bright lights and face my friends. "You guys ready?"

If the air was tense before, it's even more strained now.

"I'm ready," Kirsten finally says, starting a domino effect among our friends, who finally nod in agreement.

I nod along with them, slipping my magenta mask over my face. My friends put on their magenta masks too.

I examine my friends, their expressions as blank as Kirsten's warehouse walls once were. Maybe it's because of my nerves, but I can't stop myself from laughing. "We look ridiculous. Like we're a bunch of mimes about to attend a music festival."

And just like that, all our anxiety melts away. My friends join me in laughter, breaking into hysterics. Wyatt even snorts like a pig.

I suck in a hiccuped sigh and motion to the street. "C'mon. It's almost time. Let's head on out."

Stella climbs into her car with Wyatt in the passenger's seat and Aiden in the back. The rest of the car is loaded up with merchandise and cartons of fries, so Larry, Kirsten, and I will skate the whole way.

The sky's a pale lavender but already peppered with a few stars. There is no wind. No other noise but our deep breaths and the calming sound of our rolling wheels.

"How many people do you think will show?" Larry grunts, pushing with all his might. With his short legs, it takes him double the kicks to keep up with us.

"I don't know. People online seemed really interested. But who's to say any of them will come?" It's another reason why I'm so nervous about tonight. What if the event flops?

After about fifteen minutes of skating, Kirsten reaches the gravel pathway first. She jumps off the board, expertly picking it up in one quick swoop and, without waiting for us, jogs to the top of the hill. She stops abruptly. Dust dances around her ankles as she whirls around with her mouth dropped open. "You guys have to see this."

Larry and I give each other a quick look and rush up the hill.

Are there a lot of people waiting for us?

Are there *no* people waiting for us?

By the time I make it to the peak of the hill, my breaths are beyond labored. But once I see what's at the bottom, I completely stop breathing.

A sizeable crowd is gathered in the center lot. Though we're standing too far away, and despite the halo lights Mackabi sent us that we'd placed around the warehouses, it's too dark outside to make out their faces. I can see some skaters jumping over gaps and grinding down rails.

Kirsten's giddy with excitement and gives me a slight shove. "Well? What are you waiting for, Rivera? This is your event. Go get 'em!"

I refrain from pointing out that it's actually *our* event, too happy about the turnout and also relieved to hear Kirsten tease me again. I give her a nod and fly down the hill to greet the crowd.

# 27

I've never felt more like a celebrity. I make my way through the lot and am greeted with high fives and fist bumps. By the time I make it to the middle of the crowd, I'm almost exhausted.

My mask shifts, blocking part of my vision. Readjusting it, I look around and spot more than a few familiar faces from school seated in the spectators' area.

"Look, we got some football game skippers," I tell Kirsten the moment she steps up beside me.

"Stop gloating" is her reply, but there's no mistaking the smile in her tone. I grin back, though I know there's no way she can see it behind my full face mask.

She pinches the spot above my elbow. "What are you waiting for? Address the crowd."

My arms and legs start to tingle. But excitement overpowers my nerves.

"Hey, everyone!" I shout, but my voice gets lost in the murmurs cascading over the crowd.

I clear my throat and try again. "Yo!"

But again no one can hear me. There are too many separate conversations going on.

I'm tempted to rip off my mask and shout as loud as I can, but that would ruin my desired aesthetic. As if reading my mind, Larry pops out of nowhere again, holding a Bluetooth microphone with an attached speaker. Houdini's up to his magic tricks again, and I'm beyond grateful. "Where the hell did you get that?"

He shrugs and hands it to me. "Borrowed it from the band room. Figured we might need it tonight. Now hurry up before people start to leave."

I don't need to be told twice.

I start to pull my mask a little above my mouth, but a bright light blinds me, stopping me. I shield my eyes and hear some of the most terrifying words a teenager up to no good can ever hear: *"It's the cops! Run!"*

Everyone scatters.

Skaters fly away on their boards.

Our classmates break off on foot.

On instinct, I grab Kirsten's hand. Instead of pushing me away, she holds on to me tight.

"Come on. We need to find the others." My voice is raspy with desperation.

The aqua flyers we'd taped around the buildings rain down on us like confetti on New Year's Eve. I don't know how they got ripped off the walls, and at this point I don't have time to think about it. We run with the crowd, stomping down on already squished pieces of fries. The string on my mask breaks, revealing my face, but I pay it no mind. I'm too frantic, looking around for my friends. Luckily, I spot the taillights of Stella's car as it disappears over the hill. Larry, Wyatt, and Aiden seem to be gone as well. At least I hope they are.

Kirsten and I make it down the gravel hill, but before we can jump on our boards, we're grabbed from behind.

"You're coming with us." Tobacco-scented breath dances around my nostrils. I nearly gag, but it isn't until I see the sheriff's bright gold badge that I truly want to throw up.

# 28

I never imagined myself sitting in the sheriff's office. I'm sure a few security guards would disagree, but I'm really not a troublemaker. Okay, maybe I am a little. But life's a cat-and-mouse game, and it's your responsibility not to get caught in a trap. And I'd never been caught. Until now, at least.

If I had to imagine what being in jail would be like, I'd picture myself pretty badass. Maybe even with a cool tattoo. The kind that stretches from my neck all the way down to my well-defined pecs. Definitely not one of those stupid barbed-wire ones that wrap around the bicep. But if I did have to get one of those, I'm sure I'd rock it well.

Considering my arm's a bit too skinny to even think of getting one of those tattoos, and I by no means have a well-defined anything, my current stint in the sheriff's office leaves me feeling anything but badass. Especially since there's nothing I can do but sit and wait for my parents to pick me up.

The town precinct is exactly what you'd imagine a rural one to be. It's a mix of jail à la *Little House on the Prairie*–style and a horror movie like *The Hills Have Eyes*. To my dismay, it's also filled with two antagonists I wish I never had the displeasure of meeting.

One of Bob Marley's songs plays in my head as the deputy, who unfortunately also happens to be Grayson's older brother and the sheriff's son, perches half a butt cheek against the desk across from where Kirsten and I are seated on very uncomfortable plastic seats. His short golden-brown hair sticks out from underneath his ridiculous brown hat. In stereotypical fashion, he chews on a soggy toothpick and peers down at us from the tip of his nose. He scratches against his nostril and then points at us with the same finger. "You guys are lucky that you're still minors. Breaking and entering is a felony. Not that you'll get off easily."

I level my eyes with his but keep my mouth shut. If he thinks he can get a reaction from me, he has another thing coming.

Now Deputy Evans leans toward Kirsten. I'm worried all this is too much for her, but she lifts her chin and glares at him. Taken aback, the deputy straightens and grabs his toothpick, tossing it into the wastebasket by her feet. She still doesn't flinch. "Nelson, you're lucky your daddy's a big deal in this town," he says to her.

"Wait, did you call him?" Kirsten's voice falters, and she grips the edge of her seat.

"Of course we called him, sugar. Didn't you hear what I said? Y'all are minors." He holds out his palms and presses against the air as he repeats, "Mi-*nors*."

"But we weren't doing anything wrong."

"That sketchy meetup y'alls organized didn't seem that innocent to me." The deputy's beady eyes slide over to me. "Or should I say that Sloppy's Pit Stop organized."

I stiffen. Shit. Maybe having our family restaurant as a sponsor was a bad idea after all.

"It wasn't even like that," Kirsten argues.

"Guess we'll see what your daddy thinks, huh?" Deputy Evans snorts, clearly enjoying seeing her squirm.

She clenches her fists and mutters, "Fuck. My dad's going to love this. Just gives him another reason to be pissed at me."

The deputy continues his chuckles. "Good thing is you're not being carted straight off to jail. Bad thing is—"

"Angelo! What were you thinking?" Mom barges into the tiny building like a hurricane barreling into land.

Dad's at her heels, looking more furious than I've ever seen him. He points a trembling finger at me. "What's this they say about you organizing a mob?"

I jump to my feet. A mixture of shock and anger bubbles inside my gut. How dare my parents think so low of me? Not that it's far off from the truth, but still.

"I did not organize a mob! I was just trying to hold a skateboarding competition," I announce, ignoring Evans's disbelieving chuckle.

Dad points to Kirsten's mask on the deputy's desk. "You needed to dress like burglars to hold a competition?"

"It was purely aesthetic," Kirsten interjects. My parents glare at her.

"Skateboarding? Competition?" Deputy Evans throws back his thick head of hair and laughs. "In what world is that deviancy considered a sport?"

It's déjà vu, only this time Kirsten sniffs. "Maybe you should ask the pros."

Despite my frayed nerves, I can't help but laugh.

"Hey now. Watch it, young man," Deputy Evans warns as he stands up.

Mom's tearstained face whips in our direction, her eyes pleading for us to shut our mouths. Kirsten's obviously not taking the hint. Or at least she ignores it. She turns to Evans and asks, "How'd you find out about the event?"

The deputy addresses my parents instead of Kirsten. "These children made a website with the exact coordinates to this so-called competition. It was plastered all over the internet. Just like the Sloppy's Pit Stop logo was plastered all over the lot."

The blood drains from Mom's face. "I swear we didn't know about it."

Deputy Evans grunts and points at my mom. "You're lucky I believe you."

"Anything having to do with you is unlucky," Kirsten mumbles under her breath.

"Hey now, young lady. You're not really in the position to be a smart-ass right now. So I suggest you think twice before you piss me off."

Kirsten starts to say something, but I cut her off. This time, it's my turn to save her. "We really didn't mean any harm. We just wanted to have some fun. Get a bunch of like-minded people together for some harmless skateboarding."

"And you thought trespassing was a good way to do it? And on top of that throwing in the Sloppy's Pit Stop name?" Dad's voice trembles in rage.

I flinch. "Our restaurant needs new business."

"Angelo, stop talking," Mom hisses. Her eyes indicate the deputy. "Can't they use anything you say in court? Do you really want to make things worse? We can't afford any legal fees right now."

The younger Evans opens his mouth to respond, but Sheriff Evans walks into the room, commanding attention. Though he's probably in his mid to late fifties, he still looks as strong as an ox. Mom and Dad automatically stiffen as he approaches.

"There won't be any need for court," the sheriff says in a gruff voice that matches his leathery skin perfectly.

"There won't?" Mom crosses herself and stares at the heavens in a silent thank-you.

Sheriff Evans takes off his hat and runs his hands through his thick mess of gray hair. He points the hat at us. "Lucky for you both, I'm an understanding sort of fellow. Hell, I held my own wild parties in abandoned farmhouses when I was younger."

"It wasn't a party. It was a sporting event," I shoot back.

"Angelo! *Tigil na!*" When Mom tells me to stop doing something in Tagalog, I know I'm done for.

Sheriff Evans gives my parents a far kinder look than the one he threw me and Kirsten while we were in the back of his cruiser. "Like I was saying, I was a kid once too. I also have me two fine boys. I know how good kids can find themselves in trouble sometimes. Bad decision-making, emotional immaturity, and all that."

"Yeah, we know how Grayson is," I mutter under my breath. Apparently, not low enough.

Sheriff Evans's head turns in my direction. "However, trespassing is considered a felony in some counties." He narrows his eyes into two menacing slits. "And I'm sure a family business like Sloppy's Pit Stop can't afford its name being smeared in the mud."

Sweat breaks out along the edges of Dad's toupee. I'm sure he's picturing our already empty restaurant. Shit. Did I make things worse?

The sheriff's gruff tone breaks through my thoughts. "Consider this a warning—don't pull a stunt like this again unless you want to see the inside of a jail cell." He waits for Kirsten and me to nod and adds, "As for this current issue, there won't be any charges filed."

"Oh my God. Thank you!" Mom's accent becomes thicker when she's wound up about something, so it comes out sounding like *Oh my Gahd*.

Kirsten and I exchange a look. Something isn't right. We can't be getting off this easily. If Sheriff Evans is anything like his son, there must be a catch.

Noticing our looks, Sheriff Evans gives us a curt smile. "But don't think you're walking away without punishment. Of course, you'll be paying back your debt to society."

Dad clears his throat. "With all due respect. We're a new business. We can't afford—"

Sheriff Evans waves his hand, cutting Dad off. "I'm not talking about money, Mr. Rivera."

Kirsten's pale eyebrows furrow. "What *are* you talking about?"

The sheriff bows his head sadly. "The raucous y'all made nearly cost us the game tonight." Kirsten and I catch each other's eyes and bite back a smile. "Those poor boys played knowing they didn't have the full support of the town. If it weren't for that last field goal, we would've had our first loss of the season."

"Bummer."

"*Tigil na!*" Mom warns.

Sheriff Evans's mouth pulls down at the corners. "Seeing as how your actions affected the team, I think it's only fitting if the punishment fits the crime."

Uh-oh. This does not sound good.

"What's that supposed to mean?" Kirsten dares to ask.

"It means that starting on Monday you are cleaning up after our champion football team. Every day after school."

"Are you kidding me? No!" she protests.

A new voice joins the conversation. Stern, with a harsh crack only comparable to thunder. "Now, Kirsten, hush your mouth."

We all turn to find a slick, confident-looking man stride into the office. Dressed in a three-piece suit, he looks completely out of place in the rickety office. Dare I say, he exudes more power than both Evanses combined.

The man takes his position beside his daughter and nods at my parents. "Mr. and Mrs. Rivera, I'd say it was nice finally seeing you in person after helping you purchase your home from a distance, but given the circumstance . . ."

Dad nods back with a grim expression.

Kirsten might be scared enough to shut her mouth, but I sure as hell ain't. "The football team? Are you serious? I'd rather clean the school hallway with my toothbrush." Cleaning up after Grayson and his bully friends is probably one of the worse punishments imaginable. Besides, I wouldn't even be in this mess if they hadn't torn down our flyers to begin with.

I glance at my parents for support. "And what about my job? You increased my shifts, remember?"

Mom waves me away, but there's no mistaking the worry in her eyes. "We'll figure it out. You can come to work after your punishment."

"But what about my homework?" I ask. But what I really want to know is how I'm going to squeeze in skating.

"You'll have time to do schoolwork at Sloppy's. We're never busy." Dad's anger doesn't bother me as much as the disappointment dripping from his tone. If he only knew what drove me to hold a competition. But now's not the time to tell him that those "poor boys" from the football team have targeted Sloppy's Pit Stop from the start.

Mr. Nelson makes a clicking sound with his tongue. "As for you, young lady, first cheerleading and now this? You're on a downward spiral, Kirsten. I don't even know who you are anymore."

"Maybe if you actually took the time to understand the things I'm interested in, you would," Kirsten barks back.

"Things like him?" Mr. Nelson sniffs at me.

I blink in shock and glance at Kirsten. Her face turns red. "Dad—"

"Don't even think you're seeing this boy again, Kirsten," he snaps.

"Who are you calling 'boy,' Mr. Nelson?" Mom snaps. Of course, now she wants to jump to my defense. "He's a young man. A young man who should've known better."

Mr. Nelson holds up a placating hand. "No disrespect, Mrs. Rivera. But it was your son who dragged my daughter into this."

Fortunately, Kirsten pipes up, "It wasn't Angelo's idea."

I hold my breath. *Don't throw our friends under the bus.*

"I was also behind it from the start."

"Kirsten!" His gaze bounces between the two Evanses, who chuckle in response. Mr. Nelson kneads at his eyebrows and sighs. With a shake of his head, he motions for Kirsten. "Well, let's get on home so we can discuss this further."

"Oh, so you finally want to talk to me now?" Kirsten mumbles.

Her dad turns red and begins ushering her to the exit.

"We should get home too." Mom leans into me and whispers, "I'm not done with you."

Sheriff Evans shakes my dad's thin hand with his thick one. "I'm sure Angelo will learn a lot from being around the football team. Those are good boys." The cop turns to me and grins. "Just think. You'll lend a helping hand in making sure the Trojans keep their winning streak alive."

"Yeah. Go, Trojans. Woo-hoo." My mouth is dry.

Kirsten turns to speak to me, but Mr. Nelson practically shoves her out the door before she can get a word out. I have no doubt her real estate mogul dad will make sure we can't be anywhere near each other. My stomach rolls over. How long will it be before I get to see her again?

As I catch a last glimpse of her white-blonde hair, I feel the same way I did on my first day in Ocean Pointe.

I'm nowhere.

# 29

Saturday and Sunday go about as well as I expected. There are the expected tears (Mom's) with declarations that moving was a horrible idea. If this were weeks ago, I would have wholeheartedly agreed. But that was before my life was changed by my new crew. Friends who text me all weekend to check up on me . . . well, except for Kirsten. I haven't heard from her since we left the sheriff's office.

As much as a weekend being grounded with no skating and no TV sucks, I'm dreading Monday even more. The thought of spending the after-school hours with the very guys who drove me to hold the skating event makes me wish Sheriff Evans just charged us.

Usually the scream of the final bell leaves me ecstatic. Even flipping burgers at Sloppy's is better than listening to my Spanish teacher, Señora Mora, drone on during the last period of the day. But today the banshee's wail has my stomach in knots. My limbs are heavy, only growing heavier as I drag myself through the crowded hallway, which is full of students ready to get the hell out of here. I stare longingly at the front doors as I make the turn to the west wing where the gym is located. Thanks to my old high school's requirement of only two years of gym, I got physical education written off my schedule. I actually thought I'd never have to enter one ever again, and yet here I am.

The gym's bright-yellow door taunts me. I kick it open and it slams against the concrete wall with a frightening smack. The brightly lit gym looks almost identical to the one at my old high school.

"Why wouldn't OPHS's gym remind me of San Diego?" I mutter sarcastically, blinking quickly as my eyes adjust to the harsh fluorescent lighting.

I head for the closed locker room doors on the other side of the empty room. Muffled voices are coming from behind them. Maybe some of the players are in there. Coach Shappey's office is in there too. That's where he instructed me to meet him before practice starts.

The sour aroma of sweat intensifies as I near the locker room. Taking a moment to compose myself, I push through the door. As expected, I'm met with the stench of old gym socks, body odor, and footballs. I wind through the rows of lockers, sidestepping classmates who are half dressed with shoulder pads and those weird knee-high pants. I brace myself for a slew of insults and questions about why I'm even in here. Surprisingly, all the jocks stay mum. Not surprisingly, they look at me as if I'm dried gum crusted on the bottom of their cleats.

"Mr. Rivera! There you are. I was beginning to think you wouldn't show up." Coach Shappey leans against the doorjamb of his tiny office behind hampers full of towels. Clean ones, I hope.

I refrain from telling him that by law I technically couldn't skip out on today even if I wanted to. And good God do I want to. Forcing my customer service smile, I greet him. "Hey, Coach Shappey."

"I got some stuff to take care of in my office, so why don't you take a seat anywhere and I'll get back to you in a bit." He walks back inside, slamming the door shut behind him.

"Guess that's that." I scan the locker room, taking in the overly sculpted teenagers who are dead ringers for those "too perfect" actors on television teen dramas. The ones who aren't actual teenagers but twentysomething actors perpetually doomed to carry a backpack for the rest of their lives.

I catch a glimpse of Grayson's triceps flexing as he pulls on his shirt. Even in the locker room he's putting on a show.

He glances toward me, but I look away. It's not that I'm afraid. I just don't want him to think that for even one second I'm intimidated by him. Or worse, admiring him like one of his many minions.

A few minutes later, the coach's door flings back open. "You ready to get started?" Coach Shappey says. "Miss Nelson will be out on the field with me handing out water for the guys."

"What will I be doing, Coach?" I ask. "Handing out water bottles too?"

With a wide smile, the coach points to the hampers. "How are you with laundry?"

I briefly shut my eyes, suddenly wishing I were smacking and flipping a burger patty right now. "Do I have a choice?"

Coach chuckles in a way that makes me think he's in cahoots with the sheriff *and* Kirsten's dad. Twirling the whistle hanging from his neck, he shakes his head slowly. "Just stay in here, son. It'll be over before you know it."

I breathe out. "I hope you're right."

~

He wasn't right. A long hour later I'm head high in a pile of bleached white towels. Well, most of them are bleached. There are some nasty yellowish stains on a few grungy hand towels that no amount of washing can ever get rid of. I sit on the edge of the wooden bench, folding and refolding the towels. My hands are pruney from sticking them in the washer. I've never seen a washing machine in a locker room before, but I guess it makes sense since OPHS is hell-bent on spoiling its football team to death.

The sound of laughter cuts through the silence as the door leading to the field bursts open. Ignoring the high fives and slaps on the butt, ready to head home, I concentrate on my last pile of towels. I sort of hope Kirsten peeks her head in to say hello, but mostly I hope for her sake that she's already left for the day and is as far away from this torture as possible.

A familiar smell of musk surrounds me, and I glance up. Justin leers at me, clenching his jaw in that way all movie villains often do. I'm too exhausted to deal with him and sigh. "If you have something to say, just say it."

He snorts. "You're in my way."

"What?"

With his sweat-soaked scrimmage shirt in one hand, he gestures at the locker beside me. "You're in my way."

"Oh."

Grabbing the last armful of towels, I scoot down the bench a bit so I'm not in front of any lockers, not wanting to piss off any other football player. I glance at Justin, expecting him to say something more, but he just concentrates on opening his locker, stripping, and changing into clean clothes.

Should I remind him that even Sloppy's Pit Stop has two showers? I shake off the thought. I should consider myself lucky he's over picking on me.

As I finish folding another towel, Justin pulls his too-tight shirt over his head. Once it pops free he looks at me. "So you're Ocean Pointe's masked man."

The towel slips from my hand. "What's it to you?"

"Chill. I'm just making conversation."

"I'm sure."

He slams his locker shut and frowns down at me. "Saw a few videos posted online of your 'event'"—he makes air quotations—"and gotta say, you guys scrammed like bats out of hell when Evans showed up."

I immediately jump to my feet, ignoring the blast of pain that radiates off the side of my leg as it hits the bench. "I'm getting really sick and tired of your damn insults."

Justin isn't the slightest bit fazed. He shakes his head, grabbing on to the thin strap of his gym bag and hitching it onto his shoulder. "Hey, I'm trying to compliment you."

"How is that even a compliment?"

"Look, I know we didn't exactly start off on the right foot."

I arch an eyebrow. "You think?"

"But I gotta say, it took balls for you to go up against a football game," he grumbles as if it explains his complete 180. "I respect that."

I fall back onto the bench. I must be dreaming. "I don't understand why you're talking to me, let alone complimenting me. I thought you hated me."

He remains silent. I start to worry I've pushed his buttons again, but to my relief he explains, "Because anyone who can pull off what you did, not to mention turn those freak friends of yours into athletes, is pretty cool."

"Hey! My friends aren't freaks," I snap.

Justin abruptly sits down beside me on the bench, startling me. The long wooden slab vibrates from his weight, once again reminding me of our physical differences. He tosses his gym bag on the floor, signaling our conversation is far from over. "Listen, this isn't easy for me."

"Talking to me?"

"Asking for help from you."

"I . . . I don't know what the hell you're talking about," I admit.

"The scouts are looking at me, but I heard from Grayson who heard from Cole who heard from his dad's connection at State that I'm somewhere near the bottom rung. Apparently, I'm too slow. Stiff."

I have no idea why he's telling me all this, but I ask, "Are you sure they heard right?"

I'm no stranger to how rumors start and how things can get warped after each storytelling. Shoot, back at my old high school, Mackabi released one chicken on campus as part of a stupid prank. By the end of the week the story went he'd brought a chicken, a cow, and a goat.

"Trust me. They heard right." He licks his thick lips and frowns.

"I still don't know what any of this has to do with me."

"I'm getting to the point!" His booming voice seems to rattle the lockers surrounding us.

Everything freezes. The bustle of the locker room immediately quiets down, and without looking I feel everyone's eyes on us. Justin waves off the added attention, waiting until things are back to normal before he whips out his phone and plays a short clip from Friday night, right after the Evanses broke up our event. He pauses the video and flicks his giant fingers against the screen. "See this beanpole with the mask?"

For a second I think he's talking about me, but the more I examine the shot, I can tell it's Wyatt. "I have no idea who that is," I lie.

He rolls his eyes. "Please. We both know it's Wyatt. And would you take a look at how fast he is?" He lets the video play through, and true to his word Wyatt flies to Stella's car, his legs a blur as he dives in through the open door. "This kid's known for being slow."

"Well, he ain't slow now," I spit back.

"Exactly." Justin stuffs his phone into his bag and runs his fingers down the sides of his face. "Listen, I live near Larry—"

"You do?" I blink in surprise. After Maddie's drug-centered jab at my friend, I would never have thought she'd actually date someone from that part of town.

"So you see why I need the scouts to like me. I need the scholarship."

"Yeah. I guess so . . . ?"

"Every day when I'm heading to practice, I see Wyatt running around on the field. And every day I see him getting faster." Justin straightens and crosses his muscular arms. "At first, I thought he was juicing it or something. I mean, he does hang out with Larry."

"That's fucked up, and you know it."

Justin smirks. "But then I realized he is doing something different. He's been skating. The past couple of weeks, I've seen him skating in front of Larry's place. Lots. Skating's making him faster, isn't it?"

"Skating does give his muscles a workout—the muscles he needs to make him faster," I agree.

"I need that. I need skating."

"Are you . . . are you kidding?" I gape at him.

"C'mon, Angie. I need to build up those muscles. I need to get faster. Teach me how to skate." He zips his lips, allowing his words to hang in the air.

"You want me to teach you how to skate." I shake my head and let out a strained laugh. "You made fun of me from the first moment I stepped onto Ocean Pointe soil, and now you expect me to help you? You've got to be shitting me."

He shifts, both embarrassed and irritated. "I wouldn't be asking you if I wasn't desperate, Angie."

I lean back, crossing my arms tightly as if shielding myself from his bullshit. "Am I just supposed to forget how you tried to force me into stealing food from my own restaurant for you and your buddies?"

"That was Grayson!" As if suddenly remembering Grayson's still in the locker room somewhere, Justin looks around. For once he doesn't look as big as he pulls his bulking arms together and hunches forward.

"What about calling me a brown boy? Or bullying me in the parking lot?"

He winces. "That was sort of a welcoming thing. You know, *Welcome to Ocean Pointe* and all that."

"Right." I roll my eyes as the weight of my suspicions settles into my gut. "So was sabotaging Sloppy's Pit Stop a welcoming thing too?"

"What are you talking about?"

"You guys took down all our flyers, didn't you?" I shoot back.

Judging by the look on his face, I caught him red-handed.

"Listen, Angie—"

I shoot him a look and he corrects, "*Angelo*. You're new here."

"Oh my God. Can people stop saying that?" I run my fingers down the length of my face.

"No, listen. If you haven't noticed, Ocean Pointe doesn't take to strangers too well. Especially OPHS." I roll my eyes, but he keeps on going. "Everyone here has a role. There are the athletes, the cheerleaders, and everybody else." He holds out his hands, palms parallel to the ground. He raises one hand to eye level. "The athletes are up here." He raises the other to just below his chin. "The cheerleaders are right below them."

"Let me guess—everyone else is nonexistent?"

He thinks about it. "All I'm saying is that as the top tier, we're expected to keep up with appearances." He bounces one shoulder. "And that includes making fun of the lower tiers."

"Ripping down our flyers and, I don't know, *being racist as shit* is your definition of making fun of me?" I snap.

He shrugs. "To be honest, I thought the whole flyer thing was stupid. But Grayson thought it would be fun to see your face when you found them in your locker, so I just went along with it and tore them all down."

"Do you always do what Grayson tells you to do?" I don't know whether to be annoyed at him or feel sorry for him.

"Eh, he's been my best bud for years. But it wasn't only because of him. Maddie wanted to mess with you too."

"But why would Maddie even want to mess with me?" I ask in bewilderment.

"Because of Kirsten," he answers simply. "She hates her, so by association she hates you too since you guys are close."

"Are you freaking serious?" As dumb as Maddie's frame of thinking is, I can't deny the butterflies in my stomach at the thought of being close with Kirsten.

"I had to go along with my girlfriend. And besides, Grayson couldn't have done it himself since Larry has that video of him."

I'm relieved Grayson still thinks Larry has the video. But my Zen is short-lived because Justin adds, "At least he *had* that video. I overheard him and Wyatt arguing about it."

*Shit!*

I do my best not to react. "Okay, what about being racist?"

He cringes. "I'm really not racist."

"Right. That's what Grayson told me too—before repeating to me, on video, as it turned out, that I was a brown boy."

"No, seriously." Justin leans in, and I instinctively scoot back. "Like I said, I was making fun of you. Seemed like the easiest way to go."

"Besides the fact that you shouldn't make fun of people—period— throwing racist shit around is lower than low. What would that college you're gunning for think if they knew what a jackass you've been? Universities usually have a zero tolerance for that shit."

He blanches. "You're not going to tell the scouts, are you?"

I shrug.

"I'm sorry. I'll quit it with the insults," he says quickly. "I was being stupid . . ."

"Are you only saying that because you're afraid I'll snitch?"

He bows his head. "No . . . I really am. Sorry, I mean. It's just that I never understood people who want to be different. Why put a target on your head, you know? Why can't you just be like everyone else? Stay on your own tier."

"News flash: some people don't have a choice about being different. They don't put the targets on their own heads. It's other people that do that. They're the ones with the choice about what to do with the target."

Justin's voice is barely audible. "Yeah, I know."

"Do you? Do you know you're one of those people?"

His breaths rumble from deep within his chest. "I guess I do now." He whispers, "I'm sorry."

Though I still doubt the full sincerity of his apology, it is a step in the right direction. Besides, I never imagined I'd hear any of the bullies say those words to me, let alone Justin.

I grab one of the towels and wipe the sweat off my face. Even with the locker room emptying out, it's still too stuffy inside. "So. Justin. What do you want to get out of skateboarding? You want to be faster on your feet? Is that it?"

He lifts his gaze and whispers, "And maybe have some fun again."

I lean forward, not sure if I heard him correctly. "What? What do you mean?"

"All the football practice. Classes. A girlfriend. Lots of times I'm tired. Football used to be fun. Now it's mostly just work. But if I want to go to college, I have to grind it out. It's what's expected of me." He clenches his fist and pounds it against his tree log of a thigh. "I get angry a lot."

"Well, yeah. You don't sound too happy," I finally say after a beat of silence.

"Angie—Angelo, help me out. Skating might be like working out but without the pressure. I want to learn to do it. Please."

I bite my lip, frowning. What are the chances he'll do another 180 once he gets what he wants and become Grayson's yes boy again, insulting, nasty?

As if reading my mind, he groans, "I'm desperate. I need this scholarship. And Grayson's still my friend and my teammate. I'm still going to be his buddy. But I promise to lay off you and your friends."

I waver, but . . . "Well, even if I wanted to help you, I couldn't." My mind flashes to the warehouses, which are probably covered in yellow police tape by now, and then to a very empty Sloppy's Pit Stop. "If you haven't noticed, I'm completely busy being punished. I won't have time to teach you. Why don't you ask Wyatt to help you since you're hell-bent on being as fast as him?"

"I don't want the student when I can have the teacher."

I grunt.

"Besides, I can pull strings," he throws back without hesitation. "Get Coach Shappey to lighten up a bit."

I'm sure he can.

"I also have to work at Sloppy's Pit Stop, which you should be happy to hear is doing pretty badly." I gingerly fold a towel and smack it on top of the pile. "Who knows? Maybe I'll even be out of your hair because I'll have to move again."

"Let me repeat: Grayson was the one who wanted those flyers pulled. I don't want Sloppy's Pit Stop to close." He smiles. "I like your fries. If I knew you were giving them out for free at the event, maybe I would've come."

I snort. "Miss a game? Okay."

"And didn't you hear anything I just said? Why would I want you gone when I need your help?"

"I don't even have anywhere to teach you," I argue. "Sheriff Evans took away the one good place."

"So we'll find another place." There's no denying this kid's used to getting his way. "But preferably one where people can't see me skate. I still have a reputation to keep."

"You're not winning points here, bud."

"Angelo, please—"

I can't believe I'm actually considering helping him. Damn my parents for teaching me empathy.

"Justin, you coming?" Grayson's voice booms from the other side of the lockers. He peeks around the corner, hair dripping from the shower, and throws me an evil grin. "Why you talking to this idiot?"

He's looking for a reaction from me, but I don't flinch.

"Uh, I was . . . telling him to get out of my way." Justin clears his throat and jumps to his feet. The bench rattles underneath me, knocking over my pile of towels. "Sorry," Justin mumbles to me.

I roll my eyes.

Grayson heads to the door, never taking his eyes off me. "Don't bother apologizing to him. My dad says he deserves the punishment."

Justin doesn't respond. He grabs his gym bag, falling behind Grayson. Right when he makes it to the exit, he shoots me one last look and mouths, "Think about it."

# 30

I replay our conversation in my head. It's nearly eight o'clock, and with no customers there's nothing left to do but start closing for the night. Too bad my mind won't stop flying.

Groaning, I grab a bulging garbage bag, filled mostly with my trash, and head out the back door. Tiny flies circle the dim light bulb above the rusted dumpster. I take a moment and stare at the excess parking lot. Dad's newest, not to mention optimistic, addition rivals the restaurant in size, making the emptiness even more pathetic. Ever since it was first paved, Dad would look outside, praying for a car or two or three thousand to pull in. None ever did. Now it just serves as a grim reminder that we're no better off than we were at Rivera's Kusina.

If only there were some gaps or ramps around here. Then it'd be useful. Holding my breath, I grunt and toss the bag into the bin. Colorless juice drips from the plastic, falling onto my shirt.

Gross. Grimacing, I kick the dumpster as if it were its fault and drag my feet back inside. I'm so focused on the wet spot I don't realize I'm no longer alone.

"Rivera."

*"Ahh!"* I stumble, hitting my side against the fryer, which fortunately is turned off.

"Damn, you're jumpy." Kirsten laughs, lifting herself onto the counter. Kicking her boots against the wood, she grabs a gumball from the jar.

"Kirsten!" I don't know whether to laugh, cry, or demand she never leave me again.

I take a hesitant step toward her. "What are you doing here? Why haven't you called me? How come I haven't seen you at school?"

The questions fly out of my mouth, but what I really want to tell her is that I missed her.

She grips the edge of the counter and throws her head back. "To answer your first question, I was driving myself crazy sitting at home. You know my dad changed the Wi-Fi password? As if taking my phone wasn't bad enough."

"Oh, he took your phone?" It's almost a relief to hear. Hopefully, that explains why she hasn't answered any of my texts.

"He really doesn't want me to speak to you." She has the decency to look embarrassed.

"Great," I mutter.

"As for school, you know how he's the town's main real estate agent?"

"How can I forget?"

"He sold pretty much all the OPHS teachers their houses. I was afraid he might have roped one or twelve of them to spy on us." She shakes her head feverishly. "I couldn't take the chance."

I nod. "I guess that explains why Coach Shappey kept you outside."

"Maybe." Kirsten rakes her fingers through her hair and sighs. "My dad's been such a monster."

"Wait, he didn't hurt you or anything, did he?" I clench my fists.

"No!" Kirsten's eyes widen. "Nothing like that. I just meant that he's been extra hard on me."

"Oh." I release my breath.

"You know how I said that he stopped talking to me because of what happened with cheerleading? Well, me being hauled into Sherriff Evans's office was the trigger he needed to unload everything he kept bottled up." She rolls her eyes and sighs. "How I'm a disgrace to the family. How I'm tarnishing the Nelson name. How stupid I am for making all these mistakes that might ruin my life." She leans forward and wags a finger at me. "So you know what I told him? That I don't care what he thinks because I'm through going along with what *he* wants for my life. Mistakes or not, I'm happy and that's all that matters."

"Wow." I nod proudly. "That's so cool you said that. How'd he react?"

"He was mad, of course. Basically, grounded me for life."

I wince. "And your mom?"

To my surprise she breaks out into a smile. "I think it was the first time she actually listened to me. Obviously, she's not happy about what happened, but who knew all it took was getting arrested for her to hear me out?" She giggles and explains, "She told me that she'd get over me not being part of the squad."

"That's great."

"But she hasn't put my uniform away yet. Baby steps, I guess."

"Baby steps are better than nothing."

"You got that right." Kirsten locks eyes with me and quickly loses her smile. She clears her throat and in a cautious tone says, "Angelo, listen. I know things have been weird with us ever since . . ."

"Ever since . . . ," I repeat with a sad smile.

"But that's why I'm here."

"Why you snuck out?"

"I wanted to clear the air. Make things not so weird anymore . . . let things be normal."

"What's normal to you?" I dare to ask.

"It's . . ." She swallows hard. "Um, spending time with you."

"Oh. Okay." I should be happy. It's what I wanted. But somehow it doesn't feel like enough.

She nods. "Okay."

The rain cloud that is my own parents' disapproval hangs above my head. "Don't take this the wrong way, because I'm really happy to see you. Thrilled even. But why did you take the risk to come here? We could get in big trouble if any of our parents find out."

"First of all, my parents don't know I snuck out. They aren't home. They're at some charity function. And secondly, I know yours aren't here now. I called a few minutes ago to make sure they weren't working tonight."

My eyes bug out. "That was you who asked for a manager?"

"I changed my voice." She grins. "We have nothing to worry about."

Feeling a bit lighter, I say, "Actually, it's great you stopped by."

"Oh?" She perks up.

"Something strange happened when I was doing my time in the locker room after school today. I need to talk to you about it."

"Oh." She pouts for a bit, but her expression is fleeting. She shoots me a teasing smile. "Are you talking about having to smell all those behemoths?"

"I'm sorry?"

She cringes and plugs her nose. "It stunk on the field. I can't imagine what the locker room smelled like."

"Like flowers," I deadpan.

Kirsten snickers. "Then maybe we should trade jobs."

"Justin talked to me today," I say point-blank.

"He did? Justin?" Like I expected, Kirsten looks shocked. "About what?" She shakes her head, smacking her tongue in disgust. "Don't tell me he was trying to bully you again."

"No. Sad to say, it wouldn't have been weird if he did."

"Okay . . . so, what happened?"

I lift myself onto the counter beside her, scooting close. When our thighs touch, the tips of my ears burn, but I manage to keep my voice steady. "He wants me to teach him how to skate."

"He what?" She stares at me.

I nod. "Yeah, you heard right."

"And you told him no, right?" She scans my face. When I don't answer right away, she pulls back in horror. *"Right?"*

I wince. "Not exactly."

She jumps off the counter and whirls around. "Angelo! How can you even consider it? The guy's an animal!"

I jump down from the counter, landing just inches in front of her. I place both my hands on her shoulders and look her in the eyes. "You've seen our friends change for the better. We both have. And didn't we hold our event to incite a change?"

"I thought we held it to get back at Grayson," she snaps.

I shut my eyes. "That too. But the original idea was to take the team down a notch. Teaching Justin to skate would take the team down more than a notch. It'll topple a hierarchy."

"But Angelo . . ." She shakes her head.

I release her shoulders and step back. "Justin may not be an outsider by your original definition, but aren't we all outsiders in our own ways?"

"Wow." She whistles. "That is the corniest thing I think I've heard come out of your mouth."

"I get that this is coming out of left field—"

"And that it's freaking weird?"

"I didn't expect you to jump at the idea," I say truthfully. "Seriously. I didn't. But think about it, okay? Maybe getting Justin on board is just what OPHS needs to finally break out of tradition."

Silence blankets the two of us. Outside the wind has risen. It howls, slamming the back door against the wall.

"I guess it's up to you," Kirsten says so softly I have to strain to hear her. She lifts her head and says louder, "You're the teacher, after all."

"Nah. Remember your piece? It isn't *Just Me* anymore. It's *Just Us.*" A lazy grin spreads across my face. "It's *our* call."

My pulse races as Kirsten stares at my mouth. She smiles. After a beat, she shakes her head in a hurry. "You know what? This is too serious of a conversation for me and so not the reason why I broke out tonight."

"We need to talk about it," I point out.

"I know. And now that we did, we need to reward ourselves with something fun. We can figure things out later." Her eyes twinkle mischievously. Like I thought before—this girl is dangerous.

I sigh. "Kirsten, we can't get into any more trouble."

"Hey, we'll only get in trouble if we get caught." She grabs my hand and tugs me to the front doors. "C'mon. I'm breaking you out."

"I can't go." I take out my phone and glance at the time. "I still have thirty minutes until my shift ends."

She drops my hand and flails her arms wildly. "Look at this place. It's dead."

"Don't remind me." I grimace, scanning the empty dining room. It's been a ghost town all day, with only a sprinkling of customers coming in during the dinner rush. If I can even call it a rush. Business has been so bad that we've had to close Sloppy's early every night so that my parents won't have to pay staff. Mom's even cut back on Chad's hours. I haven't seen him in days. Weirdly enough, I'm starting to miss him.

"No, what I mean is you're about to close anyway." Kirsten elbows me in the ribs. "What's keeping you from going with me?"

I tap my chin for effect. "Oh, I don't know . . . *my parents?*"

"Okay, I didn't want to have to do this," she says, making a show of putting her hands on her hips and looking stern. "But you leave me no choice. I guess I have to pull out the big guns and ruin your surprise."

I arch an eyebrow. "What surprise?"

"What do you think about a little late-night road trip to the beach?"

"Are you crazy?" I gasp, though the idea of a beach completely thrills me. "Isn't that like two hours away?"

"Almost three," she admits. "That why it'd be best to leave now. We need to hurry if we're going to squeeze in any fun."

"Fun? Are you kidding me?" I say. "We're already in a crapload of trouble. I don't think having fun is a really good idea right now."

I expect Kirsten to argue back or even lash out at me. Instead there's a slight tremble to her bottom lip. "Please, Rivera," she pleads. "I know you don't understand right now, but I need this . . . *you* need this."

And just like that, all my resolve melts away.

As if sensing me weakening, she adds, "I got a cooler of food and some towels in the car. Let's go before it gets too late."

I throw my head back and let out a loud breath. "My parents will freak out beyond belief if I don't come home. Picture police officers and news crews."

"That's easy. Go home first. Make an appearance and sneak out the window like I did that one time."

The only time she was ever at my house.

Though I'm dying to feel sand between my toes, I pose a final argument. "Wouldn't it be smarter to wait until this whole thing blows over to visit the beach?"

"We deserve a little treat after everything we've been through." I hate how her confidence causes mine to bloom. "Besides, I need a break from everything so I'm planning to go regardless. You might as well come with me. If I go down, we go down together."

"Guess that's the running theme of our friendship, huh?"

Kirsten's eyes dance in amusement. "Stop stalling. Let's go! Your house first, then the beach."

I feel like I should argue more, but I can't.

She dances on the tips of her toes in excitement. "C'mon, already. I know you want to."

I whip off my apron and toss it on the counter. After a brief check to make sure anything that can catch on fire is turned off, I flick off the lights, lock the front doors, and lead Kirsten out the back door. Kirsten and I jump onto our boards, laughing the whole way back to my house.

I stare at this wonder of a girl. She really has turned my life upside down.

# 31

"Are you sure you know where you're going?" I stick my head out the car window, thankful to be breathing non–Ocean Pointe air for once.

"Oh, yeah. I used to drive there with . . ." Kirsten takes a hand off the steering wheel and waves it. "I've driven there plenty of times before."

I know she was going to say Grayson. Once again, the jock pops in where he's not wanted.

"Besides, my GPS will get us there," she adds weakly.

"Yeah, that's good." I nod.

I look hungrily out the window, watching the trees fly by as we hum down the empty highway. I can't wait to see the beach again. Smell it. Hear it. I picture crashing waves, remember how close we're getting, and instantly feel better.

Silence once again envelops us, but it's not the suffocating kind.

I lean back against the leather seat and grimace as my arms stick against the material despite the cool wind wafting in through the open window.

Nervous sweats. That's what Mackabi used to call the uncontrollable wetness of my armpits before competitions. But I can't help it.

If Mom and Dad find out I've snuck out, I'm beyond dead. Also, I'm alone with Kirsten again. I'm beyond excited.

It's been almost three hours since we left Ocean Pointe. We take an exit off the highway and drive past different restaurants and stores. Then, in almost a blink of an eye, the scenery changes. Multicolored beach houses line one side of the road, with the boardwalk on the other. Beside the boardwalk is the sandy beach and the water—God how I missed it!

I keep my head hanging out the window like a golden retriever. I smile, inhale the sharp air. My heart speeds up. I'm ready to jump out of my seat.

"You okay?" Kirsten glances at me with a knowing smirk. "This a bit much for you?"

I pull back from the window and settle into my seat, trying for a nonchalant shrug. "Eh, it isn't the Pacific."

Kirsten snorts and pulls into the first parking lot we come to. She unbuckles her seat belt and twists in her seat to look at me.

My face flushes. "Why are you looking at me like that?"

With a grin, she raises an imaginary camera to her face and taps the unseen button with her finger. "Just taking a mental photo of someone who's finally in their element."

"Nice. I already have a whole album of mental photos of you." The words slip out of my mouth before I can stop them, but fortunately, Kirsten isn't weirded out.

She beams. "Oh yeah? Good pictures I hope."

"You painting? Skating? Oh yeah."

It's after eleven, but the full moon might as well be the burning sun. The whole area is lit up so brightly, we don't even need our flashlights to see our way. We walk quietly toward the beach, savoring the distant rumble of crashing waves. This beach is a lot different than the ones I grew up with. The smell is odd. Less metallic. Even the heavy breeze feels strange. But hey. Different doesn't have to mean bad or even worse. It can be just as good, if not better.

We finally make it to the edge of the boardwalk.

I just stand and look. Kirsten's arm wraps around my waist, but I'm so captivated by the foaming whitewash, I almost don't notice. "Are you having fun yet?" she asks.

My throat constricts as I admire the moonlit waves. "Definitely."

I can hear the smile in her voice. "Good. Now let's get you down to the water."

I don't waste another moment. Whipping off my shoes, I jump right into the cold sand and wiggle my toes. I throw my head back with a loud, "Ahhh!"

Kirsten giggles. She steps off the boardwalk, rips off her boots, and twists and turns her hips, burying her feet into the sand up to her ankles. "I had no idea the beach can be so exhilarating."

Maybe it's the smell of the fishy air or the roar of the waves. Whatever it is, I finally let go of the insecurities I've felt since my breakup with Amanda. Grinning, I shoot Kirsten a wink. "It's probably because you never went with me."

Under the full moon, I can make out the mischievous twinkle in Kirsten's eyes. "Then what do you say we head for the water and find out how much greater this trip can be?"

"You're talking my language, Nelson." I quickly grab her hand, give it a squeeze, and practically drag her after me across the beach.

I don't know who's more excited, me or her. Kirsten tosses the one beach towel she remembered to grab onto the dry sand before we stop at the water's edge. I stare at the crashing indigo and wiggle my toes into the wet sand as the foamy water pulls away from me.

Kirsten's still holding my hand tightly, but she's an arm's length behind me, pulling back as the waves approach and then ebb. "How cold is the water?"

I shrug despite practically losing feeling in my toes. "Pretty cold."

"You seem so nonchalant about it."

"The Pacific's cold year-round." I glance over my shoulder and grin at the surprised look on her face. "Yeah, you wouldn't expect it because it's California. But that's the reason some people use wetsuits all year."

Kirsten takes a hesitant step forward, glancing down at our bare legs. "But we're wearing shorts, not wetsuits."

"We don't need wetsuits." I drop her hand and surprise us both by ripping off my threadbare shirt. Yelping, I jump into knee-high water and with chattering teeth grind out, "N-not too-oo-oo c-cold a-at a-ll."

Kirsten glances at me, then at the water, and then back at me.

"C'mon in, you wimp!" I slap the surface of the water, sending some foam flying her way.

She screeches, jumping back. "You'll pay for that, Rivera!"

I hold my breath, waiting to see what she does next. But nothing could've prepared me for the sight of her lifting her top.

The moon shines against her creamy skin, accentuating every line and curve along her torso. She yanks her shirt off completely and shakes out her white hair. Shooting me a smile, she tosses her top onto the sand beside mine and places her hands on her hips, showing off that damn gorgeous polka-dotted bra.

"Didn't think I had the guts, did you?" Losing her bravado, she squeals and hops up and down, screaming, "The wind's cold!"

"I . . . uh . . . I . . . uh . . ." I can't think much of anything with her jumping around like that.

I stare as she takes off her watch and jams it into the front pocket of her jeans and then wiggles slowly and almost seductively out of her pants. Almost as if giving me my own private show. But any seductive energy completely vanishes once she rushes into the water and screams even louder. "Ahh! I didn't know the water would be freezing!"

She thrashes around, splashing water into my face; blinking quickly, still standing knee-deep in the cold water, I shake my head.

"Wow! You're right. Didn't know you had the guts, Nelson."

An evil idea pops into my head as I watch her twirl around, still shrieking with the cold. I stalk forward with my hands outstretched.

Kirsten spots me moving toward her. Her eyes widen as she backs away. "Don't even think about it, Rivera."

"Think about what?" I tease as I take a running leap and tackle her into waist-deep water.

The cold water knocks the wind right out of me. I hug Kirsten tighter as the waves thrash above our heads and the current wraps around our bodies, pushing us closer together. Her skin is smooth against mine. Gasping, we resurface in shock and amusement and scramble to our feet.

Coughing, Kirsten slaps me against the chest. "Jerk!"

I can tell she's joking. "Ah, the water's not bad."

"You really think so?"

Before I can answer, *she* tackles *me*, and I lose my breath again as the cold water takes its turn to pound against my chest. I get back up as fast as I can and find her already standing again, laughing at me. "Okay, okay, we're even."

She crosses her arms, hugging herself tightly. Her jaw trembles as a sharp breeze cuts through us. "W-we sh-should've b-brought more t-towels."

She's probably right. But I was in such a hurry to get down here I forgot to grab another one.

"It doesn't matter. Everything's perfect the way it is," I say truthfully.

The moon continues to cast an angelic glow around Kirsten's head. I've never seen anyone so beautiful, and though I want to tell her, my mouth can't form the words.

"Why are you staring at me?" she yells above the roaring waves.

"Kirsten, I . . ." I gulp, shaking away my nerves. "I'll find a way to keep you warm."

She frowns a bit, as if it's not what she was expecting to hear. She nods and starts wading to shore. "Okay. Let's warm up."

"Turn around," I yell above the crashing waves.

She throws me a look of confusion. "What?"

"Keep your eye on the water or a wave might knock you over—"

I barely get the words out before a thigh-high wave hits Kirsten on the back of her legs, knocking her forward off her feet. I push through the water. The wave pulls away and I help her back up, wrapping my arm around her shoulders.

"You okay?" I speak into her ear.

She nods, coughing out, "Y-yeah."

"C'mon."

I keep my arm around her all the way back to the shore. I don't let go, even as we turn to sit on the sand. We opt not to put our clothes back on, going for the best way to warm up. With body heat. And the one beach towel Kirsten brought. We sit side by side, wrapping it around us. I grin down at Kirsten's head, which is pressed up against my shoulder. The tangled white strands of her hair stick to my still-damp skin.

"Angelo, I have a confession," she says.

"Oh yeah?" I try to sound casual, but she sounds so serious. She called me Angelo and not Rivera. My heart drums hard. Can she feel it through my chest?

"I planned on bringing you here so you'd see that you don't need to go back to California to experience all the things you love. You have a beach. You have skating. And you have your friends." She shifts against me and looks up at my face. "You have me."

I blink in surprise. "Kirsten, I don't want to—"

"Do you still consider San Diego your home?" She interrupts me before I can tell her what I've already figured out. I don't want to leave anymore.

"In a way it'll always be my home," I answer truthfully. "But—"

"What about Amanda?"

"Amanda?" I swallow hard and shake my head. "What about her?"

Her next question floors me. "Do you still love her? You keep going on and on about beating Tyler, but it's because you hate that he's your ex's new boyfriend, huh?"

"I don't love Amanda," I say firmly. "As for Tyler, I do hate that he's her new boyfriend, but not because I want Amanda back. It's because he beats me in everything. Winning competitions, going pro—even my love life. I told you he was my rival, but honestly that's not true, because if we were true rivals, we'd be more equally matched. I wouldn't always come in second place."

"You've always come in first place with me," Kirsten says into my shoulder.

My breaths quicken in anticipation. "Really?"

"Isn't it obvious?"

"Honestly, I don't read girls very well," I say with a wince.

"You don't read us well, or you didn't want to see what was right in front of you?" Kirsten asks slowly.

My mouth goes dry. "I guess I didn't want to see it."

"Why?"

"Because after Amanda I didn't want to be burned again." I gently push a tendril of hair away from her face. "You were also my first real friend in Ocean Pointe who made this place tolerable. I didn't want to screw things up between us."

"Angelo," Kirsten says carefully. "At the warehouse that one day . . . I thought you were going to kiss me."

"I wanted to," I admit.

Her breath hitches. "And you didn't because . . . ?"

"Like I said, I was scared."

"Are you . . . are you still scared?"

I bow my head forward. We're nose to nose. My heart beats harder as Kirsten's coconut scent swirls around my nostrils. My gaze drops to her smiling lips.

I swallow audibly. "Kirsten, I'm not trying to move back to San Diego anymore."

She straightens, twists as if she's going to look at me, but then melts back into me. "You're not? Since when?"

"Since I realized I have everything I need here. The beach. Skating. My friends." I lick my lips and whisper, "And you."

Just like in the warehouse, I want to kiss her. I've wanted to kiss Kirsten from the first moment we bared our souls to each other in the warehouse, and the feeling only intensifies the more time I spend with her.

It's about time I finally stop just wishing I can.

Pushing all second-guessing aside, I finally lean forward. I press my lips against hers. She takes a sharp breath against my mouth, stiffening for a second. Quickly, she relaxes and kisses me back, raking her fingers through my wet hair, tugging at the ends lightly.

I've had kisses before. Some good and some not so good. But none of them compare to the way Kirsten's soft lips complement my own as she nibbles and licks and caresses. In an instant we're no longer cold but hot—scorching hot.

I lose track of how long we spend kissing. Maybe time stands still for all I know. Or care.

I hug Kirsten tight and press a kiss against her cheek, trailing my lips down to her jaw and moving back up to her mouth again. Though I could probably spend forever making out with Kirsten and feeling her smooth skin pressed against mine, after a while the passion gives way to a feeling of utter peace. My eyelids start to grow heavy.

We lie back on the cool sand, turning so we're on our sides facing each other. I can't stop peppering soft kisses against this amazing girl's lips, cheeks, her neck. Kirsten smiles back at me, and there's nothing like it. She places her head on my chest and hugs me tight. I breathe slowly, so contented, and close my eyes.

# 32

W hat time is it?" My eyelids flash open. I jump up, knocking
Kirsten into the sand.

"*Oomph*. Rivera!" Sleepily, she scrambles to her feet, brushing sand
from her skin. "What's wrong?"

"We fell asleep! We need to drive home!" I grab on to my head. "My
parents are gonna flip! I'll never see the light of day again!"

Kirsten shivers and grabs her pants off our pile of clothes and digs
into the front pocket for her watch. She frowns down at the face and
tells me, "It's okay. Calm down."

"Calm down?" I repeat in disbelief.

"It's only just before five." She flails an arm above her head. "See?
The sun's not even out yet."

I take in the dark sky, relaxing for a bit. But before I'm fully comfortable, it hits me. "*It's almost five?* That means we won't get home
until eight. Which is when I usually leave for school. My parents will
definitely notice I'm not home if I'm not moving around, getting ready
for school by seven."

"I'll get us home by seven." Kirsten's already scooped up her top
and pants and is running down the beach, kicking up sand behind her.
She yells back at me, "But we have to leave now. Hurry!"

"Last time you told me to go somewhere with you, we ended up falling asleep on the beach," I grumble as I grab my shirt and run to catch up.

Now this is about the time in a movie where a hard-core song plays as our car zips in and around traffic. But no. Instead, we don't turn on the radio, and there aren't many other cars. I break out in a cold sweat, continuously glancing at the clock and at the GPS's predicted arrival time. I want to tell Kirsten to hurry up, but I also don't want to get a ticket or crash.

Kirsten grips the steering wheel like it's a life preserver, never taking her eyes off the road. Except when she briefly glances at me. "Will you just calm down and trust me? We're not gonna get in trouble."

"You sound so sure about that."

"Because I am." She loosens her grip a bit. "I may hate driving this thing, but I'm a great driver. Just sit back and stop worrying."

I slump against the seat, relaxing slightly. "Fine."

"And just stay calm." She lifts a hand off the steering wheel to pat my thigh, but I'm too high-strung to enjoy it. "While you're at it, try to grab some sleep. I got this."

"I don't know how you think I can nap at a time like this."

Sighing, I prop my elbow against the window, resting my chin on top of my fingers, and stare at the increasing rush hour traffic.

~

I wake up as the car jerks to a stop. I blink sleepily as Kirsten unbuckles my seat belt.

"It's almost seven thirty!" she growls, reaching over me to open the passenger door.

My head snaps from left to right, taking in my surroundings. We're across the street from my house. I stare at her. "How the heck did you get here so fast?"

She shakes her head. "Never mind. You need to hurry up and get inside. It doesn't look like anyone's awake yet. It's the perfect time to sneak in."

I don't need to be told twice. I open the door, but before I get out of the car, I plant a soft kiss on Kirsten's lips. They curve to a smile as they meet mine, but the euphoria's short-lived. Her palms push against my chest as she pulls away.

"Enough," she scolds. "We'll have plenty of time for that later."

I jump out of the car, slamming the door in one swift movement. For a second, I think Kirsten might have called after me, but if she did, I'll take a chance it can wait. I sprint across the street and then run around the corner of the house to my window, which I kept unlocked. Prying it open as quickly and quietly as possible, I dive in headfirst, somersaulting onto the floor. I narrowly miss Nollie's bed, but she still jerks away and barks in protest.

"Shhh!" I cringe. But Nollie will not let up with her high-pitched howls. I scramble to my feet and turn toward my bed—and my heart stops beating.

"Angelo? *Anak?* Where have you been?" As Mom rises from my bed, her bob haircut swings.

I groan in dismay at getting caught and steel myself for a tirade of harsh words, but Mom reaches out for me, bringing me in for a hug.

"Something bad happened while you weren't here, *anak.*" She sniffles, pressing her nose into my chest.

I stiffen. "Bad? What happened? Is Dad okay? Where is he?"

She pulls away. Her eyes are red, like she's been crying. "He's fine. He's at the restaurant."

"He's at Sloppy's?" I scratch my head. "Why? It doesn't open until eleven."

"Oh, Angelo," Mom wails. "Someone broke into the restaurant."

This is when a camera would zoom in on my face, blurring everything behind me so the viewer has no choice but to focus on the horror on my face. "Did they steal anything? What did they do?"

"They didn't steal anything." She releases me and snaps, "But I was worried you went back to the restaurant last night and got kidnapped!"

Ah, there's the yelling I was expecting.

"I didn't get kidnapped!"

"Obviously."

"Mom, if you were so worried, why didn't you call me?" I scold, though I have no right to be annoyed. "Then you would've known I was okay."

"I tried. No one answered." Mom narrows her eyes.

"It was probably on silent."

"You didn't return my messages either."

I pat against my pockets. Nothing. "Oh . . . shoot." I just remembered. I left my phone in Kirsten's car when we parked to walk to the beach.

"Shoot's right." Mom's eyes relax, losing her threatening expression. But just as quickly she looks as sad and disappointed as I've ever seen her. "Angelo, you never sneak out. This isn't like you."

"I just wanted to have a little fun, Mom," I try to explain, but she isn't listening.

Her head drops and she massages her forehead, kneading the deep lines. "I thought Ocean Pointe would be good for us. A small town, a cheap business to start over . . . but maybe moving here was a bad idea after all. Maybe our business doing poorly is a sign. Maybe you misbehaving is one too."

It's like she punched me in the gut.

"Mom," I say carefully.

"What were your dad and I thinking? You're still developing!"

"*Mom!*" I shift uneasily.

"And we ripped you from your home," she practically sings in dismay. "Ever since you were arrested—"

"Technically I wasn't," I interrupt, but she isn't having it.

"I've been doing a lot of thinking." She twists her thin hands together. Since when did they start looking so frail? "I think it might be a good idea to send you back to San Diego. I bet having your *lola* and all your *titos* and *titas* around you will make you think twice about breaking the rules."

I'm beyond shell-shocked. "Mom, no! You can't make me move again." I've blamed karma before, but this is ridiculous. "I don't want to leave Ocean Pointe. I want to stay here."

Mom scans my face, pausing to scrutinize my tired eyes. "I didn't expect this reaction from you." She grabs my chin and pulls my head toward her face. "Are you on drugs?" She peers at my right eye. "Is that what kind of fun you were having?"

"No!" I pry her hand off my chin and take a giant step back. "Of course I'm not. Hugs not drugs, right?"

Mom presses her lips together in a thin line and shakes her head. "You know what? Never mind. We'll talk about this later."

"No, Mom. I want to talk about this now. I don't want to move again."

But she's through listening and moves to the door. Nollie, that traitor, follows after her. "Come, Angelo. We're going to Sloppy's. The cops want a statement from you."

"B-but what about school?" I glance at the digital clock on my nightstand. The bright red numbers flash 7:40 as if taunting me.

"I already called and said you'd be late. Let's go."

It's the second time in twenty-four hours that someone's told me to go with them. Maybe if I'd said no the first time, I wouldn't be in this situation now.

# 33

We pull up to Sloppy's Pit Stop. My two pals, Sheriff and Deputy Evans, and another guy are waiting in the parking lot. I bite back a groan and exit the car. I'm sure they'll put the blame on me somehow. Fortunately (if that's even the right way to describe it), according to Mom nothing was stolen. But our restaurant was heavily vandalized.

"Well, if it isn't Angelo." Deputy Evans spits on the ground, stomping on the bubbling mess. "Can't say I'm happy to see you."

His dad, grinning, throws out his hand, whacking him against the chest. "You got that right. Twice in one week, Mr. Rivera. Doesn't look so good."

My vision narrows, tingeing in red. "Someone broke into our restaurant, Sheriff. I agree it doesn't look good. For my family and me. Don't you think I deserve a little consideration here?"

"Depends on what you know."

The double glass doors of the restaurant fling open. Dad walks out looking like a disheveled mess, like he just rolled out of bed. Which he probably did. His wig is crooked. His shirt is wrinkled. I'm surprised he had the mind to slip on his favorite pair of New Balances and isn't out here wearing *tsinelas*, his slippers.

The other guy in the parking lot, a nicely dressed man who I'm assuming is the insurance agent based on the giant logo plastered across his name tag, is busy flipping through pages on his clipboard. Dad rubs at his eyebrows and looks over, seeing me for the first time. He gasps, "Angelo. Where have you been?"

Name-Tag Man peers at me over the tip of his crooked nose. "Your son, I presume."

I step up and extend my hand to him. "It's Angelo, sir."

"Tom Jenkins." Unlike our school principal, Mr. Jenkins isn't one for niceties. He barely shakes my hand, dropping it as soon as deemed polite. "I understand you had the closing shift last night?"

I nod. "Usually there's at least two of us, but because business has been slow it was only me."

Dad clears his throat in embarrassment. "It was also part of his punishment."

The deputy and sheriff elbow each other with silent chuckles. I clench my fists.

Mr. Jenkins nods. "Did anything out of the ordinary happen last night? During your shift? Or maybe you saw something as you were leaving?"

"Shouldn't they be asking me this?" I shoot our town's finest a look of disgust.

"Angelo!" Mom scolds.

I roll my eyes. "No, sir. Nothing out of the ordinary happened. I didn't see anything weird either."

"No?" This time Sheriff Evans does step up to the plate and asks, "No one interesting came in?"

I frown, trying to decipher the look on his face. There's no way he can know Kirsten stopped by . . . is there?

Either way, I know lying will just make things worse, so I cough out, "A-a friend stopped by."

Mom's head whips around in a fury. "Who? Who stopped by?"

"A friend," I insist. If they think I'm dry snitching, they have another thing coming.

"The same friend you snuck out with last night?" Mom demands.

"Maybe . . ." I wince, waiting for Sheriff Evans's response. San Diego had a citywide curfew for teenagers. To my relief, he doesn't comment. For once Ocean Pointe's backward way of doing things works with me.

Mr. Jenkins clears his throat, commanding our attention. "Well, I think I have all I need." He stuffs his clipboard into the leather manpurse at his side. "I'll process this claim. It shouldn't take long. I'll call you as soon as I have it done. Maybe even later this morning."

Dad's defeated expression pains me. His Adam's apple bounces as he shakes the insurance agent's hand. "Thanks for getting here so quickly."

"Ocean Pointe doesn't get many complaints," he replies.

The sheriff waits until Mr. Jenkins is in his car before addressing my family again. He places his thick hands on his hips and stares at us one by one. "From what I see, this looks like a random act. But I'd like to know if you folks have had any problems with anyone in town."

"No," Mom answers at the same time Dad says, "Of course not."

But I'm nearly shaking, I want to laugh so hard. "Where do I begin?" Four pairs of eyes burn into me. I gulp but stand firm. "Yes, I've had problems."

Sheriff Evans scratches his nose and uses the same finger to point at me. "Who've you been having trouble with, son?" I open my mouth to respond, but he talks over me. "But let me remind you, any false accusations can land you in some serious trouble."

Something tells me he won't take me blaming his son very lightly. I decide to go for the more neutral approach. "Some kids at school."

Sheriff's eyebrows pull together. "What kind of problems do you have with them?"

"Oh, you know, insults, physical altercations, being threatened."

My mom's hand flies to her chest. "You were threatened? Why didn't you tell me?"

I merely shrug, and she gasps in horror. "That bruise on your face from a few weeks ago . . . I assumed it was from skateboarding. It wasn't, was it?"

"I never fall. Unless someone makes me fall." I look at Sheriff Evans. We lock gazes in what feels like the world's worst staring contest.

"Did someone make you fall, son?" He examines me quizzically.

"What do you think?"

He clears his throat. "Angelo, even the littlest bit of information might help me figure out what happened last night."

"What happened here is someone messed with our restaurant," I snap.

The sheriff ignores my jab. "Now, I understand if you're too scared to tell me who's been bothering you. But like I said, any bit of information helps."

Scared? Is he shitting me?

After all the crap I've faced since I moved here, and after everything I've had to do to make this place enjoyable, there is not one scared bone in my body.

And just like that, I no longer want to take a neutral approach. "Why don't you ask your fine boy what he was doing last night?" Knowing that Larry's video is erased and that Grayson was the mastermind behind the whole flyer debacle, I figure the agreement is null and void, so I add, "Maybe use the words 'punch,' 'locker,' and 'video' to get it out of him."

Mom nudges me. "What are you talking about?"

I shake my head as the sheriff motions to his son. "Not that son," I grumble.

While Sheriff and Deputy Evans talk together in low voices, Mom takes the opportunity to pull Dad aside and whisper, "We need to get Angelo out of here."

"Yeah." Dad sews his eyes shut and rubs against his neck. "Shouldn't he be at school?"

"No. I mean out of Ocean Pointe." My dad's eyes fly open. "We need to send him back to San Diego."

"What? Why would you want to do that, Mila?"

Mom bows her head, sadly shaking it from side to side. "This place isn't good for him. He's getting in trouble; he's getting hurt and—"

"And he's standing right here," I growl. "And *he* does not want to leave Ocean Pointe."

Mom's eyes well up. "What other choice do we have, Angelo? I see now that this place isn't good for you. And your dad does too."

Black-and-white.

Kirsten's right. It's always going to be black-and-white.

Like a life preserver thrown into rough seas, Dad's voice cuts through the static between my ears. "No, his dad does not see that. We are not sending Angelo back to California."

"But Roman—"

"No!" Dad motions to the store. "We moved here to establish our family business. *Family* business. Family isn't just Sloppy's Pit Stop's brand. Family is us. You, me, and Angelo. I'm not separating us."

I blink in surprise. Maybe "family" wasn't only one of Dad's marketing ploys after all.

"But he'll be with our extended family—"

"No. We made the decision to move out here and start over. Together."

*Wow, guess talking to Tita Marie wouldn't have done me any good,* I think, trying to hide my smile. Mom rubs her temples again, defeated, but I feel like doing Tre Flips.

Sheriff Evans clears his throat. I'm not sure how much of our conversation he heard, but it doesn't really matter. He can tell Grayson about it for all I care. At least then the jerk will know I ain't leaving.

Mom stops her sniffling and looks up. "Is there something we can help you with, Sheriff?"

For once Sheriff Evans appears to be apologetic. "Unfortunately, since there are no security cameras—"

Mom elbows Dad and hisses, "I told you we should have bought some."

"Quiet," Dad whispers back.

"—it'll be hard to pinpoint who the culprit is. There's no sign of forced entry, but given your skeleton crew I highly doubt it was an inside job."

The sheriff faces my parents and tips his hat. "We have all the information we need. We'll keep you posted."

Deputy Evans comes up from behind him and nods at my parents. "Sir. Ma'am." He looks at me with an expression I can't place. "Angelo."

My family stays in the parking lot long after the Evanses have left, almost as if we don't want to face the damage inside the restaurant. Finally, Dad coaxes, "Let's clean up."

Sloppy's Pit Stop is a zombie wasteland. It's exactly what I assume the apocalypse would look like.

Frozen on the threshold, I look around, trying to make sense of everything.

Styrofoam cups, plastic cutlery, and napkins litter the floor. Plastic trays are scattered along each table. There are different-colored puddles underneath the soda fountain. Ketchup and mustard packets are stomped on from one wall to the other. And worse, Mom's coveted candy jar is smashed to bits. Gumballs are spread out everywhere.

But those can easily be cleaned up.

What can't be cleaned up is the huge dent in Dad's beloved vent or the bent fry baskets. And what can't be saved is the contents of the open freezer.

But all those things don't make me as mad as seeing the graffiti tags spray-painted over the illuminated menus above the cash wrap. It doesn't take a genius to figure out that whoever did this probably wanted to frame Kirsten for it.

Mom catches me gawking and sidles up next to me. "Does your *friend* know anything about this?"

"Trust me. No." I turn to face my mom head-on. "I was with her all night."

"Her?" If smoke could come out of Mom's ears it would. "It was that girl you were caught trespassing with, wasn't it?"

"I plead the Fifth," I blurt out. But apparently it was the wrong thing to say.

"That's it! I don't care what your dad says. You are going back to San Diego as soon as I can get you on a plane."

"Mila." The sternness in Dad's voice surprises us both. "Angelo is not going back to California. I mean it."

Relief floods through me. Mom on the other hand . . . yikes!

Shaking her fist in the air, she stomps to my dad with a purpose. "How can you say that? He's been nothing but a troublemaker since we got here. Not to mention careless." She gestures to the back door. "He left that door open! This would never have happened if he were back at home."

I flinch. "Wait, how are you sure I left that door open? Did you see it?"

"No forced entry? How else do you think the vandal got in?" Mom's spit flies out of her mouth. "Besides, the reason we even knew about the damage so early on is because Judy saw the door wide open this morning. She thought we were open for breakfast!"

"Breakfast. Hey, that's a good business idea." I smile sheepishly, but there's no way I can smother my regret. "See? There's even a demand for it."

"Angelo, it's not the time for jokes."

I bow my head. Guilt settles into my stomach. "I'm really sorry. I didn't mean to leave the door open."

"If you didn't sneak out with that girl you wouldn't have!" Mom yells. "She isn't a good influence. Actually, this whole town is bad for you. We need to get you out of here."

Dad grabs a bucket from inside one of the showers and tosses it into our large sink. He flips on the lever and watches as the faucet sputters. "Mila, I don't ever want to hear you mention sending Angelo away again."

"But he's been acting so different," she protests.

"You're right. Ever since we moved to Ocean Pointe things have been different. We've been too worried about our store, and Angelo's been too busy dealing with things we didn't even know about." Dad shoots a look at me. "Angelo, why didn't you tell us about everything you were going through?"

"I didn't think you'd care," I answer truthfully.

Dad sucks in a breath. "Why would you think that?"

"Because you didn't care enough about what I thought before you made the decision to move to Ocean Pointe." Mom and Dad exchange looks. "And you've been so focused on making your customers happy—again—that it felt like you didn't care how *I* felt. I finally found friends and you forced me to work more shifts."

"B-but I thought that's what you wanted," Mom argues. "For your plane ticket."

"I did." I nod. "But maybe winning Streetsgiving and moving back to San Diego isn't what I want anymore."

"It's the girl, huh?" Dad eyeballs me knowingly.

I blush. "She's part of it, yeah. But now I see some things are more important than beating my old rival. Besides, I have to stay. I have this"—I motion around the restaurant—"and a bunch of new friends to look out for."

Dad smiles and nods. "See, Mila? Splitting up our family is the worst thing we can do right now. We're in this fight together. That means we're going to work hard and make sure that not only does Sloppy's Pit Stop remain open but that life in Ocean Pointe is everything we want it to be. You hear me?"

My eyes burn with the threat of tears, but I blink it away. "I agree with Dad."

"B-but Roman," Mom stammers.

"Angelo doesn't want to go anymore. What do you think people would think about us if we tossed our son out?" Dad challenges. "Not a good look for a family business."

"Once again I agree." I nod, sharing a smile with Dad.

"You know what else isn't a good look?" Mom says, more softly. "Not knowing enough about our son's life to see that he was getting bullied!"

Before Dad can reply, I raise a finger. "That was my fault too."

Mom's eyebrows raise. "Did you start the fights?"

"What? No!" I shake my head quickly. "I mean, I should've told you what was going on. I'm sorry. I thought I could deal with it myself. I should've said something."

"Yes, Angelo," says Mom firmly. "You should have."

I swallow hard and nod. "If you let me stay here, I promise I'll talk to you guys more. Let you in on what's happening."

"And not skip school or hold mobs?" Mom narrows her eyes.

"Um, yes. That too."

"Mila? What do you say?" Dad grunts, lifting the bucket and walking it over to the center table we wrap our burgers on.

Mom's quiet for far too long, but she finally nods. She grabs a towel from one of the drying racks and tosses it to me. "Wipe down the counters. You've always done a good job cleaning them."

"Yes, ma'am." I salute her dutifully.

~

"That's it? But what about our deductible? We need more for damages . . . Yes, yes. I know. But . . ." Dad groans against his phone, smacking a hand against the vent. "Okay. Thank you, Mr. Jenkins."

I wring the towel over the counter with pruney fingers. "Bad news?"

"Insurance isn't giving us enough money to cover the damages." Dad shoots Mom a worried look and walks over to the air vent, patting it as if to say everything will be okay. "We'll have to take out another loan."

"But we're already upside down on our loan as it is." Mom bows her head, but there's no mistaking her soft sobs, like the world's saddest song, played on the tiniest instrument.

I stare at the bubbles covering the counter. They seem to move, morphing into the shape of a dollar sign à la Rorschach test. In this moment, I know exactly what I have to do.

"Um, Dad?" My voice is barely a whisper.

"Yes, Angelo?" He runs a hand over his tired face. He glances at the vent as if saying goodbye to an old friend and looks back at me, putting on a brave front despite the sadness in his eyes.

If there was any doubt left in my mind, it's completely gone now. Like I told my parents, going back to San Diego for Streetsgiving isn't one of my main priorities. Not anymore.

Beating Tyler Park can wait.

Seeing my old friends can wait.

My life is here in Ocean Pointe, and I need to fight for it.

"I don't have much." I raise my voice, making sure Dad won't be able to talk over me. "But I want to give you and Mom the money I saved up for San Diego."

Dad looks shocked. "Angelo, we aren't taking your money."

"Dad—"

"No. You worked hard for it."

Now I know how Kirsten felt when she was trying to convince me to take her money for the bullies' food. Man, that seems like so long ago.

"Dad, listen. You always work hard for our family." I glance at Mom and shoot her an appreciative grin. "Both of you do. Yeah, Rivera's

Kusina may not have worked out, but Sloppy's Pit Stop will. I'm going to finally do my part. We're in this fight together, right? We're family. Let me help."

Dad comes over and pats my arm. "We are family." He takes in a deep breath and presses his lips together in an unsure smile. "Are you sure you don't mind?"

"There's nothing else I'd rather spend that money on." My stomach doesn't pinch. I don't break out into nervous sweats. I'm telling the truth, and that's that.

# 34

It's funny. But even while spending hours elbow-deep in a soap-filled bucket, my mind keeps wandering back to Kirsten. Specifically, our first kiss.

Call me sappy, but I've always wanted my own version of *the* kiss. The kiss that changes everything for the better. The kiss that defines the relationship. The kiss declaring love. Deep down I always knew my kisses with Amanda never reached that level. I hope to God my kisses with Kirsten did.

After spending all morning helping my parents out at Sloppy's, Mom decided it would be a good idea for me to go to school for my afternoon classes. Considering I'd already missed my heavier courses like AP English, Honors Calculus, and Chemistry, I don't see why missing more school would be such a big deal. But I'm not about to risk her changing her mind about San Diego by arguing with her about anything today.

A repeat of my first day, Mom drops me off in front of school.

"Bye, honey. Don't forget to get your phone back so I can reach you if I need you," Mom says.

I say goodbye, grab my bag, and jump out of the car. Unlike on my first day, I've got my skateboard strapped to my backpack, I'm thrilled to be here at OPHS, and I run up the front steps of the school in record time. My gaze bounces around the students, looking for the beautiful girl with the cowboy boots, tiny shorts, and white-blonde hair. Seeing as it's lunchtime, I'm sure she's in the cafeteria with the rest of my friends.

My heart thrums as I push through the cafeteria's double doors. I spot Kirsten at our usual table. "Kirsten!" I yell a bit too loudly. But I'm not embarrassed. She already knows how I feel about her.

She grips the edge of the table and slowly turns to look at me. An expression I can't read settles on her face, but it quickly turns to . . . anger?

I slow to a stop in front of her. Stella glances up at me, mouthing something I can't make out. I glance at Larry for clarification, but he only shakes his head.

Kirsten's teeth flash a bright white as she growls at me. "You know, I always thought Grayson was a bad guy. But at least he was honest about it."

It feels like she's slapped me in the face. "What are you talking about?"

Her voice is low. Eerie and venomous. "I trusted you. I shared my heart and soul with you. But you're nothing but a phony."

Larry scrambles to move his tuba case off the chair next to Kirsten, and I drop into it. "Why are you mad at me? What did I do?"

"Oh, you know what you did," she snaps through gritted teeth.

"I really have no idea what this is about." I blink in confusion, glancing around the table for backup.

All the guys look as confused as I do, but Stella finally speaks up. "Angelo, it would be in your best interest to leave Kirsten alone."

"But why?" Mind racing, I stare at the white-haired goddess. "I thought . . . I thought we had a good time together." I rack my brain for anything I may have said or did but come up empty. "Are you mad because I was gone this morning? Sloppy's Pit Stop was vandalized. I spent all morning helping my parents clean it up."

All my friends start talking at once. Except Kirsten.

*"Vandalized?"*

*"Do you know who did it?"*

*"What happened?"*

"It happened last night." I catch Kirsten's eyes, and she looks away. "I guess I forgot to close the door after I left and someone came in and trashed the place."

"I'm sorry that happened." Kirsten's voice is barely audible. She grabs her tote and pushes away from the table. "But that still doesn't give you an excuse to play me."

"Play you? What the heck are you talking about?" My voice wavers in desperation as she stomps off, leaving me in the afterglow of her anger.

I had thought Amanda was unreadable, but this . . .

I rush out of the cafeteria and catch up with Kirsten in the hallway. "Hey," I say, gently pulling her into the nearest empty classroom.

"Here," she says. She thrusts my phone against my chest.

I grunt at the impact, but it doesn't hurt nearly as bad as seeing the look on her face. It's an expression I've only seen once before—it was how Amanda looked when she dumped me. It's the look of goodbye. "Make sure you grab your phone next time you decide to play two girls."

I fumble for my phone, catching it before it hits the ground. "Play two girls? It's hard for me to even keep one girl!"

But she's not listening. She flies out of the room while I stare at my phone. What did she see? What the hell is she talking about? Tapping the screen, I gasp. In a text to me is a photo of Amanda's chest with nothing but a tiny bikini top covering her, um, assets. Kirsten must've seen the notification.

I knead my knuckles into my closed eyelids and groan. "Amanda, why?"

After weeks of radio silence—oh, not to mention *breaking up* with me—she chooses to text me now? Not only a text, but *that* kind of text?

I enter in my lock code and read the gray bubble underneath the photo. It's time-stamped from early yesterday morning, or around midnight Pacific time. Kirsten must've seen it after she dropped me off at home.

*Amanda Panda:* How did I get such a talented boyfriend? *muah*

"What the heck is this girl smoking?" I mumble, skimming the next text below.

*Amanda Panda:* Love you, Tyler ♥ ♥ ♥

"Tyler?" I shake my head in exasperation. "This dumb sext wasn't even meant for me!"

Anger pumps through my veins as my fingers fly across the keyboard:

Lose my number

I don't care about getting my books or even going to class. I need to find Kirsten and explain everything. After jamming my phone into my pocket, I spin around and smack into Larry.

*"Oomph."* I blink away stars. His hand juts out, barely catching his tuba case before it falls.

"Sorry." I grab his wrist to steady him. Once I'm sure he has his balance, I try to sidestep him. "Can't talk now. I have to find Kirsten."

But Larry grips my arm. "Wait."

I glance at him. "Buddy, now's really not the time."

"You didn't finish telling us about Sloppy's. Do you know who wrecked your restaurant?"

I rub my eyes with a loud groan. "I'm going to tell you all about it. I promise. But right now, I really need to talk to Kirsten."

"Why is she mad at you, anyway? Stella won't tell me."

As if on cue, our other friends walk into the classroom. All I need is one bright light shining in my face and I'm back at the sheriff's office all over again.

Wyatt jabs me with his sharp elbow. "Heard you guys went to the beach without us last night. Way to leave us out, man. Especially since we spent all weekend freaked that the sheriff would run our plates and come knocking at our door. A dip in the water would've been a nice reward."

"Trust me. The water was not nice—" I start to protest, but Larry steps in to defend me.

"They didn't need any third wheels—or make that fourth, fifth, and sixth wheels—on their date." Larry gives me a conspiratorial nod.

I shift uncomfortably as Wyatt shoots me an astonished look. "Wait. You guys are hooking up? I knew it!"

"No," I grumble.

"They will be." Larry shoots me a cheeky grin.

"Not if I don't find Kirsten and explain myself." Stella's judgmental eyes are on me. Knowing she's playing gatekeeper to Kirsten, I focus all my attention on her. "Kirsten saw a text on my phone meant for someone else and thinks I'm some player. But I'm not a player! I don't even know the first thing about playing." My nostrils flare. "My ex meant to send a photo of her boobs to her new boyfriend, but it came to me by mistake and Kirsten saw it."

"Do you still have the text? I might need to see it for evidence," Larry asks in all seriousness.

"Larry!" I complain. "Seriously. Quit joking around. My morning's already been a clusterfuck."

The screaming bell echoes above our heads. None of my friends go running for class. Not even Larry despite his perpetual need to be early.

Stella waits until the bell is done ringing and simply says, "The warehouses."

"Huh?"

"She's ditching school to try to sneak back into the warehouses. She said she needs to clear her mind and paint."

"She can't go there! Grayson—er, whoever trashed the restaurant was trying to frame her."

"*What?*"

"Okay, maybe I'm jumping to conclusions here."

"Next time lead with that." Stella taps her oxfords against the floor, irritated.

"The thing is whoever vandalized Sloppy's painted graffiti all over the menus on our walls, and the sheriff and Grayson's brother saw it, but no one in town except Grayson, and us, know Kirsten's into spray-painting graffiti. They won't make the connection. But if either of them happen to catch her at the warehouses painting, she'll be in a load of trouble."

I don't wait for my friends to respond and push through the door. I step into the hallway but immediately double back.

"What is it?" Aiden frowns.

"Mr. Holland is never around when we need him and *now* he chooses to stand in front of the exit?"

Stella sticks her head out the door to take a look and quickly pulls back into the classroom. "You're right, and he looks like he might be there for a while."

"How am I going to catch Kirsten, now?" I moan.

Larry holds up a hand like an old sage forbidding me to speak. "Calm down. We'll help you get out of here."

"How?" I peek out the door again. Mr. Holland rocks onto the tips of his wingtip shoes as if he hasn't got a care in the world. I cringe. "Doesn't look like he's going anywhere. Doesn't he have a school to principal?"

"Is that even a verb?" Larry shakes his head and nudges Aiden. "I think this calls for some music, eh?"

I stare at Larry blankly. Aiden does too.

"What are you even talking about, Larry?" I ask.

"I think it's time to show the school that little ditty we've been working on between skating practices." He addresses Aiden and not me.

"I don't even want to know," I mutter, though a tiny part of me does.

Aiden narrows his eyes for a moment and finally nods.

Larry sets down his tuba case, unclasps the buckles, and takes out his tuba. While he fidgets with it, I glance at Wyatt and Stella, who seem as enthralled, not to mention as confused, as I am.

Once Larry secures his mouthpiece, he steps into the hallway with Aiden at his side.

I shut my eyes. "Oh God. I really don't need any more weird today."

Guilt sucker punches me in the gut as soon as the words leave my mouth. My friends are anything but weird. They're awesome.

With his head held high, Larry walks into the middle of the bustling hallway and places the tuba against his lips.

"He isn't . . ." I say.

A single note carries through the hallway, followed by another and another. Soon, Larry plays a soft, sweet tune. Well, about as soft as a tuba can be. The melody is oddly familiar. Once Aiden opens his mouth and belts out the lyrics, I recognize one of my favorite punk songs.

"I-is Aiden really singing?" Stella's mouth drops open. "Out loud?"

I shake my head slowly, remembering the time he clammed up at lunch. "I knew he had it in him," I whisper.

Stella grins and points to Aiden. "You did that," she tells me. "You gave him confidence. Same for all of us."

"Duck!" Wyatt yanks us back into the classroom just as Mr. Holland walks swiftly toward the two musicians. Larry and Aiden see him and move away. The crowd of students follows them like they're the Pied Piper, with Mr. Holland nipping at their heels.

Nicely done, dudes.

"Well, what are you waiting for?" Wyatt places his palms against my back and shoves me out the door. "Go!"

I unbuckle my skateboard from my backpack and hitch the bag onto my shoulder. I rush out the door.

"Good luck," Stella calls out after me.

I throw my board onto the ground, but before I can peel away, there's a buzz in my pocket.

Fumbling with my phone, I glance down at the screen.

*Amanda Panda:* F U Loser!! I deleted your contact info a long time ago!

I roll my eyes and prepare to type a scathing response, Then why did you text me your boobs? But I decide to put my phone away—to put Amanda away—forever.

# 35

When my parents first told me we were moving to Ocean Pointe, I tried to imagine what my life would be like. As a victim of retro teen movie binges, I expected the worst and unfortunately was right about most of my suspicions. Narrow-minded classmates. Superficiality. Cliques. Even racism. But even with my ill-guided research, nothing could've prepared me for the heart-dropping sensation of falling in love again.

And the possibility of losing that love right away.

I fly down the street, hoping and praying I don't run into the Evanses. I doubt I'll be able to explain what I'm doing ditching school. But even worse would be running into them at the warehouses. If they show up there and catch Kirsten with her spray cans . . .

As if the weather is mirroring my mood, it's completely overcast and the first real cold day since I've been here. I find myself staring at the passing trees and buildings as I ride. It's like my first day in Ocean Pointe all over again. Only this time the scenery isn't a shock and doesn't strike sadness in my heart.

"No," I grumble. "There's no room for sadness in my heart anymore. At least I hope there's not."

I don't know if it's because of my lack of sleep, the calamity at Sloppy's Pit Stop, or the drama with Kirsten, but my body starts to slow. My leg muscles tighten.

But I have to hurry. I have to make sure Kirsten's okay. So I fight through the sensation and force myself to skate faster than I've ever skated before.

I'm nearly in tears by the time I catch a glimpse of white hair near an upcoming turn. Gasping, I push through my exhaustion and kick even faster. Kirsten comes into view. She's nearly to the turn leading to the warehouses, but fortunately she's on foot, dragging her feet with her skateboard tucked under her arm, giving me ample opportunity to catch up to her.

"Kirsten!" I yell.

She glances back. When she sees it's me, she drops her board. She jumps on and skates away.

"Shit." I clear my throat and shout louder. "Kirsten! Stop! Don't go to the warehouses!"

Of course she doesn't listen. This is like a skate competition, only the stakes are way higher. Mustering up the same energy I'd use on a street course, I push forward until I catch up to Kirsten. And then I skate past her.

I kick off the tail end of the board and spin around to block her.

Dust curls around her skateboard wheels as she stops. "Angelo! Leave me alone!" she insists, glaring at me.

I thought I hated maroon and yellow, but I hate brown and yellow even more. From over Kirsten's head I can see Sheriff Evans's ill-colored police car in the distance. He's driving up the road straight for us.

Without thinking twice, I push off my board and tackle Kirsten onto the grass lining the street. We crash down and find ourselves rolling into a ditch.

"Angelo! What the hell are you doing?" Kirsten slaps against me, accidentally hitting my groin area. I groan and roll over, clutching my nuts as she pushes herself up. "Can't you take a hint? I don't want to talk to you!"

"Sh-Sheriff Evans," I cough out, smacking my mouth from the phlegmy taste. "He's driving up."

"What? Shit." She drops to a squat, keeping her head low. The rumble of the car flies past us. "Do you think he saw me?"

"No." Finally catching my breath, I force myself to sit up. "At least I hope not. I think he would have stopped by now if he did."

Kirsten smiles in relief, but her happiness is short-lived. She takes one look at me and purses her lips. "Thanks for saving me. But you can leave me alone now."

With a grunt she pushes herself up and out of the ditch. My balls are still sore, but I manage to follow her.

"Kirsten, please listen to me," I plead. "I didn't do what you think I did."

She freezes. For a moment I think she wants to listen to me, but then I see what she's looking at.

My board.

"Ugh." I slump forward. "Of course."

Sheriff Evans must've run over it when I bailed out.

Kirsten picks up the two biggest pieces. Her face falls. Swallowing hard, she holds the jagged wood out to me. "Um, I guess these are yours."

"Thanks," I mumble, running a finger against the now-torn Padres sticker. "This sucks . . . but at least if any good's gonna come from this, it's that you're talking to me now."

"Or not." She shifts, prepared to turn away. I grab her wrist.

"Wait." My words fly out of my mouth. "I swear I wasn't playing you. Or Amanda."

I let go of her arm and grab my phone, pulling up Amanda's text thread. "See? She meant to text Tyler. I have no idea why she accidentally sent it to me. I'd never play you. I promise!"

Kirsten's eyes zero in on my screen, but she remains silent.

"I told her to lose my number," I spit out in a hurry. "I swear I don't know why she sent me that picture. You have to believe me! I would never do something so horrible to you. It's you I care for, not her."

Kirsten opens her mouth to speak, but before she can say anything I reach over and cup my hand over the back of her neck, pulling her into me. I press a kiss into her lips, quieting any lingering doubt she might have about me. My feelings for her. Us.

If I questioned the status of our earlier kisses at the beach, I sure as heck ain't questioning this one. This is definitely *the* kiss. I pour every single emotion into it, showing Kirsten how much she means to me.

As much as I don't want it to end, there's more I need to say to her. I pull back. Her lips stay puckered and eyes closed as I whisper, "I would never hurt you like that, Kirsten. You have to believe me. I . . . um . . . I . . . uh . . ." I shake my head. Now's not the time for my awkwardness. "It's just . . . I think—no, I know—I'm falling for you?"

I cringe at the question that falls from my mouth. I take a deep breath to try again, but before I can form a single word Kirsten's lips are against mine.

My head spins when she pulls away. "And this is why I don't understand girls. First, you're mad at me and then you're not. Then you kiss me."

"I'm sorry."

"Never apologize about kissing me," I say with a straight face.

"No, that's not what I mean." Red splotches spread across her skin. She's nervous, but why? "I should've believed you from the start. I should've never doubted you."

"But you did," I reply, but not unkindly. I take her hands into mine and squeeze them tightly. "But it's okay. The important thing is that you believe me now. Growth."

Sniffling, she laughs. "No, it's not okay. Last night . . . I knew what I was doing. I invited you to the beach for a reason."

"To convince me not to go back to San Diego, right? You told me that already."

"Yes," she admits with a wince. She pushes her hair back and lets out a strained laugh. "Gosh, I feel like I'm in junior high again."

My heart thunders against my chest in anticipation. "What do you mean?"

"I wanted to convince you not to go back to San Diego and also tell you how I felt. That I'm falling for you too." She wrings her hands together. "But I was scared. I still am. You say you don't want to go back to San Diego anymore, but what if you change your mind? I don't want this to happen if your heart is somewhere else."

"I don't have feelings for Amanda anymore," I say firmly.

She nods. "I'm not talking about her. I'm talking about California. Ever since I met you, all you wanted was to go back. Who's to say you won't change your mind again? I've liked you since you first gave me that drink of water at your restaurant. If I finally get my crush only to have him ripped away again . . . well, it would suck."

"Wait, you liked me all that time?" I rub my forehead and chuckle.

Kirsten blinks in confusion. "Wasn't it obvious?"

"I had a girlfriend," I tell her and shrug. "And like I said, I don't play. So no."

Kirsten nods. "But you still didn't notice how I felt about you even after you two broke up?"

"Maybe I did. Maybe I hoped that's what was happening. But same as what I told you at the beach. I was scared." I press my lips together into a tight smile. "Scared of my own feelings. And of trying something new. Something different. Even though it might be the best thing ever. Moving on is hard. It's probably why Ocean Pointe's full of people who don't like new things or people. Change can be scary." I gaze around the booger-colored fields, which I once thought were ugly. Now they provide me with the beauty my mom once told me to look for. "But you helped me see that some changes are necessary. Change can be good."

Looking into Kirsten's eyes, I realize change can also lead you to the right person.

"Angelo," Kirsten whispers as she pushes a lock of hair away from my eyes. "Isn't it funny?"

"What?"

"You're following me to the warehouses again." She grins. "Like on that first day. You taught me how to skate that day. It was one of my favorite days ever."

And just like that, I remember the danger she's in. I peel myself away from her, and I'm not smiling now. "Kirsten, I followed you for the same reason I followed you before. Well, besides wanting to give you my heart this time."

She grins. "Oh yeah?"

"I wanted to stop you from tagging."

Her smile vanishes. "Why?"

I nod. "You know how someone vandalized Sloppy's Pit Stop?"

"I'm sorry about that." She drops her head. "When we left for the beach . . . I didn't mean for anything like that to happen."

"I know," I say truthfully. "But the thing is, someone came in after we left and graffitied the restaurant."

"What?" Kirsten's voice rings in alarm.

"I might be reaching here, but I sort of think whoever did it might've wanted to frame you for the crime. Someone we know. Someone who knows you spray-paint." I wince, waiting for her reaction.

Kirsten starts to pace. She clenches her fists against her sides and lets out a loud groan. "My old friends know I want to study art, but there was only one of them that knew about spray-painting."

"I know," I say quietly. "But we can't prove it was him without getting you into trouble—hey! What are you doing?"

Kirsten grabs my arm. "Forget about going to the warehouses. We need to go to Sloppy's. Look for proof it was Grayson."

"Proof? I was there all day and I didn't see anything that would point to Grayson," I protest. "Besides, my parents are there. How are we going to explain ditching school?"

"We'll worry about explaining later." She hurries to grab her board from beside the ditch. "And you should know Grayson isn't exactly stealthy. You figured it out that he was the one who took down all your flyers."

"Oh. So now you're willing to admit it."

Kirsten tugs my arm and begins pulling me down the road, back toward town. "C'mon. I'm sure I'll recognize his handwriting on the graffiti. I used to proofread all his essays."

"Ah. So that's why he's in AP English." I nod.

"Stop stalling. We have a long walk ahead of us."

# 36

It takes us almost an hour by foot to get to Sloppy's. Too bad the others are still in school; otherwise I would've asked them for a ride. Sucks this town doesn't have Lyft either.

By the time we make it into the restaurant parking lot, my parents are still in the thick of cleaning. Dad took the menus' plastic barriers down from over the counter and is sitting in the middle of the parking lot trying his best to scrub them down. Bent over, eyes on his work, he doesn't see us approaching.

"That's not my hand style." Kirsten nods at the erratic script with a judgmental grimace. "Too sloppy. I mean, look at that *E*. It looks like a *P*. How's that even possible?"

She scans the menus in disgust.

I take a hesitant step to my dad. Water flows from the hose, slapping against the asphalt. I step over the stream that's already starting to pool around our gas pumps.

Dad wipes the sweat out of his eye and looks up. "Angelo! What are you doing here?"

Mom must have bionic hearing. Her head pops out of the restaurant's door. "Angelo? *Nandito siya?*"

"Yeah, I'm here, Mom," I answer.

Dad stands up. Drops of water fall from each leg of his soaked shorts. His sneakers make an uncomfortable squishing sound as he walks over to us. "Why aren't you at school? Haven't you learned your lesson?" Though he's speaking to me, he never looks away from Kirsten.

Kirsten shifts uncomfortably but looks my dad in the eye. "Sir, I—"

"I couldn't just sit around at school knowing you're stuck here cleaning the mess," I interrupt, elbowing Kirsten.

Mom stomps out of the restaurant and positions herself next to my dad with crossed arms. "Does the school know you left?"

Kirsten and I shrug sheepishly.

"*Ay naku . . .*" Mom's voice is drowned out by the rumbling of an approaching car. I glance over my shoulder and do a double take. Kirsten hurries forward, oddly taking refuge behind my mom.

Sheriff Evans pulls into one of the spots at the end of the lot but doesn't exit the car right away. I move to stand beside Kirsten, and she and I glance at each other. Is she wondering what I am—how much trouble are we in right now?

An invisible clock ticks away until the sheriff finally steps out of his car. Deputy Evans exits the passenger's side. But instead of both coming over to us, the sheriff turns and opens the car's back door, and Deputy Evans walks around the car and leans inside to say something to whoever's sitting inside.

"Why do you think they're here?" I'm sweating bullets. But I don't have to wonder for too long.

"Grayson!" Kirsten gasps, clasping her hands over her mouth as he steps out of the car.

The jock seems uncharacteristically nervous, taking his time to cross the parking lot. His dad jabs him in the back, coaxing him to hurry up.

I narrow my eyes in suspicion as the jerk stops in front of my family. "Hey," he says in a gruff tone.

"What's going on?" Dad looks to me for answers, but all I can do is shrug. "Angelo, do you know him?"

I find my voice, but it cracks as I answer. "Yeah, I know him."

"Let me ask you two what's going on." Sheriff Evans glares at me and Kirsten, who is still partially hidden behind Mom. "What are they doing here? Playing truant?" he asks my mother.

I open my mouth to respond, but Mom holds up her hand, silencing me.

"Maybe instead of questioning my son, you should pay more attention to what happened to our restaurant." Mom catches my eye. She nods so slightly that I wouldn't have noticed had it not been for sixteen years of experience. "As for my son and his friend, we already talked to the school. They're excused."

I try my best to shoot Mom a telepathic message: *He's going to know you're lying.* But Sheriff Evans seems too preoccupied to care.

"All right," he says. He pushes Grayson forward. "My son would like to tell you something."

I'm as anxious as I am excited. Kirsten must sense my weird energy and grabs my hand, squeezing tightly to calm me down. Grayson's eyes zoom in on our intertwined fingers. His cheeks turn beet red.

Sheriff Evans clears his throat. "Any day now, son."

I don't know how it's possible, but Grayson's face turns even redder. He lifts his gaze, somehow both looking at us and not. "I . . . um . . . I was the one who . . ."

The sheriff jabs a finger between Grayson's shoulder blades. "Now."

The jerk winces and finally spits out, "I vandalized your property."

"I knew it!" I blurt out before I can stop myself. Five pairs of eyes glare at me, and I shrink into Kirsten, who's trying hard not to celebrate along with me.

"Angelo. Please." Dad waves his soggy hand in front of my face and steps forward, frowning at my Ocean Pointe nemesis. "Why would you do such a thing?"

Though my dad's a good six inches shorter than Grayson, he can be intimidating when he wants to be. Grayson seems to shrivel underneath his glare and squeaks, "I . . . um . . ."

Dad points a trembling finger between Grayson's wide eyes. "You're the one torturing my son, aren't you?"

"*Torturing*'s such a strong word," I butt in, not wanting Grayson to think I'm a wimp.

As if reading my mind, Sheriff Evans clears his throat. "It took a lot of bravery for Angelo to come forward to me. I respect that."

I shift uneasily. Considering the sheriff's obviously got his eye on Grayson, I'm not too worried his son will seek revenge on me. But I still don't want the jock thinking *I* ran to his daddy.

Dad turns back to look at Grayson. To my surprise, his face relaxes, and his tone softens, "I asked you why you did it."

Grayson blinks in surprise. "I was angry."

"At my son?"

Grayson tugs at his Adam's apple. "Yes."

"Why?" Dad demands.

Sheriff Evans steps forward, pushing Grayson behind him. "Mr. Rivera, my son confessed. Is all this questioning really necessary?"

"It is necessary," Dad answers in a cool tone. "I need to know what my family and I could've done to deserve this kind of treatment. We are nothing but hardworking individuals who want nothing more than to live in peace." Dad motions to the restaurant. "Keeping a business running as the new family in town is already hard enough as it is. Why do you think we need this added stress?" he says to Grayson.

Grayson's bottom lip trembles. I doubt he's anywhere near answering, so I take the opportunity and say, "It's because we're different."

"Angelo." Once again, Mom calls out my name as if it's the only thing she can say. But unlike before, she isn't angry. Just sad.

"Everyone's so used to living in their perfect little boxes"—I catch Kirsten's eye and smile—"that they don't know what to do when someone comes and shakes everything up."

"But what have we done to shake things up?" Dad asks in bewilderment.

"For one, we're brown and stuck in the middle of nowhere." I say it like I might be joking, but we all know I mean it.

Dad stifles a laugh, but Mom's nowhere near being able to see the humor in the situation. Honestly, there really isn't any. "Let me get this straight. You hate us because of our skin color?"

"No! Of course not!" Grayson protests.

I roll my eyes. "Need I remind you of what you always call me?"

"What does he call you?" Mom demands, but I shake my head. Now's not the time to make her angrier.

Mom's eyes narrow into two menacing slits. "Is this why you destroyed our restaurant? Because of racism? What kind of town is this? It's probably why no one's eating here too!"

The blood drains from Grayson's face. "No. I promise that's not why I did it."

"Then tell us why," Dad snaps.

"I . . . I didn't plan to do it. I just got angry and it happened . . ."

Sheriff Evans clears his throat. "Son, you know you don't have to answer any of their questions until we have a lawyer present."

"There won't be any need for that," Dad cuts in, surprising as all. "At least not if we fully understand what happened last night."

Grayson's nose reddens. He looks down, sniffling. "I did it because of Kirsten."

All our heads whip in her direction. Kirsten stiffens, eyes bulging. "Me? What did I do?"

"Oh, c'mon. You know." Grayson lets out a strained chuckle when Kirsten shakes her head. "We always break up and get back together. That's our MO."

It's like all my insecurities are spoken out loud. Kirsten squeezes my hand tighter as if to assure me I have nothing to worry about. "That *used* to be our MO. But not anymore."

"I know." Grayson sniffs. "It stopped being our routine once Angelo came along."

"But we'd been broken up for months before that," she points out.

"And during summer I was having fun—"

"Ew," I mumble under my breath.

"—and I figured you were too." His nostrils flare with his deep breath. "I thought once we got our fun out of our system and school started up again, we'd get back together like we always do. But it didn't seem to be happening."

Deputy Evans snorts, pointing to Kirsten's and my joined hands. "Guess it might never happen."

"No," Grayson agrees.

Kirsten drops my hand. She stomps up to Grayson, shaking in anger. "Let me get this straight. Because of your dumb jealousy issues, you trashed my boyfriend's family's restaurant?"

Boyfriend?

Dad and I share surprised looks.

"I told you I wasn't planning on doing it," Grayson tries to argue.

"Oh. So just like you weren't planning on trying to frame me—"

"Kirsten," I interrupt. She needs to stop talking unless she wants to give her little secret away.

Fortunately, Grayson must have one nice bone in his body. He doesn't mention the graffiti and says, "I was jealous. I'm sorry. I drove past here last night and saw Kirsten walk in and . . . I don't know. I just snapped."

"Okay, that's enough of that." Sheriff Evans pulls Grayson back. The deputy stands beside his brother, shaking his head in disappointment.

Obviously pained, the sheriff clears his throat and speaks in a gar-
bled tone. "I-I know th-this is a serious matter. I'm sorry for all the
trouble my son caused."

Mom grunts.

"We can proceed with how you see fit."

Dad doesn't hesitate. "I was serious when I said there'd be no need
for lawyers."

"But Dad," I try to protest, but he waves me off.

"We don't want to press charges," Dad announces. "We want nothing but peace."

The stiffness in Grayson's neck disappears. He shuts his eyes and
releases a breath.

The sheriff also visibly relaxes, but before he can get too comfortable, Dad gives the final blow. "I was young once. I also have me a fine
boy. I know how good kids can find themselves in trouble." Dad shoots
me a wink. "But Grayson's not getting off that easy. We expect him to
pay back his debt just the way Angelo has been doing."

Dad's a freaking badass.

Sheriff Evans clears his throat. "Understood."

Even in his sopping clothes, Dad commands attention way better
than the sheriff can ever do. "Grayson, we expect you to help clean
Sloppy's Pit Stop. Every day after school."

If I'm floored, I'm nowhere near Grayson's shock. "But I have football!" He grabs at his dad's arm but is immediately shaken away. "Dad,
please. I can't miss practice. I'll be benched!"

Sheriff Evans shifts uncomfortably. "Actually, son, as you know,
there's a clear code of conduct all Trojan players are expected to follow."

"Really?" I mutter under my breath.

"I'll need to tell Coach Shappey what happened here, and I'm sure
he'll have to bench you for the remainder of this season," the sheriff
tells his son with regret.

How the mighty have fallen. Guess Grayson doesn't have a silver spoon up his ass after all.

"But Dad, it's my senior year! You're really going to tell on me? What about the scouts?" Grayson's practically in tears.

Sheriff Evans's face crumbles in remorse. "I . . . I'm sorry, son. But you did wrong. And should've thought about all that before you committed a crime." The cop nods at my parents. "You should actually be thanking these fine individuals for going so easy on you. I sure as hell wouldn't have."

Grayson cradles his face in his hands. "But football . . ."

"I know it sucks to have to give up your afternoons to clean," I tell him.

He blinks. "But?"

I shrug.

Kirsten shakes her head, trying not to grin.

Sheriff Evans scans the parking lot, stopping at the soaked menus. He cringes at the sloppy script. "Er, seeing as we're talking about debt here"—he pauses and frowns at his "fine boy"—"Grayson will also be sure to pay back whatever your insurance doesn't cover."

It's as if an invisible puppeteer yanked Grayson's head. He springs up, staring at his father in shock. "But they didn't ask for any money."

"Well, I'm asking for money. Consider this part of your punishment—from me."

The jock's mouth drops open. "How am I supposed to pay them? I don't have any money."

"Then maybe it's time you get a job. Seeing as you have more time freed up, I'm sure that won't be a problem." The sheriff reluctantly extends his hand toward my dad. "I'm really sorry about the trouble, folks."

"We just hope the problems stop." Dad grips his hand, giving it one good shake.

"I do too." Sheriff Evans sniffs. "C'mon, Grayson. We have a lot to talk about."

Deputy Evans pushes against his little brother's shoulder. "Yeah, you got that right."

Many moments in Ocean Pointe have felt like a dream. First, meeting Kirsten and the rest of my friends. Second, finding a cool place to skate. But seeing Grayson walk away with his tail between his legs really takes the cake.

Dad's heavy hand slams on my shoulder. "Looks like we won't be needing your money after all." The heavy lines on his face have almost completely gone away. "That means you can still go back to San Diego to compete in that event if you want."

I glance at Kirsten and shake my head. "Nah. I won't be going."

"Are you sure about that, son? You've always wanted to compete. I'm glad you're growing to love Ocean Pointe, but . . ."

"I'm sure I'll find an event that's closer." Even if Nobody Nowhere Skate was broken up prematurely, it was undoubtedly popular. This area's itching for a competition. It'll only be a matter of time before another one sprouts up.

Dad mumbles something about not skipping school anymore and leaves us so he can continue scrubbing down the menus.

Kirsten watches Dad for a minute, but she's frowning. I nudge her. "Why the long face? We won, Kirsten. Grayson's finally gonna get what he deserves."

"I agree with your dad. You should still compete in Streetsgiving. After all you've been through, I think you deserve some fun with your old friends."

"Nah, I have a better idea."

"And what's that?"

I shoot her a grin and lead her to the back of Sloppy's Pit Stop where our excess lot sits. The weather is continuing to reflect my mood.

The bright sun now peeks out from behind what was cloud cover. I shield my eyes and scan the parking lot, just imagining . . .

"Angelo, what's up with that look? That deranged combination of Joker and the Mask?" She reaches over to poke my cheek. I shiver with pleasure.

"Ah, I was just thinking of a new business idea. Something awesome I can invest my money in."

"Oh, that's nice."

My grin widens so much it hurts. "You have no idea how nice it will be."

# EPILOGUE

*One Month Later*

M y life is awesome.
It's full of friends constantly trying to make it better.

I'm standing here outside Sloppy's Pit Stop, but on my left, on one side of what was once our large excess parking lot, my girlfriend commands the attention of her group of students who are waiting to learn how to Ollie. Behind her are my other four comrades, each teaching a group of their own.

I stare at my new skate park in awe. Well, not my skate park. Sloppy's Pit Stop's skate park.

Though I had envisioned a much smaller park with just a few portable rails and gaps, the restaurant received a much fatter insurance check than Mr. Jenkins originally quoted. Coupled with Grayson's money, we were able to fix the restaurant up in no time, leaving a surplus of money my parents were willing to invest in my new business venture.

Multiple rails.

Grind boxes.

A mini ramp.

I was a bit surprised my parents would even consider turning the excess lot into a skate park. Especially since people have been coming to Sloppy's Pit Stop in droves. After all Dad's failed marketing exploits, who knew all it took was word of mouth to get new customers? Of course, Coach Shappey started it all when he reached out to his players' families, urging them to swing by our restaurant with their kids and their friends. He may only have been trying to save face after what his star player did, but I appreciate it regardless. Those boys can eat! If they order (and pay) as much as they do every day after practice, we'll be in business for a long time. And after getting to know most of them from my locker room cleanup duty and now their daily visits to the restaurant, I realize they really aren't such bad guys after all. Surprisingly, a few of them think skating's a sport! But anyway, after my parents calmed down about the whole "starting a mob" thing, they realized just how popular skating can be. I guess they always thought of it as my hobby, but now they see it's a hobby that attracts a lot of people, a.k.a. people who get hungry after skating, a.k.a. even more customers.

Kirsten pulls a perfect fakie kickflip and rolls back to where Justin and some of his teammates wait with their own boards. The bulky players look almost ridiculous in their football helmets and piles of safety pads. They've officially got Wyatt beat in the "overly cautious" department. But as Justin pointed out to me, they can't afford any injuries.

Justin has been a star student. I guess it helps that he's been working with Wyatt on his speed, who, by the way, is preparing to try out for the track team. The bad thing is Justin's even more impatient than I would've guessed. Especially since he's dead set on competing in Sloppy's Pit Stop Skate Park's first official competition next spring.

There won't be any masks, cryptic websites, or even glowsticks this time around—okay, maybe a few glowsticks. But there definitely won't be any hiding. We aren't nobodies anymore, and it's exactly why we want this competition to be as big as possible and why we need months to plan for it . . . it's also the reason I finally sucked it up and extended an olive branch to Tyler.

As much as I hate to admit it, Tyler's a great skater and as a new pro he's garnered quite a following. With him and Mackabi agreeing to compete in our event, it'll bring a ton of their fans to Sloppy's. My parents might even make their financial goal for the quarter in that day alone!

Or it could be just wishful thinking.

Either way, Tyler can bring Amanda if he likes. Kirsten and I won't let her spoil our fun.

I walk the perimeter of the lot one last time and grin at one of our skate park's flyers tacked onto a ramp:

## ALL OF US
## SKATEBOARDING EVENT:
### SOMEBODIES, ANYBODIES, AND NOBODIES INVITED

I cut through the lot and enter the restaurant through the back door, shooting a smile at the new security camera Dad's rigged above the entrance. A chorus of voices echo from the dining area. Though none of them speak any of the Filipino languages from our old restaurant, each conversation is just as beautiful. I shoot up a hand, greeting our regulars, and walk to the grill, immediately cringing at the sight of lopsided burger patties.

"Smack and flip! Smack and flip!" I call out as I watch Grayson push a burger patty to the edge of the greasy grill. Now that Sloppy's is all cleaned up and the damage is paid for, my parents offered the guy a permanent position.

"I'm smacking. I'm flipping." He shoots me a sheepish smile as the half-cooked patty falls onto the floor. Growling, I reach over and scoop the pinkish clump off the tile.

I toss it into the nearest trash bin and point a finger to his face. "That's coming out of your paycheck."

Grayson purses his lips. "Is that supposed to faze me? Because that'll leave me at what? Zero balance in my savings account? Sorry to say, everything's still coming out of my paycheck and going to this place. My savings account has been at zero for a month already."

I smirk right back. "You should've thought about that before you fucked up Sloppy's."

Cool air wafts inside as the glass door flies open. Kirsten struts in, looking every bit a sexy skater girl. Though she spends a lot of time with me at Sloppy's, in between skating and painting, there's still nothing like the sight of her walking into the restaurant. It brings me back to our first meeting all over again.

"Hey. You got anything to drink?" she asks with her trademark wink.

"Actually, I'll do you one better." I grab the box I'd shoved on our warmer, walk to the other side of the counter, and flip open the lid. I frown at the odd-colored patty, grimacing at the bits of yellow corn and black beans sticking out around the sides. Our supplier assured us it tastes better than it looks, but I'm still doubtful.

I hold out the box and grin. "Care to try our newest addition?"

Kirsten gasps in delight. "Omigosh! Is this it?"

"Yup." I puff out my chest in pride. "You are now the proud owner of the very first Sloppy's Pit Stop vegan cheeseburger, complete with a gluten-free bun."

"This is awesome." Kirsten whistles in amusement.

"Hell yeah it is. You know how hard it was trying to convince my parents to invest in yet another new thing so soon? It took hours staring at spreadsheets. I don't even like math!"

"They shouldn't have doubted you," she clucks. "You have a good track record for investments. Just look how well your skate park's going."

"Well, hopefully it does as well as the *lumpia* we added to the menu too."

My eyes flit up to our new illuminated menu above the counter, designed by Kirsten herself. Though I don't think her parents will ever be fully on board with her decisions, she isn't backing down and still plans to pursue her art . . . along with skating.

A loud thump echoes from outside. We look out the back door and see Justin jumping up onto his feet. "I'm okay—*whoa!*" His skateboard flies out from underneath him, crashing into the dumpster.

I rub the back of my head and grimace. "At least he's trying. And he does have that meeting with that scout from UGA, so I guess that's good . . ."

Kirsten giggles, peeling away the paper wrapping from the bun. Taking a deep breath, she lifts it up to her nose and sniffs.

I arch an eyebrow. "Seeing if it's rotten?"

Elbowing me, she laughs. "No! I like to savor my food."

"Okay, okay. Well, savor it while you taste it. You're killing me with anticipation!"

She sinks her teeth into the burger. I hold my breath.

"Well?" I demand.

"Mmm!" Her eyes roll to the back of her head. "This is amazing."

"Thank God!" I wipe a bead of imaginary sweat off my brow. "My butt was on the line here."

"And you have a very cute one, if I do say so myself." She giggles and swallows the rest of her bite as I chuckle.

Chad, our newly minted assistant manager—or brother-in-arms or honorary Rivera as he likes to call himself—walks in, nodding his head in greeting. I wait for him to say something offensive to Kirsten, but ever since I'd had a long talk with him after she and I made things official, he's been nothing but a gentleman.

"Come on." Kirsten tugs me to the door. "Your shift's over. Let's go outside and skate."

"You don't have to ask me twice." I flick my hand to say goodbye to Grayson. Though we'll never be best buds, we have an understanding.

Like I did with Justin before agreeing to teach him, I forced Grayson to listen to me tell him more about stereotypes and racism and how dangerous and damaging they are. I don't know if he really got it or even how much he was listening. But he nodded and said okay. And I won't give up. I'll sit him down for another talk in another few weeks and see if anything's sunk in.

I scoop up my new board, a joint gift from all my friends, and admire the one-of-a-kind painting on the bottom of the deck. Kirsten painted the cartoon version of me, only this time one half of Cartoon Me is standing in front of a beach landscape and the other half is standing in front of farmland.

I really like it.

We rush outside, chatting about popping a few Ollies before the sun sets. Considering the sun's already dancing on the horizon, we only have a little bit of time.

I fight back a shiver. Now that it's the end of November, it's starting to get a lot colder. Kirsten was right. I should've known better than to wish away the heat. Especially since she never wears those Daisy Dukes anymore. Then again, I'm really digging her new jeans. The back pockets are just as awesome.

Kirsten catches me staring and shoots me a sly smile. "What are you thinking about, Rivera?"

"You." Now it's my turn to wink at her.

I feel so good. Like something is ending and also beginning. Something better than good. "Hey, I have an idea." I cup the side of my mouth and yell, "Hey, everybody. Stand in front of that ramp! I'm going to take a picture to post online."

"Post a picture? I've been following your account for months now, and you haven't posted a single thing." Kirsten elbows me in the gut. "Thought you only used social media to stalk exes."

Laughing along with her, I shrug. "What can I say? I finally have something worth posting about."

"That you do."

Kirsten watches intently as I make a mock tripod out of burger boxes, skateboards, and a few football helmets. Once I frame the shot and program the self-timer, I grab her arm and tug her to the ramp while I instruct everyone to squeeze in tight.

Kirsten and I hurry over and stand behind Stella and Wyatt, who are crouched down in front. Larry grins as he squeezes in between me and Kirsten. The original Three Musketeers. Being tall, Aiden takes his place in the back with the rest of the football team. I may be counting my chickens too early, but I have a hunch he is actually considering auditioning for OPHS's spring musical. But I guess only time will tell.

I stare at the blinking light and shout, "Say 'vegan cheese'!"

"Vegan cheese!" everyone repeats with bright smiles.

The flash goes off. Even without seeing it, I murmur, "Perfect," then jog to my phone, grab it, and type in the perfect caption:

> Things aren't always black-and-white. Sometimes they're brown . . . I finally feel like I belong somewhere again.

# ACKNOWLEDGMENTS

Who knew a fun day with my family and my sister's fur baby, Mia, would lead me on this amazing adventure?

First and foremost, I want to thank God for this wonderful blessing. None of this could've ever happened without His guidance, love, and faithfulness. God is good all the time. All the time God is good. Revelation 3:8.

Since I was a little girl, I've always dreamed of becoming a writer. Thank you to Daddy, Mommy, and Janine for always praying for me, encouraging me, believing in me, and loving me unconditionally. Words can't express how much I love you. Thanks to you, my dreams came true. Can't wait to see what joys happen next. I love you to the moon and back!

My wonderful husband, Rus. You make me braver. You make me stronger. You make me believe in myself in ways I never have before. There are so many things I can write, but it'll probably be a whole new book if I do. I love you forever and a day. Thank you for your unconditional love. And for always being patient with my anxieties.

Maya and Rosie, not a day goes by when I don't think of you. I know you're with me in every rose and bee. Mommy and Daddy love you.

Roscoe, Nollie, Tobi, Mia, and Roxi—I wish you could read this. But you've all rescued me in more ways than you know. Love you, baby boys and baby girls! Good boys! Good girls!

BFF! Stephie, from the moment we bonded on the hill because of NSYNC you have always been there for me. There are so many inside jokes I can put in here, but I'll keep it serious and just say I love you and thank you for everything. Until we're old by the beach!

My girls Jen, Kat, Lek, Lorraine, and Tina. I don't know where I'd be without your constant love, support, and prayers. I am so thankful for your friendship. I am truly blessed to have you all in my life. Love you all so much!

My favorite book blogger and awesome beta reader, Heather. Thank you for everything. From our bookstore trips, all our movie nights, and our signings, you have made the literary world even more fun than it already is. Love you, girl. You are the best!

Jayne, thanks for always listening to my writer's woes and always easing my stresses. As Chuck from *Supernatural* said, "Writing is hard!"

Big, big, big thanks to my wonderful agent (and fellow early bird), Sharon Belcastro. I don't think I can ever fully express how thankful I am for you. Thanks for always believing in me, championing my work, guiding me, and for loving Angelo and his adventures as much as I do!

Thank you everyone on the Skyscape team. You all are the best. Many, many thanks to Carmen Johnson, editorial director, for acquiring *Brown Boy Nowhere* and for being so excited about this story. A big thank-you to Susan Hughes, my awesome developmental editor, for the wonderful direction. Thank you so much for helping me polish Angelo's story. A huge thanks to my copyeditors, Jon, Robin, Emma, and Liz, for all your hard work, thorough edits, and proofreading. Thank you, Kat Goodloe for your wonderful cover illustration. And thank you, Amanda Hudson for the cover design.

To my readers. Each one of you is making my dreams come true. Thank you all so much.

# ABOUT THE AUTHOR

*Photo © 2020 Roseller Lim*

Sheeryl Lim considers herself a bookworm since birth and boasts an unending TBR pile. If she isn't writing, she's eating popcorn or playing with her rescue dogs, Roscoe and Nollie. Originally from San Diego, California, the Filipino American author currently resides on the East Coast with her husband and fur babies. For more information, visit www.sheeryllim.com.